"In case... **had a ha**... **you tonig**...

"I'm sorry, b... you would be...

Hannah couldn... ...Why be? You're smart and savvy and pretty damn... to raise a child on your own and finish college at the same time."

"Keep going."

Logan could…all night. "You're a survivor and very beautiful, although you don't seem to know that. And that's not only hard to find in a beautiful woman, it's appealing."

"And?"

"Right now I'd like to kiss you," he blurted out before his brain caught up with his mouth. "But I'm not going to."

"Why not?" she asked, looking thoroughly disappointed.

"Because if I kissed you, I might not want to stop there."

* * *

From Single Mum to Secret Heiress

A... ...ion!

FROM SINGLE MUM TO SECRET HEIRESS

BY
KRISTI GOLD

Published in Great Britain 2014
by Mills & Boon, an imprint of Harlequin (UK) Limited,
Eton House, 18-24 Paradise Road, Richmond, Surrey, TW9 1SR

© 2014 Harlequin Books S.A.

Special thanks and acknowledgement are given to Kristi Gold for her contribution to the Dynasties: The Lassiters miniseries.

ISBN: 978 0 263 91466 5

51-0514

Harlequin (UK) Limited's policy is to use papers that are natural, renewable and recyclable products and made from wood grown in sustainable forests. The logging and manufacturing processes conform to the legal environmental regulations of the country of origin.

Printed and bound in Spain
by E

Kristi Gold has a fondness for beaches, baseball and bridal reality shows. She firmly believes that love has remarkable healing powers and feels very fortunate to be able to weave stories of love and commitment. As a bestselling author, a National Readers' Choice Award winner and a Romance Writers of America three-time RITA® Award finalist, Kristi has learned that although accolades are wonderful, the most cherished rewards come from networking with readers. She can be reached through her website at www.kristigold.com, or through Facebook.

To my fellow Lassiter authors, particularly
Kathie DeNosky, my good friend and brainstorming
buddy. I can always count on you to have my back, as
long as you've had your coffee. Couldn't have done
this one without you.

One

What a way to begin the end of April—with limited funds and leaky plumbing.

Yet Hannah Armstrong couldn't quite believe her sudden change in fortune. Twenty minutes after placing the 5:00 p.m. service call, and hearing the dispatcher's declaration that they would *try* to send someone out today, her doorbell sounded.

She left the flooded galley kitchen and carefully crossed the damp dining-room floor that was littered with towels. After entering the living room, she navigated another obstacle course comprised of a toy plastic convertible painted shocking pink, as well as a string of miniature outfits that would be the envy of the fashion-doll world. "Cassie, sweetie, you have to pick up your toys before you can spend the night with Michaela," she called on her way to answer the summons.

She immediately received the usual "In a minute, Mama," which came from the hallway to her right.

Hannah started to scold her daughter for procrastinating, but she was too anxious to greet her knight in shining tool belt. Yet when she yanked the front door open, she was completely taken aback by the man standing on her porch. The guy had to be the prettiest plumber in Boulder. Correction. All of Colorado.

She quickly catalogued the details—a six-foot-plus prime specimen of a man with neatly trimmed, near-black hair that gleamed in the sun and eyes that reminded her of a mocha cappuccino. He wore a navy sports coat that covered an open-collared white shirt, dark-wash jeans and a pair of tan polished cowboy boots, indicating she'd probably pulled him away from a family function. Or quite possibly a date since he didn't appear to be wearing a wedding band.

"Ms. Armstrong?" he asked as soon as she stepped onto the porch, his voice hinting at a slight drawl.

Considering her ragtag appearance—damp holey jeans, no shoes, hair piled into a disheveled ponytail and a faded blue T-shirt imprinted with Bring it On!— Hannah considered denying her identity. But leaky pipes took precedence over pride. "That's me, and I'm so glad to see you."

"You were expecting me?" Both his tone and expression conveyed his confusion.

Surely he was kidding. "Of course, although I am really surprised you got here so quickly. And since I've obviously interrupted your Friday-night plans, please know I truly appreciate your expediency. Just one question before you get started. What exactly do you charge after normal business hours?"

He looked decidedly uncomfortable, either from the question or her incessant rambling. "Anywhere from two-fifty to four hundred regardless of the hour."

"Dollars?"

"Yes."

Ridiculous. "Isn't that a bit exorbitant for a plumber?"

His initial surprise melted into a smile, revealing dimples that would make the most cynical single gal swoon. "Probably so, but I'm not a plumber."

Hannah's face heated over her utterly stupid assumption. Had she been thinking straight, she would have realized he wasn't a working-class kind of guy. "Then what are you? *Who* are you?"

He pulled a business card from his jacket pocket and offered it to her. "Logan Whittaker, attorney at law."

A slight sense of dread momentarily robbed Hannah of a response, until she realized she had no reason to be afraid of a lawyer. She gained enough presence of mind to take the card and study the text. Unfortunately, her questions as to why he was there remained unanswered. She'd never heard of the Drake, Alcott and Whittaker law firm, and she didn't know anyone in Cheyenne, Wyoming.

She looked up to find him studying her as intently as she had his card. "What's this about?"

"I'm helping settle the late J. D. Lassiter's estate," he said, then paused as if that should mean something to her.

"I'm sorry, but I don't know anyone named Lassiter, so there must be some mistake."

He frowned. "You are Hannah Lovell Armstrong, right?"

"Yes."

"And your mother's name is Ruth Lovell?"

The conversation was growing stranger by the minute. "Was. She passed away two years ago. Why?"

"Because she was named as secondary beneficiary should anything happen to you before you claimed your inheritance."

Inheritance. Surely it couldn't be true. Not after all the years of wondering and hoping that someday…

Then reality began to sink in, as well as the memory of her mother's warning.

You don't need to know anything about your worthless daddy or his cutthroat family. He never cared about you one whit from the moment you were born. You're better off not knowing….

So shell-shocked by the possibility that this had something to do with the man who'd given her life, Hannah simply couldn't speak. She could only stare at the card still clutched in her hand.

"Are you okay, Ms. Armstrong?"

The attorney's question finally snapped her out of the stupor. "I'm a little bit confused at the moment." To say the least.

"I understand," he said. "First of all, it's not my place to question you about your relationship with J. D. Lassiter, but I am charged with explaining the terms of your inheritance and the process for claiming it. Anything you reveal to me will be kept completely confidential."

When she realized what he might be implying, Hannah decided to immediately set him straight. "Mr. Whittaker, I don't have, nor have I ever had, a relationship with anyone named Lassiter. And if you're insinuating I might be some mistress he kept hidden away, you couldn't be more wrong."

"Again, I'm not assuming anything, Ms. Armstrong. I'm only here to honor Mr. Lassiter's last wishes." He glanced over his shoulder at Nancy, the eyes and ears of the neighborhood, who'd stopped watering her hedge-row to gawk, before turning his attention back to Hannah. "Due to confidentiality issues, I would prefer to lay out the terms of the inheritance somewhere aside from your front porch."

Although he seemed legitimate, Hannah wasn't comfortable with inviting a stranger into her home, not only for her sake, but also for her daughter's. "Look, I need some time to digest this information." As well as the opportunity to investigate Logan Whittaker and determine whether he might be some slick con art-ist. "Could we possibly meet this evening to discuss this?" Provided she didn't discover anything suspi-cious about him.

"I can be back here around seven-thirty."

"I'd prefer to meet in a public venue. I have a daugh-ter and I wouldn't want her to overhear our conversa-tion."

"No problem," he said. "And in the meantime, feel free to do an internet search or call my office and ask for Becky. You'll have all my pertinent information and proof that I am who I say I am."

The man must be a mind reader. "Thank you for recognizing my concerns."

"It's reasonable that you'd want to protect not only yourself, but your child." He sounded as if he truly un-derstood, especially the part about protecting Cassie.

She leaned a shoulder against the support column.

"I suppose you've probably seen a lot of unimaginable things involving children during your career."

He shifted his weight slightly. "Fortunately I'm in corporate law, so I only have to deal with business transactions, estates and people with too much money to burn."

"My favorite kind of people." The sarcasm in her tone was unmistakable.

"Not too fond of the rich and infamous?" he asked, sounding somewhat amused.

"You could say that. It's a long story." One that wouldn't interest him in the least.

"I'm staying at Crest Lodge, not far from here," he said. "They have a decent restaurant where we can have a private conversation. Do you know the place?"

"I've been there once." Six years ago with her husband on their anniversary, not long before he was torn from her life due to a freak industrial accident. "It's fairly expensive."

He grinned. "That's why they invented expense accounts."

"Unfortunately I don't have one."

"But I do and it's my treat."

And what a treat it would be, sitting across from a man who was extremely easy on the eyes. A man she knew nothing about. Of course, this venue would be strictly business. "All right, if you're sure."

"Positive," he said. "My cell number's listed on the card. If your plans change, let me know. Otherwise I'll meet you there at seven-thirty."

That gave Hannah a little over two hours to get showered and dressed, provided the real plumber didn't show up, which seemed highly unlikely. "Speaking of calls, why didn't you handle this by phone?"

His expression turned solemn once more. "First of all, I had some business to attend to in Denver, so I decided to stop here on the way back to Cheyenne. Secondly, as soon as you hear the details, you'll know why I thought it was better to lay out the terms in person. I'll see you this evening."

With that, he strode down the walkway, climbed into a sleek black Mercedes and drove away, leaving Hannah suspended in a state of uncertainty.

After taking a few more moments to ponder the situation, she tore back into the house and immediately retreated to the computer in her bedroom. She began her search of Logan Whittaker and came upon a wealth of information, including several photos and numerous accolades. He graduated from the University of Texas law school, set up practice twelve years ago in Dallas, then moved to Cheyenne six years ago. He was also listed as single, not that it mattered to Hannah. Much.

Then it suddenly dawned on her to check out J. D. Lassiter, which she did. She came upon an article heralding his business acumen and his immeasurable wealth. The mogul was worth billions. And once again, she was subjected to shock when she recognized the face in the picture accompanying his story—the face that belonged to the same man who had been to her house over twenty years ago.

That particular day, she'd returned home from school and come upon him and her mother standing on the porch, engaged in a heated argument. She'd been too young to understand the content of the volatile conversation, and when she'd asked her mom about him,

Ruth had only said he wasn't anyone she should worry about. But she had worried…and now she wondered….

Hannah experienced a surprising bout of excitement mixed with regret. Even if she had solid proof J. D. Lassiter was in fact her father, she would never have the opportunity to meet him. It was as if someone had given her a special gift, then immediately yanked it away from her. It didn't matter. The man had clearly possessed more money than most, and he hadn't spent a dime to support her. That begged the question—why would he leave her a portion of his estate now? Perhaps a guilty conscience. An attempt at atonement. But it was much too late for that.

She would meet Logan Whittaker for dinner, hear him out and then promptly tell him that she wouldn't take one penny of the Lassiter fortune.

At fifteen minutes until eight, Logan began to believe Hannah Armstrong's plans had changed. But from his position at the corner table, he glanced up from checking his watch to see her standing in the restaurant's doorway.

He had to admit, he'd found her pretty damned attractive when he'd met her, from the top of her auburn ponytail to the bottom of her bare feet. She'd possessed a fresh-faced beauty that she hadn't concealed with a mask of makeup, and she had the greenest eyes he'd ever seen in his thirty-eight years.

But now…

She did have on a little makeup, yet it only enhanced her features. Her hair hung straight to her shoulders and she wore a sleeveless, above-the-knee black dress that molded to her curves. Man-slaying curves that reminded Logan of a modern version of those starlets from days gone by, before too-thin became all the rage.

When they made eye contact, Hannah started forward, giving Logan a good glimpse of her long legs. He considered her to be above average in height for a woman, but right then she seemed pretty damn tall. Maybe it was just the high heels, although they couldn't be more than two inches. Maybe it was the air of confidence she gave off as she crossed the room. Or maybe he should keep his eyes off her finer attributes; otherwise he could land himself in big trouble if he ignored the boundary between business and pleasure. Not that he had any reason to believe she'd be willing to take that step.

Logan came to his feet and rounded the table to pull out the chair across from his as soon as Hannah arrived. "Thanks," she said after she claimed her seat.

Once he settled in, Logan handed her a menu. "I thought for a minute there you were going to stand me up."

"My apologies for my tardiness," she said. "My daughter, Cassie, had to change clothes three times before I took her to my friend's house for a sleepover."

He smiled over the sudden bittersweet memories. "How old is she?"

"Gina is thirty. Same as me."

Logan bit back a laugh. "I meant your daughter."

A slight blush spread across Hannah's cheeks, making her look even prettier. "Of course you did. I admit I'm a little nervous about this whole inheritance thing."

So was Logan, for entirely different reasons. Every time she flashed those green eyes at him, he felt his pulse accelerate. "No need to be nervous. But I wouldn't blame you if you're curious."

"Not so curious that I can't wait for the details until after dinner, since I'm starving." She opened the menu and began scanning it while Logan did the same. "I'd forgotten how many choices they offer."

He'd almost forgotten how it felt to be seated at a dinner table across from a gorgeous woman. The past few years had included a few casual flings for the sake of convenience with a couple of women who didn't care to be wined and dined. Sex for the sake of sex. And that had suited him fine. "Yeah. It's hard to make a decision. By the way, did you get your plumbing fixed?"

She continued to scan the menu. "Unfortunately, no. They called and said it would be tomorrow afternoon. Apparently pipes are breaking all over Boulder."

With the way she looked tonight, she could break hearts all over Boulder. "Do you have any recommendations on the menu?"

"Have you had bison?" she asked as she looked up from the menu.

"No. I'm more of a beef-and-potatoes kind of guy."

"Your Texas roots are showing."

She'd apparently taken his advice. "Did you check me out on the internet?"

"I did. Does that bother you?"

Only if she'd discovered the part of his past he'd concealed from everyone in Wyoming. *Almost everyone.* "Hey, I don't blame you. In this day and time, it's advisable to determine if someone is legitimate before you agree to meet with them."

"I'm glad you understand, and you have quite the résumé."

He shrugged. "Just the usual credentials."

"They certainly impressed me."

She undeniably impressed him. "Have you eaten bison before?"

"Yes, I have, and I highly recommend it. Much leaner and healthier than beef."

"I think I'll just stick with what I know."

Her smile almost knocked his boots off. "Perhaps you should expand your horizons."

Perhaps he should quit sending covert looks at her cleavage. "Maybe I will at some point in time." Just not tonight.

A lanky college-aged waiter sauntered over to the table and aimed his smile on Hannah. "Hi. My name's Chuck. Can I get you folks something to drink? Maybe a cocktail before dinner?"

Bourbon, straight up, immediately came to Logan's mind before he realized booze and a beautiful woman wouldn't be a good mix in this case. "I'll have coffee. Black."

Hannah leveled her pretty smile on Chuck. "I'd like a glass of water."

The waiter responded with an adolescent grin. "Have you folks decided on your meal?"

She took another glance at the menu before closing it. "I'll take the petite bison filet, medium, with a side of sautéed mushrooms and the asparagus."

Logan cleared his throat to gain the jerk's attention. "Give me the New York strip, medium rare with a baked potato, everything on it."

Chuckie Boy jotted down the order but couldn't seem to stop staring at Hannah as he gathered the menus. "How about an appetizer? I highly recommend the Rocky Mountain oysters."

That nearly made Logan wince. "I believe I'll pass on that one, Chuck."

"I second that," Hannah said. "A salad with vinaigrette would be good."

Chuck finally tore his gaze away from Hannah and centered it on Logan. "Can I bring you a salad, too, sir?"

No, but you can get the hell out of Dodge. "Just the coffee and a glass of water."

The waiter backed away from the table, then said, "I'll have that right out."

"What an idiot," Logan muttered after the guy disappeared into the kitchen.

Hannah frowned. "I thought he was very accommodating."

"He definitely wanted to accommodate you and it didn't have a damn thing to do with dinner." Hell, he sounded like a jealous lover.

Hannah looked understandably confused. "Excuse me?"

"You didn't notice the way he was looking at you?"

"He was just being friendly."

She apparently didn't realize her appeal when it came to the opposite sex, and he personally found that intriguing. "Look, I don't blame the guy. You're an extremely attractive woman, but for all he knows, we're a couple. The fact that he kept eyeing you wasn't appropriate in my book."

Her gaze momentarily wandered away and the color returned to her cheeks. "But we're not a couple, and he wasn't *eyeing* me."

"Believe me, he was." And he sure couldn't blame the guy when it came right down to it.

She picked up the cloth napkin near her right hand, unfolded it and laid it in her lap. "If he was, I didn't notice. Then again, I haven't been out much in the past few years."

"Since your…" If he kept going, he'd be treading on shaky ground. The kind that covered a major loss from the past. He knew that concept all too well.

She raised a brow. "Since my husband's death? It's okay. I've been able to talk about it without falling apart for the past four years."

He definitely admired her for that. Even after nine years, he hadn't been able to discuss his loss without flying into a rage. "I admire your resiliency," he said, all the while thinking he wished he had half of her tenacity.

Chuck picked that moment to bring the drinks and Hannah's salad. "Here you go, folks. Dinner will be right out."

As bad as Logan hated to admit it, he was actually glad to see the jerk, if only to grab the opportunity to turn to a lighter topic. "Thank you kindly, Chuck."

"You're welcome, sir."

After the waiter left the area, Logan returned his attention to Hannah. "So it's my understanding you recently obtained your degree."

She took a quick sip of water and sent him a proud smile. "Yes, I did, and apparently you've done your homework on me, too."

"I had to in order to locate you." Thanks to J. D. Lassiter not providing much information when they discovered the annuity's existence.

She picked up a fork and began moving lettuce around on the plate. "That old internet is a great resource for checking people out."

He only wished she would thoroughly check him out, and not on the computer. And where in the hell had *that* come from?

He cleared his throat and shifted slightly in his seat. "I take it you're satisfied I'm not some reprobate posing as an attorney."

"Yes, but frankly, I'm curious as to why you relocated from Dallas to Cheyenne, Wyoming. That must have been quite a culture shock."

He didn't want to delve into his reasons for leaving his former life behind. "Not that much of a shock. You find cowboys in both places."

"Were you a cowboy in another life, or just trying to blend in now?"

"I've ridden my share of horses, if that's what you mean."

She smiled again. "Let me guess. You were born into an affluent ranching family."

"Nope. A not-quite-poor farming family. Three generations, as a matter of fact. My parents ran a peach orchard in East Texas and raised a few cattle. They're semiretired now and disappointed I didn't stick around to take over the business."

"What made you decide to be a lawyer?"

He grinned. "When I wore overalls, people kept mistaking me for a plumber, and since clogged drains aren't my thing, studying the law made sense."

Her soft laughter traveled all the way to her striking green eyes. "Something tells me you're not going to let me live that one down."

Something told him he could wind up in hot water if he didn't stop viewing her as a desirable woman. "I'll let you off the hook, seeing as how we just met."

"And I will let you off the hook for not giving me fair warning before you showed up on my doorstep."

He still had those great images of her branded in his brain. "You know, I'm really glad I didn't decide to handle this over the phone. Otherwise, I wouldn't have met you, and something tells me I would have regretted that."

Hannah set down the fork, braced her elbow on the edge of the table and rested her cheek in her palm. "And I would have missed the opportunity to get all dressed up for a change and have a free meal."

She looked prettier than a painted picture come to life. Yep. Trouble with a capital *T* if he didn't get his mind back on business. "After you learn the details of your share of the Lassiter fortune, you'll be able to buy me dinner next time." Next time? Man, he was getting way ahead of himself, and that was totally out of character for his normally cautious self.

Hannah looked about as surprised as he felt over the comment. "That all depends on if I actually agree to accept my share, and that's doubtful."

He couldn't fathom anyone in their right mind turning down that much money. But before he had a chance to toss out an opinion, or the amount of the annuity held in her name, Chuck showed up with their entrées.

Logan ate his food with the gusto of a field hand, while Hannah basically picked at hers, the same way she had with the salad. By the time they were finished, and the plates were cleared, he had half a mind to invite her into the nearby bar to discuss business. But dark and cozy wouldn't help rein in his libido.

Hannah tossed her napkin aside and folded her hands before her. "Okay, we've put this off long enough. Tell me the details."

Logan took a drink of water in an attempt to rid the dryness in his throat. "The funds are currently in an annuity. You have the option to leave it as is and take payments. Or you can claim the lump sum. Your choice."

"How much?" she said after a few moments.

He noticed she looked a little flushed and decided retiring to the bar might not be a bad idea after all. "Maybe we should go into the lounge so you can have a drink before I continue."

Frustration showed in her expression. "I don't need a drink."

He'd begun to think he might. "Just a glass of wine to take the edge off."

She leaned forward and nailed him with a glare. "How *much?*"

"Five million dollars."

"I believe I will have that drink now."

Two

She'd never been much of a drinker, but at the moment Hannah sat on a sofa in the corner of a dimly lit bar, a vodka and tonic tightly gripped in her hand. "Five million dollars? Are you insane?"

Logan leaned back in the club chair and leveled his dark gaze on hers. "Hey, it's not my money. I'm only the messenger."

She set the glass down on the small table separating them, slid her fingers through the sides of her hair and resisted pulling it out by the roots. "You're saying that I can just sign some papers and you're going to hand me a fortune."

"It's a little more complicated than that."

After having the five-million-dollar bombshell dropped on her head, nothing seemed easy, including deciding to refuse it. "Would I have to go before some probate court?"

"No, but there are some stipulations."

She dropped her hands into her lap and sat back on the cushions. "Such as?"

"You have to sign a nondisclosure waiver in order to claim the inheritance."

"Nondisclosure?"

"That means if you take the money, by law you can't disclose your connection to the Lassiters to anyone."

She barked out a cynical laugh. "I refuse to do that. Not after living my entire life in the shadow of shame, thanks to my biological father's refusal to acknowledge me."

"Then you have reason to believe J. D. Lassiter is your father?"

Good reason. "Yes, there is a chance, but I don't know for certain because I have no real proof. Regardless, I do know I won't take a penny of his hush money."

Logan downed the last of his coffee, sat back on the opposing sofa and remained quiet a few moments. "What does your future hold in terms of your career?"

A little hardship, but nothing she couldn't handle. "I'm going to teach high-school human physiology and probably health classes as well."

He released a rough sigh. "It takes a lot of guts to stand in front of a room full of teenage boys and talk about the facts of life, especially looking the way you do."

Hannah appreciated his skill at doling out the compliments, even if she didn't understand it or quite believe it. "I assure you I can handle whatever teenage boys want to throw at me."

"I don't doubt that," he said. "But it's not going to be easy. I know because I was one once."

She imagined a very cute one at that. "Most men still retain some of those prepubescent qualities, don't you agree?"

He grinned, giving her another premiere dimple show. "Probably so. Do you have a job lined up?"

That caused her to glance away. "Not yet, but I've had my degree for less than two weeks, and that's when I immediately started the search. I expect to find something any day now."

"And if you don't?"

She'd harbored those same concerns due to the lack of prospects. "I'll manage fine, just as I've been managing since my husband died."

He sent her a sympathetic look. "That must have been a struggle, raising a child and going to school."

She'd been lucky enough to have help. Begrudging help. "My mother looked after my daughter when necessary until Cassie turned two. I lived off the settlement from my husband's work accident and that, coupled with Social Security benefits, allowed me to pay for day care and the bills while studying full-time. I obtained grants and student loans to finance my tuition."

"If you don't mind me asking, do you have any of the settlement left?"

She didn't exactly mind, but she felt certain she knew where he was heading—back into inheritance land. "Actually, the payments will end in October, so I still have six months."

He streaked a hand over the back of his neck. "You

do realize that if you accept this money, you'll be set for life. No worries financially for you or your daughter."

If Cassie's future played a role, she might reconsider taking the inheritance. "My daughter will be well provided for when she turns eighteen, thanks to my in-laws, who've established a million-dollar-plus trust fund in her name. Of course, I'm sure that will come with conditions, as those with fortunes exceeding the national debt are prone to do."

"Guess that explains your aversion to wealthy people."

Her aversion was limited to only the entitled wealthy, including Theresa and Marvin Armstrong. "Daniel's parents didn't exactly approve of my marriage to their son. Actually, they didn't approve of me. It was that whole illegitimate thing. They had no way of knowing if I had the appropriate breeding to contribute to the stellar Armstrong gene pool. Of course, when I became pregnant with Cassie, they had no say in the matter."

He seemed unaffected by her cynicism. "Are they involved in your daughter's life at all?"

"Theresa sends Cassie money on her birthday and collector dolls at Christmas that carry instructions not to remove them from the box so they'll retain their value. What good is a doll you can't play with?"

"Have they ever seen her?"

"Only once." And once had been quite enough. "When Cassie was two, they flew us out to North Carolina for a visit. It didn't take long to realize that my mother-in-law and active toddlers don't mix. After Theresa accused me of raising a wild animal, I told her

I'd find a good kennel where I could board Cassie next time. Fortunately, there wasn't a next time."

Logan released a deep, sexy laugh. "You're hell on wheels, aren't you?"

She took another sip of the cocktail to clear the bitter taste in her mouth. "After growing up a poor fatherless child, I learned to be. Also, my mother was extremely unsocial and rather unhappy over raising a daughter alone, to say the least. I took an opposite path and made it my goal to be upbeat and sociable."

He grinned. "I bet you were a cheerleader."

She returned his smile. "Yes, I was, and I could do a mean backflip."

"Think you could still do it?"

"I don't know. It's been a while, but I suppose I could don my cheerleading skirt, though it's probably a little tight, and give it the old college try."

He winked, sending a succession of pleasant chills down Hannah's body. "I'd like to see that."

"If you're like most men, you just want to see up my skirt." Had she really said that?

He sent her a sly grin. "I do admire limber women."

A brief span of silence passed, a few indefinable moments following unmistakable innuendo. Hannah couldn't recall the last time she'd actually flirted with someone aside from her husband. And she'd been flirting with a virtual stranger. An extremely handsome, successful stranger.

A very young, very peppy blonde waitress sauntered over and flashed a grin. "Can I get you anything, sir?"

"Bring me a cola," Logan said without cracking a smile.

She glanced at Hannah. "What about you, ma'am?"

"No, thank you."

"Are you sure?" Logan asked. "You wouldn't like one more round?"

She was sorely tempted, but too sensible to give in. "I'm driving, remember?"

"I could drive you home if you change your mind."

"That would be too much trouble," she said, knowing that if he came anywhere near her empty house, she might make a colossal mistake.

"It's not a problem."

It could be if she didn't proceed with caution. "I'm fine for now. But thanks."

Once the waitress left, Hannah opted for a subject change. "Now that you know quite a bit about me, what about you?"

He pushed his empty coffee cup aside. "What do you want to know?"

Plenty. "I saw on your profile you're single. Have you ever been married?"

His expression went suddenly somber. "Once. I've been divorced for eight years."

She couldn't imagine a man of his caliber remaining unattached all that time. "Any relationships since?"

"Nothing serious."

She tapped her chin and pretended to think. "Let me guess. You have a woman in every court."

His smile returned, but only halfway. "Not even close. I work a lot of hours so I don't have much time for a social life."

"Did you take a vow of celibacy?" Heaven help her, the vodka had completely destroyed her verbal filter.

When the waitress returned with the cola, Logan pulled out his wallet and handed her a platinum card to close out the tab, or so Hannah assumed. "Keep it open for the time being," he said, shattering her assumptions.

Once the waitress retreated, Hannah attempted to backtrack. "Forget I asked that last question. It's really none of my business."

"It's okay," he said. "I've had a few relationships based solely on convenience. What about you?"

He'd presented a good case of turnabout being fair play, but she simply had little to tell when it came to the dating game. "Like you, I haven't had time to seriously consider the social scene. I have had a couple of coffee dates in the past year, but they were disastrous. One guy still lived at his mother's house in the basement, and the other's only goal was to stay in school as long as possible. He already had three graduate degrees."

"Apparently the last guy was fairly smart," he said.

"True, but both made it quite clear they weren't particularly fond of children, and that's a deal breaker. Not to mention I'm not going to subject my child to a man unless he's earned my trust."

He traced the rim of the glass with his thumb. "It's logical that you would have major concerns in that department."

"Very true. And I have to admit I'm fairly protective of her. Some might even say overprotective." Including her best friend, Gina.

Logan downed the last of his drink and set it aside. "I'm not sure there is such a thing in this day and time."

"But I've been known to take it to extremes. I've even considered encasing her in bubble wrap every day before I send her off to school."

Her attempt at humor seemed to fall flat for Logan.

"You really can't protect them from everything, and that's a damn shame."

His solemn tone spurred Hannah's curiosity. "Do you have children from your previous marriage?"

He momentarily looked away. "No."

Definitely a story there. "Was that a mutual decision between you and your wife?" Realizing she'd become the ultimate Nosy Nellie, she raised her hands, palms forward. "I'm so sorry. I'm not normally this intrusive."

"My wife was an attorney, too," he continued, as if her prying didn't bother him. "Having kids wasn't in the cards for us, and that was probably just as well."

"How long were you married?"

"A little over seven years."

She started to ask if he'd been plagued with the legendary itch but didn't want to destroy her honorable-man image. "I'm sorry to hear that. I'm sure the divorce process can be tough."

"Ours was pretty contentious. But it wasn't anything compared to losing someone to death."

He almost sounded as if he'd had experience with that as well. "They're both losses, and they both require navigating the grief process. I was somewhat lucky in that respect. I had Cassie to see me through the rough times."

"How old was she when your husband died?" he asked.

"I was five months pregnant, so he never saw her." She was somewhat amazed she'd gotten through that revelation without falling apart. Maybe her grief cycle was finally nearing completion.

"At least you were left with a part of him," Logan

said gruffly. "I assume that did provide some consolation."

A good-looking and intuitive man, a rare combination in Hannah's limited experience. "I'm very surprised by your accurate perception, Mr. Whittaker. Most of the time people look at me with pity when they learn the details. I appreciate their sympathy, but I'm not a lost cause."

"It's Logan," he told her. "And you're not remotely a lost cause or someone who deserves pity. You deserve respect and congratulations for moving on with your life, Hannah."

Somewhat self-conscious over the compliment, and oddly excited over hearing her name on his lips, she began to fold the corner of the cocktail napkin back and forth. "Believe me, the first two years weren't pretty. I cried a lot and I had a few serious bouts of self-pity. But then Cassie would reach a milestone, like her first steps and the first time she said 'Mama,' and I realized I had to be strong for her. I began to look at every day as a chance for new opportunities. A new beginning, so to speak."

The waitress came back to the table and eyed Hannah's empty glass. "Sure I can't get you another?"

She glanced at the clock hanging over the bar and after noticing it was nearly 10:00 p.m., she couldn't believe how quickly the time had flown by. "Actually, it's getting late. I should probably be going."

"It's not that late," Logan said. "Like I told you before, I'll make sure you get home safely if you want to live a little and have another vodka and tonic."

Hannah mulled over the offer for a few moments. Her daughter was at a sleepover, she had no desire to watch TV, and she was in the company of a very attractive and attentive man who promised to keep her safe. What would be the harm in having one more drink?

"I should never have ordered that second drink."

Logan regarded Hannah across the truck's cab as he pulled to a stop at the curb near her driveway. "It's my fault for encouraging you."

She lifted her face from her hands and attempted a smile. "You didn't force me at gunpoint. And you had no idea I'm such a lightweight when it comes to alcohol."

Funny, she seemed perfectly coherent to him, both back in the bar and now. "Are you feeling okay?"

"Just a little fuzzy and worried about my car. It's not much, but it's all that I have."

He'd noticed the sedan had seen better days. "It's been secured in the valet garage, and I'll make certain it's delivered to you first thing in the morning."

"You've done too much already," she said. "I really could have called a cab."

In reality, he hadn't been ready to say good-night, although he couldn't quite understand why. Or maybe he understood it and didn't want to admit it. "Like I told you, it's not a problem. You don't know who you can trust these days, especially when you're an attractive woman."

She gave him a winning grin. "I bet you say that to all the women who refuse a five-million-dollar inheritance."

"You happen to be the first in that regard." Absolutely the first woman in a long, long time to completely capture his interest on a first meeting. A business meeting to boot. "I'm hoping you haven't totally ruled out taking the money."

"Yes, I have. I know you probably think I've lost my mind, but I do have my reasons."

Yeah, and he'd figured them out—she was refusing on the basis of principle. He sure as hell didn't see that often in his line of work. "Well, I'm not going to pressure you, but I will check back with you tomorrow after you've slept on it."

She blinked and hid a yawn behind her hand. "Speaking of sleeping, I'm suddenly very tired. I guess it's time to bid you adieu."

When Hannah reached for the door handle, Logan touched her arm to gain her attention. "I'll get that for you."

"Whaddya know," she said. "Looks like chivalry is still alive and well after all." She followed the comment with a soft, breathless laugh that sent his imagination into overdrive.

Before he acted on impulse, Logan quickly slid out of the driver's seat, rounded the hood and opened the door for Hannah. She had a little trouble climbing out, which led him to take her hand to assist her. Weird thing was, he didn't exactly want to let go of her hand, but he did, with effort.

He followed behind her as they traveled the path to the entry, trying hard to keep his gaze focused on that silky auburn hair that swayed slightly with each step she took, not her butt that did a little swaying, too.

Right before they reached the front porch, Hannah glanced back and smiled. "At least I'm not falling-down drunk." Then she immediately tripped on the first step.

Logan caught her elbow before she landed on that butt he'd been trying to ignore. "Careful."

"I'm just clumsy," she said as he guided her up the remaining steps.

Once they reached the door, he released her arm and she sent him another sleepy smile. "I really enjoyed the evening, Logan. And if you'll just send me what I need to sign to relinquish the money, I'll mail it back to you immediately."

He still wasn't convinced she was doing the right thing in that regard. "We'll talk about that later. Right now getting you to bed is more important." Dammit, that sounded like a freaking proposition.

"Do you want to come in?" she asked, taking him totally by surprise.

"I don't think that's a good idea." Actually, it sounded like a great idea, but he was too keyed up to honestly believe he could control his libido.

She clutched her bag to her chest. "Oh, I get it. You're afraid you're going to be accosted by the poor, single mom who hasn't had sex in almost seven years."

Oh, hell. "That's not it at all. I just respect you enough not to put us in the position where we might do something we regret, because, lady, being alone with you could lead to all sorts of things."

She leaned a shoulder against the support column and inclined her head. "Really?"

"Really. In case you haven't noticed, I've had a hard time keeping my eyes off you tonight." He was having a real *hard* time right now.

She barked out a laugh. "I'm sorry, but I'm having a difficult time believing you would be interested in me."

She couldn't be more wrong. "Why wouldn't I be?

You're smart and savvy and pretty damn brave to raise a child on your own and finish college at the same time."

"Keep going."

He could…all night. "You're a survivor and very beautiful, although you don't seem to know that. And that's not only hard to find in a beautiful woman, it's appealing."

"And?"

"Right now I'd like to kiss you," he blurted out before his brain caught up with his mouth. "But I'm not going to."

"Why not?" she asked, looking thoroughly disappointed.

"Because if I kissed you, I might not want to stop there. And as I've said, I respect you too much to—"

Hannah cut off his words by circling one hand around his neck and landing her lips on his, giving him the kiss he'd been halfheartedly trying to avoid.

Logan was mildly aware she'd dropped her purse, and very aware she kissed him like she hadn't been kissed in a long, long time—with the soft glide of her tongue against his, bringing on a strong stirring south of his belt buckle. He grazed his hand up her side until his palm rested close to her breast, and he heard her breath catch as she moved flush against him. He considered telling her they should take it inside the house before someone called the cops, but then she pulled abruptly away from him and took a step back.

Hannah touched her fingertips to her lips, her face flushed, her emerald eyes wide with shock. "I cannot believe I just did that. And I can't imagine what you must be thinking about me right now."

He was thinking he wanted her. Badly. "Hey, it's chemistry. It happens. Couple that with a few cocktails—"

"And you get some thirty-year-old woman acting totally foolish."

He tucked a strand of hair behind her ear. "You don't have to feel foolish or ashamed, Hannah. I'm personally flattered that you kissed me."

She snatched her bag from the cement floor and hugged it tightly again. "I didn't give you a whole lot of choice."

"You only did what I wanted to do." Trouble was, he wanted to do it again, and more. "For the record, I think you're one helluva sexy woman and I'd really like to get to know you better."

"But we've just met," she said. "We don't really know anything about each other."

He knew enough to want to move forward and see where it might lead. "That's the get-to-know-each-other-better part."

"We don't live in the same town."

"True, but it's only a ninety-mile drive."

"You're busy and I have a five-year-old child who is currently in school, plus I'm looking for a job."

He remembered another search she should be conducting, and this could be the key to spending more time with her. "There's something I've been meaning to ask you all night."

"Have I taken total leave of my senses?"

He appreciated her wit, too. "This is about your biological father."

That seemed to sober her up. "What about him?"

"Just wondering if you have any details about his life."

She sighed. "I only know that my mother hooked up with some guy who left her high and dry when she became pregnant with me. According to her, he was both ruthless and worthless."

Some people might describe J. D. Lassiter that way. "Did she ever offer to give you a name?"

"No, and I didn't ask. I figured that if he wanted nothing to do with me, then I wanted nothing to do with him." Her tone was laced with false bravado.

He did have a hard time believing J.D. would be so cold and uncaring that he would ignore his own flesh and blood no matter what the circumstances. "Maybe there were underlying issues that prevented him from being involved in your life."

"Do you mean the part about him being an absolute bastard, or that he was married?"

Finally, a little more to go on. "Do you know that to be a fact? The married part."

"My mother hinted at that, but again, I can't be certain."

"Then maybe it's time you try to find out the truth. You owe it to yourself and to your daughter. Because if J.D. is actually your father, you have siblings."

Hannah seemed to mull that over for a time before she spoke again. "How do you propose I do that?"

"With my help."

She frowned. "Why would you even want to help me?"

"Because I can't imagine what it would be like to have more questions than answers." In some ways he did know that. Intimately. "And since I'm an attorney, and I know the Lassiters personally, I could do some subtle investigating without looking suspicious."

"It seems to me you would be too busy to take this on."

"Actually, I have a light caseload this week." Or he would as soon as he asked his assistant to postpone a few follow-up appointments. "But I would definitely want you to be actively involved in the search."

"How do you suggest I do that from here?"

Here came the part that would probably have her questioning his motives. "Not here. In Cheyenne. You could stay with me for a few days and I'll show you the sights and introduce you to a few people. You could so some research during the day while I'm at work."

Hannah's mouth opened slightly before she snapped it shut. "Stay with you?"

He definitely understood why that part of the plan might get her hackles up. "Look, I have a forty-five-hundred-square-foot house with five bedrooms and seven baths. You'd have your own space. In fact, the master bedroom is downstairs and the guest rooms are all upstairs. We could go for days and not even see each other." Like he intended for that to happen.

"Good heavens, why would a confirmed bachelor need a house that size?"

"I got a good deal on the place when the couple had to transfer out of state. And I like to entertain."

"Do you have a harem?"

He couldn't help but laugh for the second time tonight, something he'd rarely done over the past few years. "No harem. But I have five acres and a couple of horses, as well as a gourmet kitchen. My housekeeper comes by twice a week and makes meals in advance if I don't want to cook."

"You know how to cook?" she asked, sounding doubtful.

"Yeah. I know my way around the stove."

She smiled. "Mac and cheese? BLT sandwiches? Or maybe when you're feeling adventurous, you actually tackle scrambled eggs?"

"My favorite adventurous meal will always be Italian. You'd like my mostaccioli."

She loosened her grip on her bag and slipped the strap on her shoulder. "As tempting as that sounds, I can't just take off for Cheyenne without my daughter. She won't be out of school for five weeks."

"Is there someone who could watch her for a few days?" Damn, he almost sounded desperate.

"Possibly, but I've never left Cassie alone for more than a night," she said. "I don't know how she would handle it. I don't know how *I* would handle it. Besides, I'm not sure I could accomplish that much in a few days even if I did decide to go."

He might be losing the battle, but he intended to win the war. "You could drive up for day trips, but that would require a lot of driving. If you stayed with me a couple of days, that would give us time to get to know each other better."

"Residing in a stranger's house would require a huge leap of faith."

He closed the space between them and cupped her face in his palm. "We're not strangers anymore. Not after you did this."

He kissed her softly, thoroughly, with just enough exploration to tempt her to take him up on his offer.

And once he was done, he moved away but kept his gaze locked on hers. "There could be more of that if you decide you want it. Again, no pressure. I'm just asking you to think about it. You might have the answers you need about your heritage, and we might find out we enjoy each other's company. Unless you're afraid to explore the possibilities…"

Logan realized he'd hit a home run when he saw a hint of defiance in Hannah's eyes. "I'm not the cowardly type, but I am cautious because I have to be. However, I will consider your suggestion and give you my answer tomorrow."

"Do you mind giving me your number? So I can call and let you know when your car's on its way." And in case he needed to further plead his case.

She dug through her purse for a pen and paper and scribbled down the information on the back of a receipt. "That's my home and cell number," she said as she handed it over. "Feel free to send me a text."

As Logan pocketed the paper, Hannah withdrew her keys, turned around and unlocked the door with a little effort, then walked inside without another word.

Logan was left alone on the porch to ponder why being with her again seemed so damn important. He had his choice of beautiful women back in Cheyenne, although most hadn't come close to capturing his interest like Hannah Armstrong.

He could chalk it up to chemistry, but he inherently knew that was only part of it. He did appreciate her keen sense of humor, knock-'em-dead body and those expressive green eyes that could drop a man in his tracks. He appreciated her all-fire independence and that she had the temperament of a mother bear when it came to her kid. In some ways, that attracted him more than anything else. But above all, she'd experienced the loss of a loved one. Their true common ground.

Hannah might understand his grief because she'd lived it, but if he told her his story, would she see him in the same light? Or would she turn away when she learned the truth?

Only time would tell if he'd find the courage to confess his greatest sin—he'd been partially to blame for the death of his only child.

Three

Her car was back, and so was the man who'd been foremost on her mind all morning long. All night, too.

Hannah peered out the window and watched Logan emerge from her aged blue sedan dressed in a long-sleeved black shirt, faded jeans secured by a belt with a shiny buckle and dark boots. Her heart immediately went on a marathon, the direct effect of an undeniable attraction she'd experienced all too well last night. That attraction had given her the courage to kiss him, some-thing she normally wouldn't have the audacity to do. But by golly she had, and she'd liked it. A lot.

Hormones. That had to be it. Those pesky freaks of nature that made people act on impulse. She made a point to banish them as soon as she climbed out of bed. Granted, when he'd called to say he was bring-ing the car back, she'd made certain she looked more presentable than she had during their first meeting. She'd dressed in simple, understated clothing—white capri pants, light green, short-sleeved shirt and rhinestone-embellished flip-flops. Of course, she had put on a little makeup and pulled her hair back in a sleek, low ponytail. The silver hoop earrings might be a little much, but it was too late to take them off unless she ripped them out of her earlobes.

When the bell rang, Hannah automatically smoothed her palms over the sides of her hair and the front of the blouse. She measured her steps to avoid looking too eager, even though she wanted to hurl herself onto the porch and launch into his arms. Instead, she gave herself a mental pep talk on the virtues of subtlety before she slowly opened the door.

He greeted her with a dimpled grin and surprisingly stuck out his hand. "Mornin'. I'm Logan Whittaker, in case you've forgotten."

Hannah didn't know whether to kick him in the shin or kiss that sexy look off his face. She chose option three—play along for now—and accepted his offered handshake. She noticed the calluses and the width of his palm as he gave her hand a slight squeeze before he released her. "Good morning, Mr. Whittaker, and thank you for returning my car."

"You're welcome, but after last night, you should call me Logan."

Cue the blush. "I'm trying to forget about last night."

"Good luck with that because I sure can't forget it. In fact, it kept me tossing and turning most of the night."

She'd experienced the same restlessness, not that she'd admit it to him. "Do I need to drive you back to the lodge?"

"Nope," he said. "One of the valet guys will be here in about ten minutes."

Must be nice to have people at your beck and call, but she supposed that perk came with money. "Are you sure I can't drop you off? It's the least I can do."

"I'm sure, but I'm not leaving until we discuss your inheritance and my proposal."

No amount of money would ever convince her to agree to sign a nondisclosure form, even if she had no intention of aligning herself with the Lassiters. And that's the way it would stay. "I haven't changed my mind about the money, and the jury's still out on the other, to coin a legal phrase."

"Well, since you haven't ruled it out, I think you should let me in to argue my case. I'm housebroken and I won't destroy the furniture."

The sexy dog. "I suppose that's okay, but I have to warn you, the place is a mess, thanks to my child and the plumbing problems."

He had the gall to grin again, revealing those damnable dimples and perfectly straight, white teeth. "I promise you won't regret hearing me out."

She already did when he brushed past her and she caught the subtle scent of his cologne. Even more when once they moved inside, he turned and asked, "Where do you want me?"

An unexpected barrage of questionable images assaulted Hannah, sending her mind in the direction of unadvisable possibilities. Clearly those inherent female desires she'd tried to bury in everyday life weren't completely dead. That was okay, as long as she didn't act on them. Again.

She swallowed hard and bumped the door closed

with her bottom. "Let's go in the dining room." A safe place to interact with Mr. Charisma. "Actually, the floor's wet in there, so we can stay in here." First, she had to clear the worn floral couch of kid debris.

Before she could do that, Logan presented a frown that didn't detract from his good looks one iota. "Leaky pipe?"

"You could definitely say that. I managed to cut off the water under the sink, but this morning I got up only to discover the valve is leaking, too. Now the flood waters are trying to take over my kitchen."

"Tough break."

When Logan began rolling up his sleeves, Hannah's mouth dropped open. "What are you doing?"

"I'm pretty handy when it comes to pipe problems."

"That's not what you said yesterday."

"I've learned not to reveal my skills. Otherwise I'll be hounded every time someone has a plumbing issue. But for you, I'm willing to take a look."

She'd already taken a look. A covert look at his toned forearms threaded with veins, and the opening in his collar that revealed tanned skin and a slight shading of hair she'd tried not to notice last night. "Now I get it. You're really a repressed plumber masquerading as a lawyer."

His reappearing smile had the impact of a jackhammer. "No, but I am good with my hands."

She'd bet her last buck on that. "Thanks for offering to help, but it's not necessary. A real plumber should be here today."

Now he looked plain cynical. "Good luck with that, too. They don't get in a big hurry on a Saturday." He winked. "Besides, I'll save you that weekend rate and check it out for free."

He did have a valid argument, and she really liked the free part. What would be the harm in letting him peruse her pipes, or anything else of hers he'd like to peruse? She seriously needed to get a hold on her self-control. "Fine, but you're going to get wet. I did."

"Not a problem. Getting wet isn't always a bad thing."

Logan's suggestive tone wasn't lost on her. "Since you insist, be my guest." She pointed toward the opening to the dining room. "Just swim through there and keep going. You can't miss the kitchen sink."

Hannah followed behind Logan, covertly sizing up his butt on the way. A really nice butt, not that she was surprised. He happened to be one major male specimen, and she'd have to be in a coma not to notice. Still, she refused to let a sexy, dark-eyed, dimpled cowboy attorney muddle her mind. She'd let him fix her sink and say his piece before sending him packing back to Cheyenne without her.

Logan grabbed a wrench from the counter, lowered to his knees and stuck his head into the cabinet beneath the sink. Hannah leaned back against the counter to watch, unable to suppress a laugh over the string of oaths coming out of the lawyer's mouth.

"Sorry," he muttered without looking back. "I need to tighten a fitting and it's not cooperating."

"Is that the reason for the leak?"

"Yeah. It's a little corroded and probably should be replaced eventually. But I think I can get it to hold."

At least that would save her an after-business-hours service call. "That's a relief."

"Don't be relieved until I say it's repaired."

A few minutes passed, filled with a little more cursing and the occasional groan, until Logan finally emerged from beneath the cabinet and turned on the sink. Seemingly satisfied, he set the wrench aside and sent Hannah another devastating smile. "All done for the time being. Again, it needs to be replaced. Actually, all the pipes should be replaced."

Hannah sighed. "So I've been told. The house was built over forty years ago and it's systematically falling apart. I just paid for a new furnace. That pretty much ate up my reserves and blew my budget."

He wiped his hands on the towel beside the sink. "If you claim the inheritance, you'd never have to worry about a tight budget."

She couldn't deny the concept appealed to her greatly, but the cost to her principles was simply too high. "As I've said, I have no intention of taking my share." Even if J. D. Lassiter did owe her that much. But money could never make up for the years she'd spent in a constant state of wondering where she had come from.

Logan leaned back against the counter opposite Hannah. "And what *are* your intentions when it comes to my invitation?"

"I just don't see the wisdom in running off to Cheyenne on what will probably be a wild-goose chase."

"But it might not be at all. And you would also have the opportunity to meet some of the Lassiters, in case you decide you'd like to connect with your relatives since you wouldn't be bound by the nondisclosure."

"I'm not interested in connecting with the Lassiters."

He studied her for a few moments, questions in his eyes. "Aside from your in-laws, do you have any family?"

Hannah shook her head. "No. I'm an only child and so was my mother. My grandparents have been gone for many years."

"Then wouldn't it be good to get to know the family you never knew existed?" he asked.

She shrugged. "I've gone all these years without knowing, so I'm sure I'll survive if I never meet them."

"What about your daughter? Don't you think she deserves to know she has another family?"

The sound of rapid footsteps signaled the arrival of said daughter. Hannah's attention turned to her right to see the feisty five-year-old twirling through the dining area wearing a pink boa and matching tutu that covered her aqua shirt and shorts, with a fake diamond tiara planted atop her head. She waved around the star wand that she gripped in her fist and shouted, "I'm queen of the frog fairies!"

Cassie stopped turning circles when she spotted the strange man in the kitchen, yet she didn't stop her forward progress. Instead, she charged up to Logan, where she paused to give him a partially toothless grin. "Are you a frog or a prince?"

Possibly a toad in prince clothing, Hannah decided, but that remained to be seen. "This is Mr. Whittaker, Cassie, and he's a lawyer. Do you know what that is, sweetie?"

Her daughter glanced back and rolled her eyes. "I'm not a baby, Mama. I'm almost six and I watch the law shows on TV with Shelly. That's how I learned about lawyers. They look mad all the time and yell 'I object.'"

Hannah made a mental note to have a long talk with the sitter about appropriate television programs for a kindergartner. When Cassie began twirling again, she caught her daughter by the shoulders and turned her to face Logan. "What do you say to Mr. Whittaker?"

Cassie curtsied and grinned. "It's nice to meet you, Mr. Whittaker."

Logan attempted a smile but it didn't make its way to his eyes. In fact, he almost looked sad. "It's nice to meet you, too, Your Highness."

Being addressed as royalty seemed to please Cassie greatly. "Do you have a little girl?"

His gaze wandered away for a moment before he returned it to Cassie. "No, I don't."

"A little boy?" Cassie topped off the comment with a sour look.

"Nope. No kids."

Hannah sensed Logan's discomfort and chalked it up to someone who hadn't been around children, and maybe didn't care to be around them. "Now that the introductions are over, go pick up your toys, Cassandra Jane, and start deciding what you'll be wearing to school on Monday since that takes you at least two days."

That statement earned a frown from her daughter. "Can I just wear this?"

"I think you should save that outfit for playtime. Now scoot."

Cassie backed toward the dining room, keeping her smile trained on Logan. "I think you're a prince," she said, then turned and sprinted away.

Once her daughter had vacated the premises, Hannah returned her attention to Logan. "I'm sorry. She's really into fairy tales these days, and she doesn't seem to know a stranger. Frankly, that worries me sometimes. I'm afraid someday she'll encounter someone with questionable intentions. I've cautioned her time and again, but I'm not sure she understands the risk in that behavior."

"I understand why that would worry you," he said. "But I guess you have to trust that she'll remember your warnings if the situation presents itself."

Hannah sighed. "I hope so. She's everything to me and sometimes I'd like to keep her locked in her room until she's eighteen."

He grinned. "Encased in bubble wrap, right?"

She was pleasantly surprised he remembered that from the night before. "Bubble wrap with rhinestones. Now what were you saying before we were interrupted by the queen?"

"Mama! Where's my purple shorts?"

Hannah gritted her teeth and spoke through them. "Just a minute, Cassie."

"Look, maybe this isn't a good time to discuss this…." Logan said.

She was beginning to wonder that same thing. "You're probably right. And it's probably best if I say thanks, but no thanks, to your proposal, although I sincerely appreciate your offer."

When Logan's phone beeped, he took the cell out of his back pocket and swiped the screen. "The driver's here."

"Then I guess you better go." She sounded disappointed, even to her own ears.

He pocketed his wallet then unrolled his sleeves. "Do you have a pen and paper handy so I can give you my info?"

Hannah withdrew a pencil from the tin container on the counter and tore a piece of paper from the nearby notepad. "Here you go, but don't forget, I already have your card."

He turned his back and began jotting something down. "Yeah, but you don't have my home address."

She swallowed hard. "Why would I need that?"

He faced her again, caught her hand and placed the card in her palm. "In case you change your mind and decide to spend a few days as my guest in Cheyenne."

Oh, how tempting that would be. But… "I would have to ask my friend Gina if Cassie could stay with her. And I'd have to suspend my job search, even though that's not going anywhere right now." Funny, she sounded as if she was actually considering it.

He took a brief look around before he leaned over and brushed a kiss across her lips. "If you do decide to come, don't worry about calling. Just surprise me and show up."

With that, he strode through the living room and out the door, leaving Hannah standing in the kitchen in a semi-stupor until reality finally set in. Then she snatched up the cordless phone and pounded out a number on her way to the bedroom, where she closed the door. As soon as she heard the familiar hello, she said the only thing she could think to say.

"Help!"

"He wants you to do *what?*"

Sitting in a high-back stool at the granite island in her best friend's kitchen, Hannah was taken aback by Gina Romero's strong reaction to her declaration. Normally the woman rode her mercilessly about finding a man. "I'll speak more slowly this time. He wants me to go to Cheyenne for a few days and investigate the possibility that the man I'm inheriting from might be my biological father." She sure as heck wasn't going to reveal that inheritance was basically a fortune.

Gina swept one hand through her bobbed blond hair and narrowed her blue eyes. "Is that all he wants to investigate?"

Hannah would swear her face had morphed into a furnace. "Don't be ridiculous, Gina."

"Don't be naive, Hannah."

"I'm not being naive." Even if she wasn't being completely truthful. "He really is trying to help me."

Gina handed her eight-month-old son, Trey, another cracker when he began to squirm in the nearby high chair. "So tell me what's so special about this mystery attorney who wants to *help* you."

That could take hours. "Well, he's fairly tall, has dark hair and light brown eyes. Oh, and he has incredible dimples."

Gina gave her a good eye-rolling, the second Hannah had received today. "Okay. So he's a hunk, but does he have anything else to back that up?"

"As a matter of fact, he does. He's a full partner in a very prestigious law firm in Cheyenne."

"How's his butt?" she asked in a conspiratorial whisper.

The memory brought about Hannah's smile. "Stellar."

"Well, then, why aren't you home packing?"

"You'd think that would be enough, but I still have quite a few reservations."

"Unless you're lying and he's really in his eighties and drives a Studebaker, you should go for it."

"He's thirty-eight and drives a Mercedes. But he's also childless and divorced."

"Not everyone who's divorced is an ogre, Hannah," Gina said. "You can't judge him by your experience with that Henry what's-his-name you went out with for a while."

Gina could have gone all year without mentioning that jerk. "I only went out with him twice. But you know I worry when I meet a man who couldn't make his marriage work."

Gina frowned. "There are all sorts of reasons why marriages don't work, and it might not have even been his fault."

She couldn't argue that point since she had no details about Logan's divorce. "But what if it was his fault? What if he has some horrible habits that can't be overlooked?" Or worse, what if he cheated on his wife?

When the baby began to fuss, Gina rifled through the box of crackers and handed another one to her son. "Tell me, did this attorney do anything weird at dinner like that Henry guy you dated? Did he pick his teeth and belch? Or did he try to unsnap your bra when you hugged him good-night?"

"I didn't hug him good-night."

"Too bad."

"But I did kiss him."

Gina slapped her palm on the table, sending the baby into a fit of giggles. "You've been sitting here for ten minutes and you're just now telling me this?"

"It was a mistake." A huge one. "I had a couple of drinks and I guess it stripped me of all my inhibitions."

Gina sent her a sly look. "Question is, did you strip following the kiss?"

Heaven forbid. "Of course not. I just met the guy and I'm not that stupid."

"Yet you're considering going away with him," Gina said, adding a suspicious stare.

"I wouldn't be going away with him. I'd be staying at his house, which is very big, according to Logan."

"Wonder if his house is the only thing that's big."

Hannah playfully slapped at Gina's arm. "Stop it. This has to do with filling in the missing pieces of my family history, not getting friendly with Logan."

"Sure it does, Hannah. Just keep telling yourself that and you might start to believe it."

Leave it to Gina to see right through her ruse. "So what if I am attracted to him? Is there anything wrong with that?"

Gina made a one-handed catch of Trey's cracker when he tossed it at her. "There's absolutely nothing wrong with that. In fact, it's about time you start living again, girlfriend."

Same song, fiftieth verse. "I have been living, *girlfriend*. I've finished school and raised my daughter and I'm about to start a new career."

"Don't forget you cared for your ungrateful mother during the final months of her illness." Gina reached across the island and laid a palm on Hannah's forearm. "What you've done for your family since Danny's death is admirable. Heck, I'm not sure I could do the same thing if something happened to Frank. But now you need to do something for yourself."

Hannah still harbored several concerns. "What if I make this trip, decide that he's someone I want to spend a lot more time with and end up getting hurt?"

"That will happen only if you let him hurt you."

"True, but you have no idea how I felt being around him last night. I could barely think."

"Chemistry will cloud your mind every time."

Chemistry she could handle. "I'm worried it's more than that, Gina. I wish I could explain it." How could she when she couldn't explain it to herself? "I sense he really is a compassionate person, and maybe he's had some hard times during his life, too."

Gina took Trey from the high chair, placed him in the playpen and then signaled Hannah to join her in the adjacent den. She sat on the sofa and patted the space beside her. "Come here and let's have a heart-to-heart."

Hannah claimed her spot on the couch and prepared for a friendly lecture. "Bestow me with your sage advice, oh, wise one."

Gina sent her a smile. "Look, while we were growing up, you always walked the straight and narrow, always striving to be the best cheerleader, best student and an all-around good girl."

She bristled over her friend's words. "And what was wrong with that?"

"Because you did all those things to please your mother, and it never seemed to matter. Then you married Danny at the ripe old age of twenty. You worked hard to please him by quitting college so he could go to trade school when his parents cut him off because he married you."

She could feel her blood pressure begin to rise. "I loved Danny with all my heart and he loved me."

"Yes, he did, and he appreciated your efforts, unlike Ruth. But don't you think it's time you have a little adventure?"

Adventure had been a word sorely missing from

her vocabulary. "Maybe you're right, but what do I do about Cassie?"

Gina looked at her as if she'd lost her mind. "I can't count the times you've kept Michaela when Frank and I went out of town for a long weekend, including the one when I got pregnant with Trey. It's way past time for me to return the favor and watch Cassie for however long it takes for you to thoroughly investigate the attorney."

Hannah couldn't stop the flow of sexy, forbidden thoughts streaming through her imagination, until reality came calling once more. "But you're going to be saddled with two giggling girls and a baby. That doesn't seem fair."

Gina stood and began picking up the toys bouncing across the hardwood floors while Trey kept hurling more over the side of the playpen. "I'm used to this little guy's antics, and the girls will be in school during the day. Unless you plan to be gone until they reach puberty, it shouldn't be a problem."

"If I do go—" and that was a major *if* "—I only plan to stay a couple of days. A week, tops. But you're still going to have to deal with them at night, not to mention you have a husband to care for and—"

Gina held up a finger to silence her. "Frank has been trained well. And besides, he's been talking about trying for another kid next year. I might as well get in some practice before he knocks me up a third time."

The sound of those giggling girls grew closer and reached a crescendo as one red-headed ball of fire and one petite, brown-haired follower rushed into the room dressed in too-big formal attire, their faces showing the signs of a makeup attack.

"Aren't we pretty, Mama?" Cassie asked as she spun around in the red sequined strapless grown.

"Very," Hannah lied when she caught sight of the charcoal smudges outlining her daughter's eyes. "But did you have permission to raid Gina's closet?"

"Those came out of my cedar chest, Hannah," Gina said. "Cassie's wearing my prom dress and Michaela's wearing yours, in case didn't recognize it."

Hannah did recognize the black silk gown all right, but she didn't remember giving it to her friend. "What are you doing with it?"

Gina looked somewhat chagrined. "I borrowed it and forgot to give it back."

Michaela's grin looked as lopsided as her high pony-tail, thanks to the scarlet lipstick running askew from her mouth. "Can I keep it, Hannah?"

"Yes, honey, you most certainly can." The terrible memories of her part-octopus prom date, Ryan, were still attached to the gown, so no great loss.

"Do you have something you'd like to ask your daughter, Hannah?" Gina inquired.

Hannah supposed it wouldn't hurt to get Cassie's reaction to the possibility of her traveling to Chey-enne. "Sweetie, if I decided to take a trip out of town for a few days, would you mind staying here with Michaela and Gina?"

Cassie ran right out of her oversized high heels and practically tackled Hannah with a voracious hug. "I want to stay, Mama! When are you going?"

Good question. She pulled Cassie into her lap and planted a kiss on her makeup-caked cheek. "I'm not sure yet. Maybe tonight, but probably tomorrow."

Cassie looked crestfallen. "Go tonight, please. Me

and Mickey want to have a wedding. Gina said we could use her dress."

Hannah glanced at Gina. "You said that?"

"Yes, I did. But they've been forewarned that the groom will either be a stuffed animal or the baby brother, no boys from the neighborhood."

Cassie came to her feet and gave Hannah a hopeful look. "So can I stay, Mama? I'll be good and I'll help Mickey clean her room and I'll go to bed when I'm told."

Hannah couldn't in good conscience make a promise she might not keep. "We'll see. Right now you need to wash that purple eye shadow off your lids and go for something a little more subtle, like a nice beige. But before you do that, I want to take a picture."

While she fished her cell phone from her pocket, the girls struck a pose and put on their best grins. And as soon as she snapped the photo, the pair took off down the hall, sounds of sheer excitement echoing throughout the house.

She then noticed the blinking blue light indicating she'd received a text. And she couldn't be more surprised when she noted the message's sender. "Speak of the sexy devil."

Gina moved close to her side. "Devil as in the attorney?"

"Yes."

"What does it say?"

"'Dinner should be ready around seven. Italian. I also have a good bottle of wine. The only thing missing is you.'"

"Now I'm worried," Gina said.

Hannah pocketed the phone and stared at her friend. "You have something against Italian food?"

"I'm part Italian, silly. No, I'm worried because the devil didn't mention good sex."

She elbowed Gina in the side. "Would you please get off the sex thing? We have two impressionable, minor children in the house and they hear everything within a fifty-mile radius."

Gina pushed off the sofa and picked up the whimpering baby. "Come on, Hannah. Put on your big-girl panties and get with the program."

Something suddenly dawned on her. "Oh, my gosh, all I have are big-girl panties. Not a sexy pair in the drawer."

Her friend claimed the rocker across from the sofa and positioned the baby on her shoulder. "It's not even close to noon yet, so you have a few hours left to remedy that. Have you used the department-store gift card I gave you on your birthday?"

She was somewhat ashamed she'd held on to it for three months. "No, but before you get *your* big-girl panties in a wad, I've been too busy to shop."

"You better get busy if you want to be in Cheyenne by sundown," Gina said as she set the rocker in motion and rubbed her sleepy son's back.

A barrage of memories assaulted Hannah, recollections of a time when she'd rocked her baby girl, plagued with emotions that ran the gamut from bliss to utter sadness that her daughter's father would never know those precious moments. She secretly longed to have another child someday, and to be able to share that with a special someone. She suspected Logan Whittaker might not be the one to fulfill that dream.

"What's wrong now, Hannah?"

She looked at Gina through misty eyes. "Nothing really. Just remembering when Cassie was a baby, I guess. Time has a way of zipping by before you even realize it's gone."

"True, and time's a wastin' for you," Gina said. "Go shopping and buy those sexy panties along with a few nice outfits. Then go home and pack and get thee to Cheyenne."

If only it were that easy. "Do you really think this is the right thing to do?"

Gina sighed. "I think you'll never know unless you try, so just stop thinking and do it."

Her best friend was right. Nothing ventured, nothing gained, and all that jazz.

She might live to regret the decision, but darned if she wasn't actually going to do it.

Four

Never in a million years had Logan believed she'd actually do it. But there Hannah stood on his threshold, wearing a fitted, long-sleeved blue silk blouse covering tapered jeans, a small silver purse clutched in her hands. Talk about feeling underdressed in his faded navy T-shirt, tattered jeans and rough-out work boots. She'd parked her car beneath the portico and set two bags at her feet, which sported some deadly black heels, causing Logan to think questionable thoughts he shouldn't be thinking before she even made it into the house.

"You're here," he said, slight shock in his tone.

"I guess I should have called," she replied, clear concern in her voice.

"I told you to surprise me."

"Yes, but you looked absolutely stunned when you opened the door."

He grinned. "I thought you were the maid."

Fortunately she returned his smile. "I suppose we're going to have to work on that mistaken identity thing."

He personally would have to work on resisting the urge to kiss her at every turn. "We can do that after dinner."

"As long as I don't have to cook, it's a deal."

After grabbing Hannah's bags, Logan stepped aside and nodded toward the open door. "Come inside and make yourself at home."

The minute she entered the house, Hannah's gaze traveled upward toward the two-story foyer flanked by twin staircases with modern black banisters. "Wow. This is amazing."

He'd pretty much taken the view for granted and enjoyed seeing it through her eyes. "Yeah, it's impressive. But overall the place is more comfortable than elaborate."

She shot him a cynical look. "It's practically a mansion."

He started up the wood-covered stairs to the right. "I'll show you to your room before I give you the grand tour."

Hannah followed behind him to the second floor, where Logan stopped at the landing, allowing her to move in front of him for a purely selfish, and very male reason—to check out her butt. "Just go right and keeping walking until you reach the end of the hall."

She paused to peer inside the first of the three spare bedrooms. "Very nicely appointed. I really like the navy stripes mixed with yellows."

A color pallet he wouldn't have personally chosen, but if it worked for her, it worked for him. "The house was basically move-in ready. You can thank my decorator for the finishing touches. That's definitely not my thing."

"She's very good at what she does. I'm sure she has clients lined up for her services."

"Actually, she doesn't decorate for a living. She's a good friend of mine."

"A really good friend?"

When he heard the mild suspicion in Hannah's tone, he knew exactly what she was thinking. "Her name is Marlene and she's sixty years old. I'll introduce you in the near future." He decided to withhold the fact the woman was the late J. D. Lassiter's sister-in-law.

She passed the bathroom and peeked inside, then did the same with the next guest room, and pulled up short when she came to the closed door. "What's in here?"

A room he hadn't had the heart to touch, even if it did unearth bittersweet memories he'd just as soon forget. "It's a kid's bedroom that I haven't redone yet. I figured since I have three more guest rooms, I'm not in any hurry."

When she glanced back at him, Logan could tell she wasn't buying it. "Are you sure it's not your secret man-cave?"

"That's downstairs," he said, relieved she wasn't as suspicious as he'd assumed.

"Mind if I take a look?" she asked.

"Knock yourself out."

When Hannah opened the door and stepped inside, her expression said it all. The place was a little girl's fairy tale come to life, from the four princesses painted on the walls, to the pink cushioned seat built in beneath a ceiling-high window overlooking the courtyard at the front of the house.

"Cassie would absolutely love this," Hannah said as she looked around in awe. "That was one lucky little girl."

At least someone's little girl had been that lucky. "It's not exactly my taste, but then as a kid I preferred all things rodeo and baseball."

She turned and smiled. "Is that the décor you chose for your man-cave?"

His presumed "man-cave" would suit both genders. "You can see for yourself after we get you settled in, so keep going because we're almost there."

She turned and bowed. "My wish is your command, captain."

Grinning, he headed back into the hall and strode to the door he'd intentionally kept closed just so he could enjoy her reaction when he opened it. As expected, Hannah looked completely awed when he revealed the orange-tinted skies and the Rocky Mountain backdrop in clear view through the floor-to-ceiling windows.

"That is unbelievable," she said.

So was Logan's immediate physical reaction to the breathless quality of her voice. Keeping a firm grip on his control, he set her bags on the bench at the end of the king-size bed. "I have to agree with you there. It's better than the view from my bedroom, but you'll see that for yourself." When he noticed the trepidation in Hannah's eyes, he decided to backtrack for the second time in the past five minutes. "It's included on the tour, unless you want me to leave it off."

She shook her head. "No. Since we're both grown-ups, I can go into your bedroom without the fear of being grounded."

He wouldn't mind keeping her there for an indeterminate amount of time, a fact he'd keep to himself for now. "The bathroom's to your left."

She breezed through the bedroom, opened the double doors and then looked back with a smile. "Is this where you hold all your parties?"

He wouldn't mind holding a party there for the two of them. "Nope, but I probably could fit six people in the steam shower, and at least four in the jetted bathtub."

Hannah moved inside and ran her hand over one of the two granite-topped vanities. "I feel like I've died and gone to five-star-hotel heaven."

He thought he might die if he didn't get a little lip action real soon. "It's yours to enjoy for the duration."

She turned and leaned back against the vanity. "I could use a good soak in the tub."

And he'd gladly soak with her. "If you can wait until after dinner, that would be preferable. And speaking of that, it won't be too long before it's ready."

Hannah straightened and smiled. "Great, because I'm starving."

Man, so was he—for her undivided attention. "Then let's get going with the tour." Before he suggested they say to hell with dinner and take advantage of that tub. He definitely didn't want her to believe he intended to take advantage of her.

Logan showed Hannah to the upstairs den and then escorted her downstairs. He did a quick pass through the great room, pointed out his office and the game room, pausing as he arrived at the last stop before he led her to kitchen. "And this is my favorite place, the media room," he said as he opened the heavy double doors.

Her gaze traveled over the dark gray soundproof walls as she strolled down the black-carpeted, declining aisle. She paused to run her hand along the arm of one beige leather chair before facing him again. "Media room? This is more like an honest-to-goodness movie theater. All that's missing is a popcorn machine."

He nodded to his left. "In the corner behind that curtain, next to the soda fountain."

"Of course."

Hannah sounded almost disapproving, which sent Logan into defense mode. "Hey, the whole setup was here when I bought the house, including a huge collection of movies." Most of which he'd never watched because he didn't like watching alone. He planned to remedy that…and soon.

After folding her arms beneath her breasts, she slowly approached him. "I'd love to check out your collection."

"Not a problem, but right now I better check on dinner before I burn everything to a crisp and we have to call out for pizza."

She made a sweeping gesture toward the exit. "After you."

She followed quietly behind him as he led the way back through the great room and into the kitchen. As she'd done in the media room, Hannah took a visual trek through the area, her eyes wide with wonder. "State-of-the-art appliances, enough cabinets to store supplies for an army and a stainless island that I would sell my soul to have. Are you sure you don't have a robot hidden away somewhere to prepare your food?"

At least she'd said it with a smile, and that relieved him. He'd never been one to seek approval, but for some reason her opinion mattered. "No robot. Just me and sometimes the maid. I learned to cook after the divorce. It was either that or starve."

Hannah claimed the chrome-and-black bar stool across from the oven and folded her hands before her. "I hope it tastes as good as it smells."

He rounded the island, rested his elbows on the silver counter and angled his lower body away. "The recipe's never failed me before." He couldn't say the same for his self-control because he was having one hell of a fantasy involving her and that bar stool.

"What are we having?" she asked.

He personally was having a major desire to kiss her. "The mostaccioli I told you about."

"Fantastic. I've never had it before, but it's always good to try something new."

"And it's great to share something new with someone who's never experienced it before."

"I'm looking forward to a lot of new experiences while I'm here."

As their gazes remained connected, tension as apparent as the smell of the pasta hung in the air, until Hannah broke their visual contact by leaning around him. "According to your timer, we still have five minutes."

He straightened and glanced behind him before regarding her again. "True, and it needs to rest for another ten." Now what to talk about during those few minutes that would keep him from taking an inadvisable risk. "How did your daughter feel about you coming here?"

Hannah frowned. "She couldn't get me out of town fast enough. I can't compete with best friends and their baby brothers."

"I guess sometimes kids need a break from their parents."

She sighed softly. "I agree, but this is the longest break from each other we've ever had. I am glad to know she's in good hands, and that she's going to have a great time in my absence dressing up like a teenage harlot."

"Oh, yeah?"

Hannah pulled her cell phone from her pocket, hit an app and turned it around. "I took this photo this morning of my kiddo and her best friend, Michaela."

Logan started to laugh but the urge died when he homed in on the little girl standing next to Hannah's daughter. The resemblance might be slight, but the memories overwhelmed him. Recollections of his black-haired baby girl they'd appropriately named Grace.

He swallowed hard before handing Hannah the phone. "Gotta love their imaginations."

"Yes, but I don't like the fact she's trying to grow up too fast."

He'd give up everything he owned for the opportunity to watch his daughter grow up, but she'd been torn from his life after only four brief years. Now might be a good time to tell Hannah about her, but he wasn't ready yet. He wasn't sure he would ever be ready to make that revelation. "While we're waiting on dinner, do you want a glass of wine?"

"Sure," she said with a soft smile. "As long as you're also partaking tonight. I've decided it's best I not drink alone."

He'd learned that lesson all too well. "I'm not much of a wine drinker, but I do like a beer now and then."

"Whatever works for you."

Everything about Hannah Armstrong worked for him, and he'd just have to take out that thought and analyze it later. At the moment he needed to play the good host.

Logan crossed the room to a small bar where he'd set out an expensive bottle of red and poured a glass. Then he bent down and pulled out his favorite lager from the beverage refrigerator.

He returned to his place across from Hannah and slid the wine toward her. "Let me know if this meets your standards."

"I'm sure it will since I can only afford the cheap stuff," she said. "And before you mention that I can afford the best if I take the millions, don't waste your breath. I still haven't changed my mind."

"That's fine by me." And it was, to a point. "If you do refuse the inheritance, the funds will be merged into the Lassiter Foundation and given to charity."

She looked slightly amazed. "I didn't think J.D. would have a charitable bone in his body after the way he apparently treated my mother."

"And you," Logan said. "But he always has been somewhat of a philanthropist, and a good parent, which is why I'm surprised he would ignore his child."

"Perhaps he did have his reasons, and chances are I won't know. Maybe I don't want to know."

He didn't want to spoil the evening by being bogged

down by emotional chains from the past. "Let's concentrate on the present and worry about the rest later."

Hannah grinned and lifted her glass. "Here's to procrastination."

This time Logan did laugh as he touched his beer to her wine. "And to good food, new friends and more good food."

She took a sip of her wine and set the glass down. "Just don't feed me too well. If I put on an extra five pounds that means I'll have to lose fifteen instead of ten."

"You don't need to lose weight," he said, and he meant it. "You look great."

She lowered her gaze for a moment. "Thank you, but I really need to get back in shape so I can comfortably do those backflips."

That made him grin again. "I've got quite a few acres if you want to practice after dinner."

"Do you really think that's a good idea in the dark?"

No, but he could think of several things he'd like to do with her in the dark. Or the daylight. "You're right. I have another place to show you anyway."

She bent her elbow and supported her jaw with her palm. "Where do you plan to take me?"

Places she hadn't been before, but he didn't want to jump the gun, or get his hopes up...yet. "It's my second favorite place."

She narrowed her eyes. "You aren't referring to your bedroom since you left it off the tour, are you?"

He'd done that intentionally in an effort not to move too fast. "Not even close."

"Can you give me a hint?"

Without regard to the taking-it-slowly plan, he

reached over and brushed a strand of silky auburn hair from her cheek. "You surprised me tonight. Now it's time for me to surprise you."

Hannah had to admit she was a bit surprised when Logan suggested an after-dinner walk. She was even more shocked by his skill as a chef. Never before had she sampled such great food at the hands of a culinary hobbyist, who also happened to be a man.

She imagined his skills went far beyond the kitchen, particularly when it came to the bedroom. And although she'd been curious to see his sleeping quarters, she appreciated that he hadn't presented her with that possible temptation. Of course, she had no reason to believe he actually wanted to get her in his bed. She could hear Gina laughing at her naiveté the minute that thought vaulted into her brain.

According to Logan, the temperature had dropped quite a bit and now hovered around forty-five degrees, sending Hannah upstairs to change right after they cleaned the kitchen together. Hopefully the weather would begin to warm up in the next few days with the arrival of May. She rifled through her unpacked bag and withdrew a sweatshirt. After putting that on, she exchanged her heels for a pair of sneakers, did a quick makeup check, brushed her hair and then sprinted back down the stairs.

She found Logan waiting for her at the back door right off the mudroom adjacent to the kitchen, exactly where he'd told her to be. "I'm ready to walk off all that delicious food."

He inclined his head and studied her. "You really thought it was that good?"

Men. Always looking to have their egos stroked, among other things. She would actually be game for both...and obviously she was turning into a bad, bad girl. "I believe I said that at least five times during dinner, when I wasn't making the yummy noises."

His beautiful smile lit up his intriguing brown eyes. "Just making sure."

After Logan opened the door, Hannah stepped in front of him and exited the house. She was totally stunned, and extremely thrilled, when he rested his palm on the small of her back as he guided her toward a somewhat visible rock path illuminated by a three-quarter moon.

Unfortunately he dropped his hand as they began their walk toward a large expanse of land, but the Rocky Mountains silhouetted against the star-laden sky proved to be a great distraction. "It's really nice outside, even if it's a little cold."

"Feels good to me," he said.

She glanced at him briefly before turning her focus straight ahead to prevent tripping. "I can't believe you're not freezing since you're only wearing a lightweight jacket."

"The wind's not nearly as bad as it usually is around here. And I'm also pretty hot-blooded."

She had no doubt about that. He was hot, period. "What's that building in the distance?"

"A barn."

"Is that where you're taking me?"

"Nope."

She didn't quite understand why he seemed bent on being evasive. "Are you purposefully trying to keep me in suspense?"

"Yeah, but it'll be worth it."

A roll in the hay in the barn would be well worth it to her, and she'd best keep her questionable opinions to herself.

They continued to walk in silence until a smooth-wire fence stopped their forward progress. "This is my second favorite place," Logan said as he propped one boot on the bottom rail and rested his elbow on the top.

Hannah moved beside him and waited for her vision to adjust to the dark before taking in the panorama. The lush pasture traveled at an incline to what appeared to be a stream lined by a few trees. Not far away, she noticed two shadowy animals with their heads bent to graze on the grass. "Are those your horses?"

"Yeah. Harry and Lucy."

"Didn't they star in a fifties sitcom?"

Logan's laughter cut through the quiet. "I'm not sure about that, but they both came to me already named."

After she turned toward him and leaned against a post, his profile drew her attention. It was utterly perfect, from forehead to chin. "How long have you had them?"

"I bought Harry when I turned eighteen. He was a year-old gelding. I broke him and trained him to be a pretty good cutting horse. He's twenty now."

She had no idea what a cutting horse was, but she didn't want to show her ignorance. "What about Lucy?"

He went suddenly silent for a few seconds before speaking again. "I've had her about ten years, I guess. She's a retired pleasure horse and pretty kid-proof."

"That sounds about my speed."

He lowered his foot and faced her. "You've never ridden a horse?"

She internally cringed at the thought. "Twice. The first time I was sixteen and I went on a trail ride with friends. A controlled environment is a good place to start, or so they told me. They didn't, however, tell Flint, my ride. He decided to take off ahead of the pack and it took every ounce of my strength to get him to stop. After that, the trail master tied him to his horse to make sure he behaved."

"But you still got on a horse again?"

"On a beach in Mexico. I rode a really sweet mare and by the end of the ride, I'd trusted her enough to actually gallop." She closed her eyes and immersed herself in the memories. "The wind was blowing through my hair and the sun was on my face and I remember feeling the ocean spray on my feet. It was incredible."

"You're incredible."

She opened her eyes to find him staring at her. "Why?"

"Most people aren't brave enough to get back on a horse after a bad experience. I'm starting to wonder if anything scares you."

She was scared by the way she felt around him—ready to jump headfirst into possible heartache. "Believe me, I have fears like everyone else. I've just tried not to let them paralyze me."

Logan inched closer and streamed a fingertip along her jaw. "Would you be afraid if I kissed you again?"

She might die if he didn't. "Not really."

He bent and brushed a soft kiss across her cheek. "Would it scare you if I told you that you're all I've thought about for the past two days?"

"Would it scare you if I said I've been thinking about you, too?"

"I'm glad, because I can't get thoughts of us, being really close, off my mind." When he laced their fingers together, the implications weren't lost on Hannah.

"It's been a long time, Logan. I don't take intimacy lightly."

"I respect that," he said, not sounding the least bit disappointed. "That's why I only want to kiss you. Tonight."

After he said it, he did it, and he did it very well. The first time she'd kissed him, she'd fumbled through the motions. The first time he'd kissed her, he'd been quick about it. But not now.

He explored her mouth with care, with the gentle stroke of his tongue, allowing her to capture all the sensations. She responded with a soft moan and a certain need to be closer to him. On that thought, she wrapped her hands around his waist while he wound one hand through her hair and planted the other on her back.

When Logan tugged her flush against him, the cold all but disappeared, replaced by a searing heat that shot the length of Hannah's body and came to rest in unseen places, leaving dampness in its wake.

Too long since she'd been kissed this way, felt this way. Too long since she'd experienced a desire so strong that if Logan laid her down on the hard ground beneath their feet and offered to remove her clothes, she'd let him.

Clearly Logan had other ideas, she realized, when he broke the kiss and tipped his forehead against hers. "I need you so damn bad I hurt."

She'd noticed that need when she'd been pelvis-to-pelvis with him. "Chemistry definitely can commandeer your body."

He pulled back and studied her eyes. "But I don't want to screw this up, Hannah, so we're going to take this slowly. Get to know each other better. But sweetheart, before you leave, I plan to make love to you in ways you won't forget."

Hannah trembled at the thought. "You're mighty confident, Mr. Whittaker."

"I just know what I want when I want it, and I want you." He ran the tip of his tongue over the shell of her ear and whispered, "I think you want me just as badly. So let's go before I change my mind and take you down on the ground and get you naked."

Her body reacted with another surge of heat and dampness over Logan's declaration. Yet they walked back to the house, hand in hand, like innocent young lovers who'd just discovered each other, not mature adults who were approaching the point of no return.

Hannah knew better than to cross that line too soon. She knew better than to lead with her heart and not her head. Yet when Logan said goodbye to her at the bedroom door, she almost tossed wisdom out the window for a night of wild abandon. Instead, she let him go and sought out the place where she would spend the night alone longing for things she shouldn't. Wanting, needing, Logan's words echoing through her cluttered mind...

But sweetheart, before you leave, I plan to make love to you in ways you won't forget...

Deep down she had no doubt he was a man of his word. But if she took that leap into lovemaking, would her heart suffer another devastating blow?

Five

"What do you mean you didn't do it?"

That was the last thing Hannah wanted to hear first thing in the morning, especially from her best friend.

After turning the cell on speaker and setting it on the bed beside her, she slid a sneaker onto her foot and began lacing it. "He happens to be a gentleman, Gina. And I didn't call to talk about my sex life. I called to talk to my daughter."

"You don't have a sex life, and you can't talk to Cassie because she's not here right now."

She tightened the shoestring just a little too tight. "Where is she?"

"Out with bikers she met bar-hopping last night."

Infuriating woman. "I'm serious, Regina Gertrude Romero."

"You know how I hate it when you use my middle name."

"Yes, I do," she said as she pulled on the remaining shoe. "Now tell me my daughter's actual whereabouts before I tell everyone in your book club that you want to be a pole dancer when you finally grow up."

Gina let out an exaggerated sigh. "She's with Frank at his sister's house. Since it's going to be close to eighty degrees today, and we don't know how long this heat wave is going to last, the kids are going to swim."

Hannah was poised to hit the panic button. "Are you sure it's warm enough there because it's not nearly that warm here."

"I checked the weather, Hannah. And don't forget, you're almost a hundred miles away."

She hadn't forgotten that at all, and now the distance between her and her child really worried her. "I hope the adults pay close attention because Cassie—"

"Can swim better than you and me," Gina said. "Stop being such a worrywart."

Her patience was starting to unravel. "Did you pack sunscreen? You know how easily she burns."

"Yes, I did, and I put the fire department on alert, just in case."

One more acerbic comment and she might very well come completely unglued. "Real funny, Regina. And why are you home?"

"Trey kept me up a good part of the night, so Frank let me sleep in while the baby is sleeping. I'll be heading out in an hour or so. By the way, where is your attorney now?"

He wasn't *her* attorney, but Hannah saw no reason to debate that point. "I'm not sure. I just got out of the shower and I haven't left the bedroom yet."

"I could see where you'd still be in the bedroom if

he was in there with you, but it's almost ten o'clock. Don't you think he might be wondering if you've flown the coop, leaving the rooster all alone?"

Hannah had thought about that, but so far she hadn't heard a thing coming from downstairs. "Maybe he's sleeping in, too. But I won't know until I get off the phone."

"Hint taken. Call me this evening and I'll put your daughter on the phone, unless, of course, you're engaged in some serious cross-examination."

"I'm hanging up now, Gina." As soon as she ended the call, Hannah hopped to her feet, ready to face the day—and Logan.

After a quick makeup application and hair brushing, she sprinted down the stairs, tugging at her plain light blue T-shirt and wishing she'd worn a better pair of jeans. But casual seemed to suit Logan. Very well.

She wound her way through the cowboy palace, following the scent of coffee in hopes of locating the master of the manor. When she arrived in the kitchen, there he was in all his glory, sitting with his back to her at the island. He wore a navy plaid flannel shirt and a cowboy hat, which almost sent Hannah completely into a female frenzy over her Wild West fantasy coming to life.

She stood in the kitchen opening just long enough to take a good look at his broad back before she slid onto the stool across from him. "Good morning."

He lifted his gaze from his coffee cup and smiled, but only halfway. "Mornin', ma'am. How did you sleep?"

Like a woman who couldn't get his kisses off her

blasted mind. "Pretty darn well, thank you. That mattress is as soft as a cloud."

"I'm glad you found the accommodations satisfactory." He nodded at the counter behind her. "There's some coffee left if you want me to get you a cup."

"I'll get some in a minute," she said when she noticed the keys resting near his right hand. "Have you been out already this morning?"

"Not yet, but unfortunately I'm going to have to get a move on. I got a call from Chance Lassiter. He's Marlene's son and the ranch manager at the Big Blue. He needs some extra help herding a few calves that got out of a break in the fence last night."

It figured her plans would be foiled by a Lassiter. So much for spending a relaxing Sunday getting to know him better. "How long will that take?"

"Hard to say, but it could be quite a while since we'll need to cover a lot of land. And the ranch is about thirty minutes north of here. Feel free to turn on the TV while I'm gone, or use the computer if you want to do some research on the Lassiters. If you need supplies, they're in the desk drawer."

She wondered why he would invite her—a virtual stranger—into his private domain. "You're absolutely sure you don't mind me hanging out in your office?"

He sent her a sexy-as-sin grin. "I don't have anything to hide. All my professional files are password protected, but if you have a hankerin' to hack into those, knock yourself out. The legal jargon on mergers and acquisitions is pretty damn riveting. Just be forewarned you're going to need a nap afterward."

She wouldn't mind taking a nap with him. "Do you want me to whip something up for dinner?"

"Don't worry about me. As far as you're concerned, there's quite a bit of food in the refrigerator, so help yourself."

Hannah admittedly was a bit disappointed he hadn't asked her to join him on the day trip. "Thanks."

"I really hate having to leave you, but—"

"I'm a big girl, Logan. I can entertain myself until you return."

He reached over the counter and ran a fingertip along her jaw. "When I get back, I have some entertainment in mind for you."

She shivered like a schoolgirl at the thought. "And what will that entail?"

After he stood, Logan rounded the island, came up behind her and brought his mouth to her ear. "You'll just have to wait and see, but it will be worth the wait."

After Hannah shifted toward him, Logan gave her a steamy kiss that made her want to initiate his kitchen counter. Or the floor. But he pulled away before she could act on impulse.

He snatched up his keys and winked. "I'll let you know when I'm heading home."

"I'll be here." And she couldn't think of any place she would rather be at the moment, aside from home with her daughter. Or in bed with him.

Naughty, naughty, Hannah.

After Logan left out the back door, she hurried to the great room to peer out the picture window facing the front drive. She waited until he guided the massive black dual-wheel truck and silver horse trailer onto the main road before she returned to the kitchen for coffee. She poured a cup and doctored it with lots of sugar and cream, then ate the apple set out in a fruit bowl.

Now what? TV watching seemed about as appealing as contemplating the cosmos. She did bring a book, but she wasn't in the mood to read. Doing a little research on Logan's computer called to her curiosity. After finishing off the coffee, she went in search of his office and retraced her steps from when Logan showed her around. Following a few wrong turns, she finally located the room beyond the formal dining room.

The French doors were closed, but not locked, allowing Hannah easy entry into the attorney's inner sanctum. A state-of-the-art PC sat in the center of a modern black desk that looked remarkably neat. Two walls of matching bookshelves housed several law manuals, as well as quite a few true-crime novels.

She dropped into the rolling black leather chair and scooted close to the computer, ready to start looking for more info on the Lassiters. Yet something else immediately drew her attention.

In Hannah's opinion, a man's desk drawer was equivalent to a medicine cabinet—worthy of investigation. But did she dare poke around? That would undeniably be considered an invasion of privacy. Sort of. Hadn't he said to help herself to any supplies? Of course, she didn't need any paper or pens yet, but she did have a strong need to satisfy her nosiness.

With that in mind, Hannah slid the drawer open slowly, and like the desk, the thing was immaculate. She took a quick inventory after she didn't notice anything out of the ordinary on first glance. A few pens in a plastic divider, along with some binder clips. A box of staples. A stack of stationery stamped with his name, along with coordinating envelopes.

Not quite satisfied, Hannah pulled the drawer open

as far as she could, and glimpsed the corner of something shiny. She lifted the brown address book to find a small silver frame etched with teddy bears and balloons, the bottom stamped with a date—February 15, twelve years ago. She withdrew the photo of a pretty newborn with a dark cap of hair, a round face, precious puckered lips and what looked to be a tiny dimple imprinted on its right cheek. Unfortunately, she couldn't quite determine the gender due to the neutral yellow gown, but she would guess this baby happened to be a little girl. The question was, *whose* little girl?

Logan had been adamant he had no children, leaving Hannah to assume the infant could be a sibling's child, if he had any siblings. She could clear up the mystery when he came home, but since the frame had been tucked away out of sight, she would have to admit she'd been snooping.

Right now she had another mystery that needed her focus, namely trying to find any clues indicating John Douglas Lassiter was her mother's sperm donor.

With that in mind, Hannah booted the computer and brought up her favorite search engine. She decided to dig a little deeper this time, expand her inquiries, and learn as much about the Lassiter family as possible, beginning with where it had all begun. She read articles about the self-made billionaire and his various ventures, from newspapers to cattle to his media corporation in California. He'd married a woman named Ellie, adopted her two nephews and lived through the loss of his wife, who sadly died at forty-two just days after giving birth to a daughter.

She took a few moments to study a recent publicity photo of that daughter, Angelica Lassiter, who could possibly be her sister. The sophisticated-looking woman was tall and slimly built, with dark hair and eyes—nothing that physically indicated Hannah might be kin to the reported "brains" behind Lassiter Media. Apparently Angelica had broken off her engagement to Evan McCain, interim chairman and CEO of the company, after a reported dispute over the terms in her father's will. High drama indeed.

Hannah surfed a little longer, trying to establish some connection between J.D. and her mother, yet she found nothing whatsoever to prove that theory.

Stiff-necked and bleary-eyed, Hannah noticed the time and realized a good part of the day had already passed her by. And as far as she knew, Logan hadn't returned home yet. She sat back in the chair and closed her eyes, remembering his lips fused with hers, his body pressed flush against her body, how badly she had wanted him last night. How badly she wanted him still, though she shouldn't...

The phone shrilled, startling Hannah so badly, she nearly vaulted from the rolling chair as she fumbled the cell from her pocket. Disappointment washed over her when Gina's name—not Logan's—displayed on the screen. "No, we haven't done it yet."

"Done what, Mama?"

Great. This was not the way she wanted to introduce her child to human sexuality. "Hi, sweetie. I miss you. Do you miss me?"

"Uh-huh, a little."

That stung Hannah like a hornet. "Are you back at Gina's?"

"Nope. We're still at Aunt Linda's house and we're swimming a lot."

Funny how Cassie had adopted the Romero family's relatives. But then she had very few relatives aside from Danny's parents. For the most part, they didn't count. "Are you sunburned?"

"A little on my nose. I'm gonna get more freckles, right?"

She was somewhat surprised that her daughter sounded almost happy about it. "If you continue to stay in the sun, yes, you probably will."

"Or if I swallow a nickel and break out in pennies."

"Where did you hear that, Cassie?"

"Frank told me. I like Frank. I wish he was my daddy. I mean, I love my daddy in heaven, but I want a real one. Mickey said she'd share him."

Hannah's heart took a little dip in her chest when she recalled how difficult it had been to grow up without a father. At least Cassie knew who her dad was, even if she'd never known him. She also had many pictures of Danny available to look at any time she desired. "Well, honey, maybe someday that might happen."

"Are you gonna marry your prince?"

Cassie sounded so hopeful Hannah hated to burst her fairy-tale bubble. "If you mean Mr. Whittaker, he's a lawyer, not a prince, and he's only my friend."

"But he's really cute and he doesn't have a kid. Everyone should have a kid."

From the mouth of her matchmaking babe.

Hannah heard a background voice calling for Cassie to come on, followed by her daughter saying, "Gotta go, Mama. We're eating pizza!"

"Okay, sweetie, tell Gina that—"

When she heard a click, Hannah checked to see if the call had ended, which it had. The conversation had been too brief for her liking, and too telling, yet she understood Cassie's excitement over being a part of a complete family.

At some point in time, perhaps she could provide that family for her daughter, but she didn't believe it would happen in the foreseeable future. And definitely not with Prince Logan. Though she didn't know the details of his divorce, she sensed he wasn't willing to travel that road again. Regardless, she would enjoy their time together and let whatever happened, happen. Now that she knew Cassie was faring well without her, she wasn't in a rush to head home.

"What is the rush to leave, Logan Whittaker?"

If he answered the question, it would require explaining his houseguest to Marlene Lassiter. And although she was as good as gold, she had a penchant for trying to direct his private life. "I'm just ready to take a shower and prepare for work tomorrow." And get home to a woman who'd weighed on his mind all day long.

She patted her short brown hair before pulling out a chair for him at the dining table in the corner of the kitchen area. "You've got time to eat. I made my famous meat loaf and cornbread."

Logan hadn't realized he was hungry until she'd said the magic words. Nothing like good old country cooking. He hadn't checked in with Hannah yet, so she wasn't expecting him. That didn't discount the fact he was still in a hurry to get home to her. "Do you mind fixing me a plate to go?"

That earned him Marlene's frown as she hovered above him. "Do you have a meeting of some sort?"

"Not exactly."

"Could—wonder of wonders—you have a date?"

If he didn't throw her a bone, she'd keep hounding him. "I have a friend staying with me and I'd like to get in a visit before I go to bed." Among other things.

Marlene smoothed a hand down her full-length apron. "Well then, I'll just make up two plates since I wouldn't want *him* to go hungry."

Damn. He might as well correct the gender issue. "I'm sure *she'll* appreciate it."

Marlene pointed a finger at him. "Aha! I suspected you're harboring a woman."

That sounded like he was holding Hannah against her will. He turned the chair around backward and straddled it. "Before you start getting any wrong notions, she's just a friend."

Marlene walked into the nearby pantry, returned with two paper plates and began dishing out food from the stove. "Are you sure about that friend designation? One of the hands said you seemed distracted, and nothing distracts a man more than a woman."

Double damn. "Just because I temporarily lost one of the heifers that left the herd doesn't mean I was distracted. It happens."

She shot him a backward glance. "It doesn't happen to you. But I'm glad you're finally getting back into the dating scene."

He could set her straight, or let her think what she would. He chose the first option. "Look, I'm handling a legal matter for her. That's why she's here."

After covering the plates with foil, Marlene turned and leaned back against the counter. "Is there potential for it being more than a client-attorney relationship?"

"It might, but I'm not in the market for anything permanent at this point in time." If ever.

"Does she know this, or are you leading her on?"

She had an uncanny knack for seeing right through him. "I'm not going to do anything to hurt her, if that's what's worrying you. Besides, she doesn't strike me as the kind of woman who's looking to nab a husband. Not only is she widowed, she also has a five-year-old daughter to consider."

Marlene frowned. "Have you told her about Grace?"

He should've seen that coming. "You know I don't talk about that with anyone but you, and that's only because you prodded me about my past." After he'd had a few too many during a party she'd hosted that happened to have fallen on Grace's birthday. He'd spent the night on her couch and woken the next morning with a hangover and more than a handful of regrets over baring his soul.

"Maybe you should talk to someone else about her, Logan," she said. "Keeping all that guilt and grief bottled up isn't doing you any good. You can't move forward if you stay stuck in the past."

"I'm not stuck." He tempered his tone, which sounded way too defensive. "I like to keep my private life completely private."

"And if you keep that attitude, you're never going to be happy." She took the chair next to his. "Honey, you're a good man. You have a whole lot to offer the right woman. You can't let yourself get bogged down in mistakes you think you might have made. One day you're going to have to forgive yourself, go on with your life and take a chance on love again."

He *had* made mistakes. Unforgivable mistakes.

"Isn't that the pot-and-kettle thing, Marlene? You never remarried after Charles died."

Marlene turned her wedding band round and round her finger. "No, I didn't. But that doesn't mean I cut myself off from love."

Exactly what he'd assumed, along with everyone else in town. "You mean you and J.D."

"I didn't say that."

She didn't have to. Logan saw the truth in her hazel eyes. He'd also seen something else in her at J.D.'s funeral, that soul-binding sorrow that he'd known all too well. "Come on, Marlene. You lived here with J.D. all those years after you both lost your spouses. No one would fault the two of you for being close."

"He was totally devoted to the kids and Ellie's memory." She sighed. "His wife meant everything to him and he never really got over her."

Which meant Marlene's love could have been one-sided. "Are you going to deny he cared for you, too?"

She shook her head. "No, I'm not, because he did care. But I couldn't compete with his cherished ghost. Regardless, we had some very good times."

That led Logan to believe the pair had been lovers, not that he'd ever request verification. "I tell you what, when you decide to have a serious relationship again, then I'll consider it, too." He figured he was pretty safe with that pact.

Marlene smiled sagely. "You never know what the future holds."

After checking the clock on the wall, Logan came to his feet. "I better get back to the house, otherwise Hannah might not speak to me again."

"Hannah?" she asked, more concern than curiosity in her voice.

"Yeah. Hannah Armstrong. Why?"

She attempted another smile but it fell flat. "Nothing. I've always thought it's a lovely name for a girl."

Logan wasn't buying that explanation, but he didn't have the energy to question her further tonight. He'd set aside some time later and have a long talk with her. Marlene Lassiter's relationship with her brother-in-law could be the key to solving the mystery of Hannah's past.

Yeah, he'd wait a little while before he sought more information from Marlene. If she did hold the answers, then Hannah would no longer have any reason to stay. And he damn sure wasn't ready for her to leave.

She wasn't quite ready to leave the heavenly bath, but when Hannah heard sounds coming from downstairs, she realized the dashing attorney was finally home.

After extracting herself from the jetted tub, she hurriedly dried off and prepared to get ready to greet him. And since she'd had headphones stuck on her ears until a few minutes before, and she hadn't checked her cell for messages in the past hour, she had no idea when Logan had returned.

She quickly dressed in a white tank with built-in bra and black jeans, then had a crisis of confidence and covered the top with a coral-colored, button-down blouse. She brushed her teeth, applied subtle makeup and opted to leave her hair in the loose twist atop her head. Danny had often told her she looked sexy with her hair up…and she really shouldn't be thinking about him while in the home of another man. An undeniably sexy man who'd commandeered her common sense from the moment she'd met him. And that lack of common sense had her slipping the first three buttons on the blouse to reveal the lace-edged tank beneath. An obvious indication of a woman bent on seduction.

Bracing her palms on the vanity, Hannah leaned forward and studied the face in the mirror. The same face that looked back at her every morning. Yep, she looked the same, but she felt very different. Her nerves sang like a canary and she felt as if her skin might take a vacation without her.

What was she thinking? It took a good three months for her and Danny to consummate their relationship. She'd only known Logan for three days. Yet she was older, and wiser, and lonely. She wanted to be in the arms of a man she was beginning to trust. Why she trusted him, she couldn't say. Intuition? Or maybe she was simply so foggy from lust that she wasn't thinking straight at all. That didn't keep her from sliding her feet into a pair of silver sandals and dabbing on perfume when she thought she heard him calling her name.

After rushing out of the bathroom and jogging through the bedroom, Hannah stopped in the hall to catch her breath. Seeming too enthusiastic might lead to misunderstanding. She might be happy to see him. She might be game for a little more serious necking. But she didn't know if she had the courage to go any farther than that.

She took her sweet time walking down the stairs and basically strolled to the great room. When she didn't find Logan there, she entered the kitchen to find it deserted as well. She did discover a pair of boots in the mudroom and his keys hanging on the peg, and detected the sound of the dryer in the adjacent utility room that was about as large as her den back in Boulder. At least she hadn't imagined he'd returned, but maybe she *had* imagined he'd called her.

Determined to locate the missing lawyer, she explored all the rooms he'd shown her, to no avail. That left her with only one uncharted location—his bedroom. She didn't dare go there. If he needed to speak with her, he could come and get her.

Two hours had passed since she'd eaten the ham sandwich, so she retrieved a bottle of water from the fridge and then perused the pantry for some sort of snack. She targeted the bananas hanging on the bronze holder and snapped off the best of the bunch.

Hannah had barely made herself at home on the bar stool when she heard heavy footfalls heading in her direction. The thought of seeing Logan gave her a serious case of goose bumps. When he walked into the kitchen, dressed in only a low-slung navy towel, she thought she'd been thrust into some nighttime soap opera starring a half-naked Hollywood hunk. He had a twelve-pack's worth of ridges defining his torso, a slight shading of hair between his pecs and another thin strip pointing downward to ground zero. Broad shoulders, toned biceps. Oh, boy. Oh, man.

While she sat there like a mime, appropriately clutching a phallic piece of fruit, Logan flashed her his dimpled grin. "You're here."

"You're wearing a towel." Brilliant, Hannah.

He pointed behind her. "I've got clothes in the dryer. I thought maybe you'd gone to bed already."

She noticed what looked to be a red tattoo on his upper right arm, but she couldn't see the details unless she asked him to turn toward her. Right now speaking at all was an effort, and the frontal view couldn't be beat. "It's not even six o'clock. I never go to bed that early."

"Maybe that theory was a stretch, but you didn't answer when I called you. And you didn't respond to my text."

She was surely responding to him now. All over. "I was taking a bath. The jets in the tub were going and I was listening to my MP3 player."

He cocked a hip against a cabinet and crossed his arms over his extremely manly chest. "Did you enjoy the bath?"

Not as much as she was enjoying the view right now. "Yes. Very relaxing. You should try it."

"I've got a big tub in my bathroom, but I'm not a bath kind of guy."

Maybe not, but he was one gorgeous guy. "Most men aren't into taking baths."

"True," he said. "Showers have always suited me better. A lot less effort. Easy in, easy out."

That conjured up images Hannah shouldn't be having. "I prefer showers, too, but I like a good bath now and then."

When he pushed away from the counter, she held her breath. She released it when he started toward the laundry room. "My clothes are probably dry now, so I better get dressed."

Please don't, she wanted to say, but stopped the comment threatening to burst out of her mouth. "Good idea."

The dryer door opened, followed by Logan calling, "If you're hungry, there's a plate of food in the refrigerator Marlene sent with me."

Hannah unpeeled the banana she still had in a death grip. "Thanks, but I've already eaten." She took a large bite of the fruit. Probably too large.

"Did you do any online research today?" he said over the sound of shuffling clothes.

"Yes, I did," she replied, her words muffled due to banana mouth.

"Find anything interesting?"

She swallowed this time before speaking. "Not much other than business articles." And a photo in his drawer that had piqued her interest.

While Hannah finished the fruit fest, Logan returned a few minutes later, fully dressed in beige T-shirt and old jeans. "I have an idea on how we might get some information on J.D.," he said.

She slid off the stool, opened the walk-in pantry and tossed the peel into the trash before facing him again. "What would that be?"

He leaned over the island using his elbows for support. "I'll let you know after I investigate further. It could end up being a dead end."

The man was nothing if not covert in his dealings. Must be the attorney thing—confidentiality at all costs. "Fine. Just let me know if you turn something up."

"I will." He straightened and smiled. "Are you in the mood for a little entertainment?"

She'd already been quite entertained by his re-

cent show of bare flesh. "Sure. What do you suggest
we do?"

"Watch a movie in the media room."

Not exactly what she had in mind, but what she'd
been envisioning wouldn't be wise. "I'm all for a
movie. Lead the way."

Six

Logan had chosen the lone theater chair built for two, along with a shoot-'em-up suspense film. But he hadn't bargained for the racy sex scene that came during the movie's first fifteen minutes.

He glanced to his right at Hannah, who had a piece of popcorn poised halfway to her mouth, her eyes wide as wagon wheels. "Wow. What is this rated?"

"R, but I thought that was due to the violence factor."

She popped a kernel into her mouth and swallowed. "I can't believe he didn't take off the shoulder holster when he dropped his pants. What if the gun goes off?"

"It does give a whole new meaning to 'cocked and ready.'" And he might have gone a bit too far with the crudeness.

Surprisingly, she released a soft, sultry laugh. "Ha, ha. It's hard for me to imagine a man taking a woman in an alley in broad daylight, gun or no gun."

That didn't exactly surprise him. "Anything's possible when you want someone bad enough." Exactly how he felt at the moment.

She tipped the red-striped box toward him. "Want some of this?"

His current appetite didn't include popcorn. "No thanks."

As the on-screen bumping and grinding continued, Logan draped his arm over the back of the seat, his hand resting on Hannah's shoulder. When he rubbed slow circles on her upper arm, she shifted closer to his side and laid her palm on his thigh. If she knew what was happening a little north of her hand, she might think twice about leaving it there. And if the damn movie didn't return to the run-and-gun scenes real soon, no telling what he might do.

No telling what *Hannah* might do was his immediate thought when she briefly nuzzled his neck, then brushed a kiss across his cheek. His second thought… the cheek kiss wasn't enough.

Logan tipped Hannah's face toward him and brought her mouth to his, intending only to kiss her once before going back to the film that fortunately now focused on the suspense plot. But the lengthy sex scene had obviously ignited the sparks between them, and from that point forward, everything began to move at an accelerated pace.

They made out like two teenagers on a curfew to the sounds of gunfire and cursing. He couldn't seem to get close enough to Hannah and that prompted him to pull her up onto his lap. He wound his hands through her hair and continued to kiss her like there was no tomorrow.

With Hannah's legs straddling his thighs, the contact was way too intimate for Logan to ignore. Every time she moved, he grew as hard as a hammer. To make matters worse, she broke the kiss, rose up and pulled away the band securing her lopsided ponytail. Obviously she was testing his sanity when she unbuttoned her blouse, slipped it off and tossed it aside, leaving her dressed in a thin tank top that left little to the imagination.

Seeing her sitting there with her tousled auburn hair falling to her shoulders, her lips slightly swollen and her green eyes centered on his, Logan's strength went the way of the popcorn that had somehow ended up on the floor. And just when he'd thought she was done with the surprises, she slid the straps off her shoulders and lowered the top.

He'd dimmed the lights before he'd cued the movie, but he could still make out the details. Incredible details. Unbelievable, in fact. Too tempting to not touch. That's exactly what he did—touched both her breasts lightly while watching her reaction. When Hannah tipped her head back and exhaled a shaky breath, Logan personally found it hard to breathe at all, and even harder not to take it further.

Pressing his left palm against her back, he nudged her forward and replaced his right hand with his mouth. Logan circled his tongue around one pale pink nipple, drawing out Hannah's soft groan. When he paid equal attention to her other breast, she shifted restlessly against his fly. If she didn't stop soon, it would be all over but the moaning. He damn sure didn't want to stop completely. He had a perfectly good bed at their disposal…and a perfectly good reason to halt the insanity before he couldn't. She deserved better than a quick roll in a chair, and he had no condoms available.

On that thought, he returned Hannah to the seat beside him and leaned back to stare at the soundproof ceiling while his respiration returned to normal.

"What was that?" Hannah asked, her voice somewhat hoarse.

Logan straightened to find her perched on the edge of the seat. Fortunately she'd pulled her top back into place, otherwise he wouldn't be able to concentrate. "That was uncontrollable lust."

"And, might I add, two adults acting like oversexed sixteen-year-olds," she said. "All we need now is to climb into the backseat of your car and have at it."

He didn't need to entertain that notion, but damned if he wasn't. "Hey, it happens."

"Not to me," she said. "I have never, ever been that bold."

He liked her boldness. A lot. "Not even with your husband?"

"Not really. We were both young when we met, and not very adventurous."

Interesting. "What about the men before him?"

Her gazed faltered for a moment. "Danny was my first. There wasn't anyone before him and there hasn't been anyone since."

Man, he hadn't predicted that. She kissed like someone who'd been around the block. Apparently she was a natural, even if she was somewhat of a novice. "Had I known that, I would've stopped sooner."

She frowned. "Why?"

"Because I don't want to do anything you don't want to do."

This time she released a cynical laugh. "I would think it's fairly obvious I wanted to do what I did, or I wouldn't have done it."

"Neither of us was thinking clearly." But he sure was now.

"Probably not, but since we're both consenting adults, I certainly don't consider our behavior shameful by any stretch of the imagination."

"I'm not sure I'm ready for this." He'd heard those words before, but never coming out of his own mouth.

Hannah looked perplexed. "Excuse me?"

He leaned forward, draped his elbows on his parted knees and focused on the popcorn-riddled carpet. "I'm not sure this is the right thing for either of us. More important, I don't want to hurt you, Hannah."

She touched his shoulder, garnering his attention. "I'm a big girl, Logan. I don't have any wild expectations of happily-ever-after. I want to feel desired by a man I can trust to treat me well. I know that man is you."

Yet she didn't know what he'd been concealing from her. She didn't know the demons still chasing after him. And she had no idea that his feelings for her were going beyond animal attraction.

He needed time to think. He needed to get away from her in order to keep his libido from prevailing over logic. Being the second man in her life would be a big burden to bear. He'd gained skill as a lover through experience, but he sucked when it came to the possible emotional fallout. If they continued on this course, they would only grow closer, and she might begin to have expectations he couldn't meet, regardless of what she'd said about not having any.

For that reason, he grabbed the remote from the adjacent chair, turned off the movie and stood. "I have an early day tomorrow and I'm pretty tired. We'll continue this discussion later."

Hannah stood and propped both hands on her hip. "That's it? You're going to run out on me without explaining why you've suddenly gone from hot to cold?"

He couldn't explain unless he made a few revelations that he wasn't prepared to make at this point. "I have some thinking to do, Hannah, and I can't do it with you in the same room."

"Suit yourself," she said as she moved past him and headed toward the exit.

He couldn't let her leave without telling her one important fact. "Hannah."

She turned at the door, anger glimmering in her eyes. "What?"

"I just don't want you to have any regrets."

"I don't," she said. "But I'm beginning to think you do."

Logan only regretted he might not be the man she needed. The man she deserved. And he had to take that out and examine it later before he made one huge error in judgment.

For the past two days, Hannah had barely seen Logan. He'd left for work before she'd awakened, and returned well after she'd retired to her room. She'd whiled away the lonely hours researching her possible family until she was certain her eyes might be permanently crossed. Her only human contact had come in the form of Logan's fiftysomething housekeeper,

Molly, who'd been extremely accommodating, right down to preparing meals in advance.

Of course, on several occasions she had spoken to Cassie, who had reinforced that she was having the time of her life with her best friend. Out of sight, out of mind, Hannah realized, at least when it came to her daughter and the attorney. And that hurt.

But after spending the morning in the public library perusing archived newspapers, Hannah had the perfect excuse to seek out Logan. She'd intentionally dressed in her professional best—a white sleeveless silk blouse, charcoal-colored skirt and black three-inch heeled sandals that Gina had fondly termed "do-me shoes." Hopefully she wasn't wasting those on a possible lost cause named Logan.

She didn't bother to call ahead before she arrived at the Drake, Alcott and Whittaker law firm located not far from the library. After playing tug-of-war with the strong Wyoming wind for control of the heavy wood door, she simply marched up to the very young, very pretty brunette receptionist and presented her best smile. "I need to see Mr. Whittaker please."

The young woman eyed Hannah suspiciously. "Do you have an appointment?"

She finger-combed her gale-blown hair back into place as best she could without a brush. "No, I don't. But I'm sure if you'll give him my name, he'll see me." If luck prevailed.

"What *is* your name?" the receptionist asked, sounding as if she believed Hannah might be some crazed stalker.

"It's Ms. Armstrong. Hannah Armstrong."

"Just a moment please." She picked up the phone and

pressed a button. "Mr. Whittaker, there's a Ms. Armstrong here and she... Of course. I'll send her right in." She replaced the phone and finally put on a pleasant demeanor. "His office is down the hall to your right, the second door on the left."

"Thank you."

Hannah traveled down the corridor with a spring in her step, feeling somewhat vindicated, until she realized she probably looked a whole lot disheveled. She paused long enough to open her bag for the appropriate tools, then brushed her hair and applied some lip gloss before continuing on to Logan's office. A brass plate etched with his name hung on the closed door, but the raised blinds covering the glass windows lining the hallway gave her a prime view of Logan, who happened to be on the phone.

She wasn't sure whether to wait until he hung up, or barge in. She opted to wait, until Logan caught her glance and gestured at her to come in.

Hannah stepped into the office, closed the door behind her and chose the chair across from the large mahogany desk. In an attempt not to appear to be eavesdropping, she surveyed the office while Logan continued his conversation. She had three immediate impressions—massive, masculine and minimalist. Neutral colors with dark blue accents, including the sofa and matching visitors' chairs. Blue-and-white-tiled fireplace with a barren mantel. A few modern Western paintings. Overall, a nice place to visit, but she wouldn't care to work there. The whole area could use some warming up.

Hannah couldn't say the same for herself. Seeing the sexy attorney dressed in coat and tie, his dark hair combed to perfection, his large hand gripping the phone, she had grown quite warm.

He seemed to be listening more than speaking until he finally said, "I understand, Mom, and I promise to do better with the calls. Tell Dad to stop giving you grief, and I'll talk to you next week. I love you, too." He then hung up and sent her a somewhat sheepish grin. "Sorry about that."

"I think it's nice you're close to your mother." The kind of relationship she'd wanted with hers, but never really had. "Are you an only child?"

"Actually, no," he said. "I have an older sister. She and her husband are both geologists living in Alaska with their five kids."

That could explain the picture in his desk drawer. "Wow. Five kids, huh?"

He grabbed a pen and began to turn it over and over. "Yeah. All boys."

She could have sworn that the baby in the photo she'd found in the desk had been a girl. "I suppose when you live somewhere as cold as Alaska, you have to find creative ways to keep warm."

"True, but constant procreating seems pretty extreme to me."

Hannah let out a laugh, but it died on her lips when she noticed his obvious uneasiness. "I was hoping you might introduce me to some more Lassiters."

He loosened his tie, a sure sign of discomfort. "It's been crazy busy around here."

Like she really believed that after he'd told her his schedule happened to be light this week. "Are you sure you haven't been avoiding me?"

He turned his attention back to the pen. "Not intentionally. I'm sorry that I haven't spent much time with you."

So was she. "Anyway, that's not exactly why I'm here. I came upon something at the library this morning that I found interesting." She dug through her bag and withdrew the copy of the archived article, then slid it across the desk. "This is a picture of J.D. and his brother, Charles, at a rodeo here in Cheyenne over thirty years ago. Charles won the roping competition."

Logan studied it a few moments before regarding Hannah again. "And?"

She reached across the desk and pointed at the text below the photo. "Look at the list of winners."

Logan scanned the text before looking up, sheer surprise in his expression. "Your mother was a barrel racer?"

"Yes, she was, but she gave it up after I was born." Only one more thing Ruth had blamed on her daughter. "Now I'm wondering if she met J.D. through his brother during one of these competitions."

Logan seemed to mull that over for a moment. "I planned to question Marlene Lassiter about J.D.'s past. They were very close, so she might know something about an affair."

"I'd appreciate that, Logan." She would also appreciate a better explanation for his behavior the other night in the media room. "Now that we've settled this matter, we do need to move on to our other issue."

"What issue would that be?"

She refused to let him play dumb. "The one involving our attraction to each other, and your concerns that I don't know my own mind."

"Hannah, I'm worried that—"

"I'll have regrets…I know. You're worried I'm going to get hurt. But as I told you during our last conversation, I don't have any expectations. I don't need poetry or candy or any promises. I only want to enjoy your company while I'm here, whatever that might involve."

"I don't want to do anything to hurt you."

Time to set him straight. "I'm not some fragile little flower who needs to be sheltered from life, both the good and the bad."

"I never thought of you as fragile, Hannah. But you have to know that I'm not in the market to settle down and have a family."

How well she understood that. "Fine. I get that. I'll hold off on picking out the engagement ring. Now I have a question for you."

"Shoot."

She scooted to the edge of her chair and stared at him straight on. "Do you still want me?"

He tossed the pen aside. "You really have to ask that?"

"Yes, and I want an answer."

When he rolled the chair back and stood, Hannah expected one of two things—Logan was going to kiss her, or show her to the door. Instead, he walked to a control panel mounted on the wall, pushed a button and lowered the electronic blinds, securing their complete privacy. Then he moved in front of her chair, clasped her wrists to pull her into his arms and delivered a kiss so soft and sensual, she thought her knees might not hold her. As if he sensed her dilemma, he turned her around and lifted her onto the desk.

Her skirt rode up too high to be considered ladylike, but frankly she didn't care. She was too focused on the feel of Logan's palms on her thighs, the strokes of his thumbs on the inside of her legs that seemed timed with the silken glide of his tongue against hers. *Higher,* she wanted to tell him. *Please,* she almost pleaded. But before she could voice her requests, he broke the kiss.

"Are you convinced I still want you, Hannah?"

This time she decided to play dumb in hopes he'd make more attempts at persuading her. "Almost."

"Maybe this will help." He took her palm and pressed it against his erection, showing her clear evidence of his need.

"I'm convinced." And veritably panting.

He placed her hand back into her lap. "Do you know what I really want right now?"

Hopefully the same thing she wanted—for him to have his very wicked way with her on top of his desk. "Do tell."

"Lunch."

Clearly the man was bent on driving her straight into oblivion. "Are you serious?"

Logan lifted her off the desk and set her on her feet. "Dead serious. There's a café right down the street that serves great burgers where we can eat and talk. I've been meaning to take you there."

Hannah wanted him to just take her. Now. But a talk was definitely warranted. She sent a pointed look in the direction of his fly. "Are you sure you're up to it? Oh, wait. Obviously you are."

He let go a boisterous laugh. "You'll need to walk in front of me for a few minutes. Just don't shake your butt."

Oh, how tempting to do that very thing. Instead, she picked up her purse and took her time applying more lip gloss. After she popped the cap back on and dropped the tube into her bag, she smiled. "Are you recovered now?"

"Enough to retain my dignity, so let's get out of here before I change my mind, lock the door and tell Priscilla to hold all calls while I hold you captive for a few more hours."

"Promises, promises," Hannah teased as they walked into the hall and started toward the lobby.

When they rounded the corner, an attractive sixty-something, brown-haired woman wearing a tasteful red tailored coat dress, nearly ran head-on into Hannah. "I'm so sorry, honey," she said. "I shouldn't be in such a hurry."

"You're always in a hurry, Marlene."

She patted Logan's cheek and smiled. "Not any more than you are, young man. Particularly the other evening when you rushed out of my house like your hair was on fire."

Hannah sent a quick glance at Logan, then returned her attention to the first Lassiter she'd encountered thus far.

Logan moved behind Hannah and braced his palms on her shoulders. "Hannah, this is Marlene Lassiter. Marlene, Hannah Armstrong."

The woman gave her an odd look before she formed a tentative smile and offered her hand. "It's nice to finally meet you."

Hannah accepted the brief shake, but she couldn't quite accept that the woman found the situation nice at all. "And it's a pleasure to finally meet you, too. Logan has told me a lot of good things about you."

"Well, you can't believe everything he says," Marlene added with a sincere smile directed at Logan.

"Were you here to see me, Marlene?" Logan asked.

"No," she said. "I'm having lunch with Walter, provided he's ready to go. The man still works like a field hand when he should be considering retirement."

The sparkle in Marlene's eyes, and the telling comment, led Hannah to believe the couple must know each other beyond any business arrangements. "I suppose that comes with the territory."

Marlene fiddled with the diamond necklace at her throat. "Yes, I suppose it does. And I better see if I can hurry him along."

"Again, it's nice to meet you," Hannah said as Marlene hurried past them.

"You, too, Hannah," she said over one shoulder before disappearing into the office at the end of the hall.

Hannah and Logan remained silent until they exited and stepped foot onto the sidewalk, where Logan turned to Hannah. "I suspect there's a story there with Walter and Marlene."

Considering Marlene's uneasy expression when they met, Hannah wondered if the woman might actually know the story of her life.

Before Logan could open the glass door to the Wild Grouse Café, a brown-haired man walked out, blocking the path. At first he didn't recognize him, until he realized the guy happened to be a client, a premiere chef, and the second Lassiter he'd encountered that day. "Are you checking out the competition, Dylan?"

"Hey, Logan," he said with a smile as he shook Logan's offered hand. "Actually, I grabbed a bite here because it's still one of the best eateries in town, at least until the grand opening of our newest restaurant. I've barely had time to eat since I've been working on grabbing some good press for this venture to circumvent the bad press over the will dispute."

Bad press compliments of Dylan's sister, Angelica. "I hear you on the bad press, and finding time to eat. I'm actually going to have lunch for a change."

"So they do let you out of the law cage?"

"It happens now and then." When he remembered Hannah was behind him, he caught her arm and drew her forward. "Dylan, this is Hannah Armstrong. Hannah, this is Dylan Lassiter, CEO of the Lassiter Grill Corporation, a veritable restaurant empire."

Dylan grinned. "Pleased to meet you. And where have you been hiding her out, Whittaker?"

"I'm his maid," Hannah said as she returned his smile.

Dylan frowned. "Seriously?"

Leave it to Hannah to throw out a comeback, but then he'd really begun to appreciate her easy wit. "She's a teacher during the day."

"And Logan actually moonlights as a plumber," she said.

They exchanged a smile and a look over their inside joke, interrupted by Dylan clearing his throat. "Logan, as a word of warning, I just had lunch with my sister. She's still loaded for bear over the will, in case you want to reconsider and find somewhere else to dine."

Great. Another Lassiter, and this one wasn't going to be pleasant. "I can handle Angelica." As long as he used kid gloves. He just hoped she wasn't wearing boxing gloves.

Dylan slapped him on the back. "Good luck, Whittaker. And it was damn good to see you again. Nice to meet you, too, Hannah."

After Dylan rushed away, Logan escorted Hannah into the restaurant and walked up to the hostess stand to request a table. He glanced across the crowded dining room and immediately spotted Angelica Lassiter sitting alone, wearing a white tailored business suit and a major scowl. Unfortunately, she spotted him as well. Too late to turn tail and run, he realized, when she slid out of the booth and approached him at a fast clip.

She bore down on him like a Texas tornado, her dark hair swaying and brown eyes flashing. "Logan Whittaker, you didn't return my last call."

An intentional oversight, not that he'd tell her. "I've been busy, Angelica, and you should address all questions regarding the will to Walter."

"Walter won't listen to me," she said. "He keeps saying there's nothing I can do to change the paltry percentage of Lassiter Media I inherited and I should learn to live with the fact Evan controls the majority of the shares, and the voting power that affords him. I still can't believe Daddy did this to me."

Frankly, neither could Logan. Nor could he believe how Angelica, a strong, independent businesswoman, reportedly the spitting image of her mother, could sound so much like a lost little girl. "I'm sure he had his reasons, and I know they don't seem logical or fair. All I can say is hang in there."

This time Hannah stepped forward on her own volition. "Hi, I'm Hannah Armstrong, a friend of Logan's."

Angelica gave Hannah's offered hand a gentle shake and presented a pleasant smile. "It's truly a pleasure to meet one of Logan's friends. Perhaps we can have dinner at some point in time."

"I'd like that." And she would, for reasons she

couldn't even reveal—namely this woman could actually be her sister.

Angelica turned back to Logan. "I'm asking you as a friend to talk to Walter and see if I can somehow contest the will. That company should be mine, not Evan's." And with that she was gone as quickly as she'd come, fortunately for Logan and for Hannah.

Once they were seated across from each other in the booth Angelica had just vacated, Hannah folded her hands on the table before her. "What were the odds I'd meet two of J.D.'s offspring in one day?"

Slim to none. "Now that you have met them, what do you think?"

She seemed to mull over that query for a minute. "Well, Dylan seemed nice enough, and so did Angelica, although she did seem pretty angry. I assume it had something to do with the breakup and that will dispute that I came across in a newspaper article. Am I right?"

He wasn't at liberty to hand her all the dirty details. "That's part of it. But just so you know, she's actually a very nice woman. Smart and savvy and she spends a lot of time involved in charity work."

"Don't forget she's very pretty," Hannah added.

"Yeah, you could say that." And he'd probably said too much.

"Have you dated her?" Hannah asked, confirming his conjecture.

"No. She's ten years younger and not my type."

She braced her bent elbow on the table and propped her cheek on her palm, reminding him of that first night they'd had dinner together. "Exactly what is your type?"

Hard to say, other than she seemed to be fitting the

bill just fine. "Keen intelligence, a nice smile. Green eyes. And most important, a smart-ass sense of humor."

Hannah leaned back and laid a dramatic hand above her heart. "I do declare, Mr. Whittaker. You sure have high standards."

He narrowed his eyes. "And you're getting a Texas accent."

"I wonder why." She went from smiling to serious in less than a heartbeat. "It's really hard for me to believe the people I met today could be my half siblings. And it makes me angry that my mother withheld vital information years ago, preventing me from making my own decision whether or not to connect with them."

If she only knew the vital information he'd been withholding from her, she wouldn't be too thrilled with him, either. But little by little, he'd begun to think he could trust her enough to tell her about his own sorry past. Eventually. "If you did decide to sign the nondisclosure, you'd never have a chance to get to know them. And since you're determined not to sign it, you really should give getting to know them a shot."

Hannah pondered that statement for a few moments before speaking again. "That's an option I'm not ready to explore. And signing the nondisclosure waiver would be the price I'd pay if I claimed my inheritance."

He wondered if she'd come to her senses and changed her mind. "Are you reconsidering taking the money?"

She shook her head. "No. Although it's tempting, I still don't feel I can claim it in good conscience, or sign the nondisclosure. Knowing the annuity will be turned over to charity does make my decision much easier."

She didn't sound all that convincing to Logan. "You

still have some time to think it through before you have to leave." And he wasn't looking forward to her leaving, though he had no right whatsoever to ask her to stay.

After finishing their food, they engaged in casual conversation, covering movies and music they liked, before their discussion turned to Hannah's child. Logan listened intently while Hannah verbally demonstrated her devotion to her daughter. Not a day had gone by when he hadn't thought about his own daughter, Gracie, and what she would look like now at age twelve. If she'd be chasing boys, or chasing cows with her grandpa. If she'd be smart as a whip like her mom, and love all things horses like him. The signs had pointed to that equine love, but he'd never known for sure, and never would. Gracie had only ridden Lucy one time, and that was a shame on many counts. A mare that willing and able and gentle should be ridden more often....

"Did I lose you somewhere, Logan?"

His thoughts scattered and disappeared after Hannah made the inquiry. "Sorry. I just came up with a really good idea." And he had. A banner idea.

"What would that be?" she asked.

He stood, held out his hand and helped her out of the booth. "I'm going to take the rest of the day off and we're going to have some fun."

"What, pray tell, do you have in mind, Mr. Whittaker?"

"Sweetheart, we're going to take a long, long ride."

Seven

This wasn't at all what Hannah expected when Logan mentioned going for a ride. She'd envisioned satin sheets and afternoon delight in his bedroom that she had yet to see. She *hadn't* expected to be sitting atop a plodding mare that kept stopping to graze as they headed toward the creek.

"You're doing fairly well for someone who hasn't been on a horse for a while."

She shot him a withering look. "Remind me of that when I have a sore butt for the next few days."

Logan's rich, deep laugh echoed across the pastureland. "Nothing a good soak in the tub won't cure. Or a massage."

"Know a good massage therapist?"

That question brought a frown to Logan's face. "Why would you need one when you have me?"

Her day suddenly brightened significantly, along with the sun. "Are you good at giving massages?"

"So I've been told."

She didn't care to ask who had told him. "That's nice to know in case I do need your services."

He winked. "Oh, you're going to need them all right. And I promise you're going to enjoy them."

"I'm counting on you to make good on that promise." And counting on herself not to let her heart get tangled up in him. Of course, that would be easier said than done.

They continued to ride in companionable silence, and after traveling over most the surrounding land, Logan finally dismounted in one smooth move a little farther away from where they'd stood the other night. Hannah did the same with much less poise, grabbed the reins and tugged a single-minded Lucy in Logan's direction before the mare launched into another grass attack. "Why did we stop?"

Logan guided the gelding to the gate opening up to the pasture that led to the creek. "I want to show you another special place."

"Good," Hannah replied. "My bottom was just about to give out."

After leading the horses through the gate, Logan turned and closed it, then said, "Let Lucy go for now."

As predicted, the mare went to the nearest clump of grass. "She's a regular chow hound."

"She needs to be ridden more often," Logan said as he detached a rolled blanket from the back of his saddle and tucked it beneath his left arm. "We can take another ride this weekend on my nearest neighbor's property. He has a larger spread and he told me to feel free to use it anytime."

Hannah's spirits plummeted when she realized she was set to leave in three days. "I plan to go home on Saturday."

He clasped her hand in his and gave it a gentle squeeze. "You can stay until Sunday."

She just might at that. One more day wouldn't matter to Cassie. If anything, her daughter might be disappointed to see her if it meant going back to her normal routine. "We'll see."

Logan guided her down the incline a hundred yards or so from the fence and stopped beneath a cottonwood tree not far from the narrow creek. He released her hand to spread the blanket over the ground. "I've been known to come here to think."

Hannah looked around the area, amazed at the absolute quiet. "It does seem to be a good place to clear your head."

"Among other things."

She turned to see Logan had already planted himself on the blanket, removed his boots and reserved a space beside him. "Take off your shoes and take a load off," he said.

She really wanted to remove more than her shoes. More like her clothes. And his. It had now been confirmed—she could star in her own made-for-TV movie about a very bad girl titled *Hannah and Her Outrageous Hormones*.

After she toed out of her sneakers, she dropped down next to Logan as a little flurry of butterfly nerves flitted around in her belly. "So are we going to meditate now?"

Logan's eyes appeared to grow darker in the shade, and undeniably more intense. "That's up to you."

With that, he brought her down onto the blanket in his arms, where she rested her head on his chest. They stayed that way for a time, the sound of his heart beating softly in Hannah's ear, his arm stroking her shoulder back and forth in a soothing rhythm.

She lifted her head to find him staring at the overhead branches. "Dollar for your thoughts. To account for inflation."

His smile made a short-lived appearance before he turned sullen again. "I was thinking how quickly life can change in one moment."

Hannah returned her head to his chest. "I know that all too well. One day you're sending the man you married off to work, the next you learn you'll never see him again."

"What exactly happened to him?" he asked. "If you don't mind talking about it."

She didn't mind, at least not now. "He was rewiring a commercial building that was under renovation and something went wrong. After the electrocution, they rushed him to the hospital and tried everything they could to save him, but it was too late."

"Does anyone know what went wrong now?"

"At first the insurance company claimed Danny was at fault, but his coworkers said he did everything he should have been doing in accordance with the wiring diagram. So they offered me a two-hundred-thousand-dollar settlement and I took it."

"You should have sued them."

Spoken like an attorney. "With a baby on the way and a new mortgage, I couldn't afford to ride it out, possibly for years, or risk losing the suit and ending up with nothing. Danny had a small insurance policy, but it barely covered funeral expenses, let alone any hospital bills I incurred after having Cassie."

"And your mother couldn't help out financially?"

A cynical laugh slipped out before she could stop it. "She always acted as if she didn't have a dime. However, she gifted us the down payment on our house out of the blue. I was able to repay her in a manner of speaking when I took care of her after her cancer diagnosis."

"You did that and attended school?" he asked, his voice somewhat incredulous.

"She only lasted two more months during the summer, so I wasn't in school." Hannah thought back to that time and the bittersweet memories. "Funny, I always felt as if I'd been a burden to her because she was so unhappy and bitter. Yet the day before she died, she told me thank you, and said she loved me. I don't recall her telling me that the entire time I was growing up. She was never the demonstrative type."

He released a rough sigh. "I can't imagine a parent not telling a child they loved them. But maybe she was so consumed by anger over being jilted by your father, she couldn't see what a gift she had in you."

Hannah's heart panged in her chest. "I don't know about being a gift, but I tried my best to be a good girl so I could win her approval. Unfortunately it never seemed to be enough."

He gave her a gentle squeeze. "As hard as it was, her attitude probably made you a stronger person. Definitely a good person. One of the best I've met in a long time."

He was saying all the right things, and he'd said

them with sincerity. "You're kind of remarkable yourself."

"Don't kid yourself, Hannah. I'm just an average guy who's made more than my share of mistakes."

Those mystery mistakes he had yet to reveal, leaving Hannah's imagination wide open. "Haven't we all screwed up a time or two, Logan? You just have to learn from those mistakes and move on. And eventually you have to stop blaming yourself for your shortcomings. That was fairly hard for me."

"Why were you blaming yourself?"

She truly hated to drudge that up, but soul-cleansing seemed to be the order of the day. "The morning Danny died, I got on him about leaving his shoes on the living room floor and missing the clothes hamper. I should have said I loved him, but the last words he heard from me had to do with cleanliness. I can count on one hand the times I didn't say I loved him before he left for work."

He brushed a kiss over her forehead. "You had no way of knowing he wouldn't be coming home."

If only she had known. "I finally acknowledged that, but it didn't lessen the guilt for a long time. If it hadn't been for Gina verbally kicking my butt, I might still not be over it."

"She's a good friend, huh?"

The very best and one of the few people she'd trust with her child. "Yes, she is. Granted, she does like to throw out advice whether I ask or not."

"How does she feel about you being here with me?"

She thought it best to hand him the abridged version. "Oh, she's all for it. In fact, if she'd had her way, we would've been having wild monkey sex from the minute I walked through your door."

"That would've worked for me."

She looked up to see his grin and poked him in the side. "That's rich coming from the guy who left me high and dry in his home theater."

"Believe me, that wasn't an easy decision."

Revelation time. "Just so you know, the way you make me feel…well…I thought I might never feel that way again."

He tipped her chin up and said, "That's my goal right now, to make you—" he kissed her forehead "—feel—" he kissed her cheek "—real good."

When Logan finally moved to her mouth, all Hannah's pent-up desire seemed to come out in that kiss, a hot meeting of tastes and tongues and mingled breath. Soon they were not only lip-to-lip, but also facing each other body-to-body until Logan nudged Hannah onto her back. He kissed the side of her neck as he slid his calloused hand beneath her T-shirt, at first breezing up her rib cage until he found her breasts. When he kissed her thoroughly again, he also circled her nipple with his fingertip through the lacy bra, and she reacted with an involuntary movement of her hips. Dampness began to gather in a place too long neglected, and she felt as if she might spontaneously combust due to the heat his touch was generating.

Her breathing, as well as her pulse, sped up as he skimmed his palm down her belly. She would swear her respiration stopped when he slipped the button on her jeans and then slid the zipper down.

Logan left her lips and softly said, "Lift up," and when Hannah answered his command, he pushed her pants down to her thighs, leaving her brand-new, leopard-skin panties intact.

For a few minutes, he seemed determined to keep
her in suspended animation, toying with the lace band
below her navel without sliding his hand inside the
silk, no matter how badly Hannah wanted it. He finally
streamed a fingertip between her thighs and sent it in
a back-and-forth motion. He knew exactly how and
where to touch her, but he only continued a brief time
before he took his hand away. She responded with a
somewhat embarrassing groan of protest, yet she soon
discovered she had nothing to complain about when
Logan worked her panties down to join her jeans.

From that moment forward, every bit of her sur-
roundings seemed to disappear. The only sound she
heard happened to be Logan whispering sensual words
in her ear about what he wanted to do to her, what she
was doing to him right then. Some of the comments
could be considered crude, but she regarded them as the
sexiest phrases she'd ever heard. He knew all the right
buttons to push and, boy, did he push them well. The
pressure began to mount, bringing with it pure pleasure
on the heels of an impending climax, compliments of
Logan's gentle, right-on-target strokes. And when the
orgasm hit all too soon, Hannah inadvertently dug her
nails into his upper arm and battled a scream bubbling
up from her throat.

She'd never been a screamer. She'd never been in a
pasture with her pants down around her knees either,
being tended to by one outrageously gorgeous, sexy
guy who knew exactly how to treat a woman.

Hannah was suddenly consumed by the overwhelming need to have him inside her. Yet when she reached
for his fly, he clasped her wrist to stop her. "Not here,"
he said. "Not now. This was all for you."

She focused on his beautiful face, the deep inden-
tations framing his mouth. "But—"

"It's okay, sweetheart. I'm going to be fine until we get back to the house."

She lifted her head slightly, with effort, to look at him. "What are we going to do when we get there?"

"I'm going to show you my bed." He favored her with a grin. "That is, if you want to see it."

Who was he kidding? "I seriously thought you would never ask."

Logan could have gone with spontaneity, but he wanted this first time between them to be special. More importantly, he needed Hannah to know she meant more to him than a quick roll on the ground, instant gratification, then over and out. She'd begun to mean more to him than she probably should.

Taking her by the hand, he led her into the master bedroom and closed the door behind them, determined to shut out the world and any lingering reservations.

Hannah remained silent when he tossed back the covers then guided her to the side of the bed. "Take off your shoes." And that would be the last thing she'd remove by herself if he had any say in the matter, which he did.

While she sat on the edge of the bed and took off her sneakers, he sat in the adjacent chair to pull off his boots. Once that was done, he lifted her from the bed and back onto her bare feet. He saw absolute trust in her eyes after he pulled the T-shirt over her head and tossed it aside. He noticed some self-consciousness in her expression as he removed her bra, and unmistakable heat when he slid her jeans and panties to the floor. She braced one hand on his shoulder for balance as she stepped out of the remaining clothes, a slight blush on her cheeks when he swept her up and laid her on the bed.

The sun streamed in from the open curtains covering the windows facing the pasture, casting Hannah's beautiful body in a golden glow. He needed to touch her. Had to touch her. But first things first.

Her gaze didn't waver as Logan stripped off his shirt, but she did home in on the ink etched in his upper arm. He'd have to explain that later. Right then he had more pressing issues. After shoving down his jeans and boxer-briefs, he opened the nightstand drawer, withdrew a packet and tossed it onto his side of the bed. He returned his attention to Hannah, who looked more than a little interested in his erection, her eyes wide with wonder.

She caught his glance and smiled. "I didn't realize you were that happy to see me."

Happier than he'd been in a long, long time. "I'm ecstatic to be here."

"So am I."

Relieved to hear that confirmation, Logan claimed the empty space beside Hannah and remained on his knees to allow better access. As he slid his fingertip between her breasts, pausing to circle each nipple, then moved down her torso, Hannah's breath caught. And when he replaced his hand with his mouth to retrace his path, he would swear she stopped breathing altogether.

When it came to sex, the advantage always went to women—they required little to no recovery time. And although his own body screamed for release, he was bent on proving that fact.

Logan nudged her legs apart to make a place for himself, then planted a kiss right below her navel. He didn't linger there long because he had somewhere more interesting to go. An intimate place that needed tending. When his mouth hit home, Hannah jerked from the impact. But he didn't let up, using his tongue to tease her into another climax. And as far as he could tell, this one was stronger than the last, apparent when she dug her nails even deeper into his shoulder.

He'd waited as long as physically possible to make love to her completely, and that sent him onto his back to reach for the condom. In a real big hurry, he tore the packet open with his teeth and had it in place in record time. He moved over her, eased inside her and called up every ounce of control to savor the feel of her surrounding him.

He'd learned long ago how to take a woman to the limits, but he also learned how to shelter his emotions in recent years. His sexual partners—and they'd been very few and far between—had been a means to an end. No commitments. No promises. Only mutual physical satisfaction. Up to that moment, he hadn't realized how empty his life had become. Until Hannah.

He minimized his movements as he held her closely. He wanted it to last, if not forever, at least a little while longer. But nature had other ideas, and the orgasm crashed down on him with the force of a hurricane.

Logan couldn't remember the last time he'd shaken so hard, or the last time his heart had beaten so fast. He sure as hell couldn't recall wanting to remain that way for the rest of the day, in the arms of someone he'd known for such a short while. But at times, he'd felt as if he'd known Hannah for years.

When she moved slightly beneath him and sighed, he took that as a cue his weight might be getting to her. But after he shifted over onto his back, she asked, "Where are you going?"

He slid his arm beneath her and brought her against his side. "I'm still here, Hannah."

She rose up and traced one half of the broken-heart tattoo on his upper arm, etched with an *A* on one side, and a *G* on the other. "Are these your ex-wife's initials?"

He'd expected that question, and he decided on a half-truth. "No. They belong to a girl I used to know." His baby girl.

She rested her cheek on his chest, right above his heart, which was pounding for a different reason now. "She must have been very special, and I'm sorry she broke your heart."

After another span of silence passed, Logan thought she'd fallen asleep. She proved him wrong when she asked, "You've never really considered having children of your own?"

Alarm bells rang in his head. "I'm not cut out for fatherhood."

She raised her head again and stared at him. "How could you possibly know that if you haven't even tried it? Or do you just not like kids?"

"I like kids a lot. They're way the hell more honest than adults. But it takes more than liking a child to raise them right."

She settled back on the pillow. "I personally think you'd be good at it, for what it's worth."

In a moment of clarity, Logan realized Hannah deserved the truth. She had to know the real man behind the facade. It pained him to think about reliving those details. He'd be tearing open an old wound that still refused to heal. He also could be inviting her scorn, and that would be even worse. Still, he felt he had no choice but to be open and honest.

"Hannah?"

"Hmmm…" she murmured as she softly stroked his belly.

"There's something I need to tell you, and it's not going to be pretty."

Hannah sensed he'd been concealing a secret all along, but was she prepared to hear it? She certainly better be, she realized, when Logan handed her the T-shirt and panties, then told her to put them on with a strange detachment that belied the sadness in his brown eyes.

While she dressed, Logan pulled on his jeans before sitting on the bed's edge and turning his back to her. A long period of silence passed and for a minute she wondered if he'd reconsidered confessing whatever it was he felt the need to confess.

"I had a daughter at one time."

Hannah bit back an audible gasp. She'd expected an affair, a business deal gone bad. Maybe even bankruptcy, although that didn't make much sense considering he'd purchased a million-dollar home. But she could not have predicated he'd lied about being a father. Then again, that could explain the framed photo she'd found in his desk drawer. "Did you lose custody?"

"I lost her because she died."

And Hannah only thought she couldn't be more stunned. "When did this happen, Logan?"

"Almost eight years ago," he said in a weary tone. "She was only four years old."

She swallowed around her shock right before her

ability to relate to his loss drew her to his side. She laid a hand on his shoulder. "I'm so sorry, Logan." It was all she could think to say at a moment like this. Now she understood why so many people had been at a loss for words following Danny's death.

He leaned forward, hands clasped over his parted knees as he kept his eyes trained on the dark hardwood floor beneath his feet. "Her name was Grace Ann. I called her Gracie."

The truth behind the tattoo. Devastating loss had broken his heart. Not a woman, but a precious child. "I know how badly it hurts to lose a husband, but I can't even begin to imagine how difficult it would be to lose a child."

"That's because it's unimaginable until it happens to you." His rough sigh echoed in the deathly quiet room. "When Jana got pregnant, we'd barely been out of law school. We were both ambitious and career-minded. A kid hadn't been a part of the plan. But when Gracie was born, and they put that tiny baby girl in my arms, I thought I'd be terrified. Instead, I was totally blown away by how much I loved her at that moment. How I would've moved mountains to keep her safe. And I failed to do that."

Hannah desperately wanted to ask for details, but she didn't want to push him. "Things happen, Logan. Horrible things that we can't predict or prevent."

"I could have prevented it."

Once more Hannah didn't know how to respond, so she waited until he spoke again. *If* he spoke again.

A few more seconds passed before he broke the pain-filled silence. "I bought her one of those little bikes for her fourth birthday. The kind that still had training wheels. She loved that bike." He paused as if lost in the memories before he continued. "A couple of days later, I was supposed to be home early to help her learn to ride it. I'd just made junior partner, and I was assigned the case of a lifetime that would've netted the firm a windfall. The pretrial hearing went on longer than expected that afternoon, so I wasn't going to make it home before dark. My job took precedence over my daughter."

The guilt in his tone was instantly recognizable to Hannah. "You're not the first man to put work over family when the situation calls for it. Danny missed dinner many times because he had to put in overtime to secure our future."

"But I had earned plenty of money by then, and so had my wife. I could have turned the hearing over to the associate working the case with me, but I was so damn driven to prove the senior partners had been justified in choosing me over two other candidates. And that drive cost my child her life."

She truly needed to know what had happened, but did she dare ask? "Logan, I'm really trying to understand why you feel you're to blame, but I'm having some problems with that with so little information to go on."

Logan glanced at her again before returning his focus to the floor. "When I drove up that night, I saw the ambulance and police cruiser parked in front of the house. I tried to tell myself one of the neighborhood teens had been driving too fast and had an accident. But my gut told me something inconceivable had happened, and it turned out I was right." He drew in a ragged breath and exhaled slowly. "I pulled up to the curb, got out of the car and started toward the ambulance, only to be met by an officer who told me not to go any farther. He said Grace had ridden the bike into the street and a woman driving by didn't see her, and she didn't even have time to put on her brakes."

Hannah felt his anguish as keenly as if it were her own. "Oh, Logan, I don't know what to say." And she honestly didn't. Again.

"Her death was instant, they told me," he said, as if he couldn't stop the flow of words. "She didn't suffer. But we all suffered. My marriage definitely suffered. Jana screamed at me that night and told me she'd never forgive me."

That threw Hannah for a mental loop. "She blamed you?"

He forked both hands through his hair. "We blamed each other. She blamed me for the bike and not being at a home on time. I blamed her for not watching Gracie closely enough. We both blamed the nanny for leaving early."

While Hannah pondered all she had learned, Logan went silent for a few more seconds before he released a ragged breath. "We had an alarm on the pool," he said. "We bought a top-rate security system and had every inch of the house child-proofed. But it wasn't enough. It came down to one unlocked door to the garage and Gracie climbing on a step stool to open the garage door, and she'd never been a climber."

Hannah had one burning question she had to ask. "Where was your wife at the time Gracie left the house?"

"Checking her email. She said Gracie was watching a DVD in the den only minutes before she went into the home office, and I had no reason not to believe her. Jana had always been a good mother, even if she had the same drive to succeed as I did. Basically, a few minutes of inattentiveness on Jana's part, and blind ambition on my part, irreparably changed our lives forever."

To Hannah, Logan's wife seemed more at fault than he did. But then she really couldn't completely blame her when she had been guilty of the same inattentiveness. "Children can be natural-born escape artists, no matter how vigilant the parent. Cassie got away from me in the grocery store once when I wasn't paying attention to her. It took a half hour and a security guard to find her. I was lucky someone didn't kidnap her when it would have been so easy."

"Gracie knew better than to leave the house without an adult," he said. "Until that night, she never had. I should have suspected she might pull something with the bike when I talked to her that afternoon."

"You spoke to Gracie?"

He smiled a sad smile that shot straight to Hannah's heart. "Yeah. I called Jana to say I was going to be late and she put Gracie on the phone so I could explain. When I told her I couldn't help her ride the bike that night, she was mad as a wet hen and told me she'd do it herself. I said that wasn't allowed and if she tried it, I'd take the bike away. She pouted for a few minutes but when I promised to help her the next day, and take her to the zoo that weekend, she seemed happy enough. Her last words to me were 'I love you, Daddy Bear.' She had a thing for Goldilocks."

Hannah's eyes began to mist like morning fog. "I know it's not the same thing as having her in your life, but at least you'll always have Gracie's wonderful last words to keep in your memory bank."

"But it's never been enough," he said, his voice

hoarse with emotion. "I finally did forgive Jana, but it was too little, too late. And when it came right down to it, she'd been right. I never should have bought Gracie the damn bike."

A solid stretch of logic, but logic didn't count for much when it came to guilt and grief. "When are you going to forgive yourself, Logan?"

He looked at her as if she'd presented a totally foreign concept. "Forgiveness is earned, Hannah. I'm not there yet."

She wanted to inquire as to how long it might take before he reached that point, but he looked completely drained. "I can tell you're tired." Of the conversation and the pain.

He swept both hands over his face. "I'm exhausted."

Hannah stretched out on her back on the bed and opened her arms to him. "Come lie down with me for a little while."

For a split second she thought he might ignore her request, but instead he shrugged out of his jeans and surprisingly accepted the solace she offered.

Curled up together, they slept for a while, until the sun had been replaced by darkness. Logan made love to her again, at first slowly, gently, completely, before a certain desperation seemed to take over. "I can't get close enough," he said, even though they were as close as two people could be.

"It's okay," she kept telling him, until his body went rigid and he released a low moan.

In the aftermath, he brought his lips to her ear and whispered, "Stay with me, sweetheart."

She caressed his shadowed jaw and almost started to cry over the tenderness in his request. "I'm not going anywhere, Logan."

"I meant don't leave on Saturday. Stay another week."

Temptation came calling, but wisdom won out. "I need to get home to Cassie."

"I know I don't have any right to ask, but I need you to be here for a little longer."

I need you....

Those three powerful words shattered Hannah's resolve. Cassie would be fine without her for another week, perhaps even happy to have the extra time with her best friend, that much she knew. Gina would be okay with her extended stay as well.

Logan needed her, and it felt so good to be needed. She instinctively knew she couldn't save him, but maybe if she loved him enough…

Loved him? If she wasn't completely there, she was well on her way, perhaps to her own detriment. She might regret giving in to that emotion, but she would never regret knowing him or what they had shared. What they would share.

"All right, Logan. I'll stay."

Eight

"Logan Whittaker, what brings you all the way out here in the middle of the week and the middle of the day?"

A quest for information he sensed Marlene held. He'd revealed his sorry secrets to Hannah several days ago, and now he wanted Marlene to do the same. "I'm taking a late lunch. Guess I should have called first."

"Don't be silly," she said as she held open the door. "You're practically family."

After he stepped through the door, Marlene pointed to the doors leading to the outdoor entertainment area. "Since it's such a lovely day, let's talk outside," she said as she showed Logan onto the flagstone deck adjacent to the massive great room. He settled on a rattan chair while she took the one to his left.

The 30,000 acres comprising the Big Blue ranch

spread out before them as far as the eye could see. The original homestead where J.D. and Ellie Lassiter had raised their family, now occupied by Marlene's son, Chance, sat in the distance beneath the blue sky that inspired the ranch's name. He'd learned the history early on, but it had never impacted him like it did today. "I'd like to build a house on a place like this in the future. Far away from everything with no signs whatsoever of the city." No suburban streets where playing kids could get hurt, or worse, and that unexpected thought gave him pause. He didn't intend to have any more kids. Not now. Not ever.

"It is peaceful," Marlene said. "All the Lassiter children enjoyed living here."

Speaking of Lassiter children...

Logan glanced back and peered inside through the uncovered floor-to-ceiling windows, looking for signs of other life—namely J.D.'s only daughter. "Is Angelica staying here right now?" Not only did he not want a repeat of their last conversation, but he also didn't want to risk her accidentally overhearing that her own father had taken a mistress, and produced a child. That would categorically send her over the edge. Of course, that would only happen if Marlene came clean.

"Angelica is back in L.A. for a couple of days," she said. "And quite honestly, that's a good thing. That girl has been in a constant tizzy lately. She needs a break. *I* need a break."

"I totally understand. J.D.'s decisions on who inherits his millions have created a lot of questions." Especially for Hannah.

Marlene reached over and patted his arm. "Now why are you here, honey?"

A perfect lead-in to the reason for his impromptu visit. "It's actually about those aforementioned questions. I'm pretty sure you have information about Hannah Armstrong's parentage, namely her connection to J.D. And if you do know anything about that, tell me now because she has a right to know."

She began to wring her hands like an old-time washer. "It's probably past time Hannah learns the truth, and I do know the details. But I wouldn't feel right discussing those particulars with you before I speak with her."

His suspicions had been upheld, and the answers were within Hannah's grasp. A good thing for Hannah because she would know the truth. A bad thing for him because she'd have no reason not to return to Boulder immediately. But delaying the revelation would be selfish on his part. "If I bring her by, will you tell her the whole truth?"

Marlene raised a brow. "She's still here?"

"Yeah. I asked her to stay another week." An unforgettable week of lovemaking and conversation and making a connection with a woman who'd become very special to him. A week that had passed way too fast. But since he had so little to offer her, he would be forced to let her go eventually.

"What makes this one so different from the rest, Logan?" Marlene asked, cutting into his thoughts.

He could recite every one of Hannah's attributes, but that would take hours, so he chose to list only a few. "She's funny and kind but also damn tough. Not many people could handle losing a husband, raising a child on their own, caring for an ill parent and finishing college in the process. Without even trying, she also has the means to make a person want to tell their life story." Much like the woman sitting next to him.

She raised a brow. "Did you tell her yours?"

He streaked a palm over his neck. "Yeah. She knows about Grace." And it had almost killed him to tell her.

Marlene smiled a mother's smile. "I am so glad, Logan. And since she's still sticking around, I assume that she holds the opinion you're not to blame, like I do. Am I right?"

"Yeah, you are." Even if he still didn't agree with that lack of blame assumption. "But she's also compassionate."

"She's a woman who understands loss," Marlene said. "I do as well. We're all unwitting members of a club drawn together by that loss, and sadly that also includes you, too. Hannah intimately understands your pain, and you're very lucky to have found her."

"Don't read too much into this relationship. On Saturday, she's going back to her life and I'll go back to mine."

"Your currently lonely life?" She topped off the question with a frown. "You'd be a fool to let her go, Logan, when she could be a part of your future."

Here we go again. "We had this conversation last week."

"And we'll continue to have it until you listen to reason."

If that's the way she wanted to play it, he'd reiterate all the reasons why a permanent relationship wouldn't work with anyone, especially Hannah. "Marlene, my job doesn't allow for a personal life, and I don't intend to quit for another twenty years, if then."

"Work isn't everything," she said. "Family is."

His profession had indirectly destroyed one family. He wasn't going to risk that possibility again. "Look, I enjoy being with Hannah, but I'm not sure I'll ever be able to make a serious commitment again. I've already been through one divorce and I don't want a repeat. And most important, Hannah's a single mom. She's going to have expectations I might not be able to meet."

Marlene narrowed her eyes and studied him for a few moments. "Part of your reluctance has to do with her daughter, doesn't it?"

Only someone as astute as Marlene would figure that out. "Could you blame me for being concerned? What if I became close with Cassie and my relationship with Hannah doesn't work out? That would be like—"

"Losing Grace all over again?"

She'd hit that nail on the head. "It wouldn't be fair to either one of them."

Marlene leaned forward, keeping her gaze on his. "Honey, life is about balance and a certain amount of chance-taking when it comes to matters of the heart. But life without the possibility of love isn't really living at all. We aren't meant to be alone. Just keep that in mind before you dismiss Hannah due to your fears."

"I'm only afraid of hurting her, Marlene." Afraid he might fail Hannah the way he'd failed his former wife and daughter.

"Maybe you should let her decide if she wants to take a chance on you."

Needing a quick escape, Logan checked his watch and stood. "I have an appointment in less than an hour, so I better get back to the office. When do you want to have that talk with Hannah?"

Marlene came to her feet. "Bring her over for lunch

on Saturday. I'll take her aside after that and speak with her privately. Better still, why don't you bring her daughter, Cassie, too? You could surprise her as a Mother's Day gesture, and give yourself some extra time with her as well."

He'd totally forgotten about the holiday. Marlene's suggestion would buy him more time with Hannah, and he knew she would appreciate the gesture. "I'd have to figure out how I could manage that without her knowing."

Marlene patted his cheek. "You're a smart man, Logan. You'll come up with a plan."

And that plan suddenly began to formulate in his mind. Marlene's suggestion just might work after all. But could he deal with being around a little girl so close in age to Grace when he'd lost her? He wouldn't know unless he tried, and this time he needed to consider Hannah, not himself.

Logan gave Marlene a quick hug. "Thanks for doing this for Hannah. She really needs to know how she came to be."

"You're welcome, honey. And once she learns the whole truth, she's going to need you to lean on."

Being there for her, like she had been there for him, was pretty much a no-brainer. "She's already figured out J.D. was her father. You'll only ease her mind if you confirm it."

Marlene sighed. "On second thought, maybe it's better I provide you with some information first so you'll be prepared. As long as you promise not to say anything to her before I do."

He just wished she would make up her mind. "Fine,

as long as you tell me everything, down to the last detail."

"J.D. didn't father Hannah."

Apparently they'd been traveling straight down the wrong-information path. "Then who was it?"

"My husband, Charles."

She'd spent the day doing laundry and packing her clothes—her final day in Cheyenne.

When Logan sent her a text saying he'd be home by 3:00 p.m., Hannah waited for him on the great-room sofa, wearing only his white tailored button-down shirt. She felt somewhat foolish, but what better way to greet him on their last night together? Even after days of nonstop searching, tomorrow she would return home with no answers about her father and no idea if she would ever see Logan again.

He'd seemed somewhat distant the past two days, or at the very least distracted. She couldn't help but believe he'd been planning his goodbye, and she should be preparing for it now. As soon as she implemented her current and somewhat questionable plan, she would. In the meantime, she refused to think about the impending heartache brought on because she'd been naive enough to fall in love with a man who might never love her back.

Ten minutes later, when she heard the front door open, Hannah stretched out on the cushions on her side and struck what she hoped would be deemed a sexy pose. Logan strode into the room, tossed his briefcase aside and stopped dead in his tracks when he caught sight of her. "Howdy, ma'am."

She brushed her hair back with one hand and smiled. "Howdy yourself."

He walked up to the couch and hovered above her. "I have never said this to a woman before, but you're going to have to get dressed."

She pretended to pout. "You don't like what I'm wearing?"

"Oh, yeah," he said. "But I have a surprise for you and it requires that you put on some clothes."

She straightened and lowered her feet to the floor. "I have a surprise for you, too. I'm not wearing any panties."

He hesitated a moment, his eyes growing dark with that familiar desire. "We don't have a whole lot of time, and I need to take a shower."

Hannah slipped two buttons on the shirt, giving him a bird's-eye view of her breasts. "Imagine that. So do I. We could go green and do it together."

His resistance dissolved right before her eyes, and he proved he was no match for their chemistry when he clasped her hands and tugged her off the sofa. "Then let's go conserve some water."

They rushed through the house, pausing to kiss on the way to Logan's bedroom. Once there, they began to shed their clothes article by article, until they reached the bathroom, completely naked and needy.

He pressed a series of buttons on the nearby chrome panel, sending several showerheads set into the stone walls into watery motion.

While the digital thermostat adjusted the temperature, Hannah stood behind Logan, her arms wrapped around his bare waist. "If I use your soap and shampoo, I'm going to smell like a guy."

He turned her into his arms and grinned. "Better than me smelling like a girl. Of course, you could go get your stuff, but that would take time we don't have." He punctuated the comment by placing a palm on her bottom and nudging her against his erection.

What a man. A sexy, incredible man. "I get the point. Now don't just stand there, take me in the shower."

"That's precisely what I plan to do."

All talk ceased as they took turns washing each other with soap and shampoo that smelled like Logan— clean, not cologne-like. For all intents and purposes, Hannah didn't care if she carried the trace scent of him on her flesh all night, or back home with her tomorrow for that matter. She rejected all thoughts of leaving, and fortunately for her, Logan aided in that cause with his gentle caresses and persuasive kisses that he feathered down her body. He kneeled before her and brought her to the brink of climax with his mouth, then suddenly straightened and pressed the control that cut off the sprays.

His rapid breathing echoed in the large stone shower before he groaned the single word, "Condom."

Hannah did a mental calculation and realized it would be the worst time to take a chance. "We absolutely have to have one before we go any further."

"I know. Getting you pregnant is the last thing I need."

She couldn't deny that his firm tone stung a little, but she also acknowledged he had his reasons for being so resolute—he wanted no more children, period. "Should we take this to the bedroom?"

"Good idea."

They had barely dried off before Logan gathered her

up in his arms, carried her to the bedroom and didn't even bother to turn down the covers. He simply deposited her on the navy comforter and put the condom in place in record time, then faced her on the mattress, one arm draped over her hip.

"I want to really see you when we make love," he said, followed by a brief yet stimulating kiss.

With the room bathed in sunlight, Hannah didn't view that as an issue. "It's still daytime."

"I want you to be in charge."

She gave him an intentionally furtive grin. "You want me on top."

"You got it."

Not a problem, she thought, as she rose up and straddled his thighs. Quite an extraordinary fit, she realized after he lifted her up and guided himself inside her. From that moment on, instinct took over as Hannah took the lead. She suddenly felt as if she'd become someone else—a truly sensual being with the capacity to be completely in control. Yet that control began to wane as Logan touched her again and again, and didn't let up until the last pulse of her orgasm subsided. Only then did she realize he was fairly close to losing it, and she took supreme advantage, using the movement of her hips to send him over the edge. She watched in wonder as the climax began to take hold. His respiration increased, his jaw locked tight and he hissed out a long breath as his body tensed beneath her, yet he never took his gaze from hers.

Feeling physically drained, Hannah collapsed against Logan's chest and rested her head against his pounding heart. He gently rubbed her back with one hand and stroked her hair with the other, lulling her into a total sense of peace.

After a time, he rolled her over onto her back, remained above her and touched her face with a reverence that almost brought tears to her eyes. "You're phenomenal, sweetheart."

But not phenomenal enough to figure into his future. "You're not so bad yourself, sexy guy."

She took his ensuing smile to memory to bring back out on a rainy day. "I wish…" His words trailed off, along with his gaze.

"You wish what?"

"I wish I'd met you years ago, back when we were both young and unattached."

Before his life had taken a terrible turn, she assumed. "Well, since you're eight years older, and I married at the ripe old age of twenty, that would have made me jailbait if you'd dated me before I met Danny."

"I guess you're right about that, and from what I gather, you loved your husband very much."

"I did," she said without hesitation. "But I also know he'd want me to be happy and go on with my life."

He turned onto his back and draped an arm over his forehead. "You deserve to be happy, Hannah. And someday you're going to find someone who will do that for you."

Clearly he believed he didn't qualify, when in truth he did. Not exactly goodbye, but pretty darn close.

She sat up and scooted to the edge of the bed so he wouldn't see the tears starting to form in her eyes.

"Hannah, are you okay?"

No, she wasn't. Not in the least. But she would be because she was a survivor. "I'm fine. I just thought

I'd get dressed since I do believe you mentioned we have some place to be."

When she started to stand, Logan caught her wrist before she could come to her feet. "Believe me, if things were different, if I were the right man for you—"

She pivoted around to face him and faked a smile. "It's all right, Logan. I told you before this thing started between us I had no expectations where we're concerned." And, boy, had she lied without even realizing it.

"You're one in a million, Hannah, and never forget that."

One thing she knew to be true, she would never forget him.

An hour later, Hannah climbed into Logan's Mercedes and they set out for who knew where. She dozed off for a bit and awoke to find they were close to Fort Collins in Colorado, heading in the direction of Boulder.

She hid a yawn behind her hand before shooting a glance at Logan. "If you wanted me to go home, all you had to do was ask."

He gave her a quick grin before concentrating on the road. "That's not where we're going."

"Do you mind telling me were we *are* we going?"

"You'll see real soon."

Five minutes later, he exited the interstate and pulled into a rest stop, leading Hannah to believe Logan needed a break. He shut off the ignition, slid out of the sedan without saying a word, rounded the hood and then opened her door. "Time to get out and take a walk."

"I don't need a walk."

"You'll want to take this one whether you need it or not."

She tapped her chin and pretended to think. "Let me guess. You've arranged for an intimate dinner to be catered at a roadside park."

"Not hardly."

"A picnic beneath the halogen light set to the sights and sounds of eighteen-wheelers, complete with the smell of diesel fuel?"

He braced a hand on the top of the door. "You can sit there and crack jokes, or you can come and see your surprise."

She saluted like a practiced soldier. "Whatever you say, Your Excellency."

Hannah exited the car with Logan's assistance and followed behind him, completely confused over where he could be taking her. Then she saw the familiar silver SUV, the sweet, recognizable face pressed against the back window, and it all began to make sense.

Gina came around from the driver's side, opened the door and released a squealing redhead dressed in white sneakers, floral blue shorts and matching shirt, and of course the tiara planted on her head. "Mama!"

Hannah kneeled down and nearly fell over backward due to her daughter's voracious hug. "I missed you so much, sweetie!" she said as she showered Cassie's cheeks with kisses. "But what are you doing here?"

The little girl reared back, wiped her wet face and displayed her snaggletoothed grin. "It's an early Mother's Day gift. Gina told me I'm gonna spend the weekend with you and the prince!"

"And it was all His Royal Hotness's idea," her best

friend said as she approached carrying Cassie's suitcase and booster seat.

Hannah straightened and turned to Logan. "How did you manage to make this happen without my knowledge?"

He streaked a hand over his nape. "It took some work and some sneaking around. I had to steal your phone when you weren't looking so I could get Gina's number."

"Then he called and asked me to bring Cassie halfway," she added. "Now here we are and Frank's at home with a crying son and a pouting daughter who's mourning the temporary loss of her best gal pal."

Only a short while ago, Logan had claimed he couldn't be the kind of man she needed, and then he did something so wonderfully considerate and totally unselfish to prove himself wrong, wrong, wrong. "This is a very welcome surprise, Mr. Whittaker. Thank you very much."

He took the bag and seat from Gina. "You're very welcome."

Cassie tugged on Logan's shirt sleeve to garner his attention. "I'm hungry, Prince Logan."

"Then we should probably get on the road so we can get the queen something to eat." His follow-up bow brought back Cassie's vibrant grin.

Hannah took the suitcase from Logan's grasp. "If you don't mind getting her settled into the car, I'll be along in a minute right after I receive a full report from Gina." She then set her attention on her daughter. "And Cassie, stay close to Logan when you're crossing the parking lot."

"You can count on that," he said with all the determination of a man who believed he'd failed to protect his own little girl.

When Cassie slid her hand into Logan's hand, Hannah saw the flash of emotion in his eyes and she could picture how many memories had assaulted him in that moment. After they walked away—the cowboy attorney with the slow, easy gait, and the bouncing queen wannabe—she turned back to her friend. "*Your Hotness?* Really?"

Gina shrugged. "Seemed pretty appropriate to me."

"You know, I'd be mad at you over that comment if I didn't so appreciate everything you've done. Not only this evening, but over the past two weeks."

"The question is, Hannah, was it worth it? Did you finally find what you were looking for?"

She shook her head. "I still don't know who my father might be, and I've accepted the fact I might never know."

Gina rolled her eyes. "I don't mean only the thing with your long-lost dad. I'm referring to you and the lawyer. Do you see a future with him in it?"

Sadly, she didn't. "He's not the kind to settle down, Gina. He's a remarkable man who's been through a lot, but he's closed himself off emotionally. And that's okay. I didn't expect anything to come of it anyway."

Her friend nailed her with a glare. "You did it, didn't you?"

This time Hannah rolled her eyes. "We had this discussion at least three times last week and once this week. Yes, we did it. Often."

"I'm not talking about the sex," Gina said. "You've gone and fallen in love with him, haven't you? And don't hand me any bull because I can read it all over your face, you ninny."

Hannah's hackles came to attention. "I am not a ninny, and I didn't fall in love with him." Much.

"You lie like a cheap rug."

"You're too meddlesome for my own good." Hannah hooked a thumb over her shoulder. "My daughter is waiting for me."

Gina held up both hands, palms forward, as if in surrender. "Fine. Go with your daughter and the hunk. But when you get home tomorrow, we're going to have a long talk about the virtues of emotionally safe sex."

That worked for Hannah, and after that talk, she could very well need to have a long, long cry.

By the time they arrived home, Logan had been steeped in so many recollections, he'd begun to feel the burn of regret. Watching Cassie at the café ordering a kid's meal and coloring on the menu, he remembered Gracie at every turn. And he missed her. God, did he miss her.

The ache grew worse when he carried a sleeping Cassie up the stairs and to the second surprise of the evening.

"You can put her in my bed," Hannah said from behind him.

That wasn't a part of the plan. "She'll sleep better in here." He opened the door to the room he'd kept as a tribute to his own daughter.

Hannah gaped when she saw the double bed covered by a white comforter imprinted with pink slippers to match the décor. "When did you do this?" she whispered as she turned down the covers.

He laid Cassie carefully on the sheets, her thumb planted firmly in her mouth, her eyes still closed against the light coming from the lamp on the nightstand. "I'll tell you in a minute."

After Hannah pulled off her daughter's shoes, then gave her a kiss on the cheek, they walked back into the hall.

Logan closed the door and turned to her. "The owner of a furniture store in town happens to be a client. I arranged to have the bed delivered right after we got on the road tonight."

"And the bedspread?"

"I bought it yesterday during lunch." Another gesture that had rocked him to the core.

Hannah folded her arms beneath her breasts. "I don't mean to seem ungrateful, because I do appreciate your consideration. But my question is, why would you buy a bed when we're only going to be here one night?"

"I thought maybe you'd agree to stay another night."

She sighed. "I need to get home and resume my job search."

He started to grasp at hopeless straws. "Maybe you and Cassie could visit now and then when you have the chance. I could teach her to ride Lucy."

"What would be the point in that, Logan? You've already established this relationship isn't going to go anywhere. So why would I get my daughter's hopes up and lead her to believe there could be more between us?"

She evidently wanted him to say there could be more, and he couldn't in good conscience promise her that. "I guess you're right."

"Yes, I am right. Now that we've cleared that up,

I'm going to get ready for bed and I'll see you in the morning."

He shouldn't be surprised by her curt dismissal, since he'd made it perfectly clear earlier that he couldn't be the man in her life, but he hadn't expected this rejection to twist his gut in knots. However, despite his wounded male pride, he still could provide the information she'd sought from the beginning. "Marlene Lassiter wants us to have lunch at the Big Blue ranch tomorrow."

She frowned. "I really planned to get on the road early."

"Can you wait to leave until later?" he asked, trying hard not to sound like a desperate idiot. "The ranch is a great place for a kid to play. Cassie would enjoy it." He'd learned long ago if you wanted to melt a good mom's heart, you only had to mention her kids.

He realized the ploy had worked when she said, "I guess a few extra hours won't matter. Besides, I might grab the opportunity to ask Marlene a few questions about J.D., if you don't think I'd be overstepping my bounds."

She had no idea that's exactly what Marlene intended to do—answer all her questions—and he couldn't help but feel guilty over not being forthcoming with what he knew. "Actually, it's a real good idea. Since you haven't signed the nondisclosure, I'm sure she'd be willing to tell you what she knows."

"Provided she actually knows something."

Little did she know, tomorrow she would not only learn about her real father, she would also discover she had a brother. "You might be surprised."

"Probably not," she said. "But I guess I'll find out."

When she started away, he caught her hand and pulled her into his arms. She allowed it for only a moment before she tugged out of his hold and said, "Sleep well, Logan."

For the first time in several days, Hannah retired to her own bedroom, and Logan left for his, without even a kiss good-night.

Sleep well? No way. Not with the prospect of letting her go hanging over his head. But he still had another day in her presence. He would make it his goal to show her and her daughter a good time, and try one more time to convince himself why he didn't deserve her.

Nine

When Marlene Lassiter showed her into a private study at the main house for an after-lunch chat, Hannah could barely contain her curiosity. She wondered if perhaps the woman might hand her the third degree about her relationship with Logan. If so, Marlene would be encountering a major dead end with that one. Truth was, after today, the relationship would be null and void.

"Have a seat, dear," Marlene said as she gestured to one of two brown leather chairs before she crossed the room, nervously tugging at the back hem of her white cotton blouse that covered her black slacks.

After Marlene paused at what appeared to be a bar, Hannah took a seat and conducted a quick visual search of the room. The office was rustic and large, like the rest of the Lassiter family homestead, with bookcases flanking another stone fireplace. That fireplace was much smaller in scale than the one in the great room, where they'd left Logan watching some animated film with Cassie, who'd adhered herself to his side like kid glue. He'd spent most of the morning keeping her entertained by letting her climb up to her castle—in this case, huge round bales of hay—under his watchful eye. If he'd minded the make-believe, or the recollections the interaction had most surely produced, he hadn't let on. He'd just patiently played the knight to the imaginary queen, wielding an invisible sword while sporting a sadness in his eyes that couldn't be concealed, at least not from Hannah.

"How big is this place?" she asked when Marlene bent down and opened the door to the built-in beverage refrigerator.

"Eight bedrooms, at least ten baths, I think because I always lose count, and around 11,000 square feet."

She'd known the glorified log cabin was huge when they'd driven through the gates of the Big Blue, but not that huge. "You have enough room to establish your own commune."

Marlene smiled over one shoulder. "Would you like a glass of wine, dear?"

Hannah normally didn't drink in the middle of the day, but it was well after noon, so what the heck? "Sure, but just a little. I have to head home this evening."

"I'll pour just enough to take the edge off."

Hannah wanted to ask why on earth she should be edgy, yet when Marlene returned with the drinks, looking as solemn as a preacher, she assumed she would soon find out.

She accepted the wine and said, "Thanks," then took

a quick sip. The stuff was so dry it did little to wet her parched throat.

Marlene took a larger drink then held the glass's stem in a tight-fisted grasp, looking as if she could snap it in two. "You might be wondering why I asked you in here, Hannah."

That was a colossal understatement. "I assume it has something to do with Logan."

"Actually, no, it doesn't. It has to do with—"

"Mom, are you in there?"

Marlene sent her an apologetic look before responding to the summons. "Yes, Chance, I'm here."

The door opened wide to a six-foot-plus, brown-haired, athletically built man wearing a chambray shirt with the sleeves rolled up to his elbows, worn leather boots and faded jeans. "Just wondering if the coals are still hot on the grill."

"Yes, they are," Marlene said. "And Chance, this is Logan's new girl, Hannah. Hannah, this is my son, Chance, and if he doesn't learn to wipe his boots better at the back door, I'm going to ban him from the house."

Hannah wanted to correct her on the "Logan's girl" thing, but when Chance Lassiter turned his gaze on her, she was practically struck mute. She met eyes the exact same color of green as hers, and although his hair was a light shade of brown, the resemblance was uncanny. Not proof positive she could be a Lassiter, but pretty darn close.

She had enough wherewithal to set the glass down on the coffee table and offer her hand. "It's nice to meet you, Chance."

He leaned over and gave her hand a hearty shake.

"Pleasure's all mine," he said before regarding his mother again. "Did you have burgers or steak?"

Marlene shrugged. "Steaks, of course. What I always have when we have guests. I saved you one in the fridge to cook to your liking. Two flips on the grill and it's done." She turned her attention back to Hannah. "Chance owns and runs the whole ranching operation, including developing the cattle breeding program. He raises the best Black Angus in the country, but I hope you know that after sampling our steaks."

Fortunately she hadn't been formally introduced to the cows before she'd literally had them for lunch. "Unequivocally the best."

Chance grinned with pride. "We aim to please. So now I'm going to leave you ladies to your girl talk while I go grab a bite. I take it that little redheaded girl napping on the sofa beside Logan belongs to you, Hannah."

Clearly Cassie had finally wound down, a very good thing for the poor lawyer. "Yes, she's all mine, and she's quite a live wire."

"She's as pretty as her mama," he said. "Logan is one lucky guy. Think I'll go tell him that before I grab a bite and get back to riding the range."

Chance Lassiter could talk until he was blue in the face, but luck had nothing to do with their inevitable parting a few hours from now.

After Chance closed the door behind him, Hannah smiled at Marlene. "He seems to be a great guy. Is he your only child?"

"Yes, he is. And he's done very well considering he lost his father when he was only eight. I believe you were around six years old at the time."

How would she possibly know that? Unless… "Marlene, has Logan mentioned anything to you about why I'm here in Cheyenne?"

She momentarily looked away. "Yes, he has, but don't hold that against him because he was only trying to help."

Logan's determination to come to her aid only impressed Hannah more. "Then you know about the annuity J.D. bequeathed to me?"

"I do, although no one else in the family knows about it."

"And the nondisclosure I have to sign to accept it?"

"J.D. added that clause to protect me."

And that made no sense to Hannah. "Why would he feel the need to protect you?"

Marlene downed the rest of her wine and set the glass aside on the end table positioned between the chairs. "Because my husband, Charles, was your father."

Hannah's mind reeled from the shocking revelation, jarring loose a host of unanswered questions. "And you knew about this for how long?"

"Charles came to me and told me about his brief affair with Ruth a few days after he ended it," she said. "Both of us learned about the pregnancy two weeks after you were born."

She didn't know whether to apologize to Marlene for her mother's transgressions, or scold her for not saying something sooner. "And you're absolutely sure Charles was my father?"

"I demanded a paternity test, and when it confirmed he was without a doubt your dad, Charles insisted on being a part of your life."

Hannah took a moment to let that sink in. "Apparently that never happened since I don't remember any man claiming to be my father spending time with me."

Marlene fished a photo from the pocket of her slacks and handed it to her. "You were two years old when this was taken."

She could only stare at the lanky yet handsome cowboy seated on a park bench, a smiling little girl on his lap. She didn't recognize him, but she positively recognized herself. "I have no memories of this or him." And she hated that fact with a passion.

"That's because your mother quit allowing visits when Charles refused to leave me for her."

Her fury returned with the force of an exploding grenade. "She used me as a pawn?"

"Unfortunately, yes," Marlene said. "If Charles wouldn't give in to her demands, then she wouldn't let him see his daughter."

Hannah wasn't sure she could emotionally handle much more, but she had to ask. "And he didn't think to fight for me?"

"No, dear, that's not the case at all. Charles consulted several lawyers on several occasions through the years. Ironically, he even spoke with one family law attorney who used to work at Logan's firm. They all basically told him the same thing. A mother's rights, especially a mother who'd conceived a child and was essentially *dumped* by a married man, would trump the biological father's rights."

She couldn't fathom the time she'd lost getting to know her father, all because of the law. "That's archaic."

"That's the way it was in that day and time." Marlene laid a hand on Hannah's arm. "But Charles never stopped hoping that might change, and he never stopped sending you money up until his death. I took over the payments after that."

Hannah was rapidly approaching information overload. "My mother claimed my father never gave her a penny of support."

Marlene sent her a sympathetic look. "I am so sorry you're learning this now, but Ruth received a monthly check every month from the day you were born, until J.D. learned you'd left college and married, which she failed to tell him."

Obviously all-consuming bitterness had turned her mother into the consummate liar. "She failed to tell me any of this." And now for another pertinent question. "Do you happen to know why J.D. came to our house when I was in the first grade? I remembered him when Logan first approached me about the annuity and I did an internet search."

"He went to tell her about Charles's death in my stead," she said. "Ruth only wanted to know who was going to sign the check. J.D. insisted on contributing the full amount and then some, but I refused to let him. That's when he established the annuity in your name."

"But why on earth would he list my mother as the secondary beneficiary?"

"I assume he believed it would allow him control over the situation. I honestly believe he didn't want to create a scandal for me, since he didn't know Charles had confessed to me about the affair and you. Regardless of what my husband had done, Charles and J.D. were always thick as thieves."

And that left one very important consideration—

the wronged wife. "Marlene, I can't imagine what you went through all those years, knowing your husband created a baby with another woman. And then you were charitable enough to see to that child's welfare." Even if the child had never known. And how horrible to learn her own mother had betrayed her. At least now she knew how Ruth had come by the down payment for the house. A weak gesture in light of the lies.

"Believe me, Hannah," Marlene continued, "I'm no saint. It took me years to forgive Charles, and I resented the hell out of your mother. I also resented you in many ways, and for that I am greatly ashamed."

Hannah set the photo next to her wineglass and clasped Marlene's hand. "I don't blame you at all. I *do* blame my mother for the deceit. Although it does explain why she never seemed happy, especially not with me. No matter what I did, I never felt it was good enough."

"Yet somehow you turned out so well, dear," she said. "I can tell you're a wonderful mother and a genuinely good person. Believe me, Logan knows that, too."

Regardless, that wasn't going to be enough to keep him in her life. "Logan is a very good man with a wounded soul. I hope someday he realizes he deserves to be happy again."

"With your help, I'm sure he will."

If only that were true. "I hate to burst your bubble, Marlene, but when I leave here, I doubt I'll be coming back anytime soon."

Marlene frowned. "I was hoping you'd return now and then to get to know your brother."

Her brother. She'd been so embroiled in the details she hadn't given Chance a second thought. "Does he know about me?"

"No, but I plan to tell him in the very near future. And I hope you'll tell Logan how you really feel about him before you go."

Time to admit the agonizing truth. "He's only going to be a special man I had the pleasure of meeting, and that's all he'll ever be."

Marlene had the skeptical look down to a science. "Don't try to fool an old fool, Hannah. I can spot a woman in love at fifty paces."

Hannah fixed her gaze on the almost-full glass next to the photo, but she had no desire to drink, only sob. "It doesn't matter how I feel about him. Logan has all but given up on love. And that's sad when he needs it so very much."

"I'm asking you not to give up on him," Marlene said. "Men have been known to come around, once the woman of their dreams has flown the love nest. But before you do that, you need to tell him how the cow ate the cabbage and convince him that you're worth fighting for. Then make sure you turn around and leave so he'll have time to chew on it awhile."

"I suppose I could give that a shot."

"You'd be surprised how effective it can be."

Hannah could only hope. That's about all she had left to hold on to. Actually, that wasn't exactly the case. She picked up the photo and studied it again. "Do you mind if I keep this?"

"Not at all, dear." Marlene stood and smiled. "Now let's go find that hardheaded attorney so you can have the last word."

Hannah had the strongest feeling it could very well be her last stand.

* * *

"Looks like it's going to rain."

In response to Logan's observation, Hannah looked up. The overcast skies reflected her gloomy mood, but she needed to snap out of the funk in order to tell Logan exactly what had been brewing in her mind, with a little help from Marlene.

She kicked at a random stone as the two of them walked a path leading away from the house. "Hopefully it won't be more than a spring shower. Just enough rain that lasts long enough for Cassie to get in a good nap."

"Chance is hoping for a deluge."

"You mean my *half brother,* Chance?" she asked, as she took a glimpse to her right to gauge Logan's reaction.

"I figured Marlene told you everything."

His poker face and even tone told Hannah he'd been privy to that knowledge. "How long have you known Charles Lassiter was my father?"

"Since Wednesday."

"And you went three days without telling me?" She'd thought she'd meant more to him than that. Obviously she'd been wrong.

"Now before you get all worked up," he said, "Marlene made me promise I wouldn't say anything to you before she could explain. It was damn hard keeping you in the dark, but I had to respect her wishes."

She shrugged. "What's three days when compared to thirty years? I still cannot believe my own mother never told me about him, or the fact that she received checks from Charles and then Marlene during my formative years and beyond."

Finally, Logan showed something more than detachment to her disclosures. "That part I didn't know, Hannah. I'm sorry you had to find out after the fact."

She was sorry she couldn't change his mind about settling down. Or having children. Yet expecting someone to alter their ideals made little sense. "It's done, and I'm over it. I have a great daughter, own my home and a degree. Now I just need to find a job and my life will be complete." That rang false, even to Hannah's ears.

"You know, you could look for a job here," Logan said.

The suggestion took her aback, and gave her hope. "Why would I do that when my life is in Boulder?"

"So you can get to know your new family since you're not going to take the inheritance."

So much for hoping he might actually see a future with her. "That really only includes Chance, since I have no idea how my cousins will take the news." And who was to say her brother would even want to have a relationship with her?

"I still think that if you moved closer, we could get together every now and then."

Not at all what she wanted to hear. "For the occasional booty call?"

He scowled. "You know me well enough to know I respect you more than that. I just thought we could see where it goes."

She knew exactly where it would go. Nowhere. "Let's review, shall we? I eventually want to marry again and have at least one more child. You, on the other hand, would prefer to live your life alone, moving from one casual conquest to another with no commitment, in typical confirmed-bachelor fashion. And since I don't intend to follow in my mother's footsteps and wind up as someone's mistress, that puts us directly at odds. Do you not agree?"

He stopped in his tracks to stare at her, anger glinting in his dark eyes. "I've never seen you as some kind of conquest and definitely not as a potential mistress. I only thought that if we spent more time together—"

"You'd suddenly decide by some miracle to become a family man again?"

"I told you why—"

"You don't want to settle down. I know. You're too wrapped in guilt and grief to give me what I need. But what about *your* needs?"

He shifted his weight from one leg to the other. "What do you think I need?"

He'd asked for it, and she was glad to give it to him. "You need to get over yourself. You're not the only one who's lost someone they loved more than life itself. But life does go on unless you say it doesn't. And that's what you've been saying for the past eight years. Do you think keeping yourself closed off to all possibilities is honoring your daughter's memory? Believe me, it's doing just the opposite."

His eyes now reflected pent-up fury. "Leave Grace out of this."

"I can't, Logan, because deep down you know I'm right. And if I never see you again, it's going to be tough, and it's going to break my heart just like that memorial tattoo on your arm. But I'm not a quitter, and I didn't peg you as one, either, when I stupidly fell in love with you."

He looked astonished over her spontaneous admission. "You what?"

No need to stop when she was on a roll. "I love you.

Oh, I fought it with everything in me. I chalked it up to lust and liking your home theater. And of course my appreciation of your plumbing skills. What woman wouldn't want a man who could fix her leaky pipes? And I really valued your determination to make sure I found out the truth about my heritage." She hitched in a breath. "But do you know when I quit questioning my feelings?"

"No."

"Today, when I watched you playing with my daughter, and I saw this longing in your eyes that took my breath away. Whether you believe it or not, you're meant to be a father, and somewhere beneath that damned armor you've build around your heart, you want to be one again. But that will never happen unless you stop beating yourself up and being afraid of making a mistake."

Tension and silence hung between them despite the whistling wind. Hannah allowed the quiet for a few moments before she finished her diatribe. "Logan, I only want what's best for you, believe it or not. And I hate it that I hurt you by laying out the truth. I also pray you find the strength to love again. Maybe I'm not the woman you need, but you do need someone."

For the first time ever, he appeared to be rendered speechless. Either that, or he was simply too irate to speak.

When he failed to respond, Hannah decided to give up, though that went against her nature. But she wasn't too stubborn to recognize when it was time to throw in that towel. "If it's not too much of a bother, I'd like to go back to your place, collect my things and my car, and get back to Boulder before dark."

This time she didn't bother to wait for his answer. She simply spun around and headed back to the house to gather her child in order to go home and lick her wounds.

Yet as she afforded a glance over her shoulder, and she saw him standing there in the rain, looking forlorn instead of furious, she wondered if maybe she'd expected too much from Logan too soon. Given up on him too quickly. She wanted desperately to believe he might eventually come around to her side.

And that possibly could be too much to ask.

Yesterday afternoon, Logan had told Hannah goodbye after giving her and Cassie a brief hug, not once giving away the sorry state of his heart. Since then, he'd been carrying around a brand-new bushel full of regrets that kept running over and over in his head. He wound up spending the night seated on the floor in the now-vacant child's room, alone and lonely. He dozed off now and then, always awakening with a strong sense that he'd made the biggest mistake of his life when he let Hannah go without putting up a fight.

He'd blamed her for treading on his pride, when all she'd done was shine a light on the hard truth. In many ways, he had stopped living. But he hadn't stopped loving, because he was—without a doubt—in love with her. He loved her wit and her gentle ways. He loved the way she made love to him. He loved the fact she could melt his heart with only a smile. He hated that he hadn't uttered one word of that to her before she'd driven away, and now it might be too late.

Although he was dog-tired, that didn't keep him from sprinting down the stairs when he heard the doorbell chime. He hoped to see Hannah on his doorstep, but instead he peered through the peephole and found Chance Lassiter. As much as he liked and respected the guy, he wasn't in the mood for company. But when he noticed the wind had begun to push the rain beneath the portico, he decided he should probably let him in.

Logan opened the door and before he could mutter a greeting, Chance said, "You look like hell, Whittaker."

He ran a hand over his unshaven jaw and figured he looked like he'd wrestled a bear and lost. "Good to see you, too, Lassiter."

Chance stepped inside without an invite, shrugged off the heavy weatherproof jacket and shook it out, sprinkling drops of water all over the travertine tile. He then dug a pair of tiny blue socks from his jeans pocket and offered them to Logan. "Mom told me Cassie left these at the house. Is Hannah still here?"

He wished that were the case. "She went home yesterday afternoon."

"Damn. I really wanted to talk to her. When's she going to be back?"

"I don't think she'll be coming back anytime soon." Voicing it made the concept all too real. "At least not to see me."

"Trouble in paradise?"

Paradise had disappeared the minute she'd walked out his door. "Guess some things aren't meant to be."

"That's really too bad," Chance said. "I was hoping maybe you'd be my brother-in-law in the near future, that way I wouldn't hesitate to call you when I need help with the cows."

Chance's attempt at humor sounded forced to Logan, and with good reason. Suddenly learning you have a sister because your late father was a philanderer would be a damn bitter pill to swallow. "You don't hesitate to call me for help now, and I take it Marlene told you the whole story about your father and Hannah's mother."

"Yeah, the whole sorry story." Chance let go a caustic laugh. "You spend your life idolizing your dad, only to learn the guy was a good-for-nothing cheater. But at least I got a sibling out of the deal. That's if she wants to acknowledge me as her brother. Had I known the facts before she took off, I would've spoken with her yesterday while she was still at the ranch."

Had Logan known how bad he would hurt, he might not have let her take off. "I've got her phone number and address if you want to get in touch with her."

"I'll do that," he said. "Question is, what are you going to do about her?"

"I'm not sure what you mean."

Chance shook his head. "For a man with a whole lot of smarts, you're not real good at pretending to be stupid."

He didn't much care for the stupid designation, even if it might ring true in this instance. "Didn't know you planned to deliver insults along with the socks."

"Well, if the shoe fits, as Mom would say."

Logan also didn't appreciate the pun. "Look, Hannah and I had a good thing going, but now it's over."

Chance narrowed his eyes, looking like he was prepared to take his best shot, or throw a punch. "You do realize you're talking about my sister. If you used her and then threw her away like garbage, that's grounds to kick your ass."

"I don't use women and I sure as hell didn't use

Hannah, so simmer down. In fact, I stayed awake all night thinking about her."

Chance seemed satisfied by that response, at least satisfied enough to unclench his fists. He also looked a little too smug. "Man, do you have it bad for her."

Dammit, he'd walked right into that trap. "That's one hell of a major assumption, Lassiter."

"Are you going to tell me I'm wrong?"

Not unless he wanted to hand Chance one supersized lie. "No, you're not wrong."

"Well, hell, that sure explains why you look like something the mountain lion dragged in that the bloodhound couldn't stomach."

He really should have checked a mirror on his way downstairs. "Are you done deriding me now?"

"Nope. Not until you admit how you really feel about Hannah."

"I love her, dammit." There, he'd said it, and a hole in the tiled entry hadn't opened up and swallowed him. "Are you happy now?"

"As happy as a squirrel in the summer with a surplus of nuts. Do you still want to be with her?"

More than he could express. "Yeah, I do."

"Now what are you going to do about it?"

Logan didn't have a clue. "I'm sure you're itching to tell me."

"I don't even begin to understand what makes a woman tick," Chance began, "but I do know if you want her back, you've got to do it soon, before she has time to think about how you've wronged her."

"I'll call her as soon as I call my mom." Talk about serious avoidance.

Chance glared at him like he'd just proposed a plot

to commit murder. "Man, you can't do this over the phone. You have to go see her. Today."

"But—"

He pointed a finger in Logan's face. "You're going to show up at her house with something that will force her to forgive you."

"Flowers?"

"Yeah. Flowers are good, especially since it's Mother's Day. Do you have any planted in some garden?"

"Hell no. I'll have to buy them somewhere." Fortunately he had a connection who could accommodate him.

"What about one of those fancy silk suits?"

Logan's patience was wearing thin. "I'm an attorney, Chance. I have a damn suit."

"Sorry, but I had to ask because I've never seen you wear an entire suit, bud. Anyway, you'll show up in your suit with flowers—"

"For a die-hard bachelor, you're sure quick to dole out the advice."

"I just want my sister to be happy," Chance said in a surprisingly serious tone.

So did Logan. But would all the frills be enough to persuade Hannah to give them another chance? "What if she throws me out before I have my say?"

Chance slapped his back with the force of a steamroller. "Whittaker, according to Mom, Hannah loves you something awful, too. If you play your cards right, she'll let you come crawling back to her. Now I'm not saying you need to propose marriage because you've known each other a short time. My mom and dad only knew each other a month before they tied the knot and we now know how that one worked out."

Funny, Marlene hadn't mentioned that to Logan during their many conversations. "No kidding? Only a month?"

"No kidding," he said. "And then he cheated on his wife, not that I think you'd do that to Hannah."

"Not on your life." She was all he needed. All he would ever need.

"And to top it off," Chance continued, "Mom told me yesterday that in spite of my father's faults and weakness, she never doubted his love for her. It's just hard for me to believe love that strong exists."

Logan was beginning to believe it existed between him and Hannah, provided she hadn't fallen out of love with him overnight. "I hope you eventually forgive Marlene. She was just trying to protect you from the ugly truth."

"I'll forgive her eventually," Chance said. "As far as my dad's concerned, I'm not sure that will ever happen."

Logan knew all about that inability to forgive, and he could only hope Chance eventually came around like he had. But Hannah… "I hope like hell Hannah forgives me for taking so long to realize we need to be together."

"She'll forgive you the minute you show up at her door wearing your heart on your sleeve."

"Guess that's better than eating crow."

"You'll be doing that, too, Whittaker, so pack some salt. And groveling couldn't hurt. Hope that suit isn't too expensive in case you have to get down on your knees when you beg."

The suit didn't mean as much to him as Hannah. His pride no longer mattered much where she was concerned, either. "Are you sure you don't want to go with me, Lassiter? In case you want to talk with her after I do."

Chance grinned, grabbed his coat and backed toward the door. "You're on your own with this one, bud. Now go get a shower and shave, then go get your girl. Who knows? She might even be waiting for you."

Ten

Hannah walked out the door to meet Gina for their traditional Mother's Day brunch, only to stop short of the sidewalk when she caught sight of the black Mercedes parked at the curb. And leaning against that sedan's driver's door was the beautiful, wounded, brown-eyed man who'd invaded her thoughts the majority of the night. He wore a beige silk suit with matching tie and a white tailored shirt, a bouquet of roses in one hand, a piece of white paper in the other. If not for the dress cowboy boots, she might believe this was Logan Whittaker's clone. Yet when he grinned, showing those dimples to supreme advantage, that was all the confirmation she needed. But why was he here? She aimed to find out.

Hannah stepped across the yard, her three-inch heels digging into the grass made moist by the deluge that had arrived during the night. Fortunately the clouds had begun to break up, allowing the sun to peek through.

When she reached Logan, she shored up her courage and attempted a smile. "What are you doing here, Mr. Whittaker?"

"Thought you might need a plumber."

"My pipes appear to be holding, so no more water in the floor." On the other hand, her heart was flooded with a love for him that just wouldn't leave her be. "Since you're wearing a suit, I thought maybe you got lost on your way to some wedding."

"Nope, but I was pretty lost until I found you."

Her flooded heart did a little flip-flop in her chest. But she wasn't ready to give in to his pretty words and patent charms. Yet. "Who are the flowers for?"

"You," he said as he handed them off to her. "Happy Mother's Day."

She brought the roses to her nose and drew in the scent. "Thank you."

He leaned around her. "Where's Cassie?"

"Two houses down at the Romeros'. She's going to spend a few hours there while Gina and I have lunch together."

"Who's going to be watching her?"

His protective tone both surprised and pleased Hannah. "Gina's husband, Frank. He's used to watching their baby and the girls when Gina and I have plans."

"That sounds like a damn daunting job."

"He's a great dad, but he's had lots of practice." *And you would be a great dad, too,* she wanted to say.

Amazingly the familiar sadness didn't show in his eyes. "I guess practice makes perfect."

He still had a lot to learn. "Not perfect, Logan. No parent is ever perfect."

"I'm starting to realize that."

Oh, how she wanted to believe him. Yet she continued to resist the notion he had finally seen the light.

Hannah pointed at the document now clenched in his fist. "What's that?"

"The annuity terms that include the nondisclosure clause." He unfolded the paper, tore it in half and then tossed the remains into the open back window. "And according to your wishes, it's no longer valid."

Hannah couldn't resist teasing him a little. "Darn. I decided last night to sign it and take the money."

"Are you serious?"

She stifled a laugh. "No, I'm not serious. I could always use that kind of money, but I have everything I need without it, especially since Cassie's future is secure, thanks to my in-laws."

He inclined his head and looked at her as if he could see right through her phony assertion. "Everything?"

Except for those things money couldn't buy—like his love. "Enough to get by until I find a job. And mark my words, I will find a job even if I have to flip burgers."

"Marlene told me there's an opening at one of the rural high schools between my place and the Big Blue. They need a biology teacher. You should go for it."

"You're saying I should just uproot my child, sell my house and move to the middle of nowhere?"

"As I mentioned earlier, you'd have the opportunity to get to know your brother. We can continue to get to know each other better, too."

And he would have to do better than that. "We've already had this discussion, Logan. I want—"

"A man who can promise you a solid future and more kids."

"Exactly."

Some unnamed emotion reflected in his eyes. "I can be that man, Hannah. God knows I want to be."

The declaration tossed her into an emotional tailspin. "If that's true, then what made you suddenly change your mind?"

"What you told me about not honoring Grace's memory. I sat up all night in that room with the princesses on the wall and had a long talk with my daughter, as crazy as it seems."

How many times had she had those conversations with Danny in the distant past? "It's not crazy at all. It's long overdue."

"Anyway, for the first time since the funeral, I cried like a baby. But that meltdown didn't occur last night only because of Gracie. It had a lot to do with losing you."

Hannah could tell the admission was costing him as much as it was costing her. She wanted to throw her arms around him, tell him it would be okay, but she wasn't quite ready to do that yet. "Are you sure you're prepared to make a commitment to me and Cassie if and when the time comes?"

"I'm all in, Hannah," he said adamantly. "I also know I can be a good dad to Cassie. And do you want to know how I figured that one out?"

"Yes, I would."

He looked down and toed a random clump of grass before bringing his gaze back to hers. "When I was playing with Cassie yesterday on the hay bales, she slipped a few times and I caught her. Once I couldn't reach her, but she managed to pick herself back up after she tumbled to the bottom. Granted, it scared the hell out of me for a few minutes, but it also made me acknowledge that kids are actually pretty resilient, and the truth is, you can't logically be there for your children all the time." He exhaled roughly. "You can only do the best you can to protect them, and sadly sometimes that isn't enough, but you can't spend your life being paralyzed by a fear of failure."

A lesson everyone should learn. Unfortunately, he'd learned it the hard way. "Cassie's completely enamored of you, Logan. She told me on the drive home that you would make a good daddy, and she's right. But I've known that all along. I'm just glad you finally realized it."

His smile was soft and sincere. "She still thinks I'm some kind of prince."

"So do I. Or maybe I should say a prince in progress. You still need some work, but the flowers helped your cause."

He reached over and clasped her hand. "If I tell you I can't imagine my life without you, would that help, too?"

Hannah held back the tears, with great effort. "Immensely."

He brought her closer. "How about if I tell you I love you?"

So much for keeping those tears at bay. "Really?"

He gently kissed her cheek. "Really. I didn't expect to fall so hard and so fast for someone, because I never have. Hell, I didn't expect you at all. And although neither of us knows what the future will bring, I do know what I want."

Hannah sniffed and hoped she didn't look like a raccoon. "For me to buy waterproof mascara from now on?"

He responded with that smile she had so grown to

adore. "No. I want to give us a fighting chance. I promise to do everything in my power to make it work."

"I promise that, too." And she did, with all her heart and soul. "I love you, Logan."

"I love you, too, sweetheart."

Then he kissed her, softly, slowly, sealing the vow they'd made at that moment, and those vows Hannah believed were yet to come.

"I guess this means brunch is off."

She broke the kiss to find Gina standing in the middle of the sidewalk, gawking. "I suppose we'll have to postpone until next year."

Gina shrugged. "That's probably for the best. Frank's been complaining of a cold all morning and Trey's teething. I'd feel guilty if I left him with three kids, and even more guilty if I spoiled this wonderful little reunion. However, it does pain me to break a long-standing tradition."

"Tell you what, Gina," Logan said as he kept his arms around Hannah. "If you'll let me take my lady to lunch, I'll give you and your husband a night on the town, my treat. We'll even keep the kids."

Gina's eyes went as wide as saucers. "How about tonight? That would so cure Frank of what ails him."

He returned his attention back to Hannah. "Works for me, if it works for you."

With one exception. "Sure, as long as we have a few hours alone before we're left in charge of the troops."

"It's a deal," Gina said as she backed up a few steps. "Have a good lunch, and have some of that wild monkey sex for dessert, too."

As soon as her friend left the immediate premises, Hannah gave Logan another quick kiss. "You're mighty brave, taking on three kids."

He responded with a grin. "Hey, I've got to get into practice for when we have our three. Or maybe four."

Sweet, welcome music to Hannah's ears. "Don't get ahead of yourself, buster. You'll have to marry me first, Logan Whittaker, my repressed plumber."

"You know, Hannah Armstrong, my maid-in-waiting, I just might do that sooner than you think."

The past six weeks had whirled by in a flurry of changes. She'd sold the house, moved into the Big Blue for the sake of her minor child, spent every day with Logan, and even a few nights alone with him, thanks to Marlene's generosity. Aside from that, the saintly woman hadn't even flinched when Cassie had begun to call her Grandma.

Best of all, Hannah had learned that morning she'd been awarded the high school biology teaching job and would begin in the fall. Things couldn't be going any better, and tonight she and Logan planned to celebrate with a night on the town and a hotel stay in Denver. But she'd better hurry up with the preparations, otherwise Logan might leave without her.

On that thought, she inserted the diamond earrings he'd given her two weeks ago on the one-month anniversary of their meeting. Admittedly, and ridiculously, she'd secretly hoped for jewelry that fit on her left ring finger, but she had no doubt that would eventually come. She had no doubts whatsoever about their future.

After a quick dab of lipstick and a mirror check to make sure the white satin dress was properly fitted, Hannah grabbed her clutch in one hand and slipped the overnight bag's strap over one bare shoulder. She then rushed out of the bedroom and down the hall of the wing she shared with Marlene.

She was somewhat winded when she reached the staircase, and her breath deserted her completely when she saw Logan standing at the bottom landing. He'd donned a black tuxedo with a silver tie, and he was actually wearing Italian loafers, not the usual Western boots.

She couldn't help but smile as she floated down the stairs and took his extended hand when she reached the bottom. "Okay, what did you do with my cowboy lawyer?"

"According to your daughter, tonight I'm supposed to be a prince. This is as close as I could get because I refuse to wear those damn tights and a codpiece."

She reached up and kissed his neck. "I'd buy tickets to see you in tights."

He sent her a champion scowl. "Save your money 'cause it ain't happenin'."

"That's too bad."

He grinned. "You like bad, especially when it comes to me."

Oh, yeah. "I won't argue with that."

He crooked his arm for her to take. "Are you ready, Ms. Armstrong?"

"I am, Prince Logan. Take me away."

Instead of heading toward the front door, Logan guided Hannah down the corridor and into the great room, where an unexpected crowd had gathered. A crowd consisting of Marlene wearing a beautiful white chiffon dress, Chance dressed in a navy shirt and dark jeans, Cassie decked out in her pink princess gown, complete with pretty coat and feather boa, and of all people, senior law partner, Walter Drake, who had debonair down pat. Hannah had to wonder if they were going to pile all these people into a car caravan and head to Denver together.

"Did you plan a party without me knowing?" she asked when Logan positioned her next to the floor-to-ceiling stone fireplace.

"That's somewhat accurate," Logan said. "And you're the guest of honor."

A frenzy of applause rang out, accompanied by a few ear-piercing whistles, compliments of Chance. Her half brother had become very special to her, and he'd proven to be a stellar uncle to Cassie, evidenced by the fact he'd picked up his niece and held her in his arms.

"First, thank you all for being here," Logan began, sounding every bit the attorney, with a little Texas accent thrown in. "But before we get to the celebration, I have something important to ask a very special lady."

Surely he wasn't going to… Hannah held her breath so long she thought her chest might explode, until Logan said, "Cassie, come here."

While Logan took a seat on the raised heart, Chance lowered Cassie to the ground. She ran over as fast as her little pink patent leather shoes allowed. She then came to a sliding stop, plopped herself down in Logan's lap and draped her tiny arms around his neck.

"Darlin'," Logan began, "you know I love your mama, and I love you, right?"

She nodded emphatically, causing her red ringlets to bounce. "Uh-huh."

"And you know that I'm never going to try to take your daddy's place."

"My Heaven daddy."

"That's right. But I sure would like to be your daddy here on earth, if that's okay."

"I'd like you to be my earth daddy, too," Cassie said.

Hannah placed a hand over her mouth to stifle a sob when she saw the look of sheer love in both Cassie's and Logan's eyes.

Logan kissed her daughter's forehead before setting her back on her feet. "Now I have to ask your mom a few questions."

Cassie responded with a grin. "You betcha." She then looked up at Hannah, who could barely see due to the moisture clouding her eyes. "I told you so, Mama. Logan is your prince."

Cassie ran back to her uncle while Logan came to his feet. He moved right in front of Hannah, his gaze unwavering. "Sweetheart, I want to wake up with you every morning and go to bed with you every night. I want to find a good balance between work and family. I don't want to replace Cassie's real dad, but I want to be the best father I can be to her. And I want, God willing, for your face to be the last one I see before I'm gone from this earth. Therefore, if you'll have me, Hannah Armstrong, I want more than anything for you to be my wife."

The room had grown so silent, Hannah would swear everyone could hear her pounding heart. This was no time for smart remarks. For questions or doubts. This precious request Logan had made only required one answer. "Yes, I will be your wife."

Following a kiss, and more applause, Logan pulled a black velvet box from his inner pocket and opened it to a brilliant, emerald-cut diamond ring flanked by more diamonds. "This should seal the deal," he said as he removed it from the holder, pocketed the box again, then placed it on her left finger.

Hannah held it up to the light. "Heavens, Logan Whittaker, this could rival the Rocky Mountains. I might have to wear a sling to hold it up."

Logan leaned over and whispered, "Always the smart-ass, and I love it. I love you."

She sent him a wily grin. "I love you, too, and I really and truly love the ring."

The pop of the cork signaled the party had begun as Marlene started doling out champagne to everyone of legal age. When Cassie asked, "Can I have some?" Logan and Hannah barked out, "No!" simultaneously.

She turned to Logan and smiled. "You're going to come in handy when she turns sixteen and the boys come calling."

"She's not going to date until she's twenty-one," he said in a gruff tone.

"And I'm the Princess of Romania," she replied, although tonight she did feel like a princess. A happy, beloved princess, thanks to her unpredictable prince.

Following a few toasts, many congratulations and a lot of hugs and kisses, Logan finally escorted Hannah out the door and into the awaiting black limousine, just one more surprise in her husband-to-be's repertoire. Then again, everything about her relationship with Logan had been one gigantic surprise.

After they were seated side by side, and the partition dividing the front and back of the car had been raised, Logan kissed her with all the passion they'd come to know in each other's arms.

"How did you enjoy that proposal?" he asked once they'd come up for air.

"It was okay. I really hoped you would have dressed like a plumber and presented the ring on a wrench."

He grinned. "Would you have worn a maid's uniform?"

"Sure. And I'd even pack a feather duster."

The levity seemed to subside when Logan's expression turned serious. "I've set up a trust fund in Cassie's name, in case you want to tell your former in-laws thanks, but no thanks."

"I'd be glad to tell them to take their trust fund and control and go to Hades. And if I did, frankly I don't think they'd care. But if they do decide they want to see her again, it wouldn't be fair to keep her from them." The same way she'd been kept from her father.

"We'll deal with it when and if the time comes. Together." Logan pulled an open bottle of champagne from the onboard ice bucket, then filled the two available glasses. "To our future and our family."

Hannah tipped her crystal flute against his. "And to weddings. Which reminds me, when are we going to do it?"

He laid his free hand on her thigh. "The seat back here is pretty big, so I say let's do it now."

Spoken like a man who'd spent a lot of time with a wise-cracker. She gave him an elbow in the side for good measure. "I meant, as if you didn't know, when are we going to get married?"

He faked a disappointed look that melted into an endearing smile. "I'm thinking maybe on July Fourth."

That allowed Hannah very little time to plan. But since this would be both their second marriages, it wouldn't require anything elaborate. "You know something? People will speculate I'm pregnant if we have the ceremony that soon."

He nuzzled her neck and blew softly in her ear. "Let's just give them all something to talk about."

Lovely. More rumors, as if the Lassiter family hadn't had enough of that lately. Oh, well. It certainly kept things interesting. So did Logan's talented mouth. "Then July Fourth it is. We can even have fireworks."

He winked. "Fireworks on Independence Day for my beautiful independent woman works well for me."

An independent woman and single mom, and a one-time secret heiress, who'd had the good fortune to fall in love with a man who had given her an incredible sense of freedom.

Now, as Hannah gazed at her gorgeous new fiancé, this onetime secret heiress was more than ready for the lifetime celebration to begin. Starting now.

* * * * *

"Sleep well, Taylor."

When Lane slowly released her and took a step back, it took a moment for her to realize he was looking at her expectantly. "Um…good night…Lane," she finally managed.

Forcing herself to move, she opened the screen door and didn't stop until she was upstairs with her bedroom door shut firmly behind her. As she leaned back against it, she had to remind herself to breathe. Lane had more raw sensuality in his little finger than most men had in their entire bodies.

Her heart suddenly began to pound against her ribs. When had she started thinking of him by his first name? It had been much easier and a lot less personal to keep him compartmentalized as Donaldson, her adversary—the very man who stood between her and her goal of owning all of the Lucky Ace.

* * *

Your Ranch…Or Mine?
is part of The Good, the Bad and the Texan series:
Running with these billionaires will be
one wild ride.

YOUR RANCH...
OR MINE?

BY
KATHIE DeNOSKY

Published in Great Britain 2014
by Mills & Boon, an imprint of Harlequin (UK) Limited,
Eton House, 18-24 Paradise Road, Richmond, Surrey, TW9 1SR

© 2014 Kathie DeNosky

ISBN: 978 0 263 91466 5

51-0514

Printed and bound in Spain
by Blackprint CPI, Barcelona

Kathie DeNosky lives in her native southern Illinois on the land her family settled in 1839. She writes highly sensual stories with a generous amount of humor; her books have appeared on the *USA TODAY* bestseller list and received numerous awards, including two National Reader's Choice Awards. Kathie enjoys going to rodeos, traveling to research settings for her books and listening to country music. Readers may contact her by e-mailing kathie@kathiedenosky.com. They can also visit her website, www.kathiedenosky.com, or find her on Facebook, www.facebook.com/Kathie-DeNosky-Author/278166445536145.

This book is dedicated to my poker playing friends Chris Doss, Jeremy Miller and Michele Hudson. Over the years I've had a ton of fun playing poker with you and hope we get to play again soon.

One

Lane Donaldson couldn't help but laugh as he watched the five men he called brothers acting like a bunch of damned fools.

It was funny how a baby could do that to otherwise intelligent grown men. And whether he wanted to admit it or not, he was no different. He had done his fair share of making faces and odd noises to try to get a smile out of the kid, as well.

He had invited his family and friends to the barbecue to celebrate his winning half of the Lucky Ace Ranch in a poker game last fall. But because of the birth of his nephew a few months back, the celebration had turned into a party to welcome the new baby to the family as well as to commemorate his big win.

"Y'all are going to scare the pudding out of little

Hank," Nate Rafferty complained as he made another face at the infant in his brother Sam's arms.

Nate and Sam were as different as night and day, even though they were the only two biological siblings out of the band of foster brothers who had spent their adolescence together on the Last Chance Ranch. While Sam was happily married with a three-month-old son, Nate was too busy trying to date the entire female population of the southwest to settle down. In fact, of the four remaining confirmed bachelors, Lane included, Nate was hands down the wildest of the bunch.

"And I suppose you think you're not scaring the kid with that sappy grin of yours, Nate?" Ryder McClain asked, laughing. "I play chicken with two thousand pounds of pissed-off beef every weekend and you're still enough to scare the hell out of me." A rodeo bull fighter, Ryder was without question one of the bravest men Lane had ever had the privilege of knowing—and Ryder was also the most laid-back, easygoing of his foster brothers.

"How much longer before you become a daddy, Ryder?" T. J. Malloy asked, taking a swig from the beer bottle in his hand. A highly successful saddle bronc rider, T.J. had retired at the ripe old age of twenty-eight and in the ensuing years had started raising and training champion reining horses.

"The doctor told us the other day that it could be just about any time," Ryder answered, glancing uneasily over to where his wife, Summer, sat talking to Sam's wife, Bria, and Bria's sister, Mariah. "And the closer it gets, the more I feel like a long-tailed cat in a room full of rocking chairs."

"Getting a little nervous, are you?" Lane asked, grinning.

"More like a lot," Ryder said, glancing again at his wife as if to assure himself she was still doing all right.

"I know exactly how you feel, Ryder," Sam said, nodding. "About a month before Bria had little Hank, I mapped out the quickest route to the hospital and made several practice runs just to be sure I could get her there in time."

"Both of you have helped cows during calving season for years," Nate said, his tone practical. "If you'd had to, you could have delivered little Hank, Sam. And you could deliver your and Summer's baby, Ryder."

Every one of them gave Nate an unimpressed look, then, shaking their heads, resumed their conversation.

"What?" Nate asked, obviously confused.

"I want the best for my wife when the time comes for her to have our baby and I'm man enough to admit I'm not it," Ryder answered, his disgusted expression stating louder than words what he thought of Nate's logic.

"Have you given in and asked the doctor if the baby is a boy or a girl, Ryder?" Jaron Lambert asked, staring across the yard at the women.

"We really don't care as long as the baby is healthy and Summer is okay," Ryder answered, shaking his head. "She wants to be surprised and I want whatever she wants."

"Well, I hope it's a girl," Jaron said flatly.

Lane couldn't help but chuckle. "Mariah still not talking to you, bro?"

Jaron shook his head. "She's still pissed off about what I said when Sam and Bria told us they were having a boy."

Jaron and Mariah had been arguing from the time they learned that Bria and Sam were expecting. Jaron had been sure the baby would be a boy, while Mariah had insisted it would be a girl. Apparently, Mariah had taken exception to Jaron's gloating after he'd been proven right.

"Yeah, women don't like it very much when a man says 'I told you so,'" Lane said, grinning.

"You think, Dr. Freud? I figured that out all by myself right after she stopped talking to me, genius." Jaron's sour expression and reference to Lane's psychology degree caused Lane to laugh out loud.

"When are you going to stop beating around the bush and take that girl out for a night on the town?" Lane asked.

"I've told y'all before, I'm too old for her," Jaron answered sullenly.

"That's bull and we all know it," T.J. shot back. "She's only eight years younger than you. It might have mattered when you were twenty-six and she was eighteen, but she's in her mid-twenties now. Your ages aren't that big a deal anymore."

"Yeah, and it's not like she wouldn't go," Ryder added. "She's had a crush on you from the time she met you. Although I can't for the life of me figure out why."

Taking a sudden interest in the tops of his boots,

Jaron shrugged. "It doesn't matter. I've got a world championship to win and I don't need the distraction." Competing in bull riding and bareback events, Jaron was a top contender to win the All-Around Rodeo Cowboy Championship for the third year in a row.

"While you guys try to talk some sense into Jaron, I see a lady who looks like she could use a trip around the dance floor," Nate said, grinning. "And I can't think of a man here who is better at doing the Texas two-step than me."

When they all turned to see which woman Nate was talking about, Lane felt as if he had taken a sucker punch to the gut. A little above average in height, the leggy redhead in question wasn't just pretty, she was absolutely breathtaking. Her long, straight, copper-colored hair complimented her creamy complexion to perfection and he couldn't help but wonder what it would feel like to run his fingers through the silky strands.

"Who is that?" T.J. asked, sounding as awestruck as Lane felt.

"I've never seen her before," Lane answered, looking around. It didn't appear she was with any of the other guests.

"She had to have just arrived," Nate added, sounding quite certain of the fact. "Otherwise, I would have noticed her before now."

As Nate started across the yard toward the woman, Lane couldn't say he was sorry she had decided to crash the barbecue he was throwing to celebrate winning half of the Lucky Ace Ranch. He would have thrown the party when he first became a partner in the place, but it had been so late in the fall he had decided to wait until spring, when it was warmer and they could celebrate Texas style—with an outdoor barbecue and dance. And now he was glad that he had. She was without question one of the prettiest women he'd ever seen and a welcome addition to the view in his ranch yard.

Lane frowned at the uncharacteristic stab of envy coursing through him as he watched Nate introduce himself to her, then take her in his arms to move around the temporary dance floor Lane's hired hands had installed for the festivities. He'd never been envious of any of his brothers before, but there was no denying that was exactly what was wrong with him at the moment.

When the country band took a break, Lane watched Nate talk with the woman for a moment before he shrugged and sauntered back to the group. The woman glanced at him and his brothers standing on the opposite side of the dance floor, then walked over to the refreshment table.

"It doesn't look like that went exactly the way you planned, Nate," T.J. said, laughing.

Looking as if he couldn't quite believe what had happened, Nate shook his head. "I must be losing my touch."

"Why do you say that?" Sam grinned. "Has she heard about your love-'em-and-leave-'em reputation?"

"No, smart-ass." Nate gave Sam a dark scowl before turning his attention to Lane. "All she did was ask me questions about *you*."

"Me?" It was the last thing Lane had expected to

hear. Why would she be inquiring about him? "What did she want to know?"

Nate shrugged. "She mainly wanted to know how long you've lived on the Lucky Ace and if you intend to stay here or sell out and move on." He frowned and glanced over his shoulder at the woman. "She didn't even know which one of us you were. I had to point you out."

Lane was more bewildered than ever as he stared across the yard at the woman surveying the array of food the caterer had prepared for his guests. He supposed she might have been in the gallery at one of the high-stakes poker tournaments he'd played over the years. But he rejected that idea immediately. If she had, she wouldn't have needed Nate to identify him.

"Looks like you might have an admirer, Lane," Ryder said, grinning like a six-year-old kid turned loose in a toy store.

"I doubt it," Lane answered, shaking his head as he stared across the yard at the woman. "If that was the case, she wouldn't have had to ask Nate about me."

His brothers all nodded their agreement as they continued to stare at her.

Deciding that he could speculate all evening and still not come up with any firm answers as to why the woman would be so curious about him, Lane took a deep breath. "No sense in standing here wondering about it. I'm going to ask her."

"Good luck with that," Jaron said.

"If you strike out like Nate, let me know and I'll give my luck a try," T.J. added, laughing.

Ignoring his brothers' teasing comments, Lane crossed the dance floor to the opposite side of the yard, where the woman had seated herself at an empty table. "Mind if I join you?" he asked as he pulled out a chair and started to sit down. "I'm—"

"I know who you are. You're Donaldson." She was silent for a moment, then, without looking up from her plate, shook her head. "You might as well join me. It wouldn't do me a lot of good if I told you that I did mind."

Her cool tone, obvious hostility and refusal to look directly at him caused him to hesitate. He was almost certain they had never met. What could he have possibly done to offend her? And why had she crashed his party just to give him the cold shoulder?

"Forgive me for not being able to recall, but have we met before?" he asked, determined to find out what was going on.

"No."

"Then why the chilly reception?" he asked point-blank as he pushed the chair back under the table without sitting down. He had no intention of sitting beside her when it was obvious she didn't want his company. But for the life of him, he couldn't figure out the reason for her attitude toward him.

"I'm here to discuss something with you and I'd rather not get into it in front of your guests," she said, pushing the food around on the plate in front of her with her fork. When she finally looked up at him, her emerald-green eyes sparkled with anger. "We'll talk after the party is over."

Lane studied her delicate features as he tried to get a read on what she might be up to. She had never met him before. She'd shown up to his party uninvited, and she was extremely angry with him. Now she was refusing to tell him why?

He had no idea what her agenda was, but it was more than a little apparent she had one. He had every intention of finding out what was going on, but she was right about one thing. Getting to the bottom of things would have to wait until the party started winding down. He wasn't about to ruin the rest of his guests' good time by getting into an argument with her now. And there was no doubt in his mind that an argument was exactly what was going to happen.

Nodding toward her plate, he gave her what he hoped, considering the circumstances, was a congenial enough smile. "I'll let you get back to your meal and I'll see you after the party."

As he turned to walk away, Lane checked his watch. Being a professional poker player for the past ten years, he'd long ago learned the fine art of patience. But it was sure as hell failing him now. He suddenly couldn't wait for the party to end so he could find out who the woman was and what she wanted. Then he'd send her on her way.

As Taylor Scott waited for the last of the guests to leave the barbecue, she gathered her anger around her like a protective cloak and reminded herself she was on a mission. Donaldson was a scheming, cheating snake in jeans. Villains in the old Western movies her grandfather used to watch always wore black hats and, quite appropriately, Donaldson's wide-brimmed Resistol was as black as his heart. But the one thing she hadn't counted on was how darned good-looking he would be.

Watching him bid farewell to an extremely pregnant woman and her husband, Taylor couldn't help but notice how tall he was, how physically fit. From his impossibly wide shoulders to his trim waist, long, muscular legs and big, booted feet, he had the body of a man who spent his days doing manual labor. Not the look she'd expected of someone who sat for endless hours at a poker table. But what had really thrown her off guard was the warmth and sincerity she'd detected in his chocolate-brown eyes. Framed with lashes as black as his hair, they were the kind of eyes a woman could feel safe getting lost in.

Taylor gave herself a mental shake. Donaldson might be Mr. Tall, Dark and Drop-Dead Gorgeous, but he wasn't a man who could be trusted any farther than she could pick him up and throw him. He was a con man, a swindler—a conniving thief. There was no way he could have won half of the Lucky Ace Ranch in a card game with her grandfather if he hadn't cheated. For over sixty years her grandfather had been considered one of the best players in the world of high-stakes professional poker, and he would never have risked any part of his ranch if he hadn't been certain he could beat the man.

"Let's go inside," Donaldson said when he reached the table where she was sitting.

"Why?"

She hadn't been inside her grandfather's home in several years and she worried her emotions would get the better of her when she walked into the house without him being there. That was something she would rather die than allow Donaldson to see.

He pointed to the catering staff as they cleaned up. "I thought my office might be a little more private." He shrugged. "But it's up to you how much privacy you think we need."

Grinding her back teeth over the fact that he'd called her grandfather's office *his,* Taylor pushed her chair back. She could deal with her feelings later—after she'd ousted the interloper.

"The office is fine," she said, rising to her feet. "I doubt that you'll want anyone to hear what I have to say anyway."

He stared at her for several long seconds before he nodded and stepped back so she could lead the way across the yard.

Taylor felt his gaze on her back as she walked up the steps and crossed the porch, but she ignored the little shiver of awareness that streaked up her spine. She had come to Texas for one reason. She was going to confront the man who had stolen part of her grandfather's ranch, buy it back, then take great pleasure in ordering him off the property.

But when she entered the kitchen, she forgot all about Donaldson and his disturbing gaze as emotion threatened to swamp her. Being in her grandfather's ranch house, knowing that he wasn't there and never would be again, was almost more than she could bear.

"The office is just down the hall and to your…"

"I know where it is," she snapped, cutting him off. To have a rank stranger try to direct her through a house that held the happiest memories of her childhood irritated her as little else could.

Her heart ached with unshed tears when she walked into her grandfather's office. How could everything look the same and yet be entirely different from the last time she was here?

"Please have a seat, Ms...."

"My name is Taylor Scott," she answered automatically.

Nodding, Donaldson motioned toward one of the two big leather armchairs in front of the desk. "Would you like something to drink, Taylor?"

The sound of his deep baritone saying her name caused an interesting little flutter in the pit of her stomach. She took a deep breath to regain her equilibrium and lowered herself onto the chair. "N-no, thank you."

He placed his hat on the credenza, then walked around the desk to sit in the high-backed chair. "What is it that you wanted to discuss with me?"

Maybe if she waited to reveal her identity she could get him to incriminate himself as having cheated her grandfather. "I'd like to know what you intend to do with your interest in the Lucky Ace," she stated, meeting his dark brown gaze head on.

She wasn't surprised when his expression remained unreadable. After all, he was a professional poker player and well practiced at keeping his emotions concealed.

"I'm not in the habit of discussing something of this

nature with a stranger," he said as if choosing his words carefully.

"I understand you won half of the ranch from Ben Cunningham." When he nodded, she went on. "I'm here to make you an offer for your share."

He slowly shook his head. "It's not for sale."

"Are you sure, Donaldson? The offer I'm willing to make is quite generous."

"Please, call me Lane," he said, giving her a smile that caused her heart to skip a beat. Several of Hollywood's leading men were among her clients. They'd spent thousands of dollars on dental and cosmetic surgery and still couldn't come close to having his perfect smile.

Giving herself a mental shake, she decided to focus on the fact that he was a swindler and ignore his good looks, as well as his request to call him by his first name. That was more personal than she cared to get with the man.

"I'm prepared to pay you well above market value if you can vacate the property within a week," she pressed.

"I'm quite happy here, and even if I weren't, I wouldn't consider selling my share of the Lucky Ace without consulting my partner first, and he's currently in California." He silently stared at her, as if analyzing the situation, before he spoke again. "Why do you think you want my share of the ranch?"

"I don't *think* I want the ranch. I *know* I want it," she said impatiently.

"Why?" he demanded. She could tell she was getting

to him when he sat forward, showing the first signs that he was becoming irritated with the situation.

Confident that she was gaining the upper hand, she couldn't help but smile. "Before we get into that, could I ask you a couple of questions, Donaldson?"

He stared at her for a moment before he answered. "You can ask, but I'm not guaranteeing that I'll give you the answers you want to hear."

"How did you manage to get Ben Cunningham to wager any part of this ranch in that poker game last fall?" she queried.

"Why do you think it was my idea that he use the Lucky Ace to cover his bet?" he asked, slowly leaning back in the desk chair.

"Are you saying he voluntarily put it up?" she shot back.

"Why do you think otherwise, Taylor?" he asked, sounding irritatingly calm.

She had heard that he was a licensed psychologist, and it seemed that the rumor was true. Instead of answers, he followed every one of her questions with one of his own—like any good therapist would do. Taylor decided right then and there that if he asked her how she felt about the situation, she was going to reach across the desk and bop him a good one.

"I happen to know that he wouldn't have wagered the ranch unless he was certain he had the winning hand," she stated flatly.

"So you know Mr. Cunningham?" he asked, his expression still as bland as dry toast.

"Yes, I know him quite well. But we'll get to that

later." She was getting nowhere fast and it infuriated her no end that Donaldson remained calm and collected when she was filled with nothing but frustration and anger. She was ready for a verbal battle, but he wasn't taking the bait. "What I'd like to know is why you're living here in his house."

"That's none of your business, Ms. Scott." Addressing her in a more formal way was the only outward indication he was losing patience.

"You've won several of the larger poker tournaments and I would think that with your wealth you would prefer something a bit more urban than a ranch house in the middle of nowhere," she said, hoping he would give her an indication of why he had taken up residence in her grandfather's home.

"Nice try, Taylor." To her surprise, a slow smile curved his mouth. "Now, why don't we start over and you tell me what you've been dancing around since we came in here?"

Deciding that he wasn't going to divulge anything without her telling him who she was, she took a deep breath. "I'm Ben Cunningham's granddaughter and I want to know how you got him to bet half of the ranch in that poker game, why you're staying here and what it will take to get you to sell your interest and get off the Lucky Ace for good."

"Since you're here grilling me, I take it that Ben hasn't supplied you with the answers to your questions?" he asked, raising one black eyebrow.

"No."

"I'm sure he has his reasons for not telling you, and

I'm not going to betray his trust." He shook his head. "But I can tell you that he suggested I move into the house to watch over the place while he was in California visiting with you and your parents."

"What about getting him to bet half of the ranch?" she demanded, not at all satisfied with his unwillingness to tell her what she wanted to know. "How did you manage that?"

"I had nothing to do with him putting up any part of the ranch. It was his idea and his alone," Donaldson answered.

"I have a hard time believing that, Donaldson." Unable to sit still any longer, Taylor rose to her feet to pace back and forth in front of the desk. "He bought this land sixty years ago with his first poker winnings. It was his pride and joy and when he and my grandmother married, they built this house and raised my mother here. In all that time, he never once considered risking any part of it. Why would he suddenly change his mind last fall?"

"You'll have to ask Ben." He smiled. "I haven't heard from him in a couple of months. How is your grandfather? Is he enjoying his time in sunny California? Has he mentioned when he'll be coming back to the ranch?"

Taylor stopped pacing and turned to face him. Her eyes burning with tears she refused to allow her nemesis to see, she took a deep, steadying breath. "Grandpa passed away about three weeks ago."

Donaldson's smile immediately disappeared. "I'm really sorry to hear that. Ben was a good man and the best poker player I've ever had the privilege to know. You have my deepest sympathy."

"T-thank you," she said, sinking into the armchair. Talking about her grandfather, knowing he was gone and that she had been powerless to stop the inevitable, was overwhelming.

"Here, drink this," he said, handing her a glass tumbler as he lowered himself into the armchair beside her.

Lost in her misery, she hadn't been aware that he'd risen from the chair behind the desk. "What is it?" she asked, looking at the clear liquid in the glass.

He gave her a sympathetic smile. "It's just water."

"Oh."

"How did Ben die?" he asked softly.

"He had a massive heart attack," she said woodenly. "He'd apparently known about his heart condition for quite some time, but didn't tell anyone. When I learned about it, I insisted that he see the top cardiologist in Los Angeles. But it was too late. He went into cardiac arrest the day before he was scheduled for open-heart surgery."

They sat in silence for some time before he commented. "I wonder why the poker federation failed to announce Ben's passing last week at the tournament in Vegas?"

Finishing the glass of water, she placed the tumbler on the desk. "It wasn't announced because they don't know about it. He asked that his death be kept quiet until after his ashes were scattered here at the ranch."

"Is that why you're here now?" he asked. "To tell me you're going to scatter Ben's ashes?"

"No." She determinedly met his questioning gaze. "I took care of his request yesterday evening at sunset."

He looked doubtful. "If you were here yesterday, why didn't I see you?"

"Because I know this place like the back of my hand," she answered. "There's a road two miles west of here that leads to the creek on the southern part of the ranch. Grandpa told me that if something happened to him he wanted his ashes released at sunset down by the creek where he asked my grandmother to marry him." She stared at her hands, clasped tightly in her lap. "I'm sure you can understand that it was a private moment for me."

"Of course," he said quietly.

Suddenly feeling drained of energy, she hid a yawn behind her hand. "Now that you know about my grandfather's death, there's no reason not to answer my questions." She gave him a pointed look. "Besides, I inherited the other half of the Lucky Ace Ranch and as the co-owner, that gives me the right to know everything. And the first thing I intend to find out is how you managed to swindle my grandfather."

Two

Lane stared at Taylor for several long seconds as he worked to control his anger. He was still trying to come to terms with losing a good friend, as well as his partner in the ranch. The last thing he wanted was to be defending his integrity. But it appeared that was exactly what he was going to have to do.

"Before this goes any farther, let me set you straight, Ms. Scott," he said, wondering how he could still find her attractive when he was angry enough to bite nails in two. "I have never been a cardsharp, nor will I ever be. I take my poker games very seriously and I can guarantee you that I don't have to cheat to win. I pit my skill against other players' and I'm good enough to be quite successful at it—just as your grandfather was."

"But he had more years of experience than you are

old," she insisted. "How could you possibly beat him unless the game was rigged?"

"I know this is probably hard for you to believe, but your grandfather and I had a lot in common," he stated. "We had a mutual respect for the game and for each other as worthy opponents. I'm sorry if you can't accept that I had the skill to beat your grandfather, but I wouldn't cheat at cards any more than Ben would have."

Suddenly needing a drink, he rose to his feet, walked over to the credenza and poured himself a shot of bourbon. Downing the amber liquid in one gulp, he let the warmth spread throughout his chest before he turned to face her.

"The day I won an interest in this ranch, I had the better hand." He shook his head. "We could have played another day and he might have come out the winner. That's the game and a chance you take any time you sit down at a poker table."

"I realize that there's always a risk of losing," she said, sounding a little less confident. She hid another yawn behind her delicate hand then continued, "But my grandfather was arguably the best poker player in modern history. He could tell at a glance what his odds of winning were and how much he could safely wager. He would have never bet half of the ranch if he hadn't been certain he would win."

"And because of his miscalculation that makes me guilty of cheating?" Lane demanded.

She yawned yet again. "He wouldn't have risked—"

"I think we've adequately covered that already," he interrupted. He took a deep breath in an effort to cool the fury burning in his gut. She wasn't listening and he was tired of beating his head against a brick wall trying to convince her of his innocence. "Look, it's past midnight and we're getting nowhere. Let's put this discussion on hold until tomorrow morning."

She stared at him for a moment before she finally nodded and rose to her feet. "That would probably be best."

"Where are you staying?" he asked. "I'll drive you to your hotel."

Looking suspicious, she asked, "Why?"

"You're too tired to be behind the wheel of a car," he stated flatly.

"I'm staying right here," she said, her stubborn tone indicating that hell would freeze over before she budged on the issue. Resigned, he followed her out into the hall.

"I'm assuming that you have a bedroom you used when you visited your grandfather?"

"My room is the one with the lavender ruffled curtains and bedspread at the opposite end of the hall from the master suite," she answered. She started toward the kitchen. "I'll just get my overnight bag from the car."

"Give me your keys and I'll get it for you," he said, holding out his hand.

Even though she had made him angry enough to want to forget his manners, he couldn't ignore the code of conduct his foster father had taught him and his brothers about how a man was supposed to treat a woman. When a woman had something that needed to be carried, a man stepped forward and took care of it for her—no matter how small or lightweight the object was. No excuses.

"I can get it," she insisted, taking a set of keys from the front pocket of her jeans.

He took them from her and tried to ignore the tingling sensation that streaked up his arm when he brushed her fingers with his. "You're tired and it's probably heavy," he said through gritted teeth. "Go on upstairs and I'll leave it outside your door."

"It's the blue backpack on the front passenger seat," she called after him as he left the house. She said something else, but instead of turning back to ask what it was, he continued on to the little red sports car parked by his truck.

At the moment, it was better to put a little distance between them. If he didn't, he couldn't be certain he wouldn't lose his temper and tell her what he thought of her and her ridiculous accusations—or grab her and kiss her until they both forgot that she was a lady and he was trying to be a gentleman.

He stopped short. Where had that thought come from? He would just as soon cozy up to a pissed-off wildcat than to get up close and personal with Taylor Scott. She might be one of the hottest women he'd seen in all of his thirty-four years, but she represented the kind of trouble that a man just didn't need.

Shaking his head at his own foolishness, he unlocked the Lexus and reached inside to get Taylor's backpack. The light, clean scent of her perfume assailed his senses and reminded him of just how long it had been since he'd lost himself in the charms of a willing woman. The scent only added an unwelcome element to the level of his frustration and he cussed a blue streak when his lower body began to tighten. And it didn't help matters one damned bit knowing she would be sleeping in the room directly across the hall from the one he had been using since moving to the ranch six months ago.

He clenched his teeth as another wave of heat surged through his body. How could he possibly feel this level of desire for a woman when she irritated the living hell out of him? For that matter, how had she managed to make him forget everything he'd learned in seven years of studying to become a psychologist?

He had known immediately that she was fishing for information and he'd successfully evaded answering her by turning the tables and asking questions of his own. He'd even found her interrogation mildly amusing. But what he couldn't quite come to terms with was the fact that when she'd started making accusations, he had let her get to him.

Lane had played poker with men who made it a point of talking smack in an effort to throw him off his game, and not once had he ever let any of it affect him. For one thing, he recognized the insults as a psychological ploy and simply tuned the men out. And for another thing, they all had better sense than to cross the line and accuse him of cheating. But when Taylor made it clear that she thought he had swindled her grandfather out of his ranch, she had unknowingly touched on one of his hot buttons and he'd damned near gone off like a Roman candle in a Fourth of July fireworks display.

He was a psychologist specializing in human behavior. He had been schooled not only in how to be a patient and observant listener but also how to keep his emotions in check. The last thing a client wanted to see from his therapist during a session was a judgmental expression or outright shock when they revealed some of their darkest secrets. Those psychology tools had served him well over the years and he had used them quite successfully as a professional poker player to keep from alerting his opponents to the cards he had been dealt.

But when it came to Taylor, it was as if his skills didn't even exist. All she had to do was look at him with those big green eyes of hers and his training seemed to go right out the window.

The first time he'd noticed his uncharacteristic reaction to her had been when she told him that she wanted the other half of the ranch. She'd looked him square in the eye and the passion and determination in her striking green gaze had sent a streak of heat straight to the region south of his belt buckle. He had even found himself wondering if she would be that passionate when he made love to her.

His body tightened to an almost painful state and he rattled off every curse word he could think of. He forcefully slammed the car door and locked it with the remote. As he walked back to the house, he glanced down at the small bag in his hand. She couldn't have put much more than a few changes of clothes in it, indicating that she wouldn't be staying more than a night or two. That suited him just fine.

The sooner she went back to California and left him

alone, the better. Then maybe he could figure out what the hell had gotten into him and what he was going to do to get rid of it.

Well before dawn, Taylor rolled over in bed and glanced at the clock on the bedside table. She hadn't been able to sleep more than a couple of hours and those had been filled with fitful dreams of the tall, dark-haired man sleeping in the bedroom directly across the hall from hers.

Deciding she couldn't stand another minute of tossing and turning, she sighed heavily, threw back the covers and sat up on the side of the bed. How was she going to get Donaldson to sell her his interest in the ranch and leave the Lucky Ace for good? And why on earth did she find him so darned attractive?

She still wasn't entirely convinced that he hadn't somehow managed to cheat her grandfather in that poker game. But Donaldson had presented a compelling argument for his innocence and even though she knew how good her grandfather was at the game, she was starting to have her doubts. After all, he was human and as much as she hated to admit it, he could very well have made a mistake when he mentally calculated his odds of winning that fateful hand.

But what disturbed her the most about Donaldson was her reaction to him. The moment he'd approached her at the party to introduce himself, she had caught her breath, and she wasn't entirely certain she had breathed normally since. She had never experienced that kind of reaction to any of the men she'd dated in the past, let alone one she had just met and didn't trust.

Exhausted from the emotional roller coaster she had been on for the past three weeks and unsettled by her reaction to the man across the hall, she decided to do the one thing that always helped her put things in perspective. After a quick shower, she was going to start cooking.

Twenty minutes later, Taylor tied her damp hair back in a ponytail as she walked into the spacious kitchen. After washing her hands and starting the coffeemaker, she prepared to get to work. Checking the pantry and refrigerator for available ingredients, she decided on what she would make for breakfast then reached into one of the cabinets for a set of mixing bowls.

"Do you mind if I get myself a cup of coffee?" a deep male voice asked from close behind her.

Jumping, she almost dropped the bowls she held as she spun around to face Donaldson. Her heart racing, she took a deep breath. "I think you just took ten years off my life."

"Sorry," he said, hanging his hat on a peg by the door before pouring himself a mug of coffee. "I didn't mean to scare you. I thought you heard me." His deep chuckle sent a wave of goose bumps shimmering over her skin. "It's kind of hard not to make noise in a pair of boots on a hardwood floor."

Her heart skipped a beat as her gaze traveled the length of him, down to his scuffed cowboy boots. No man had a right to look that good so early in the morning.

Last night at the party, she had thought he was extremely handsome in his dark blue jeans, white oxford-cloth shirt and expensive caiman-leather boots. But that was nothing compared to the way he looked now. Wearing well-worn jeans and a chambray work shirt, he was downright devastating. With his dark eyes, black hair and a fashionable day's growth of beard stubble, Donaldson had that bad boy appeal about him that was sure to send shivers up the spine of any woman with a pulse.

Disgusted with herself and her wayward thoughts, Taylor set the metal mixing bowls on the counter and reached for a carton of eggs. "Where's my grandfather's housekeeper?"

"Marie retired right after the first of the year and I just haven't gotten around to hiring another one," he answered.

She wasn't surprised. The woman her grandfather had hired after her grandmother died had to be getting close to seventy. But on the other hand, she wouldn't have put it past Donaldson to have fired the woman, either.

"I'll have breakfast ready in a few minutes," she said, cracking eggs into one of the bowls with one hand while she reached for a whisk with the other. "Why don't you have a seat at the table?"

"What are you making?" he asked as he sat down at the head of the oak trestle table that had been in her grandmother's family for over three generations.

"Blueberry and ricotta–stuffed French toast with blueberry syrup, link sausage and blueberries and cantaloupe covered with vanilla sauce," she said, dipping extra thick slices of bread in the cinnamon-spiced egg mixture before placing them on the heated stovetop griddle.

"Sounds good, but isn't that a little fancy for a typical ranch breakfast?" he commented. "You must really like to cook."

She shrugged. "Since I graduated from the California School of Culinary Arts, then went to Paris for a year to study pastry, you might say I'm rather fond of it."

"Do you have your own restaurant?"

Arranging the food on two plates, she shook her head. "No, I'm a personal chef. I'm mainly hired for dinner parties and other special in-home occasions, like graduation and anniversary celebrations."

"That sounds like an interesting job," he said conversationally. "Do you have many clients?"

Nodding, she poured vanilla sauce over the fruit. "When I first started, I registered with the personal chef association and they referred clients to me. Now the majority of the calls I get are referrals from clients or from people who have attended the dinner parties I've prepared."

"You must be good at what you do," he said, sounding thoughtful.

Taylor carried the plates over to the table and sat down. "I'll let you be the judge." She watched him eye the food in front of him as if he wasn't sure it was safe to eat. Barely resisting the urge to laugh, she asked, "Is something wrong?"

"You made your opinion of me quite clear last night, so I'm sure you can understand my hesitation," he said, giving her a deliberate smile.

"It's true that I don't completely trust you, but that doesn't mean you can't trust *me*." She switched his plate with hers. "Now you have no reason not to try it."

Picking up his knife and fork, he cut into the French toast. "What do you say we start over?" he suggested. "The least we can do is be civil to each other until you go back to Los Angeles."

"I agree that being polite to each other would make negotiations for my buying your share of the ranch a lot easier," she agreed, taking a bite of fruit.

"I told you last night I'm not selling. But you could always sell your half to me," he said, taking a bite of toast.

"Absolutely not. I love the Lucky Ace. It represents the best part of my childhood." Irritated by his offer to buy her share, Taylor put her fork down to glare at him. "My grandfather knew how much this place meant to me and he intended for me to have it. I'm not selling it to you or anyone else."

Donaldson calmly took a sip of his coffee. "Then before you go back to Los Angeles, we'll have to work out an agreement on how I run the day-to-day operations and how often you want to receive dividend checks."

"I'm not going back to L.A.," she said, taking great satisfaction in the annoyed expression that came over his handsome face.

A forkful of toast halfway to his mouth, he slowly lowered it back to his plate. "What do you mean you aren't going back?"

Her appetite deserting her, she rose from the table to scrape the contents of her plate in the garbage disposal.

"I have every intention of making the Lucky Ace my permanent home."

"What about your clients back in Los Angeles?" he asked, looking more irritated with each passing second. "And that backpack wasn't big enough to hold more than a handful of clothes."

"I informed my clients of the move over a week ago and arranged for another chef to cover the dinner parties I had scheduled," she said, watching the frown lines on his forehead deepen further. "I sublet my apartment, stored my furniture, and the clothes I was unable to bring with me in the car, I shipped here. Those cartons should arrive sometime next week. I told you last night when you went out to get my backpack that I was here to run the ranch and would get the rest of my things from the car today."

He suddenly got up from the table, walked over to scrape his plate, then reached for the hat hanging beside the back door.

"Will you be back for lunch?" she asked.

"No."

"Then I'll have plenty of time to clean my room this morning before I bring my things in from the car and put them away this afternoon," she said thoughtfully.

"I'll go over to the bunkhouse and see if I can get one of the men to help you with that," he answered without turning around.

Before she could thank him for his thoughtfulness, he opened the door to walk out onto the porch then forcefully pulled it shut behind him.

"He took that better than what I thought he would,"

she murmured as she started rinsing their dishes to put into the dishwasher. She wasn't sure what she had expected, but Donaldson's passive acceptance of her moving into the ranch house hadn't been it.

Of course, she wasn't foolish enough to think that he had given up trying to get her to sell her part of the ranch to him. But maybe now that he knew she was serious about living at the ranch, he was giving a little more thought to selling her his.

Lane rode his blue roan gelding across the pasture toward the barn at a slow walk. He had to find some way to get Taylor to sell him her share of the ranch. Or if that wasn't something she was willing to do, at least get her to go back to Los Angeles and leave him the hell alone.

He could appreciate her sentimentality about the place her grandfather owned. But he had become attached to the property as well. For the first time in over twenty years he had a place he could truly call his own. It felt good and he wasn't willing to give that up.

As he stared off across the land, he thought about the plans he had for the future. He'd made a fortune playing poker and having invested wisely, he never had to work another day in his life if he didn't want to. But he didn't consider playing poker or ranching actual jobs. Poker was a pastime. He enjoyed the challenge of competing with other equally skilled players and if he ever lost interest in it, he'd quit with no regrets. But ranching was a lifestyle, and up until six months ago, he hadn't even realized how much he had missed it. That's why he intended to improve the Lucky Ace by introducing a herd of free-range cattle, as well as start raising and training roping horses for rodeo.

But all that could change if Taylor insisted on living on the ranch and taking an active role in running it. That's why he spent the entire day riding fence, repairing windmills and tightening gates, whether they needed it or not. Keeping busy helped him think. Unfortunately, he didn't arrive at any conclusions other than that Taylor was just as stubborn about selling her share of the ranch as he was.

When he'd won half of the Lucky Ace last fall, he had fully intended to sell it back to Ben. But the old man had asked that Lane move in and oversee the day-to-day running of the ranch while he spent the winter with his family in California. Ben had told him they would talk again in the spring and Lane could let him know if he still wanted to sell the property back to him. It had seemed like a reasonable request and Lane had agreed. But the past six months had reminded him of his time at the Last Chance Ranch and he'd decided that he might have been a little too hasty about offering to sell his interest back to Cunningham.

Lane stared off into the distance. As it turned out, being sent to the Last Chance Ranch as a teen and placed in the care of his foster father, Hank Calvert, had been the best thing that had ever happened to Lane and he had nothing but fond memories of the time he'd spent there.

Hank had been the wisest man Lane had ever had the privilege to know. He'd not only taught the boys in his care to work through their anger and self-destructive behavior by using ranch chores and rodeo, he had taught them a code of conduct that they all adhered to even as adults. Lane and the men he still called his brothers had all become honest, productive members of society because of their time with Hank. Along the way, they had bonded into a family that remained as strong, if not stronger, than any traditional family tied together by blood.

He drew in a deep breath. Even though he had overcome his past, gained a family he loved and, with Hank's help, managed to save enough money from his junior rodeo earnings to make restitution to the people he had conned or stolen from, Lane didn't particularly like being reminded of his youthful problems.

Of course, he hadn't had much of choice in what he'd done. But stealing was stealing and whether he'd had a good reason or not, being a con artist and a thief was still wrong.

That's why he'd had such a strong reaction when Taylor accused him of swindling her grandfather. She had unwittingly reminded him of what he had been and what he might have continued to be if he hadn't straightened up his act.

Riding into the ranch yard, he dismounted Blue and led the gelding into the barn. As he removed the horse's saddle and began brushing the animal's bluish-gray coat, Lane reviewed his options.

He supposed he could sell Taylor his half of the ranch, then look around for another property. But he rejected that idea immediately. Texas might be a huge state, but there weren't that many ranches the size of the

Lucky Ace up for sale. Nor were any of them located close enough that he would be able to see his brothers regularly or be there for them if they needed him. Besides, he had won his half of the ranch fair and square and no one was going to guilt him into selling it—not even a hot-as-hell redhead with the greenest eyes he'd ever seen and a figure that made him want to spend endless hours exploring it.

When his body stirred from just thinking about her, he stopped grooming the roan and cursed his neglected libido as he led the horse into its stall. That did it. When Lane started to find a woman who frustrated him to the brink of insanity attractive enough to incite a case of lust, it was time to do something about it. As soon as he took a quick shower and got ready, he was going to make a trip over to that little honky-tonk in Beaver Dam and see if he couldn't find a warm, willing female to help him scratch this itch. Maybe then he would be able to forget how desirable Taylor Scott was and start thinking of her as he would think of any other business partner.

With a firm plan in place, he walked purposefully across the ranch yard and climbed the porch steps. "Taylor, I won't be here for supper," he said as he entered the kitchen. "I'm going over to—" He stopped short when she vigorously shook her head. "What's wrong?" he asked, walking over to where she stood at the counter mixing something in a bowl.

She nodded toward the hall. "I can't get rid of the cowboy you assigned to help me carry my things in from the car," she whispered.

"I didn't assign him to do anything," Lane said, careful to keep his voice low. "When I mentioned you needed help, he volunteered."

"Whatever. I can't get him to leave," she insisted. "We finished unloading the car over an hour ago, but he keeps coming up with excuses to stick around. I even gave up putting my clothes away because I wasn't comfortable with him lurking in the doorway watching me."

Standing so close to her, breathing in the light scent of her herbal shampoo and noticing the perfection of her coral lips, caused every nerve in Lane's body to come to full alert. He took a step back, then another.

To distract himself from the temptation she posed, he asked, "Where's he now and what is he doing?"

"He's in the living room building a fire in the fireplace," she answered.

"It's May and the air conditioning is on. The last thing we need is to heat up the house with a fire," Lane said, frowning. "Whose bright idea was that?"

"Mine." She set the bowl aside and reached for some small white ceramic ramekins. "I had to think of something to keep him busy until you got back from wherever it was you went this morning."

"I was out riding fence and repairing some of the windmills," he answered defensively. He didn't owe her an explanation of his whereabouts, so why did he feel compelled to give her one?

"It's Sunday and after they tend to the livestock, even the hired men have the day off," she said, her tone disapproving. "Couldn't those chores have waited until tomorrow?"

It suddenly occurred to Lane that the impatience in Taylor's voice stemmed from her uneasiness about being around the man in the other room, not because she was annoyed by his daylong absence from the house.

"I'll get rid of him," he said, turning toward the hall. When he walked into the living room he found Roy Lee Wilks kneeling beside the fireplace, failing miserably at building a fire in the stone firebox. "Don't worry about the fire, Roy Lee. I don't think we'll be needing it. It's well over eighty degrees outside."

"Hey there, boss," the young man said, sitting back on his heels. "I wondered why Ms. Scott wanted me to build a fire." He removed his sweat-stained ball cap to run a hand through his shaggy blond hair. "I wasn't having much luck at getting it started anyway."

Lane checked his watch. "Marty should just about have supper ready over at the bunkhouse. It would probably be a good idea to get over there before Cletus eats his share and yours, too."

Putting his cap back on, Roy Lee rose to his feet and nodded. "I'll do that as soon as I check with Ms. Scott to see if she needs me to do anything else."

Lane shook his head. "Thanks, but you've spent most of your day off helping her and I'm sure you'd like to rest up before you move that herd of heifers over to the north pasture tomorrow morning. If she wants something else done, I'll take care of it."

The man looked as though he might want to argue the point, but apparently he decided that crossing the boss might not be a wise choice. "I guess I'll see you in the morning then," he finally said, turning toward the hall.

Lane leaned one shoulder against the kitchen doorway and waited for Roy Lee to bid Taylor a good evening and leave before he walked over to where she stood at the counter finishing the dessert she was working on. "Now that your problem is solved with Roy Lee, I'm going to take a shower and drive over to Beaver Dam for the evening."

"You won't be here for dinner?" she asked, looking disappointed. "I'm making prime rib, twice-baked potatoes with herbs and cheese, asparagus spears with hollandaise sauce and crème brûlée for dessert."

She had apparently been too distracted by wanting to get rid of Roy Lee to have heard him tell her earlier that he was leaving for the evening. He shifted from one foot to the other as he stared into her crystalline green eyes. She was going to a lot of trouble making dinner and if the look on her pretty face was any indication, she was going to be extremely disappointed if he didn't stick around to eat it. He decided right then and there that if he wanted to talk her into selling her share of the ranch to him, or at the very least convince her to go back to L.A., he was going to have to placate her. Otherwise, he wouldn't have a snowball's chance in hell of getting her to agree to anything.

"I thought you might not feel like making dinner after spending the day unpacking and arranging your things," he lied.

She gave him a smile that caused a hitch in his breathing. "Cooking is one of the ways I relax."

"Do I have time to take a quick shower before dinner?" he asked, unbuttoning the cuffs of his work shirt.

"Sure." She placed the ceramic ramekins in a pan with water in the bottom, then began to fill them with the crème brûlée mixture. "Everything should be ready by the time you come back downstairs."

Nodding, Lane clenched his jaw as he walked out of the kitchen and headed upstairs. He wasn't the least bit happy about the change in his plans for the evening. But there wasn't anything he could do about it now. It was one of those damned if he did and damned if he didn't situations where no matter what he chose to do, he'd be the one suffering the consequences.

Taylor would take it as a deliberate insult if he didn't have dinner with her and insulting her would make it impossible to talk to her about the future of the ranch. And then there was the matter of the itch he needed to scratch. Just being in the same room with her seemed to charge the atmosphere with a tension that sent hormones racing through his veins at the speed of light, reminding him that he was a man with a man's needs.

When his body tightened in response to that thought, he muttered a guttural curse and headed straight into the bathroom to turn on the cold water. Stripping off his dusty clothes, he stepped inside and hoped the icy spray would clear his head, as well as traumatize his body into submission.

As he stood there with his teeth chattering like a pair of cheap castanets, a plan began to take shape in his mind. If successful, it would settle things once and for all. And the sooner he got Taylor to agree to it, the better.

If he didn't, he had a feeling one of two things would happen. She would either drive him completely insane or he would end up suffering frostbite on parts of his body that no man ever wanted to think about freezing.

Three

"Thank you for getting rid of Roy Lee for me," Taylor said as she sat down in the chair Donaldson held for her. "I was so relieved to finally have him out of the house, I forgot to thank you earlier."

He shrugged as he sat down at the head of the table. "I don't think he meant any harm."

"Probably not," she admitted. "He's just always seemed a little creepy to me, even as a teenager."

"So you've known him a long time?"

She nodded. "He started working summers here before he got out of high school." Pausing, she had to think back. "That would have been about twelve years ago."

"Besides overstaying his welcome this afternoon, has Roy Lee ever said or done anything else that made you feel uncomfortable?" Donaldson asked, taking a sip of the cabernet she'd had him open and pour for them.

"Not really." Pushing the asparagus spears around her plate with her fork, she tried to put into words how she felt whenever she was around the man. "I know it's probably just my imagination, but he seems to watch every move I make." Looking up, she added, "You know, like those paintings with eyes that follow you around the room." She couldn't keep from shuddering. "He's that kind of creepy."

"I'll try to make sure he stays away from the house," Donaldson said, taking a bite of his prime rib. Swallowing the tender beef, he smiled. "This is really good."

"Thank you," she answered, hoping her cooking worked its magic and put him in a good mood. "I'm glad you like it."

They fell into an awkward silence for the rest of the meal and by the time they finished dessert, Taylor's nerves felt ready to snap. Yesterday she had tried talking him into selling his share of the ranch to her and that hadn't worked. Hopefully there was something to the old adage that the way to a man's heart was through his stomach. Only in this case, she was hoping to appeal to his sense of justice. The Lucky Ace had been in her family for years and her grandfather had known just how much the place meant to her. He'd always told her that one day he wanted it to be hers and not once had he mentioned that he intended for her to share it with someone else.

"After we get the kitchen cleaned up, I'd like to discuss something with you," Donaldson said, interrupting her troubled thoughts.

"About the ranch?" she asked, afraid to hope that he had changed his mind and was going to be reasonable about it.

He nodded as he rose to his feet and reached for her empty ramekin. "It's a nice evening. I thought we could go out on the front porch and watch the sun go down while we talk."

Getting up from the table, she walked over and began rinsing their dishes to put into the dishwasher while he put the leftover prime rib in a plastic storage container and placed it in the refrigerator. As they worked side by side to clean the kitchen, Taylor's nervousness increased tenfold, and it had nothing whatsoever to do with their upcoming discussion about the ranch.

Why did she have to notice how handsome Donaldson looked in his black shirt and jeans? And why did he have to smell so darned good? There was something about the combination of expensive leather and the scent of clean male skin that was just plain sexy.

Their fingers touched as he handed her their wineglasses and Taylor felt a streak of longing course straight through her. She came dangerously close to dropping one of the delicate crystal goblets.

"It won't take me more than a few minutes to finish up here." She cleared her throat and hoped her voice didn't sound as husky to him as it did to her. "Why don't you go on out to the porch?"

"Are you sure?" Was that relief she detected in his

deep baritone? Had he felt the tension surrounding them as well?

Forcing a smile, she nodded. "I won't be long."

When he turned and walked down the hall toward the front of the house, Taylor placed her forearms on the sink and sagged against it. How could one man exude so much sex appeal? And why on earth wasn't she impervious to it?

Lane Donaldson was the intruder—the enemy—and the very last man she should find appealing. But as she finished wiping off the counters, she had to admit that beyond his devastating good looks, there was a certain charm about him that any woman would find hard to resist. How many men still had the manners to hold a chair for a woman when she sat down at the table? Or insist on retrieving her bag from the car and carrying it upstairs, especially after she had accused him of stealing part of her grandfather's ranch?

She did feel a bit guilty about that. But at the time she had been angry and certain that her grandfather had been victimized by Donaldson. But now?

She still wasn't sure that he hadn't exploited her grandfather. But there was one thing she was certain of—he wasn't going to take advantage of her.

"All finished in the kitchen?" Donaldson asked over his shoulder when she pushed the screen door open and walked out onto the porch a few minutes later. He was sitting on the steps with his forearms propped on his knees, staring out at the sun sinking low in the western sky.

"There wasn't really much left to do," she answered, walking over to sit in the porch swing.

They were both silent for several long minutes before he finally spoke again. "I've been thinking about our situation," he said slowly. "And I'm pretty sure I've come up with a solution."

"Are you going to sell me your share of the ranch?" she asked. As far as she was concerned, that was the only acceptable answer.

His deep chuckle sent a shiver streaking up her spine. "No. And I'm betting you aren't willing to sell me yours."

"Not a chance," she shot back.

"I figured as much." He got to his feet and walked over to lean one shoulder against the porch support post in front of her. "But I think the one thing we do agree on is the fact that the way things are now is unacceptable."

She nodded. "You're right about that. There's nothing about this that I find even remotely acceptable."

"Before I tell you what I have in mind, I'd like to ask that you hear me out before you give me your answer," he said, folding his arms across his wide chest. "Do you think you can do that, Taylor?"

His deep baritone voice saying her name caused her to catch her breath. "A-all right. What have you come up with?"

"I want us to play poker," he said, meeting her questioning gaze. "If you win, I'll sell you my share of the Lucky Ace and you'll be rid of me for good."

Taylor's heart sank. Her grandfather might have been a world-class poker player, but she had never taken an interest in the game and didn't have a clue about how to play. What chance would she have against someone like Donaldson?

Besides, she wasn't entirely certain she could trust that he would play honestly. And even if he did, he was a professional and in the same elite category as her grandfather had been. She wouldn't have a prayer of winning against him.

"And if you should happen to win?" she asked, knowing she wasn't going to like his answer.

He smiled. "If I win, you go back to California and I stay right here."

"Absolutely not," she said, shaking her head. "I'm not taking a chance of losing my share—"

He held up his hand to stop her. "You promised to hear me out."

Glaring at him, she folded her arms beneath her breasts. "All right," she conceded. "Continue."

"I didn't mention anything about you losing your interest in the ranch," he said calmly. "If I win, you would retain your half of the place, go back to California and be content with occasional visits. And I'm sure we can come to an agreement on how often you want to receive reports and dividend checks, as well as sign documents stating that if either of us ever decide we want to sell our share, we'll give the other the first right of purchase."

Suspicious, she asked, "Why are you willing to be so generous? You told me that if I won, you would sell me your half. Doesn't that work both ways? Wouldn't you want my share if I lost?"

"It's true that I'd like to own the entire property,"

he admitted. "But I know this land belonged to your grandfather and that you have a sentimental attachment to it. I respect that and wouldn't ask you to give it up if it means that much to you."

"Why do you want it?" she demanded. There had to be a reason behind his stubbornness about not selling his part of the ranch and she was determined to find out what it was. "You don't have the same ties to it that I do."

He paused for a moment as he stared down at his boots. When he looked up, he shrugged his broad shoulders. "I finished growing up on a place a lot like this one and until I moved here last fall, I didn't realize how much I missed living on a ranch."

"Surely there are other places you could buy," she said, hoping he would see reason. "Texas isn't the only state with ranch property. I'm sure you could find something suitable somewhere else. And you wouldn't have a business partner. You would be the sole owner."

"All of my brothers have ranches that are close by or within a few hours' driving distance from here and there's nothing the size of the Lucky Ace for sale that isn't at least a day's drive away." He smiled. "I'm sure you can understand my wanting to be close to my family, as well as not wanting to settle for something that isn't what I really want."

Staring at him, she couldn't help but wonder what it was like to want to be close to family. Being the only child of a couple who should have never married, the only family member she had ever been close to was her grandfather. Spending all of her summers with him on the Lucky Ace until she enrolled in cooking school after high school graduation had been her only reprieve from her parents' constant arguing. That's why it meant so much to her. It represented the tranquility that she'd never had at home. But that wasn't something she felt comfortable sharing with just anyone, and especially not with Donaldson.

"So what do you think?" he asked when she remained silent. "Would our playing a game of cards for the ranch be a viable solution to our problem?"

"I'm going to have to give it a lot more thought before I decide," she said, wondering if there was a poker gene that she might have inherited from her grandfather. She knew there probably wasn't, but all things considered, it would have been nice if there had been.

He smiled. "Neither one of us is willing to go anywhere else, so there's plenty of time for you to make your decision."

"I think I can safely say I'll have an answer for you within the next day or so." Taylor rose from the swing and started toward the front door. Turning back, she started to add that she'd like the issue settled as soon as possible, but she forgot what she was about to say when she ran headlong into his broad chest.

He immediately wrapped his arms around her to keep her from falling. "Sorry. I didn't…expect you to switch directions."

As she stared up into his dark brown eyes, her breath lodged in her throat. She felt completely surrounded by him and the feeling wasn't at all unpleasant.

Her heart skipped several beats.

"I...um...I think I'll...turn in for the night," she stammered, unable to think clearly. What on earth was wrong with her?

He brought one of his hands up to brush a strand of hair that had escaped her ponytail from her cheek. The tips of his fingers lingered on her skin just a bit longer than was necessary and sent a tingling sensation pulsing through her.

When he lowered his head, she held her breath a moment as she awaited his kiss. But instead of covering her mouth, Lane's lips lightly brushed her ear as he whispered, "Sleep well, Taylor."

When he slowly released her and took a step back, it took a moment for her to realize he was looking at her expectantly. "Was there something else?" he asked.

"Um...good night...Lane," she finally managed.

Forcing herself to move, she opened the screen door and didn't stop until she was upstairs with her bedroom door shut firmly behind her. As she leaned back against it, she had to remind herself to breathe. Lane had more raw sensuality in his little finger than most men had in their entire bodies.

Her heart suddenly began to pound against her ribs. When had she started thinking of him by his first name? And why?

It had been much easier and a lot less personal to keep him compartmentalized as Donaldson, her adversary—the man she had suspected of cheating her grandfather. The very man who stood between her and her goal of owning all of the Lucky Ace.

Taylor scrunched her eyes shut as she tried to wipe

out the image of him holding her gaze as he leaned toward her. She had thought he was going to kiss her. And heaven help her, she hadn't made a single move to stop him.

"Get a grip on yourself," she muttered as she pushed away from the door. She wasn't interested in a one-night stand, a relationship or any other kind of entanglement with a man. She had watched her parents and the miserable existence that their marriage had become for the past twenty-eight years. And if there was one thing she had learned it was what she didn't want in life.

Grabbing her nightshirt, she headed into the adjoining bathroom. As she changed clothes and brushed her teeth, she tried to tell herself that she had been distracted by his proposal and hadn't been thinking clearly. But staring into the mirror, she shook her head at the woman staring back at her. She could try to justify her reaction all she wanted, but the fact of the matter was, she was attracted to him. And she wasn't the least bit happy about it.

Stepping out of the shower, Lane shivered and reached for a towel to wipe away the rivulets of cold water running down his body. Two cold showers in less than twelve hours was more than any man should have to endure, and he for damned sure had no intention of suffering through a third.

After Taylor ran into him on the porch and he had put his arms around her, he'd seen the anticipation in her emerald eyes. As a result, he had spent the entire night wide-awake and feeling as if he was going to climb the walls. Walking into the bedroom now, he quickly got dressed and pulled on his work boots. He was going downstairs and over breakfast, he was going to tell Taylor that he definitely wouldn't be home for dinner. If he didn't scratch this itch, there was a very good chance he would be a complete lunatic and a straitjacket away from being committed by the end of the week.

His only hope of any kind of reprieve from the situation would be for one of them to leave the Lucky Ace. That's why he had proposed a game of poker for control of the ranch. It had been the only thing he could think of that she might agree to.

If his instincts about her were correct, Taylor would want to win the Lucky Ace back by playing the same game Ben had lost. Lane was sure that in her mind it would vindicate her grandfather once and for all, as well as give her the satisfaction of beating him at his own game.

His conscience had reminded him that he was a professional and might have an unfair advantage. But surely Ben had taught Taylor his strategy and style of playing during her many visits to the ranch. If anything, that would make the game more interesting, and he hoped that she took him up on his offer to decide the fate of the ranch that way.

When he walked into the kitchen a few minutes later, instead of finding Taylor making breakfast, he found her talking on the phone. Who in the Sam Hill could she be carrying on a conversation with at five in the morning?

"He just came downstairs for breakfast," she said, smiling. "Would you like to tell him yourself?"

Lane frowned. "Who is it?"

"One of your brothers," she said, handing him the cordless phone.

As she turned toward the counter and whatever it was she was preparing for their meal, Lane cringed as he put the phone to his ear. The last time he'd received a phone call from one of his brothers this early in the morning, it was to tell him that his foster father had died from an undiagnosed heart problem.

"What's up?" he asked, walking down the hall to the study. He wasn't sure which one of his brothers was on the other end of the line, but it didn't matter. They were always there for each other and always would be.

"You're talking to the proud daddy of a healthy baby girl," Ryder said, sounding happier than Lane could ever remember.

Relieved that the news wasn't something bad, Lane grinned as he lowered himself into the desk chair. "Congratulations! How are Summer and the baby doing?"

"They're both doing just fine," Ryder answered. "Summer is understandably tired, but things couldn't have gone any better for either of them."

"That's great. And how are you holding up?" Lane asked, laughing.

"I face two thousand pounds of pissed-off beef on a regular basis without so much as blinking, but watching Summer go through labor was the most intense thing I've ever experienced," Ryder said, sounding as if he was glad everything was over with. "Let's just say I'm recovering and leave it at that."

"Glad to hear it. What's my new niece's name?" Lane asked, settling back in the chair.

"I'm leaving that up to Summer." Ryder paused as if a wave of emotion threatened. When he finally continued, his voice was extremely husky. "I don't care what she decides to name the baby. I swear I didn't think it was possible to fall in love with something so tiny so damned fast."

"You're going to be a great dad," Lane said, feeling his own chest tighten. Clearing his throat, he teased, "I can just see you now, sitting on a little chair with your knees threatening to bump your chin while you sip imaginary tea out of a tiny pink teacup."

Ryder laughed. "I'll be more than happy to do it. Whatever my little girl wants, my little girl gets."

"When do we all get to meet the newest member of the family?" Lane asked, hoping it would be soon. Since Sam and his wife had little Hank, he had really started to get into being a proud uncle.

"When I talked to Sam a few minutes ago, he said that Bria and Mariah have been planning a family dinner for the past couple of weeks in anticipation of Summer having the baby," Ryder answered.

"That doesn't surprise me," Lane said. "You know how much Bria loves family get-togethers. Just let me know when they're planning on having it and I'll be there."

"I sure will, bro," Ryder assured him. "Now, before I hang up and call the rest of the guys to tell them about the baby, would you like to let me in on who Taylor Scott is and what she's doing answering your phone at this time of morning?"

"It's a long story," Lane hedged, not all that eager to try explaining the situation.

"Why don't you give me the thumbnail version?" Ryder pressed.

Lane sighed heavily. He should have known better than to think he could end the call without his brother wanting to know what was going on. He'd do the same thing with any of his brothers if their roles were reversed.

"She's Ben Cunningham's granddaughter," Lane said, hoping that would satisfy Ryder's curiosity.

"Did she come back from California with Ben?" his brother asked.

"No, Ben passed away about three weeks ago." Lane ran his hand over the tension building at the back of his neck. He wasn't surprised that his brother wanted more of an explanation. If he was in Ryder's shoes, he would want details, too. "And before you ask when she arrived, Taylor is the redhead who crashed the party the other night. Ben left her his share of the ranch."

"I'm sorry to hear that about Ben. I know the two of you became pretty good friends after you won half of the Lucky Ace," Ryder said, his tone sympathetic. "But you don't sound all that thrilled about being in the ranching business with his granddaughter."

"We'd be just fine if she'd go back to California where she belongs and leave me alone," Lane admitted. "She's decided that she is going to take up residence here and actively run the ranch."

"Oh, this sounds like a story I've got to hear," Ryder said, sounding a little too happy about Lane's predicament.

"You're not going to let this go, are you?" Lane asked, already knowing the answer.

"Hey, Freud, you didn't let things go when I was being a stubborn jackass before I finally asked Summer to marry me," Ryder shot back.

Lane should have known that the intervention he and his brothers staged when Ryder had decided he wasn't good enough for Summer would come back to bite him in the butt. "There are absolutely no similarities between the situations," Lane said, shaking his head at his brother's erroneous comparison. "You were head over heels in love. I'm not." He snorted. "Hell, I'm not even sure if I like her. She's stubborn, opinionated and about as prickly as a cactus patch."

"In other words, she's a challenge and that makes her all the more attractive to you, doesn't it?" Ryder asked knowingly.

Lane gritted his teeth. "Have I told you lately what a smart-ass you can be?"

"No. But whether you wanted to or not, you just answered my question," Ryder said, sounding quite smug.

If he could have reached into the phone and got hold of his brother, Lane would have cheerfully throttled him. "Goodbye, Ryder."

"Later, bro."

Ryder's laughter echoed in Lane's ear long after he

ended the phone call. He loved all of his brothers, but sometimes they irritated the life out of him. Ryder was reading way more into his partnership with Taylor than was there. And before the sun cleared the eastern horizon, the rest of his brothers would know all about it.

Lane groaned. There wasn't a doubt in his mind that along with announcing the birth of his daughter, Ryder was already spreading the word that Lane was living under the same roof with Taylor. And once his brothers put their spins on the facts, the next time they all got together, Lane's life would be a living hell from all of their good-natured ribbing.

But they'd have it all wrong. Any attraction he felt for Taylor had more to do with his long dry spell of being without the warmth of a woman than anything else. She was beautiful and had a smoking-hot body. He was a healthy adult male who had neglected his basic needs. And they were stuck in a house together because they were both too stubborn to give on the issue of who was going to live on the ranch. It just stood to reason that until he released some of his built-up tension he was going to find her desirable.

Confident that his perspective had been restored, he rose to his feet and walked straight to the kitchen. "Taylor, I won't be home for dinner this evening. I have to make a trip over to Beaver Dam."

Lane parked his truck next to Taylor's little red sports car, switched off the lights and muttered a word he reserved for the direst of situations. His trip to the Broken Spoke over in Beaver Dam had turned out to be a huge waste of time. And it wasn't because there weren't any interested women present. There was one cute little brunette in particular who'd made it crystal clear she was available for an evening of no-strings-attached fun. But he hadn't even been able to work up enough enthusiasm to ask her to dance.

What the hell was wrong with him? He still felt edgy enough to jump out of his own skin. The woman had been more than willing and he'd made the hour's drive over to the watering hole specifically for just such an encounter.

But as he got out the truck and slowly walked up the porch steps, he decided that he wasn't going to do any kind of self-analysis in an effort to understand his reaction to the situation. He had a feeling that he wouldn't be overly happy with what he discovered about himself if he did.

"I didn't expect you back this soon," Taylor said when he entered the kitchen. Sitting at the kitchen table, she had a laptop set up in front of her. She quickly closed it as if there was something on it that she didn't want him to see. "Would you like a cup of coffee?" she asked.

"Why not?" he muttered. It wasn't as if the caffeine would prevent him from sleeping. The woman staring at him had taken care of that ever since her arrival. When she started to get up, he shook his head. "I'll get it."

"I've been thinking," she said as he poured his coffee, then walked over to sit down at the head of the table.

He wasn't sure he wanted to know, but taking a sip from the mug in his hand, he asked, "About?"

"Your suggestion that we play cards for the Lucky Ace," she answered.

She caught her lower lip between her teeth as if she was still trying to make up her mind. It was all Lane could do to keep from groaning. He'd like nothing more than to do a little nibbling of his own on her perfect coral lips.

The thought caused his heart to stall. Where had all this desire to kiss a woman been when the brunette at the Broken Spoke had flirted with him? With sudden clarity, he knew exactly what the problem had been. The woman at the Broken Spoke hadn't been a redhead with the greenest eyes he'd ever seen.

He came dangerously close to repeating the word he'd muttered when he parked his truck and prepared to enter the house.

"If I agree to your terms, I would definitely want an impartial observer to witness the game and verify the outcome," she said, oblivious to his turmoil.

"Absolutely," he said, thankful that she had distracted him from his sudden realization. "With the stakes this high, I wouldn't have it any other way."

"Where would the game be held?" she asked. "Here or somewhere neutral?"

"Since gambling is illegal in the state of Texas, we'd have to go over into Louisiana," he said, shaking his head. When he won, he wanted to make sure that everything was aboveboard and there was no question about the validity of the game.

"Why not go to Las Vegas?" she asked, looking a bit suspicious.

He shrugged. "It's fine with me if that's where you want to go. I just figured it might be easier to go to Shreveport, since it's just a few hours away and won't involve extensive travel arrangements."

She frowned. "I hadn't thought about it being so much closer. That probably would make it the obvious choice."

"I have a friend who owns one of the finest casinos over there." Confident now that she was going to agree to his plan, he smiled. "I could talk to him about setting up a private room for us, with our own dealer, of course."

"Is that where you played my grandfather when you won part of the ranch?" she asked suddenly.

He didn't like her tone or the suspicion in her green gaze. "Yes."

"Then I'd rather not play there," she said, shaking her head.

"Why not?" he demanded. He had a good idea what she was driving at and he didn't like it one damned bit.

"Nothing against the man, but I'm sure you can understand that I'd feel more comfortable with someone who wasn't one of your friends taking care of the arrangements," she said determinedly as she got up to get herself more coffee.

Lane set his mug on the table with a thump and rose to face her. "Let me set you straight on something right now, babe. Cole Sullivan is one of the most honest men I've ever known. He's not only a trusted friend of mine, he was a good friend of your grandfather's, as well."

When she took a step back, he took a step forward. "In fact, Ben knew Cole for years before I met him."

"Oh, I didn't realize…I, uh, just want to make sure the game isn't compromised…" Her voice trailed off as she once again began to worry her lower lip.

"In other words, you want to make sure that I don't cheat," he said, advancing on her.

"I didn't…say that," she stammered, backing up until her retreat was stopped by the kitchen cabinets.

Bracing his hands on the countertop on either side of her, he leaned forward to make his point, effectively trapping her. "I know it's hard for you to believe, but I didn't cheat your grandfather and I have no intention of cheating you." As he stared down at her, the anger in his gut evolved into heat of another kind. Lowering his tone to a more intimate level, he reached up to trace her jawline lightly with his index finger. "Believe me, Taylor, if it isn't going to be a clean, honest game, I won't play."

He noticed the same anticipation in her eyes that had been there the evening before. This time, Lane couldn't have stopped himself if his life depended on it.

"I'm going to do what I should have done last night." Holding her gaze with his, he slowly began to lower his head.

"W-what…is that?" she asked, sounding delightfully breathless.

"I'm going to kiss you," he said, covering her mouth with his.

Four

Lane's lips molded to hers and Taylor couldn't work up so much as a token protest. The truth was, she had wanted him to kiss her the night before and been disappointed when he hadn't. Her reaction was totally insane, considering that she still wasn't entirely sure she could trust him, not to mention that it was completely out of character for her. But there was no denying that she felt a level of attraction to him that she'd never felt for any other man. And it appeared there wasn't anything she could do to keep from giving in to it.

But when Lane closed his arms around her and drew her close, she abandoned all contemplation of her atypical behavior. Teasing her lips with his, he sought entry to deepen the kiss, and his soft exploration, the gentleness of his tongue stroking hers, caused a delightful little quiver deep in the pit of her belly. When she placed her hands on his broad chest, the strength she detected in the hard contours beneath his shirt reminded her of the contrasts between a man and woman and set her pulse to racing. What would it be like to feel those muscles pressed to her much softer body as he made love to her?

The thought stunned her out of her daze. Why was she fantasizing about Lane Donaldson? He was the man who stood between her and having what she wanted—the entire ranch. Quickly she pushed against his chest.

"I…uh, that…shouldn't have—" Why couldn't she get her mind and vocal cords to work in unison?

Instead of releasing her, Lane continued to hold her against him. "I'm not going to apologize for something we both wanted," he said, shaking his head.

"I didn't want…I mean, I suppose I was curious, but—" She clamped her lips together and rested her head against his chest in defeat when it was apparent that her thoughts were still too scattered to be coherent.

His low chuckle vibrated against her ear, sending warmth spreading throughout her body. "Now who's being less than honest?"

Not trusting that she wouldn't make a bigger fool of herself than she already had, she simply shrugged.

"So are we agreed that I'll call Cole Sullivan tomorrow and have him set up the game for us?" he asked.

"I'm not sure what to do." How was she going to play a card game with the stakes so high when she had no idea what she was doing?

Placing his finger under her chin, he tipped her head

up until their gazes met. "What aren't you sure of, Taylor? Me? The integrity of the game we'll play? What?"

As she stared up into his dark brown eyes, she sighed heavily. "I'm not sure I'll be able to play with you or anyone else," she finally said, shaking her head.

He frowned. "Why not?"

His gentle tone was playing havoc with her senses and before she could stop herself, she blurted out, "I don't know the first thing about poker."

"You've never played?" he asked, looking as if he couldn't quite believe it. "Didn't Ben at least teach you the basics?"

She shook her head. "I know it sounds bizarre, considering that he was a legendary player and considering how much time I spent here, but I was more interested in doing other things with him, like going horseback riding or fishing down at the creek."

"Then playing for the Lucky Ace is out of the question," he said slowly.

"Yes, we are going to play, eventually. While you were away this evening, I've been doing some research online and it doesn't look like the game of poker would be all that difficult to learn. I'm just unsure of how long it will take me to master it," she said, walking over to the table to open her laptop. "I'm not missing my only chance to get your half of the ranch."

It irritated her no end when Lane threw back his head and laughed out loud. "You've got to be kidding."

Snapping the laptop shut, she turned to glare at him. "I couldn't be more serious."

"Poker isn't something you learn overnight," he said,

grinning, as he shook his head. "Besides the fact that there are several different card games referred to as poker, you also need to learn the rank of the different hands, when to stay and when to fold, how to bet and how to read the other players. And that's just the tip of the iceberg, babe."

"Are you so arrogant you think there's too much for a woman to learn?" she asked, her anger increasing with each passing second.

"Not at all." His easy expression was replaced by a dark scowl, indicating that he took her accusation as an insult. "Some of the best and most challenging players I know are women. So don't accuse me of thinking women aren't intelligent enough to learn the game, because that's not the case."

"Then what *are* you trying to say?" she asked.

"I'm trying to tell you that it isn't as easy as just learning the fundamentals of the game." He picked up his coffee cup from the table and walked over to empty it in the sink. "A website or a book can't teach you how to recognize a player's tell or how to conceal your own. And don't think that's something you can learn by reading something online. It takes practice, patience and learning to be extremely observant of the other players."

Taylor nibbled her lower lip. She had no idea what he was talking about. What was a tell? But she wasn't going to let her lack of knowledge deter her. Even if one of the poker websites couldn't furnish her with a definition and show her how to recognize it, she was certain if given enough time she could figure it out.

"We don't have to play the game tomorrow," she said,

wondering how long it would take her to find a website explaining the skills he'd outlined and then how much longer it would take to become good enough to beat him.

He smiled. "If you want to go back to California and take the time to learn how to play, we can always set up things when you think you're ready."

"What do you hear when I tell you something?" she demanded, propping her hands on her hips.

His frown deepened. "What do you mean?"

"Either my voice comes out at a decibel you can't hear or you have a serious listening problem," she stated flatly. "I told you that I'm not going back to California, unless of course the outcome of the game goes in your favor. Then I'll hold up my end of the bargain and move. But only then." Her confidence restored, she smiled. "You might as well accept it, Lane. I'll be staying right here until we play that game."

She could tell by the muscle working along his lean jaw that he wasn't the least bit happy. But that was just too darned bad. She had every right to stay at the ranch and nothing he could say would convince her to do otherwise.

Deciding that she needed to do more research, she picked up her laptop and started toward the hall. But a sudden thought had her turning back. "You said there are several card games that fall into the poker category. Which one will we be playing?"

"Texas Hold'em," he answered tightly.

She nodded. "Then that's the one I'll concentrate on learning. And at some point before the game, I'll draw up a document with the details of our agreement. We'll both sign it and have it witnessed by an outside party."

His lips flattened into a line. "You still don't trust me, do you?"

"At this point, I'm not sure whether I do or not. But I've always heard it's smart to get things of this nature in writing," she said, turning to go upstairs. "Let's just call it insurance against either of us changing our minds about the game we'll be playing or against a misunderstanding of what we get if we win."

As she went upstairs to her room, she hoped there really was some kind of skill or natural talent for playing poker that she might have inherited from her grandfather. It would make everything so much easier. She could not only learn the game quickly, she might be able to hold her own playing cards with Lane and quite possibly beat the socks off of him.

She couldn't help smiling at the thought. Nothing would please her more than to beat Lane at his favorite game. She would not only make the Lucky Ace whole again, but she would be avenging her grandfather's lapse in judgment for betting the ranch in the first place.

As she plugged in her laptop and sat down on the bed, Taylor nibbled on her lower lip. All things considered, she probably should have turned Lane down and requested they do something else to determine who would control the ranch. But she hadn't been willing to take the chance that he would withdraw his offer completely. And the last thing she wanted was for him to own any part of the ranch for an extended period of time.

Besides, she was intelligent and learned things quickly. It was perfectly reasonable for her to believe she had a fighting chance at winning.

When Lane went upstairs for what he knew for certain would be another sleepless night, he glanced at the closed bedroom door across the hall. He could see a narrow strip of light reflected on the hardwood floor beneath it and he'd bet every dime he had that Taylor was visiting websites, researching how to play Texas Hold'em.

If he had known that she'd never played before, he wouldn't have suggested a poker game to decide the fate of the ranch. But when he'd given her the opportunity to call it off, she'd refused.

He released a frustrated breath. The woman was too stubborn for her own good. There was no way it could be a fair game. Not when he was a professional and she had no idea what she was doing. So what was he supposed to do?

Trying to go the fair and honorable route hadn't worked, and his conscience wouldn't allow him to take advantage of her inexperience. But it appeared elephants would start roosting in trees before she backed down. The way he saw it, there was only one thing he could do that might come close to solving the problem.

Shaking his head at the ridiculousness of the entire situation, he stepped across the hall and knocked on Taylor's door. He couldn't believe what he was about to do, but there wasn't any other choice.

"Is something wrong?" she asked when she opened her door.

She looked absolutely adorable in her lime-green midlength gym shorts and a hot pink T-shirt with butterflies screen printed across the front. On any other woman he wouldn't have found the outfit all that appealing, but Taylor somehow managed to make it look sexy. Real sexy.

His mouth went as dry as a Texas drought when he realized she wasn't wearing a bra. "No, nothing's wrong," he finally managed as he shifted his weight from one foot to the other in an effort to relieve the pressure beginning to build behind the fly of his jeans. "I've been thinking that if you insist on playing cards for the ranch, you're going to need someone to give you a crash course on how to play."

"The only person I knew who could play well enough to teach me how to beat you at cards was my grandfather," she said, shrugging one slender shoulder.

He nodded. "And since that's no longer possible, I see no other alternative but to teach you myself."

Her eyes widened and he could tell she was thoroughly shocked by his offer. "Excuse me?"

"It's the only option that makes sense," he insisted, wondering if she had finally driven him over the edge. Even he was finding the idea absurd. "We both know you can learn all you need to know about the rules of the game and the ranking of the hands from a website. But it can't teach you what to expect when you're facing me across the table in a live game."

"Do you think I've lost my mind?" she asked, laughing. "Why would you want to help me learn to play a game that I fully intend to win? And what guarantee would I have that you'd be honest about what you teach me? For all I know, you might teach me something that will ensure that you come out on top."

"First and foremost, your grandfather was a good friend. I'm making the offer to help you because of the admiration and respect I had for him. And secondly, contrary to what you think of me, I have a conscience and a set of ethics I live by." For reasons he didn't quite understand himself, he was determined to set her straight about his morals once and for all. "When we play for the ranch, I want it to be a fair game and one that we both have a chance of winning. Otherwise, you might as well pack your bags and head back to L.A. now."

She raised an eyebrow. "Oh, so you think you're that good, huh?"

He grinned. "I know I am, babe. That's why I'm willing to help you out."

When she started to nibble on her lower lip, he reached out and placed his finger to her mouth, stopping her. "Lesson number one. Stop worrying your lower lip when you're trying to decide what to do. That's one of your tells and lets me know that you're unsure."

"I have more than one?" she asked.

Staring down into her expressive green eyes, he nodded. "When you think you have the advantage, you smile." He cupped her face with his hands. "And when you think I'm going to kiss you, your eyes widen slightly in anticipation." He slowly began to lower his head. "Just like they're doing right now."

As he covered her mouth with his, Lane knew he was flirting with disaster. They were rivals for the Lucky Ace and she could very easily accuse him of trying to use their attraction to convince her to sell him her share. Or worse yet, she might think he was trying to win her trust only to betray it later when he taught her how to play poker.

He didn't like either prospect, but there didn't seem to be anything he could do to stop himself. Every time he got within arm's length of her, all he could think about was kissing her the way she was meant to be kissed—and a whole lot more.

Tracing her lips with his tongue, Lane coaxed her to open for him. When she sighed softly and allowed him entry, he didn't think twice about deepening the kiss to stroke her inner recesses. Never in all of his thirty-four years had he tasted anything as erotic or sensual as Taylor's sweetness. When she circled his neck with her arms and leaned into him, he pulled her more fully against him and the feel of her lithe body pressed to his had him harder than a chunk of granite in less than the blink of an eye.

His heart stalled and a surge of heat shot straight through him when a tiny moan escaped her parted lips as she sagged against him. He had expected her to pull out of his arms and give him hell for his reaction, but to his immense satisfaction, it appeared that she was as turned on as he was. With sudden clarity, Lane realized that the tension between them had just as much

to do with an undeniable chemistry drawing them together as it did their rivalry over who would own all of
the Lucky Ace.

The discovery wasn't something he was at all comfortable with. Needing time and distance to think, he
eased away from the kiss and took a step back. "I should
probably let you get some sleep," he said, knowing he
was facing another cold shower and another night of
feeling as if he could climb the walls.

Staring down at her, he couldn't help but notice the
blush of desire on her creamy cheeks and the slightly
dazed look in her emerald eyes. He knew beyond a
shadow of doubt that she would be as passionate about
making love as she was about getting his share of the
ranch.

The thought sent a surge of heat knifing through him
and he quickly turned to cross the hall to his bedroom.
"We'll get started on you learning the fundamentals of
the game after breakfast in the morning."

"I haven't agreed to let you teach me how to play,"
she reminded him.

With his hand on the doorknob, he turned back. "If
you have a better idea, I'd like to hear it."

"I...well, no," she admitted.

"Do you think you can win on your own without me
teaching you?" he asked, knowing full well she couldn't.

She started to nibble on her lower lip, then stopped
herself and shook her head. "I suppose it wouldn't hurt
for you to show me a few things about the game." She
paused for a moment and then shrugged, adding, "If
that's what you want to do."

He almost laughed out loud. If he hadn't realized before how fiercely independent she was, he did now. She had to make it sound as if she would be doing him a favor to let him teach her how to play so she could beat him. Normally, that attitude would irritate the hell out of him. But coming from Taylor, he just found it cute and…endearing?

Quickly opening the door to his room before he crossed the hall and took her back into his arms, he grinned. "Pleasant dreams, Taylor. I'll see you in the morning."

The following morning, Taylor yawned as she finished loading and starting the dishwasher. She had spent most of the night visiting websites and researching all she could on the game of Texas Hold'em. At least, that was the excuse she was going to use if Lane asked her why she was so sleepy. She wasn't about to admit to him or anyone else that after that kiss at her bedroom door last night, she couldn't have slept if her life depended on it.

Both times Lane had kissed her, she'd felt as if she would melt into a puddle at his big booted feet. And neither time had she been able to work up the slightest resistance. All Lane had to do was start lowering his head and every ounce of sense she possessed seemed to desert her. Never in her entire life had a man had such a drugging effect on her.

A shiver slid up her spine when she closed her eyes and thought about how his lips felt as they explored hers. He wasn't aggressive the way some men were.

Lane's firm lips softly moved over hers with such care—it was as if he worshipped her. Her lips tingled from just the memory of it.

Taylor opened her eyes and shook her head. She needed to get her mind off Lane and his addictive kisses. Her full attention needed to be focused on what she had learned about the card game they would be playing. His lips on hers might be the most erotic thing she'd ever experienced, but he was still her rival and she had every intention of beating him at his own game in order to regain all of the Lucky Ace.

Forcing herself to concentrate on the information she'd read on the internet, she still wasn't sure about the ranking on a couple of hands, but for the most part it seemed pretty straightforward and fairly easy. They would each be dealt two cards facedown, known as their "hold," then three community cards called the "flop" would be dealt faceup. They would be given the opportunity to bet, then the next card, called the "turn," would be dealt faceup and they would be given the chance to make another wager. When the last card, called the "river," was dealt, they would once again bet and the object was to make the best five-card hand out of their hold cards and the five community cards face up on the table.

Now all she had to do was let Lane teach her when and how much to bet on the different hands and what to look for when she was trying to discover someone's tell.

Yawning again, she poured herself a cup of coffee and walked over to sit at the kitchen table to wait for her first poker lesson. Lane had gone to the barn right after he helped her clear the table to have Judd, the ranch foreman, call the farrier to come to the ranch to put new horseshoes on the working stock. He should be back soon, and she wanted to be ready.

Taylor nibbled on her lower lip before she could stop herself. It appeared he knew more about ranching than she had first thought. He'd mentioned that his brothers had ranches in the area and that he had finished growing up on one. Did that mean they had all lived in a town or city before moving to a ranch?

"What's running through that overactive mind of yours now?" Lane asked, walking over to the table.

Lost in thought, she hadn't even realized he'd entered the house. "You mentioned that you finished growing up on a ranch," she said, choosing her words carefully. "Was it around here?"

He shook his head as he sat down beside her. "It was up close to Dallas—about eight miles southeast of Mesquite."

"I've been to the rodeo up there," she said, remembering the times she and her grandfather had made the two-hour trip for the weekly summer events.

Lane smiled. "I used to compete in that rodeo every weekend when I was home on summer break."

"Really?" The more she learned about him, the more she was finding Lane to be one surprise after another. She would never have guessed he'd been a rodeo contestant.

Nodding, he reached for the deck of cards lying on the table in front of them. "My foster brother T.J. and I competed in the team roping event until he decided to concentrate on the bareback bronc riding."

It suddenly occurred to her why he had mentioned that he finished growing up on a ranch. Lane had been a child of the foster care system.

"And before you ask, yes, I was a foster care kid," he said, as if reading her mind. He peeled the cellophane wrapper from the new deck of cards and took them out of the box. "I was sent to the Last Chance Ranch when I was fifteen—right after my mom passed away from breast cancer."

"I'm sorry, Lane." She reached over to place her hand on his forearm. "That's such a young age to lose your mother. But what about your father? Couldn't you have lived with him?"

The only outward sign that she might have touched a nerve was the muscle working along his lean jaw. "He died a couple of years before my mom."

"Didn't you have any other family you could have lived with?" she asked. Even though her mother and father's parenting had been far from stellar, Taylor couldn't imagine not having anyone.

"No, both sets of my grandparents were dead. My dad did have a brother in the military, but he got killed in the Middle East. And my mom was an only child." He shrugged as he began to shuffle the cards. "But it all worked out. When I went to live on the Last Chance Ranch, I gained five brothers and a father that anyone would be proud to call family, and I consider myself one of the luckiest men alive to have them."

"So you still stay in touch with your foster father as well as your brothers?" she asked.

He shook his head. "Hank Calvert died several years ago. Much like your grandfather, he had a heart problem that he chose to ignore instead of getting the medical treatment he needed."

They were silent for a moment before she frowned. "But how did you know I was curious about your being a foster child?" she asked. Was the man psychic?

He reached over to trace her lower lip lightly with his index finger. "Remember what I told you last night about worrying your lip when you're unsure or trying to decide something?"

"My tell," she murmured.

His gaze held hers as he slowly nodded. "I could see you were curious about my brothers, but that you couldn't decide if you should ask about them." He smiled. "What about you? Ben mentioned he had family in California, but he didn't say if you had siblings."

"I used to think it would be nice to have a brother or sister." She shook her head. "Then the older I got, I decided it was just as well that I was an only child. I wouldn't wish my childhood on anyone."

Lane put the cards down. "Why do you say that?" His eyes narrowed and his voice held a hard edge when he demanded, "Were your parents abusive?"

"No. Not at all." Taylor took a sip of her coffee. She didn't like to talk about her parents, but since Lane had shared details about his upbringing, she felt it was only fair to share hers. "My mother and father are the most mismatched couple you'd ever care to meet and they should have never married. They have nothing in common, lead separate lives and when they are together, they argue constantly." She sighed. "The only peace I ever had as a child was the summers I spent here on the Lucky Ace with my grandfather."

"Did they ever talk about getting a divorce?" he asked, his tone gentle.

She nodded. "They've hurled that word at each other on a daily basis for as long as I can remember. But neither one of them ever intend to carry through with it."

Lane frowned. "Was it because of not wanting you to come from a broken home?"

"No, it was something much simpler than that," she answered. "In fact, I don't think my becoming a child of divorce even crossed their minds."

"How could it not?" he asked, frowning.

"They were too busy trying to figure out a way to get around the state divorce laws." She smiled at his skeptical expression. "California is a community property state and they would have had to divide everything equally. Neither of them wanted the other to get any part of their assets. They both wanted it all."

"I'm sure they would both have wanted you," Lane said, sounding more sure of that fact than she was.

"Maybe if they had ever come to an agreement about the bank accounts and property, they might have discussed it," she said, rising from her chair to refill her coffee. Taking a mug from the cupboard, she poured Lane a cup of the steaming brew as well, then set it in front of him. "But I've often wondered if they would have argued as passionately about who got custody of me as they did over the money and the house—if they'd ever gotten that far along in the discussion."

When she sat down, he reached over to cover her hand with his. "I'm sure you were their most important consideration, Taylor. I know it didn't seem that way at the time, but I'm betting that you never doubted that they loved you."

She shook her head. "No, that was never an issue. I always knew they both loved me very much."

"And they're still together?" he asked. "Even now that you're grown and have a place of your own?"

"Yes." She shrugged. "I assume it's because whoever outlives the other wins and gets everything."

"That could be," he admitted, lightly touching her cheek with his knuckles. "But it might be that's just the type of relationship they have. They bicker a lot, but deep down they love each other. I'm not saying that's definitely the case with your parents, but there is that chance."

"I suppose it's a possibility," she admitted, stopping herself just before she started nibbling on her lower lip.

Lane's slow grin caused her pulse to race. "Now, I'm going to move to the opposite side of the table."

Confused, she frowned. "Why? Aren't you supposed to be showing me how to play?"

"That's why I'm moving across the table from you." His deep chuckle as he moved to the chair opposite her caused warmth to spread throughout her body. "If I don't put a little distance between us, I'm going to be tempted to take you in my arms and kiss you until a poker lesson is the last thing on either of our minds."

Five

Two hours after he moved to the other side of the table, Lane sat back in his chair and smiled at the woman seated across from him. "I don't know about you, but I'm ready for a break," he said, rotating his shoulders. "It's a nice day. What would you say about going for a horseback ride?"

"Actually, that sounds pretty good," she said, smiling. "It's getting close to lunchtime. I could pack some sandwiches and we could find a nice shady spot for a picnic down by the creek."

"While you get those ready, I'll go saddle the horses," he said, rising to his feet. "Was there a particular horse you rode when you were here to visit Ben?"

She nodded. "The buckskin mare is mine. Grandpa

gave her to me for my sixteenth birthday." Looking uncertain, she asked, "Has anyone been riding her?"

"I think Judd told me someone tries to ride her at least once a week," he said, referring to the ranch foreman. "Why?"

"Horses that haven't been ridden in a while can get ornery," she said, smiling. "I just wanted to know what to expect."

Lane grinned as he grabbed his hat from the peg beside the door and put it on. "Not in the mood for a rodeo, huh?"

Her laughter sent a shaft of heat straight through him. "I haven't ridden in several years and I'm going to be sore enough as it is. I'd rather not end up with a broken bone or two on top of that."

"There's a set of insulated saddlebags in the pantry and there should be a couple of ice packs in the freezer," he said, reaching for the doorknob. "When you get everything ready, call the barn and I'll bring the horses up to the house."

"Why?" she asked, opening the refrigerator.

"The saddlebags are going to be heavy and I don't want you to have to carry them," he said, quickly stepping out onto the back porch before he grabbed her and kissed her until they were both numb from lack of oxygen.

He muttered a curse and walked across the ranch yard toward the barn. The entire time he had been teaching her which poker hands to keep and which ones to fold, all he'd been able to think about was how much he wanted to do a whole lot more than just kiss her.

He shook his head at his own foolishness. What in hell was wrong with him? He'd gone over to Beaver Dam to get some much needed female attention and quickly discovered that none of the women appealed to him. Yet all he could think about was Taylor and the attention he'd like for them to give each other.

"Hey there, boss," Roy Lee greeted him when Lane entered the barn. "Judd told me to tell you that he called the farrier and he'll be here tomorrow to put new shoes on the working stock."

Lane nodded as he walked down the barn aisle toward the man. "Thanks for letting me know. Where's Judd now?"

Roy Lee took off his cowboy hat to wipe the sweat from his brow. "He took Cletus with him to check out the grazing conditions in the north pasture."

"What did you do to piss Judd off?" Lane asked, eyeing the wheelbarrow and pitchfork Roy Lee was using to muck out the stalls.

"Oh, I'm not in hot water," he said, shaking his head. "I volunteered to clean out the stalls."

"Why?" Lane asked, frowning. If there was anything a cowboy hated more than just about any other ranch chore it had to be mucking out stalls.

"Somebody had to do it," Roy Lee said, shrugging. "And Cletus was complaining that he'd cleaned the stalls for the last three days. I just thought I'd give him a break."

Lane had a good idea why the cowboy was being so accommodating and it had nothing whatsoever to do with giving the other hired hand a break. "Blue will be gone for a while, so you'll have plenty of time to get this one done," he said as he opened the half door, snapped the lead rope onto the gelding's halter, then led him out of the stall.

"Going for a ride?" Roy Lee asked, sounding a little too curious.

"We'll be gone until sometime this afternoon," Lane said, nodding.

"I'll hang around close," Roy Lee offered, his tone almost giddy. "You know, in case Ms. Scott needs help with anything."

The man had just confirmed Lane's suspicions. He was hanging around close to the house on the off chance he would get the chance to talk to Taylor.

"That won't be necessary," Lane said, tying Blue to a grooming post.

He started back toward the buckskin mare's stall when Roy Lee insisted, "I don't mind at all, boss." He laughed. "You know how women are. They're always changing things. She might decide she needs to rearrange furniture and wants me to move some of the heavier stuff for her."

"Not today," Lane said, leading the mare to the hitching post to be saddled along with his roan. "She's going to be with me."

Roy Lee's cheerful expression quickly changed to one of disappointment. "Well, I guess I'll get back to work then, boss."

Lane almost felt sorry for the poor guy as he slowly walked back to the stall he'd been cleaning. It was clear the man had a huge crush on Taylor and had hoped to spend some time with her. But Roy Lee had no way of knowing that he made Taylor extremely uncomfortable by staring at her.

Of course, Lane had to admit that the young cowboy wasn't the only one who couldn't take his eyes off Taylor. Several times while they'd been playing cards, Lane had caught himself gazing at her, and not just to observe her tells. He'd noticed how her copper-colored hair framed her heart-shaped face and complimented her peaches-and-cream complexion. And he'd never seen eyes so green or filled with so much expression. He could tell exactly what she was thinking just by looking into their emerald depths and he couldn't help but wonder how they would look filled with passion as he made love to her. His body twitched and his jeans suddenly became a little too tight in the stride.

Not at all happy with the direction his thoughts had taken, he yanked the cinch tight on Blue, causing the roan to grunt. "Sorry, buddy," he muttered, patting the gelding's bluish-gray coat.

Quickly saddling the mare, Lane untied the reins of both horses and led them out of the barn. He'd do well to stop daydreaming about his business partner and focus on teaching her to play poker. The sooner they played that game and the fate of the Lucky Ace was decided, the better off he would be. Otherwise he was going to be in a perpetual state of arousal and completely out of his mind in very short order.

A sudden thought caused him to slow his steps. His and Taylor's situation was not unlike her parents' and their selfish refusal to share their assets. Wasn't that what he and Taylor were doing with the Lucky Ace? They were both too stubborn to give in, sell their interest in the ranch and move on to find something else.

But he rejected that train of thought immediately. He and Taylor weren't tied together by the bonds of marriage or in any other way, except for joint ownership of the property. They both had their reasons for wanting to hang onto it and none of those reasons had anything to do with an egotistical game of one-upmanship.

By the time Lane reached the house, he decided not to give it any more thought. He needed a break and fully intended to relax and enjoy the rest of the day without thinking about which one of them would end up controlling the ranch.

When he tied the horses to a hitching post by the steps, he crossed the porch and went inside. "Are you ready to go?"

Taylor was nowhere in sight, but he could hear her voice as she came down the hall. "That sounds very nice," she said, walking into the kitchen with the phone. When she saw him, she mouthed, "It's one of your brothers."

Lane immediately shook his head. The last thing he wanted to do was listen to whichever one of them was on the other end of the line rib him about living under the same roof with a hot-as-hell redhead.

"Okay, I'll be sure to tell him," Taylor said, ending the call. Smiling, she placed the cordless unit on the charger. "That was your brother Sam. He said to tell you that the dinner they're having to welcome the new baby is a week from Sunday at Ryder and Summer's place."

"Sounds good." Lane smiled. "We can ride over there together." He didn't have to ask if she would like to go with him. He knew his brother well enough to know Sam had already issued the invitation.

"I don't know," she said, sounding uncertain. "Sam asked me to join the celebration, but I don't want to intrude on your family gathering."

Lane shook his head. "It wouldn't be an intrusion at all." He stepped forward and without giving it a second thought, took her into his arms. "I can guarantee you'll enjoy yourself, especially getting to know the three women."

He barely stopped a groan from escaping when he watched her nibble on her lower lip for a moment before she finally nodded. "All right. I'll think about it."

Taking a step back, he decided that it would be in both of their best interests for them to start that horseback ride sooner rather than later. "Are you ready to go?"

"Absolutely," she said, giving him a smile that sent his blood pressure soaring.

Lane picked up the packed saddlebags from the kitchen island and followed her out of the house. As he watched her put her foot in the stirrup and swing up into the mare's saddle, his heart stalled and the pressure in his jeans increased. The sight of her slender legs straddling the mare had him wondering what it would feel like to have them wrapped around him as he sank himself deep inside of her.

Mentally running through every curse word he'd ever heard, he tied the bags to the back of his saddle and mounted the roan. He immediately had to shift to a more comfortable position or risk emasculating himself.

What was it that Taylor had that other women didn't? Why was she more attractive to him than any other woman he'd ever known? And what in the name of all that was holy could he do to stop it?

As a trained psychologist, he had the tools to fight what he suspected was a growing addiction to her. But as a man looking at a desirable woman, that same knowledge was proving to be completely useless.

"I can tell I haven't been on a horse in a while," Taylor said when they stopped at the creek and dismounted. Her thigh muscles and backside were sore, but riding her mare again was well worth a little discomfort. "I'm just glad Cinnamon has such a smooth gait."

"Otherwise you'd be sitting on a pillow for the next few days?" Lane guessed.

Laughing, she nodded as she waited for him to untie the saddlebags from the back of his horse. "A nice, hot soaking bath tonight should help."

"Some liniment probably wouldn't hurt," he said, carrying the saddlebags to a spot beneath a grove of cottonwood trees along the bank.

She reached for the blanket she had tucked inside one of the compartments to spread it out on the grass. "I wasn't sure what sandwiches you prefer, so I made a couple of different kinds."

"I'm pretty easy to get along with," he said, smiling. "I'm sure whatever you've made will be just fine. Besides, there hasn't been anything you've fixed yet that wasn't absolutely delicious."

His compliment pleased her more than she would have thought. "I'm glad you've gotten over your reticence about my cooking."

"Yeah, I owe you an apology for that." He grinned as he knelt beside her to help unpack their lunch. "But you were pretty clear that you wanted me off the ranch one way or another. As angry as you were the night before, I wasn't sure you hadn't decided to tamper with my food."

"I suppose I owe *you* an apology for that," she admitted. "I was tired and angry and might have overreacted just a bit."

"More like a lot, babe," he said, unwrapping a ham-and-cheese sandwich.

"I did make some pretty serious accusations, didn't I?" She wasn't proud of it, but her temper had gotten the better of her that night. "I'm sorry for bringing your integrity into question, Lane. But I just couldn't understand why Grandpa would jeopardize any part of the ranch. I still don't. It just doesn't make sense to me."

He put down his sandwich and wrapped his arms around her, pulling her to his broad chest. "Don't beat yourself up, Taylor. I got over it and after I cooled down, I realized that you'd had a tough few weeks. You'd just lost Ben, learned that he had lost part of the ranch you expected to inherit, then had to fulfill his last wish and bring his ashes back here." He ran his hands along her back in a soothing manner. "That kind of emotional roller coaster would put anyone on edge."

If Lane hadn't been so understanding, she might have

been able to stop herself. But his insight into what she had gone through with the loss of her beloved grandfather was more than she could bear. For the first time since her grandfather's passing, Taylor felt tears flow freely down her cheeks.

She hated to cry and had managed to hold the grief at bay until now. But once she acknowledged it, there was no way to stop it. Lane held her close as she sobbed against his chest and when the emotion finally subsided, he wiped away the last traces of her tears with one of the napkins she'd packed for their lunch.

Embarrassed by her uncharacteristic display, she stared down at her tightly clenched fists. "I'm so… sorry. I didn't…mean to do…that."

Placing his index finger under her chin, he lifted her gaze to meet his. "Don't ever be sorry for mourning someone you love, Taylor. It's part of the healing process. Was that the first time you've cried since you lost Ben?"

She nodded. "I don't like…being weak."

"Shedding tears for your grandfather's passing doesn't make you weak," he said gently. "It shows the strength of your love for him. And you should never apologize for loving someone that much."

His tender tone and the understanding she detected in his dark brown eyes caused a warmth like nothing she'd ever known to spread through her. With no thought to the consequences, Taylor pressed her lips to his.

She'd never in her entire life been the one to initiate a kiss, but Lane didn't seem to mind her assertiveness. Pulling her more fully against him, he took control and lightly teased her with nibbling kisses that were both thrilling and frustrating. She wanted him to deepen the caress, to kiss her like he'd done before.

Apparently sensing what she wanted, he coaxed her to open for him and her heart skipped a beat. At the first touch of his tongue to hers, stars burst behind her closed eyes and a streak of longing coursed through her.

As he softly stroked her inner recesses, he slid his hand under the tail of her T-shirt and the feel of his callused palm against her smooth skin sent ribbons of desire twining to the most feminine part of her. But when his hand covered her breast and his thumb grazed her nipple through her thin bra, a shiver of anticipation coursed through her and left her feeling weak with longing. The sensation was so strong it frightened her with its intensity.

"It's okay, babe," Lane said, apparently sensing her panic. He moved his hand from beneath her shirt, then, straightening the garment, added, "Nothing is going to happen that you don't want to happen."

That's what bothered her. She did want something to happen. She wasn't comfortable with it and she certainly wasn't about to tell him about it.

"I think it would be a good idea...if we stopped doing that," she said, sounding anything but convincing as she put some space between them on the picnic blanket. "We're rivals."

"Yeah, it's probably not wise," he said, his tone as unenthusiastic as hers. The slow, sexy grin curving the corners of his mouth made her feel warm all over. "But there's nothing wrong with a little *friendly* rivalry."

"Your kisses are way too sensual to be considered friendly." As soon as the words were out of her mouth, she wished she could call them back. She hadn't intended to let him know how his kiss affected her.

"What do you say we stop playing games and be honest with each other?" he asked, taking her by surprise. "We're both fighting an attraction that neither of us is comfortable with, but that both of us seem powerless to stop."

As she stared at him, she started to deny there was any kind of chemistry between them, but she couldn't. There was no sense lying about something they both knew to be the truth.

"Is that your professional opinion?" she asked, picking up one of the soft drinks.

"Just an observation," he said, shrugging.

They sat in silence as they finished their sandwiches before curiosity got the better of her. "So what do you propose we do about this so-called attraction?" she asked, wondering if she'd lost her mind. The smart thing to do would have been to change the subject and ignore his comment.

"I've given it some thought and the way I see it, we've got two options," he said, capturing her gaze with his. "We can either continue to let things go the way they've been going and be frustrated beyond reason, or we can explore this thing between us and see where it goes." His smile took her breath away. "It's my opinion that we should choose the latter."

"You've got to be kidding," she said, laughing. Surely he couldn't be serious.

"Think about it, Taylor." He gathered their empty sandwich wrappers and stuffed them into the saddlebags. "Trying to pretend it doesn't exist hasn't worked."

She couldn't argue with him on that point. It had been the elephant in the room, so to speak, practically from the moment they'd met. But she had studiously avoided a romantic entanglement with any man for so long, it was difficult for her to consider doing anything else.

"Are you saying you think we should start dating?" she asked, wondering if that's all he was suggesting.

He stared at her for several long moments as if trying to discern what she was thinking. "Are you interested in more?" he finally asked.

"No!" She hadn't meant for her answer to come out quite so forcefully. "I mean, I'm just not interested in a relationship."

"I'm not, either." He raised one black eyebrow. "I know what my reasons are. Would you care to share yours?"

"You know about my parents and the constant turmoil they're in. I would think it would be obvious," she stated flatly. "If that's what being part of a couple is, I'd rather not bother." She frowned. "Now it's your turn. Why are you resistant to the idea?"

He remained silent until they had the last traces of their lunch packed away in the saddlebags. "Playing poker is all about taking chances and accepting that sometimes you're up financially and sometimes you're down. I don't have that particular worry, nor will it ever be an issue for me because of the investments I've made.

I have the freedom to do whatever I want, when I want, without having to worry. But most women want stability, not a man who plays a game just for the fun of it," he said, getting up from the blanket. He held his hand out to help her to her feet. "I haven't met a woman yet who tempted me enough to consider giving that up."

"Did you always want to be a gambler?" she asked, folding the picnic blanket.

He shook his head. "I have a master's degree in psychology and had every intention of working in that field. But while I was in college there always seemed to be a poker game going on somewhere in the dorm and I'd join in after I got out of class for the day." He smiled. "After I won everybody's spare change, I figured out I was pretty good at it. Then my roommate suggested that I enter a tournament over in Shreveport." He tied the bags on the back of his gelding's saddle. "I did and the rest, as they say, is history."

As she mounted the mare, she thought about what Lane had told her. Why had she been disappointed when he mentioned that he'd never met a woman who'd made him think about giving up being a professional gambler? She certainly didn't want him to be tempted by her, did she?

"So what do you want to do?" he asked as they rode away from the creek.

Distracted with her disturbing thoughts, she asked, "About what?"

"Are we going to continue on as things are?" He smiled. "You know my take on the situation. I'd like to know yours."

"I'll give it some thought and let you know," she said evasively. She had never been one to make hasty decisions and she wasn't about to start now.

Six

Hurrying down the hall toward the front of the house, Taylor hoped whoever was knocking on the door turned out to be the delivery service with the things she'd shipped to herself from California. But her smile faded when she found Roy Lee standing on the porch.

"Sorry to bother you, Ms. Scott," he said, smiling. "But I was on my way back from a trip to the feed store and I thought I'd check to see if you need me to help you with anything today."

"No, but thank you for asking, Roy Lee," she said, wondering why he wasn't doing whatever work the fore-man had assigned him for the day.

"Okay," he said, looking disappointed. He stood star-ing at her as if waiting for her to issue an invitation to come inside the house.

"Was there anything else, Roy Lee?" she asked, wishing the cowboy would just leave. She didn't want to be rude, but he was making her extremely uncomfortable.

"No. I just wanted to make sure you know I'm available if you need me." He continued to look at her for several long moments before he finally added, "I guess I'll let you get back to whatever you were doing." He started down the steps, then suddenly turned back. "If you do find something you need help with, just call the barn. I'll be more than glad to come back and take care of it for you."

"I'll remember that," she said, watching him walk to the ranch truck he'd parked next to the house.

Closing the door, she felt a chill slide through her. On impulse, she reached down to secure the lock. She wasn't sure what it was about the man, but she didn't trust him.

"Who was that?" Lane asked, coming out of the office.

"Roy Lee," she answered. "He wanted to know if I needed his help with anything today."

Walking over to her, Lane put his arms around her waist. "You know what his problem is, don't you?"

She shook her head as she tried to ignore the warmth that spread from the top of her head all the way to her toes from his touch. "If you have any kind of insight into what he's up to, please enlighten me."

"Roy Lee has a huge crush on you and unless I miss my guess, he's had it since you were teenagers," he said, smiling.

"That's ridiculous," she insisted. "I haven't been here for a visit in several years and besides, I've never given him the slightest bit of encouragement."

Lane grinned. "Let me clue you in on the way this works, babe. When a man finds a woman attractive, he's a lot like a banty rooster strutting around the hen house. He'll do whatever he thinks will get her to notice him. For Roy Lee, it's offering to help you out. He's trying to prove to you that he's handy to have around and that you need him."

"The only thing he's accomplishing is giving me a major case of the creeps," she said, shuddering. "I can't put my finger on what it is about him, but I'm just not comfortable being around him."

Pulling her to him, Lane hugged her close. "I'd be the last person to tell you not to trust your instincts, Taylor. But he's done nothing that would warrant me firing him."

"I'm not saying he should be fired." She rested her head against Lane's broad shoulder. "I just don't want to be around him."

"You don't have to be." He kissed the top of her head. "I'll be here to run interference while I help you practice your poker skills. And as added insurance that he doesn't bother you, I'll have Judd assign him to chores on another part of the ranch."

Feeling a little better about the situation, she tilted her head back to kiss his lean jaw. "Thank you."

"That's completely unacceptable," he said, smiling as he lowered his head. "If you're going to kiss me, I want the real deal."

As his mouth came down on hers, Taylor immediately melted against him. In the past couple of days she'd thought a lot about his suggestion that they acknowledge the magnetic pull between them, but she still wasn't sure what to do. Lane didn't want a relationship any more than she did, but a casual liaison had never been her style.

Unfortunately, it didn't seem that she had a lot of choice in the matter. Every time she was close to Lane, she forgot all the reasons she didn't want to get involved with him or any other man. All she could do was think about the way he made her feel.

When he traced her lips with his tongue and coaxed her to open for him, she gave up on trying to understand why she couldn't resist him and lost herself to the myriad sensations flowing through her. Her blood pulsed through her veins and an empty ache began to pool in her lower belly when he moved his hand to cup her breast. Even through her clothing, his touch had the magical effect of making her feel as if he truly cherished her. But when she felt his hard arousal pressed to her, she had to cling to him for support.

"Have you come to any conclusions on what we should do about this?" he asked, easing away from the kiss.

Gazing up at his handsome face, she shook her head. She would like nothing more than to throw caution to the wind and live for the moment. But that wasn't who she was and she wasn't about to pretend otherwise.

"I don't want you to think that I'm pressuring you, Taylor," he said, tucking a strand of hair that had escaped her ponytail behind her ear. "Nothing is going to happen unless that's what you want. But I'm not going to hide the fact that I want you, either."

They gazed at each other for several long moments before the ringing of the phone intruded. "I'll get that in the office," Lane said, kissing her forehead before he released her to go answer the call.

As she walked back into the kitchen, Taylor nibbled on her lower lip. There wasn't a doubt in her mind that it was just a matter of time before they both reached the limit of their frustration and gave in to the chemistry between them. A thrilling hum vibrated through every part of her at the thought.

Taylor sighed as she removed a roast from the refrigerator and began to cut it into cubes for the beef bourguignon she'd planned to make for their dinner. She only hoped when the moment came that she could keep things in perspective and not let her emotions get the better of her. Otherwise she had a feeling there was a very real chance she could get her heart broken.

After another one of Taylor's delicious dinners, Lane sat at the table watching Taylor glance at the five cards face up on the table between them, then at the two cards she was holding. For the first time since he'd started teaching her how to play, she wasn't giving her hand away with her tells. He couldn't help but be proud of her. She had caught on to the game quickly and her skills were progressing nicely. It wouldn't be too much longer and they would be playing for the ranch. So why did that thought leave him with a keen sense of dread? That was what he wanted, wasn't it?

The sole purpose of him teaching her to play poker was so they could engage in a game for control of the ranch. A game he had every intention of winning. But the thought of Taylor leaving the Lucky Ace to go back to California didn't hold nearly as much appeal as it had a week and a half ago.

"I'm *all in*," she said as she shoved all of her chips to one end of the community cards.

She was betting everything she had on the single hand and the odds were he had her beat. He had a full house, while the best she could hope for was a straight. He fleetingly thought about folding the hand and letting her win, but he'd never thrown a game in his life and she wouldn't want him to do that now. She was determined to win on her own and he admired that. Besides, she needed to learn to consider all the possible hands he could be holding and place her bet accordingly.

Counting out the equivalent number of chips, he added them to the pot. "I call."

He watched her take a deep breath as she turned over her two hold cards. "I have a jack-high straight," she said proudly.

"Very nice hand," he said, smiling. When she started to pull the pile of chips to her side of the table, he shook his head. "Unfortunately, it's not quite good enough." He flipped over his hold cards. "I have a full house. Jacks full of nines."

"Well, drat!" She frowned. "I really thought I had you that time."

He nodded. "You had a good solid hand and a damned good chance of winning. But you also needed to consider that with two jacks on the table, I could be holding a jack and that the other community cards would give me the full house."

"Which was exactly what happened," she said with a sigh.

"Hey, don't feel bad." Standing up, he walked around the table to pull her from her chair and into his arms. "If I'd had the straight, I would have had to consider going all in, too."

She tilted her head slightly. "But you wouldn't have, would you?"

"It depends." He kissed the tip of her nose. "In a tournament with other professional players, there are more cards in play and the odds are better that one of them would have the full house. But with just the two of us, the odds were in your favor of winning with the straight."

"So I didn't make a bad play?" she asked, snuggling against him.

With her delightful body aligned with his, he was finding it hard to draw his next breath, let alone think about playing poker. "No," he finally managed.

"When do you think I'll be ready to play you for the ranch?" she asked, leaning back to look up at him.

"I'd say within the next week or so," he answered evasively. He had a feeling that either way the game went, he would come out feeling as though he'd lost. But he didn't want to think about settling who would live on the ranch. With her in his arms, he had more pleasurable things on his mind. "Why don't we take a break and go out onto the front porch to watch the sun go down?"

"I think I'd like that," she said, giving him a smile that sent his blood pressure up a good ten points.

Ten minutes later, as they sat in the porch swing watching the last traces of daylight fade into the pearl-gray of dusk, Lane held Taylor to his side. They were both silent for some time and he couldn't get over how right it felt to be enjoying something so simple with her.

"Could I ask you something, Lane?" The sound of her soft voice saying his name caused heat to gather in his loins.

"Sure." Turning slightly to face her, he smiled. "What would you like to know?"

"Why did you go ahead and become a psychologist when you had already started playing poker profession-ally?" she asked.

He stared at her a moment before he answered. She had been truthful with him about her situation at home and her parents' constant turmoil, which he knew wasn't easy for her. He supposed it was only fair to tell her why he had chosen to study psychology.

"I wish I could tell you my reasons were noble and that I had wanted to help people. But I can't," he said, shaking his head. "I went into the field for one purely selfish reason. I was looking for answers."

"May I ask what you were questioning?" she said cautiously.

He didn't think about his biological father all that much anymore. After he'd been sent to live on the Last

Chance Ranch, Hank Calvert had become his dad and had been more of a parent to him than his real father ever had. Ken Donaldson had been too busy wining and dining clients in order to climb the corporate ladder in the world of high finance to be a good husband and father.

"I told you that my father died a couple of years before my mother," he said, choosing his words carefully. When she nodded, he went on. "What I didn't say was that he died by his own hand."

"Oh, Lane, I had no idea," she said, hugging him. "That must have been horrible for you and your mother."

He did his best to swallow the anger that always accompanied thinking about his father's death. "I went into psychology because I wanted to understand what he might have been thinking and how he could cause his family that kind of devastation."

She laid her soft hand on top of his. "Did you find the answers you were looking for?"

"Not really." Shrugging, he twined their fingers. "It would have been easier to accept if it had been something he couldn't help, like an undiagnosed chemical imbalance or some other psychosis that impaired his reasoning. But it wasn't."

"Did he leave an explanation why he thought death was his only answer?" she asked.

Lane clenched his jaw until his teeth hurt as he nodded. "My father selfishly took his own life because he was a coward." Unable to sit still, he released her and stood up to walk over to the porch rail. Gripping the board so tightly he wouldn't have been surprised if he'd left dents in the wood, he kept his back to her as he finished. "The note was with him when I came home from school and found him hanging from one of the rafters in the garage."

"Oh, my God, Lane! That must have been so awful for you," she said, her tone quavering.

"It was a sight that I'll never forget, as long as I live," he admitted. He took a deep breath. "He explained in the note that he was facing legal issues over some bad financial decisions and couldn't bear the loss of his reputation and financial ruin because of it." He paused a moment before he could force words past the resentment that choked him. "It was all about him and his pride. He didn't consider what it would do to my mother and me. Either that, or he just didn't give a damn about all of the emotional pain taking his own life would put us through."

"I'm so sorry, Lane," Taylor said, placing her hand on his back. Wrapped up in his anger, he hadn't even heard her get up from the swing. "I didn't mean to bring up something so painful for you."

Turning, he took her in his arms and held her to him like a lifeline. "It's all right. You had no way of knowing," he said, closing his eyes as he tried to wipe away the last traces of the memory. "It's been over twenty years and it's not something I allow myself to think about all that often. As far as I'm concerned, it's in the past, where it needs to stay."

When she framed his face with her palms and raised up on tiptoe to kiss him, his heart slammed against his rib cage. The kiss was brief and one of comfort more than anything else, but a need stronger than anything he'd ever experienced shot through him.

Lane couldn't have stopped himself if he'd tried as he pulled her more fully against him to deepen the caress. Heat streaked straight to the region south of his belt buckle as he explored her and reacquainted himself with her sweetness. He might not have known her for all that long, but he sensed that Taylor could very easily become his anchor—the one person who would renew his strength and help keep him grounded.

At any other time, the thought would have scared the hell out of him and would have sent him running as hard and fast as he could go in the opposite direction. But all he could think of, all he wanted, was to forget the ugliness of his past and lose himself in the beauty he knew he would find in her arms.

Her soft moan when he moved his hand to her breast and the way she pressed herself into his touch caused his heart to race and his body to harden so fast it left him feeling light-headed. He'd never been as aroused as he was at that moment and he knew he was going to go out of his mind if they didn't make love soon.

Easing away from the kiss, he took one deep breath after another in an effort to relieve some of the tension gripping him. "I think I'll go...for a walk," he finally managed.

"W-why?" Taylor's eyes were bright with desire, and the passion coloring her creamy cheeks was almost his undoing. Nothing would please him more than to see her look like that as he sank himself deep inside of her.

"I need you, Taylor," he said roughly. "And if I don't walk away now, I'm not going to be able to."

Instead of telling him to take a long hike off a short pier as he expected her to, she gazed up at him for several long seconds before she whispered, "I want you, too, Lane. I know it's probably not wise. But I do."

When Lane pulled her to him, shivers of anticipation coursed through her. Taylor wasn't about to think of the consequences of making love with Lane. He wanted her, and at the moment, she needed him more than she needed her next breath.

"Are you sure, Taylor?" he asked, kissing the side of her neck. "I don't want you feeling pressured. I'd rather go for a jog and take a cold shower than have you regret making love with me."

"The only thing I'll regret is if we don't make love," she said truthfully.

She watched him close his eyes and take a deep breath then, taking her by the hand, he led her into the house. Neither said a word as they climbed the stairs and walked down the hall toward their rooms. She wasn't at all surprised when he opened the door to his bedroom and stood back for her to enter. Very few men were comfortable amid ruffles and lace and besides, from everything she'd heard when she and her friends talked about relationships, men had a thing about taking women to their beds.

Looking around, she realized that her first impression of Lane had been correct. He was not only a Texan from the top of his Resistol all the way to his big leather boots, he was a cowboy through and through. He had painted the walls a soothing sage that complimented the Native American artwork and printed drapes perfectly.

As she continued to peruse the room, her gaze landed on the rustic king-size bed and her heart skipped a beat. The natural shades of red in the cedar logs were in sharp contrast to the black satin pillows and comforter. His choice of bedding wasn't what she expected, considering the rest of the decor. But as she stared at the bedding, she had to admit that the sheer sexiness of it suited the man she was about to make love with.

When he slipped his arms around her waist from behind, she leaned back against him. "It's all right if you're having second thoughts," he said, nuzzling the side of her neck. "I don't want you doing anything you aren't comfortable with."

Turning in his arms, she shook her head. "I'm not having second thoughts," she said, wondering if what she was about to tell him would have him changing his mind. "I'm not on any kind of birth control."

"Don't worry, babe. I'll take care of everything," he said, kissing the side of her neck.

Shivering from the delightful feeling of his mouth on her sensitive skin, she nibbled on her lower lip. "There's something else."

"What?" He sounded distracted as he bent down to remove her tennis shoes and his boots.

"I've…never done this before."

He went completely still a moment before he straightened to face her. "You're a virgin." It wasn't a question. He looked as if the concept was completely foreign to him.

"Yes. I believe that's what a woman is called when she's never had sex," she said defensively.

He looked doubtful. "You're twenty-eight."

"Yes, I am, and you're thirty-four." She frowned. "So what's your point?"

"I just thought you would have met someone you wanted to be with before now," he said, gently touching her cheek.

"I didn't say I haven't been tempted a few times," she admitted. "I just never felt I was with the right guy."

"And you think I'm the right man?" he asked huskily as he lightly ran his index finger along her jaw.

Taylor nodded. She couldn't explain it, but making love with Lane just felt right.

"If I take your virginity, it's not something I can give back, babe," he warned, capturing her gaze with his.

"I—I...know." The look in his dark brown eyes and the intimate deepening of his voice made it hard to catch her breath.

She watched him close his eyes a moment before taking a deep breath. When he opened his eyes, he stared down at her. "I should send you across the hall to your room."

"But you aren't going to do that, are you?" she asked, her heart thumping so hard against her ribs, she thought it might burst.

Lane slowly shook his head. "I'd like to do the right thing, but I want you too damned much to be gallant about this." He lowered his head to give her a kiss so tender it brought tears to her eyes. "Are you really sure this is what you want, Taylor? If not, say so now."

Reaching up, she took her hair down from her ponytail. "There are a lot of things I'm not sure of, but right
now making love with you isn't one of them."

When she tugged her tank top from the waistband
of her jeans and started to take it off, he smiled and
caught her hands in his. "I can take things from here."

Normally, she was very independent and wanted to
do things for herself. But whether it was the situation
or the man, allowing Lane to take the lead felt completely natural.

"I want you to tell me if anything we do makes you
uncomfortable or if you change your mind," he said as
he slowly lifted her top over her head.

Instead of reaching for the front clasp of her bra as
she thought he would, he unsnapped the front of his
chambray shirt and tossed it on top of her turquoise tank
top. The sight of his well-developed chest and abdomi-
nal muscles sent a wave of goose bumps shimmering
over her skin. Lane's body was absolutely beautiful.

Unable to stop herself, she ran her fingers along the
ridges and valleys of his smooth skin. "You don't work
out, do you?"

He shook his head as he allowed her to explore the
well-defined sinew. "Any exercise I get is either from
ranch work or shuffling cards," he said, his low chuckle
seeming to vibrate all the way to her soul.

Fascinated by the contours of his upper body, it took a
moment for her to realize that he had unhooked her bra.
He parted it and slid the straps over her shoulders and
down her arms. "You're absolutely beautiful, Taylor."

Cupping her breasts with his palms, his tender touch

sent a wave of heat flowing through her and she closed her eyes as she savored the erotic feeling. "I...that... what you're doing. It feels...amazing," she said, suddenly extremely short of breath.

"It's only going to get better, babe," he whispered as he lowered his head to take one of her nipples into his mouth.

The feel of his tongue circling and teasing her while his thumb gently chafed the other tight tip caused her body to pulse with a need stronger than anything she'd ever experienced. When he lifted his head to pay homage to her other breast, Taylor's heart sped up and her knees felt as if they were made of rubber.

Unsure how much longer her legs would support her, she placed her hands on his chest to brace herself. The feel of his warm masculine skin and his heart beating in time with her own sent a delicious heat coursing through her.

"Are you doing okay?" he asked as he reached for the button at the top of her jeans.

"I—I...think so," she answered, wondering if she would ever breathe normally again.

His appreciative smile as he eased the zipper of her jeans down made her feel as if she was the most cherished woman on earth. "Tell me what you're feeling."

"Warm and—" She paused as she searched for the right word to describe how she felt. "—restless. And my knees feel weak."

Instead of taking her jeans and panties off, he surprised her when he stepped back to unbuckle his belt. As she watched him unfasten his jeans, then slide them and his boxer briefs down his long, muscular legs, she realized he was taking the rest of his clothes off first in order to make her feel a bit more comfortable. An unfamiliar tightness spread through her chest at his thoughtful consideration.

When he kicked the rest of the garments toward the growing pile of their clothing, her heart stopped then took off beating double time. His body wasn't merely beautiful, it was magnificent.

As she appreciated his taut physique, her gaze traveled from his impossibly wide shoulders down his washboard abdomen and beyond. But her heart stalled and her eyes widened at the sight of his arousal and the heaviness below. Although she didn't have any experience and couldn't make an accurate comparison, she sensed that Lane wasn't a small man.

Her concern must have been apparent, because he closed the distance between them. He took her into his arms, kissing her tenderly. "We'll fit together just fine, babe."

Most of the time, she took exception to men calling her anything but her name. She felt it was insincere and condescending. When Lane used the endearment, though, it was genuine and made her feel as if she was truly special to him.

But she abandoned all speculation when he ran his hands along her sides, then beneath the waistbands of her jeans and panties. Capturing her eyes with his, he slowly caressed her hips and thighs as he slipped the denim and lace down her legs to her feet. When she stepped out of them, he straightened and stood back, caressing her with his heated gaze.

"You're...perfect," he said, taking her into his arms.

The feel of having all barriers between them removed, the excitement of skin against skin, caused every nerve in her body to tingle to life. Gasping from the intense desire coursing through her, Taylor wrapped her arms around Lane's waist to keep from melting into a puddle.

"Let's lie down," he said, kissing her collarbone.

When he pulled back the covers, she got into bed and marveled at how sensual the black satin sheets felt against her bare skin. It seemed to heighten the anticipation of what they were about to do. As she watched Lane remove a foil packet from the bedside table and tuck it under his pillow, she shivered from the wave of desire that swept through her.

"We're going to go slow," he said, stretching out on the bed beside her. Reaching to draw her to him, he sealed their lips in a kiss so poignant that it stole her breath. "And I'm going to try to make this as easy for you as I can, babe. But I'm afraid our lovemaking tonight won't be as pleasant for you as it will be the next time we make love."

"I know it can't be helped," she said truthfully. "But I also know you'll do everything you can to ease the discomfort."

Even though she'd had her doubts about him in the beginning, she knew it was true. The realization might have disturbed her if she'd had the time to think about it, but Lane was too busy creating a need in her like no other.

"You have no idea how much your trust means to me," he said, his eyes darkening to a deep coffee-brown.

Lowering his head, he kissed his way from the pulse at the base of her throat to the valley between her breasts and Taylor lost the ability to think. At the moment, she was too caught up in the way Lane was making her feel.

As he nipped and teased his way down her abdomen to her navel, the exquisite fluttering in the most feminine part of her transformed into the empty ache of desire and she knew for certain it was one only Lane could satisfy. But when he slid his palm over her hip, then down her thigh and back up to touch her intimately, she felt as if she would burn to a cinder.

"P-please…Lane."

"Does that feel good, Taylor?" he asked, rising up on one elbow to stare down at her.

"Y-yes…but it's making…me crazy," she said, grasping the sheet on either side of her.

"Do you want me to stop?" He kissed her and held her close as he continued his gentle stroking.

"N-no…I need…"

Her voice trailed off as she felt waves of pleasure begin to course through her. Moaning, she moved restlessly against him as the delicious sensations spread to every part of her being then slowly released her from the tension, allowing her to float back to reality.

"I've got you, Taylor," he whispered as he kissed the hollow below her ear.

"T-that was…amazing," she said, trying to catch her breath.

"I wanted to make sure you experienced some degree of pleasure this first time," he said, smiling. "That's just a glimpse of the way it will feel when we make love again."

Her chest swelled with emotion. Lane was one of the most giving men she'd ever known and she couldn't believe she hadn't seen it before now.

Placing her hands on his lean cheeks, she kissed him. "Thank you, Lane." She felt his body stir against her leg and she knew his need was as great as hers had been.

"I'm going to love you now," he said, reaching beneath his pillow for the foil packet. He quickly removed the condom, arranged their protection, then nudged her knees apart and rose over her. "I promise I'll be as gentle as I can, babe."

"I know," she said, closing her eyes and bracing herself for the unknown.

"Open your eyes, Taylor," he commanded as he positioned himself to enter her.

When she did as he directed, the look on his face caused her body to tingle and her heart to beat double time. He eased his body forward with such tenderness in his expression that she was robbed of the ability to think, much less worry about any discomfort she might feel.

As his blunt tip slowly slid into her, Lane held her gaze with his. When he breached her barrier, she barely noticed. So caught up in the moment was she that she only experienced mild discomfort when he sank into her completely and gathered her to him.

Kissing her, he asked, "Are you okay?"

She nodded. The renewed desire filling her due to the intimacy they were sharing rendered her speechless.

"I'd like to give you more time to adjust." His voice sounded strained and she could hear the toll his restraint was taking on him. "But I've wanted you since the night we met, babe."

"And I want you again, too," she admitted softly.

"I'll try to be gentle," he said as he began to rock softly against her.

She immediately responded and in no time, Taylor felt herself climbing toward the pinnacle of fulfillment. But this time the feeling was different. Having Lane deep inside of her, his body coaxing hers to join him in the wonderment of the moment, was her undoing. Clinging to him to keep from being lost, she gave in to the need he created within her. Once again, she experienced the amazement of complete release.

A moment later, she felt Lane grow still before he thrust into her one final time. As he groaned her name, his body pulsed and she knew he had found his own relief from the delicious tension.

When he collapsed on top of her, she wrapped her arms around his shoulders and held him to her. She had never met anyone as selfless as Lane or as patient. He had done everything he possibly could to make her first time a pleasurable experience. And at no small cost to himself. She'd seen the strain on his handsome face and knew he had put off his own satisfaction until she could find hers.

"Are you okay?" he asked when he finally raised his head. "I tried not to—"

"Really, I'm fine," she interrupted. "That was wonderful." She kissed his shoulder. "You were wonderful."

Levering himself to her side, he wrapped his arms around her and pulled her to him. "Thank you."

"What for?"

"For trusting me to be the first man to touch you and make love to you," he said, sounding as if he truly meant what he said.

With her head pillowed on his shoulder, she kissed his lean jaw. "I'm glad I waited," she admitted. She started to add that she was glad she had waited for him, but the thought startled her.

Why *had* she given herself to him? Why had she been willing to trust Lane with her body when she still wasn't entirely certain he hadn't somehow manipulated her grandfather?

In her heart, she knew why she had given herself to Lane after resisting temptation for years. Making love with him had felt natural and right. She didn't want to think about what that might mean. She wasn't sure she was ready for the answers.

But as she drifted off to sleep, she knew that if she was honest with herself, she would have to admit she was starting to fall for Lane and there didn't seem to be anything she could do to stop it. More importantly, she didn't really want to.

Seven

The following morning when Lane came downstairs for breakfast, he didn't hesitate to walk up behind Taylor, wrap his arms around her waist and kiss the hollow beneath her ear. "How are you feeling this morning?" he asked, loving the way her lithe body felt aligned with his.

She set down the mixing bowl she had been holding and turned to face him, her smile causing a serious hitch in his breathing. "I'm wonderful." She raised up on tiptoe to give him a quick kiss. "But I'm afraid breakfast is going to be a little late. It seems that someone kept me up last night and I ended up oversleeping this morning."

"I slept pretty well myself," he admitted, nodding. After they made love, he'd held her close and enjoyed the first good night's sleep he'd had in almost two weeks. "In fact, I slept so well, I think we should try the same arrangement tonight."

He felt a shiver course through her. "Is lovemaking always that amazing?" she asked, melting against him.

His body responded to hers so quickly that it took a moment for him to find his voice. How could he tell her that he'd never experienced anything as exciting or meaningful as what they'd shared together? Or that he had a feeling he never would experience the same with any other woman? It wasn't something he had allowed himself to think about because he wasn't sure he was ready for the answers.

"It's only going to get better, babe," he answered evasively.

Her eyes widened. "Really?"

Before he could reply, the phone rang. "This early it has to be one of my crazy-ass brothers," he said, kissing the tip of her nose. "I'll take it in the study."

As he walked down the hall, Lane decided that he wasn't all that upset by the interruption. He needed to give some serious thought to why he felt Taylor was the only woman who could excite him in ways he'd never dreamed possible.

"Talk to me, T.J.," he said, after checking the caller ID.

"You sound like you just drew an inside straight," T.J. said, laughing. "I guess you got everything settled with your new partner, huh?"

"Not exactly." Lane hesitated a moment before he

admitted, "We'll be playing a game of poker for control of the ranch in another week or so."

"Well, something has you in a good mood. You sound like you just got la—" T.J. grew quiet and Lane knew his brother had figured out why he was in such a good mood. "You do know you're playing with fire, don't you, bro?"

"Don't worry about me," Lane said, irritated by his brother's perceptiveness. "What did you need?"

"Uh-oh."

"What?" Lane demanded.

"You're pissed off. That tells me there's more going on than just a little friendly fun with your business partner," T.J. said knowingly. "So when do we get to meet the future Mrs. Donaldson?"

"Shut up and tell me why you called or I'm going to hang up," Lane snapped. He loved his brother, but he suspected that T.J.'s observations were hitting too close to home.

"All right, all right. Simmer down, Freud. I've got a heap of trouble brewing with that woman next door. Her stallion keeps jumping the fence to romance my mares and I need you guys to help me out," T.J. said, his voice tight with anger.

"How many more of your brood mares has he bred this time?" Lane asked, understanding his brother's frustration. T.J. raised championship reining horses and having a rogue stallion impregnate his brood stock would cost him hundreds of thousands of dollars and set his breeding program back several years.

"He covered four more of my mares yesterday before

I discovered him in the pasture," T.J. said disgustedly. "That makes ten in the past four months."

"What can the guys and I do to help?" Lane asked, knowing he and his brothers would all drop whatever they were doing to help out T.J.

Over the past year or so, T.J. had tried talking to the woman about checking and mending her fences more often. When that failed, he had requested that she keep the stud on another part of her ranch. Since that hadn't netted the desired result, it appeared that he'd come up with another plan.

"I figure with the six of us and my two hired hands, we can get a six-foot-tall woven-wire fence put up between my place and hers by nightfall," T.J. said determinedly.

"That should take care of your problem," Lane agreed. "I'll be there right after breakfast."

"Thanks, Lane," T.J. said sincerely. "I owe you one."

"See you in about two hours," Lane added, ending the call.

As he walked back into the kitchen, Taylor had just set two plates of eggs Benedict with smoked salmon, hash browns and fresh mixed fruit at their places at the table. "It looks delicious," he said, holding her chair for her. "I haven't eaten this well in years."

"Just wait until you see what I plan for dinner," she said, smiling.

"I'm afraid I'll probably be late for dinner tonight," he said, taking a drink of the freshly squeezed orange juice by his plate. "My brothers and I are going to help

T.J. put up a boundary fence between his place and another ranch today."

"Is he having problems with his neighbor?" she asked, sounding genuinely interested.

Telling her about the woman's stallion and the cost to T.J.'s breeding program, he gave her an apologetic smile. "I'm sorry, but I won't be able to help you practice playing poker today, either."

"Don't worry about that," she said, placing her soft hand on his forearm. "I realize how important it is to stop the neighbor's horse from visiting your brother's mares. I'll just plan to have dinner ready a couple of hours later than usual."

Lane took hold of her hand and scooted his chair back so he could pull her over to sit on his lap. "I promise I'll be back as soon as I can."

She kissed him and he thought he might go up in a puff of smoke at the need the simple caress created within him. "While you're helping your brother, I'm going to call the shipping company and find out where my things are. They should have been here at the end of last week. If I can run them down, I'm going to spend the day putting everything away."

"So you're that sure you're going to win the big game?" he teased.

Grinning, she nodded. "I'm going to knock your socks off."

"You accomplished that last night, babe." He kissed her, then set her on her feet and rose from his chair. "I think I'd better get going."

"But you haven't finished breakfast," she said, looking at the uneaten food on his plate.

"As delicious as I know those eggs would be, what I'd really like to have isn't on the menu," he said, going over to the cabinet to get a travel mug to fill with coffee.

"I could make you something different," she said, looking a bit uncertain.

Walking back over to her, he set the mug on the table and took her in his arms. "What I want for breakfast involves you and me, upstairs with our clothes off," he said, kissing her soundly. When he raised his head, he gazed down into her passion-glazed emerald eyes. "But I have work to do, and I can't afford to get distracted. I'll see you this evening, Taylor."

Forcing himself to put one boot in front of the other, he grabbed his hat from the peg beside the door and walked out of the house without looking back. He had to. Otherwise, he would have carried her upstairs and spent the entire day making love to the woman who was quickly becoming as important to him as his next breath.

His heart hammered hard against his rib cage as he climbed into his truck and started the engine. Now he definitely knew he needed some time away from Taylor in order to do a little self-analysis and figure out what the hell he was going to do about the feelings he'd discovered.

Taylor alternated between outright fury and fear as she waited for Lane to return home. By the time she saw his headlights cut through the darkness as his truck came down the road leading to the house, she was surprised she hadn't worn a trench in the hardwood floor from her pacing. Deciding not to wait until he came into the house, she unlocked the back door, marched out onto the porch and down the steps.

"We have a problem," she said when he opened the driver's door. As angry as she was, relief flowed through her at the sight of him. Now that Lane was home, she felt safer and more secure than she had the entire day.

"What's wrong?" he asked, getting out of the truck.

"It's Roy Lee," she said, unable to keep from shuddering. Just saying the man's name gave her a case of the creeps.

"Are you all right?" Lane demanded, placing his hands on her shoulders.

His concern was touching, but at the moment she needed to tell him what had happened. "We have to fire Roy Lee Wilks," she stated flatly.

"Why?" Lane's eyes narrowed, making him look dangerous. "What's he done this time?"

"He stole all of the things I shipped from California." Every time she thought of what the cowboy had done, a fresh wave of anger burned through her. "When I called the shipping company, I was told that they had delivered the containers last week and Roy Lee was the one who signed for them."

"What did he do with them?" Lane asked, propping his fists on his hips and turning to stare hard at the bunkhouse.

"I don't know." She shook her head. "I haven't talked to him about it."

"I'm glad you didn't confront him," Lane said, putting his arms around her and pulling her to his chest.

"I wanted to talk to you first and see how you thought I should handle it," she admitted.

"You're not going to take care of this," he said firmly. "I am."

She frowned. "But it was my things he took. I should be the one to talk to him about it."

"I understand that you want to have your say and I respect that," he said, as if choosing his words carefully. "But in this case, I wouldn't advise it." When she started to protest, he held up one hand to stop her. "Consider this. Roy Lee's behavior wouldn't, by any stretch of the imagination, be considered stable. I'm not saying he's dangerous, but that's one chance I'm not willing to take."

"What are you going to do?" she asked, suddenly concerned that they might be dealing with more than she'd realized.

"I'm going over to the bunkhouse to find out where Roy Lee put your things, then I'm going to tell him to pack his gear and get off the property," Lane answered. He pointed toward the house. "I want you to go inside and lock the door."

"I've had them locked all day, even though I knew he was working away from the house with the other men," she admitted.

He nodded. "Go on inside while I take care of getting rid of Roy Lee."

"Be careful," she said as a shudder ran through her.

"Don't worry about me, babe. I'll be fine." He gave her a quick kiss. "I may not be in for a while. I'm going to make sure Roy Lee gets everything packed and loaded into his truck. Then I'm going to see that he drives away."

An hour later, Taylor breathed a sigh of relief when Lane used his keys to let himself into the house. "Did you have any trouble getting Roy Lee to leave?" she asked, walking over to wrap her arms around Lane's waist. His arms immediately closed around her and pulled her close.

"No. At first, he tried to talk his way out of it, but when I told him we knew that he had signed for the boxes, he explained that he stored them in the hayloft in the barn." Lane shook his head. "He was waiting for a chance to bring them to you when I wasn't around."

"I don't like the sound of that," she said, snuggling against his solid chest.

"He wanted to ask you to go dancing with him and decided that he'd have a better chance of you agreeing if you thought he'd found your missing things." Sounding tired, Lane finished, "Roy Lee is socially awkward and clearly has a few issues with reasoning, but I still don't think he meant any harm. He was just trying to impress you because of a deep infatuation."

"Is that your professional opinion?" she asked, leaning back to look up at him.

He grinned. "Sure, if you want to call it that."

For the first time since he had returned from helping his brother, she noticed how exhausted he looked. "I'm so sorry you had to deal with this, Lane, especially after such a long day. You look like you're ready to drop in your tracks. I'm afraid I was too upset to make the dinner I had planned, but while you take a shower, I could make some sandwiches for us."

"That sounds good," he said, yawning. He kissed her forehead, then stepped back to unsnap his sleeves and the front of his shirt. "I won't be long."

While Lane went upstairs, Taylor set to work and in no time had several sandwiches prepared for them. When she looked at the clock on the stove, she frowned. Lane should have finished with his shower and been back downstairs by now.

Deciding to check on him and find out what was keeping him, she headed to his bedroom. She started to knock on his door and discovered it was partially open. "Lane?"

Her heart skipped several beats when she found him lying on the bed sound asleep beside his clean clothes. His nude body was every bit as magnificent as she remembered from the night before and even completely relaxed, his physique was impressive.

Taylor's chest filled with an emotion she was determined to ignore as she moved his clothes, then reached to pull the comforter over him. He had been thoroughly exhausted from working on his brother's fence all day, yet when he returned home he had insisted on coming to her rescue and dealing with Roy Lee.

Quietly leaving the room, she went back downstairs to the kitchen. She wrapped and put away the sandwiches she'd made in the refrigerator, then she cleaned the kitchen. After checking the door to make sure it was locked, she turned out the light and headed back upstairs. When she reached the doors to their bedrooms, she looked from one to the other. She knew where she should sleep. But that wasn't where she wanted to be.

Entering her bedroom, she changed into a nightshirt, then walked across the hall, entered Lane's room and climbed into bed beside him. Even in sleep, he turned toward her to put his arm over her.

She refused to dwell on why it seemed so right to be sleeping in his arms. It was where she wanted to be and felt as natural as taking her next breath. Besides, she was tired of fighting what she had suspected for the past couple of days. Whether she wanted it to be true or not, she was falling head over heels for Lane Donaldson.

Three days after the incident with Roy Lee, Lane found himself taking a deep fortifying breath as he parked his truck beside his brothers' and got out to walk around and open the passenger door for Taylor. Facing an entire day of listening to his brothers rib him about his relationship with his new business partner was about as appealing as trying to climb a barbed-wire fence buck naked. But there hadn't been any question about him attending the family dinner to welcome his new niece, nor had he considered—not even for a second— not bringing Taylor with him to the gathering.

"I hope the gift I got for the baby is something they need," she said when he helped her down from the truck.

"They'll love it," he said, knowing Ryder and Summer would be extremely appreciative of Taylor's thoughtfulness. He and his brothers had all done well after college and had become extremely wealthy, but thanks to their foster father, they had their priorities straight. They remembered what was important in life.

As they walked across the yard, he could tell that Taylor was apprehensive about meeting his family. He could understand her insecurities. But she had nothing to fear. They were going to love her just as much as...he did?

His heart stalled and he wasn't sure he'd ever breathe again.

Where the hell had that come from? And why of all times did it have to occur to him right now?

"Lane, are you all right?" Taylor asked, her concern evident.

"Uh, yeah, I'm fine," he finally managed, even though he was struggling to assimilate his new self-awareness.

"Hey there, bro!" Nate called from the gathering of men on the covered patio. "We've got a beer over here with your name on it."

"Glad you could make it, Lane," Ryder said, walking over to them.

"You know I wouldn't miss it," Lane answered.

Completely ignoring Lane, his brother turned toward Taylor. "We talked on the phone the morning my little Katie was born and I'm happy to finally meet you. I'm Ryder McClain, this big lug's better-looking brother."

"You wish," Lane shot back, forcing a grin.

He would just have to deal with the discovery about his newfound feelings later. Right now, he needed to concentrate on hiding them before one of the other men figured out what was going on with him. And there wasn't a doubt in his mind that if he wasn't careful, one of them would. That was one of the hazards of knowing each other so well.

"Nice to see you again, Taylor." Nate laughed as he handed Lane a bottle of beer. "And don't listen to these two sidewinders. They both know I'm better-looking than the two of them combined."

"That's just what we let you think, Nate," T.J. said, stepping forward. "Hi, Taylor. I'm T.J."

When he shifted the baby in his arms to his shoulder, Sam smiled and nodded. "I'm Sam and this is my son, little Hank. We're all happy you decided to join our celebration."

"Thank you for inviting me," Taylor said, smiling. "It's nice getting to know all of you."

"Sam, do you want me to take little Hank and get him down for a nap? Dinner will be ready in about ten minutes," Bria said from the back door. When she noticed Taylor standing beside him, she smiled. "Lane, why didn't you show Taylor inside? I'm sure she'd rather talk to me, Summer and Mariah than listen to you men discuss your cattle or argue about which bucking bull you think will be champion this year."

Placing his hand on her back, Lane walked Taylor over to the door. "Taylor this is Sam's wife, Bria. She's the glue that holds us all together." He kissed Bria's cheek. "We all love her for it, too."

"Come on inside," Bria said, hugging Taylor. She took the baby from her husband and motioned for Taylor to follow her. "I'll introduce you to my sister, Mariah, and Ryder's wife, Summer."

As Bria took Taylor inside to get acquainted with the other two women, Lane rejoined his brothers. Looking around, he asked, "Where's Jaron?"

Ryder nodded toward the road. "Here he comes now."

When Jaron parked and got out of his truck, they all greeted him much like they'd greeted Lane.

"Mariah is in the house with the other women if you want to go in and tell her you're here, Jaron," Sam said, grinning from ear to ear.

"Stuff it, Rafferty," Jaron shot back as he accepted the beer T.J. handed him. "She's probably still pissed off at me anyway."

"If you don't stop dragging your ass and ask that girl out, you're going to miss your chance," Nate advised.

"Is that what happened when you stopped seeing that little blonde down in Waco?" Jaron asked, giving Nate a knowing look.

"That's different and you know it," Nate said, his expression turning serious. Glaring at Jaron, he shook his head. "That was a low blow and not something I expected from my best friend."

Lane and the other four men looked from one brother to the other. Jaron and Nate had been best friends since meeting at the Last Chance Ranch and they still traveled the rodeo circuit together. Their personalities were completely different, but they had always seemed to balance each other out. While Jaron was quiet and brooding, Nate was outgoing and rarely encountered a situation he couldn't joke his way out of. Nate could always bring Jaron out of his shell and Jaron helped keep Nate grounded. But this was the first time any of them had seen tension between the two men.

"Look, I'm sorry, Nate," Jaron apologized, looking contrite. "It's just that I don't want to talk about Mariah. I'm too old for her and that's that."

Nate nodded. "Apology accepted, bro."

"Here we go again," T.J. said, shaking his head. "Methuselah is back to his old self."

Just when Lane thought he was in the clear and wouldn't have to dodge his brothers' questions or listen to their good-natured speculation about his relationship with Taylor, Ryder asked, "So what's the story with you and Taylor?"

"Yeah, when are you supposed to play the poker game that will decide which one of you gets control of the Lucky Ace?" Sam asked.

"I'll be setting that up for next week," Lane answered, glancing toward the house. What was taking so long for the women to call them in for dinner?

"You know there is a way for both of you to keep the ranch," T.J. said, rocking back on his heels.

Lane knew where his brother was going with that train of thought and he didn't care for it one damned bit. "I'm not going to marry the woman just to keep the ranch."

"So you'll marry her for other reasons?" Ryder asked, laughing.

Taking a swig of his beer, Lane almost choked. "I don't ever expect to get married."

"Never say never, bro," Ryder said, tempting Lane

to wipe away his brother's ear-to-ear grin with a good right hook. "If you'll remember, I said that just before I woke up and figured out that Summer was the best thing that ever happened to me." He laughed. "After that, I couldn't put my ring on her finger fast enough."

"That was different," Lane said stubbornly, shaking his head.

"I've got a hundred bucks that says Lane and Taylor are married by the Fourth of July," T.J. said, laughing like a damned hyena.

"I say it'll be next month," Nate said, digging in his pocket for the money to place his bet.

"I'll take Labor Day," Jaron stated.

"Who's going to take care of the prize pool?" Sam asked.

"I'll hold onto it," Ryder volunteered.

While his brothers placed their bets on when they thought he and Taylor would be tying the knot, Lane checked his watch. Groaning, he shook his head. He and Taylor hadn't been there more than thirty minutes and his brothers already had them walking down the aisle. No doubt about it. It was going to be one of the longest evenings of his life.

After dinner, Taylor laughed as she watched the five proud uncles argue over who would be the first to hold their new niece.

"I'm the most experienced at holding a baby," Sam said, his tone practical. "I think that makes me the obvious choice."

"Yeah, but I have a way with females," Nate argued. "If she starts to cry, I can charm her into a good mood."

T.J. rolled his eyes as he shook his head. "That goofy grin of yours would scare the bejesus out of her. I should be the one to hold little Katie first."

"What makes you say that, T.J.?" Jaron asked, frowning. "You can't even get along with that neighbor lady of yours. What makes you think you can do any better with a baby girl?"

As she watched the men argue their cases, Taylor noticed Lane quietly scoot his chair back, rise to his feet and walk to the head of the table to take the baby from Ryder. "You all just keep on arguing," Lane said, sounding smug as he cradled the infant to his broad chest. "In the meantime, I'm going to get acquainted with our new niece."

"Now see what you did?" Nate complained to T.J. "Lane's getting to hold Katie first."

"Me?" T.J. shook his head. "I didn't do anything. You were the one…"

While the two brothers bickered good-naturedly, Taylor's pulse skipped a beat as she watched Lane with the tiny pink bundle in his arms. Unlike a lot of men, he looked completely natural and at ease holding the baby. What was there about a big, strong man gently holding an infant that melted a woman's heart? More importantly, why was her chest tightening with emotion?

She had never given having children a second thought, nor had she ever thought a baby would be in her future. But something about watching Lane with the little girl had her wondering what it would be like to see him holding their baby.

Her heart stalled and she had to set her iced tea glass back on the table to keep from dropping it. What in the world had brought that thought to mind? She wasn't actually daydreaming of becoming *that* involved with Lane, was she?

When he looked up to see her watching him, his smile made her catch her breath. "Taylor, have you had the chance to hold little Katie yet?"

"N-no," she said, shaking her head. "Your brothers should have their turn first."

"We don't mind." Nate spoke up, smiling. "Ladies first."

"That's right," T.J. agreed. "We'll all have our chance and before you know it, she'll have us wrapped around her little finger just like little Hank does."

To Taylor's utter disbelief, Lane walked over and placed the infant in her arms, then sat down in the chair at the dining room table beside her. "I'm going to be her favorite uncle," he stated, resting his arm along the back of her chair.

"I've never held a baby before," she said, marveling at how tiny and sweet the child was.

"Never?" Bria asked, her tone filled with disbelief.

"I don't have siblings and none of my friends have children," Taylor answered as she gazed down at the sleeping little girl. "This is nice."

When she looked up to see the smile on Lane's face, a warm feeling spread throughout her body. "You're a natural," he whispered, tenderly touching the baby's tiny hand.

"Now we know who to call when little Hank is fussy and I'm busy with the livestock and you're trying to fix supper, Bria," Sam said, laughing.

"I'll put the Lucky Ace's number on speed dial with Mariah's." Bria laughed as she rose to take her and her husband's plates into the kitchen.

"Taylor, it looks like you and I have found ourselves a couple of babysitting jobs," Mariah said with a laugh.

"There's only one problem," Taylor said, nodding. "Beyond holding a baby, I don't know the first thing about taking care of one."

Summer smiled as she confided, "I didn't either until Katie was born. Thank goodness for motherly instincts. Not to mention all the parenting sites on the internet."

When little Hank started making discontented noises from his baby carrier, Bria handed Sam a baby bottle. "Why don't you men take the babies into the family room? After you feed little Hank you can all argue over who gets to hold the munchkins while we clean up the kitchen."

Taylor handed the newborn back to Lane as she rose from her chair to help the women clear the table. As she watched them file out of the dining room, she couldn't help but feel envious of the closeness they all shared. They might have started out on a rocky path in life, but the men had bonded into a family that was as strong and loving as any she had ever seen.

"I noticed that you and Jaron still aren't speaking,"

Summer said to Mariah as Taylor entered the kitchen. "You still haven't forgiven him?"

"Nope." Mariah shook her head. "He shouldn't have gloated over being right about little Hank's gender."

"Don't you think you've punished him enough?" Bria asked.

"I want a formal apology," Mariah insisted. "Until I get that, I have nothing to say to Jaron."

"She's been in love with Jaron since she was a teenager and I suspect he's in love with her," Summer whispered to Taylor. "But he has some crazy idea that he's too old for her."

"I noticed that he couldn't take his eyes off of her during dinner," Taylor admitted.

Summer nodded. "It's that way every time we get together."

"Maybe one day they'll work it out," Taylor offered.

"Maybe," Summer said, smiling.

As talk turned to babies, breast-feeding schedules and the lack of sleep both new mothers were experiencing, Taylor smiled. Even the wives of the men were close, making the blended family all the more special.

Several hours later as they drove away from Ryder and Summer's ranch, Taylor glanced over at Lane. "I love your family," she said, sincerely. "Everyone is so friendly and nice. I really enjoyed getting to know them."

"I'm lucky to have them." Lane shrugged. "Even though there are times I'd like to muzzle them to shut them up, there isn't one of them that wouldn't be there for me in a heartbeat if I needed them, the same as I will always be there for them."

"I think it's wonderful that you all have stayed so close over the years." She had friends, but the bond between the men she'd met tonight went beyond friendship. They had chosen to become a family and were closer than some people she knew who were related by blood. "I would have loved to have a family that got along that well."

Reaching across the truck's console, he covered her hand with his. "We're just like any other family. Most of the time we get along. But other times it can be a zoo," he said, smiling. "Just because you see us getting along, don't think that we don't have our arguments sometimes."

"But you always get over it and you're right back to getting along?" she guessed.

"Always," he admitted.

"That's something my parents never do," she said, sighing. "They just continue to shout at each other."

"But they love you," Lane said gently.

She nodded. "I guess everyone has a different family dynamic," she admitted. "Some are just more harmonious than others."

Staring out the windshield at the star-studded night sky, Taylor still couldn't help but be envious of Lane's family. Besides the fact that they all got along so well, listening to Bria and Summer talk about their husbands almost made Taylor wish she could have a relationship like that.

She had never entertained the idea of getting married and starting a family because of her parents and their hostilities toward each other. But seeing Lane's brothers and their wives and the loving way they treated each other was eye-opening for her. It had shown her what a relationship based on love and respect could be like.

"I'll be setting up the poker game over in Shreveport for the end of this coming week," Lane said, breaking into her musings.

"Do you think I'm ready to match my skills against yours?" She wasn't overly thrilled by the news. For one thing, she wasn't entirely certain she would be a worthy opponent. And for another, no matter who won, the other would be leaving the ranch. So why did that make her sad?

Over two weeks ago, all she'd wanted—all she could think about—was winning back his half of the ranch and ordering Lane off the property. But now?

"You still have to watch your tells," he answered. "But yes, you're ready to play me for the ranch."

They were both quiet for the rest of the drive and by the time Lane parked his truck next to the Lucky Ace ranch house, Taylor decided not to think about what would happen when they played poker for the ranch. She was determined to enjoy whatever time they had left together.

"I don't know about you, but I'm damned glad to be home," he said, giving her a look that caused her insides to feel as if they had turned to warm pudding. "I think turning in early would be a good idea."

"Really? I thought you told your brothers you were going to come home and watch the baseball game," she said, feigning innocence. She knew exactly what he meant and her heart sped up at the thought of once again being loved by him.

"What I tell my brothers and what I do are some-times two different things," he said, getting out of the truck to come around and help her from the passenger side. Putting his arm around her shoulders, he leaned down to whisper close to her ear as they walked to the porch. "I would much rather take you upstairs and hit a home run than watch some overpaid athlete only make it to second or third base."

"Don't you think the Rangers will score at least once or twice tonight?" she teased.

Laughing, he shook his head. "Not the kind of scor-ing I intend to do when we go upstairs, babe."

"Oh, so you intend to race around the bases?" she asked as they entered the house.

He locked the door behind them and immediately took her into his arms. "Not a chance. I have every in-tention of taking things slow and enjoying every base I touch." He kissed her until she felt as if her limbs had been replaced by limp spaghetti. "And I'm going to make sure you enjoy every one of them, too."

Eight

Taking Taylor by the hand, Lane led her across the foyer and up the stairs. He had spent a miserable afternoon and evening checking his watch to see how much longer it would be before he could whisk her away from his family and bring her home to make love to her.

When they reached his room, he walked over and lit a group of candles he had placed on the nightstand before they left to go to Ryder's. "I'm going to make this a night you'll never forget," he said, turning to put his arms around her.

"You've got my attention," she said, rising up on her tiptoes to kiss him. "What do you have in mind?"

"You'll see," he answered as he pulled off his boots and unbuttoned his white oxford-cloth shirt. When she started to take off her blue silk blouse, he shook his head. "I want the pleasure of doing that for you."

After quickly stripping off the rest of his clothes, he knelt to remove her shoes. He caressed her slender ankles and massaged the arches of her bare feet. He had every intention of taking his time to touch every part of her delightful body and build the energy within her.

As he reached for the buttons on her shirt, he smiled. "I want you to close your eyes and concentrate on how I'm making you feel while I take off your clothes."

"All right," she murmured as she did as he commanded.

Releasing the top button, he kissed her satiny skin down to the next button and then the next. By the time he reached the waistband of her navy linen slacks, she had goose bumps and he was certain they weren't from cold.

"You're…driving me…crazy," she said, sounding delightfully breathless.

He put his index finger to her lips as he whispered close to her ear. "Shh. I want you to promise you'll keep your eyes closed and won't talk. I want you to get lost in the way I make you feel. Okay?"

When she nodded, he slipped the garment from her shoulders, then took his time kissing her arms—from her shoulders to the tips of her fingers—before he reached for the clasp of her bra. Unfastening the satin and lace, then tossing it aside, he used his palms to support her full breasts as he kissed one hardened nipple while he chafed the other with the pad of his thumb. By the time he finished giving his full attention to both tight tips, a tiny moan escaped her perfect lips.

"Let me hear you, Taylor," he whispered, skimming her satiny skin with his lips.

Without saying another word, he unbuttoned her slacks and slowly slid the zipper down, kissing his way along her lower belly much the way he'd done when he removed her shirt. When he reached the waistband of her bikini panties he stopped to slide her slacks down, then kissed her from her thighs all the way to her ankles. Kissing his way back up along the inside of her legs, he paused to remove the scrape of lace between him and his goal.

"Lane?"

"You promised," he said, kissing her intimately.

When she moaned and began to sway, he caught her hands in his to place them on his shoulders. As he continued his sensual assault, her nails scored his skin and he knew she had almost reached her limit.

Rising to his feet, Lane swung her up in his arms and carried her over to the bed. His body burned to make her his once more, but this night wasn't about him. It was all about Taylor and bringing her the most pleasure a man could give to the woman who owned his heart.

If he had given himself enough time to think about that and what it meant, he might have run like hell. But he concentrated on the woman in his arms as he placed her on the bed, then he reached for a foil packet from the drawer in the nightstand.

When he had their protection in place, he sat on the bed beside her and lifted her to straddle him. He gritted his teeth as he eased her down onto him and she slowly took him in.

"Open your eyes, Taylor," he commanded. When she did, the passion in the emerald depths robbed him of breath.

Taking her hand in his, he placed it over his heart while at the same time he covered her heart with his palm. "I want you to feel our hearts beat while I make love to you."

As they stared into each other's eyes, he urged her to wrap her legs around him and begin a slow rocking motion against him. Without hesitation she moved her body with his and in no time their hearts united to beat as one. In time with the rhythm of their lovemaking, the beat increased along with their movements. As the tension built, Lane knew that they were both reaching the summit they both sought.

With hearts pounding to the same cadence, her body clenched him tightly and he felt them both let go and give in to the release of complete fulfillment. Feeling as if he might pass out, Lane held her to him as they rode out the storm of pleasure engulfing them.

As the last waves of passion coursed through them, he knew beyond a shadow of doubt that the woman in his arms had changed his life forever. She had not only drained him of every ounce of energy he possessed, she had just taken away his will to fight his feelings any longer. He was in love with her and as soon as they settled ownership of the ranch, he fully intended to tell her.

The following morning at breakfast, Taylor smiled when Lane twined their fingers on top of the table. He seemed to take every opportunity to touch and kiss her. And she loved every single minute of it.

"What do you have planned for today?" she asked as she took a sip of her coffee.

"Right after I set up the poker game, I'll be helping Judd in the north pasture," he answered, giving her a smile that caused her pulse to take off at a full gallop. "He needs somebody to help him cut several cows from one of the herds and bring them up to the holding pen."

"Why? Is something wrong with them?" she asked, knowing they sometimes separated cattle from the herds because of a health issue.

Lane nodded. "He noticed some cattle yesterday that looked like they might be coming down with pinkeye."

"That's highly contagious," she said, remembering hearing her grandfather talk about how the disease could be passed on to the entire herd if the infected cows weren't separated and treated immediately.

"We'll get it taken care of," he assured her.

"Why isn't one of the other men helping him?" she asked, knowing they had several cowboys working for them.

"After we fired Roy Lee, we're a man short," he explained. He rose from the table to take his breakfast plate to the sink for rinsing, then put it into the dishwasher. "Besides, Judd knows I'm pretty good at roping and thought I might come in handy if one of the cows is reluctant to go into the chute on her own."

Joining him at the sink, she wrapped her arms around his waist to give him a hug. "Should I plan on you being back for lunch?"

"I wouldn't count on it," he said, kissing her until

she felt completely breathless. "But I'll definitely be here for dinner."

He kissed her again, then grabbed his hat and walked out of the house. Standing there watching him leave, she couldn't help but wonder what would happen when they played the poker game to decide who would control the ranch.

If he won would he be opposed to the idea of her staying longer than they had agreed on? Or in the event that she won, would his pride allow him to accept her invitation to remain on the ranch until the attraction between them ran its course?

Starting the dishwasher, she finished cleaning up the kitchen and started upstairs to unpack some of the cartons Lane had rescued from the hayloft in the barn. She was optimistically going to unpack her clothes and the few personal items she had shipped to herself with the hope that things would work out no matter who won the game.

Three hours later, Taylor came back downstairs to take a break and had just made herself a mocha latte when someone knocked on the front door. She had no idea who the visitor could be, unless it was one of Lane's brothers or their wives. Either way, she'd enjoyed talking to them the night before and a visit from any of them would be more than welcome.

But when she opened the door, Roy Lee Wilks stood on the other side. "Good morning, Ms. Scott," he said, taking his sweat-stained hat off in a gentlemanly manner.

"What are you doing here, Roy Lee?" she demanded.

"I thought Lane told you to clear off the property and not come back."

He nodded. "I'm real sorry about taking your stuff like I did, but I wanted to bring it to you myself." A dark scowl replaced his friendly expression. "He ruined that idea."

"Okay, fine. Apology accepted." Deciding not to tell the man that she had been the one who'd discovered what he had done, she pointed to Roy Lee's truck. "Now please leave and don't come back."

She started to close the door, but he wedged his boot against it. "Telling you I'm sorry is only part of the reason I'm here," he said, removing some papers from the hip pocket of his jeans. His expression turned outright nasty. "I just thought you'd like to know a few things about the son of a bitch you're playing house with. I've seen the two of you cozied up together here on the porch and you don't have any idea what kind of man he is."

"You were watching us?" Outraged, she shook her head. "Get off this property right now and don't you ever step another foot on the Lucky Ace again. If you do, I'll have you arrested for trespassing, harassment and anything else I can think of."

"Not before I give you these," he said, shoving the papers he held into her hand. "If you're smart, you'll read up on Donaldson. He's not the man you think he is. You're sure that I'm the bad guy here, but some of the things he's done makes me look like a saint."

Before she could throw the papers back at him, he moved his foot and turned to jog down the steps. He got into his truck and drove away, the tires squealing.

Her hands shook as she closed and bolted the door. Her instincts had been correct about Roy Lee. He was without a doubt one of the creepiest men she'd ever had the misfortune to meet.

Walking straight into the kitchen, she started to throw the papers he'd given her into the trash can under the sink. But something caught her eye and she closed the cabinet door instead.

The papers were copies of news articles from several of the Houston newspapers. There was one article detailing the suicide of Lane's father and his embezzlement at the financial institution where he had been employed. He had been facing years in prison for stealing his clients' money and chose to end his life rather than spend the majority of the rest of it behind bars.

Sitting down at the table, she read on and learned that Ken Donaldson's only son, thirteen-year-old Lane Donaldson, had found the man hanging from the rafters of their garage, just as Lane had told her. But the information in the next article was what caused her heart to stall and her stomach to feel as if she would become physically sick. The son of a disgraced financial advisor who had committed suicide had been arrested two years later for running confidence schemes and selling stolen goods to several pawn shops in the Houston area. Because he was a juvenile at the time, the newspaper was prohibited from releasing his name, but there was no doubt they were reporting on Lane. The article went on to say that the boy had pled guilty to the charges and because of extenuating circumstances had been placed into the custody of the foster care system instead of being detained in a juvenile detention facility. There wasn't a doubt in her mind the newspaper referred to Lane.

He had mentioned being sent to a foster care home called the Last Chance Ranch, but she had assumed the ranch name was just something someone had come up with. She hadn't believed it had a literal meaning. Apparently, she'd been wrong.

Her first instincts had been right about Lane. He must have manipulated her grandfather into wagering half of the ranch and then cheated to win the game.

Why had she let down her guard? How could she have been so gullible?

Normally, she wasn't nearly as trusting as she had been with Lane. Nor did she take everything someone said at face value. But Lane had been so convincing when he swore he wasn't guilty of the things she had accused him of doing. She knew now that he wasn't just a swindler; he was a consummate liar as well.

With her heart feeling as if it had shattered into a million pieces, she went upstairs to get her laptop and spent the rest of the day searching every newspaper archive she could find that might give her additional details about Lane and his past. There wasn't much more, other than his mother's brief obituary and the details of the real estate and personal possessions auction that was held to recover some of the money Lane's father had stolen from his clients.

But by the time Lane returned to the house after helping the ranch foreman with the sick cattle, Taylor was waiting for him, armed with all the information she needed. She felt like a fool. Over these last few weeks, she had convinced herself that she'd been wrong about him and that he was trustworthy after all. She'd even given herself to him and all the while, he was probably laughing himself silly at what an easy mark she had been.

"Did you set up the poker game?" she asked when he opened the back door and hung his hat on the peg beside it.

Opening the refrigerator to get a beer, he nodded. "I called Cole Sullivan and he's agreed to let us use the VIP poker room at the End of the Rainbow Casino on Friday." He walked over to sit at the table with her. "He said that he just heard about your grandfather and that he has something Ben left for him to give to both of us when he passed." Lane frowned. "Do you have any idea what that could be?"

"Why would I have the slightest clue what my grandfather gave to a man I've never met?" she asked, unable to keep an edge from her voice.

He reached across the table to cover her hand with his. "Is something wrong?"

"You could say that," she said, removing her hand from beneath his.

"Tell me what's bothering you, babe." He looked sincere, but she knew better than to trust him.

"First of all, I don't want you calling me 'babe' anymore," she said, folding her arms beneath her breasts. "I'm not your babe, your honey, your sweetheart or anything else."

He had his beer bottle halfway to his mouth, but he

slowly set it back on the table. "Okay. Would you like to tell me what's going on and why you suddenly take exception to my calling you that when it didn't seem to bother you before?"

"I learned something about you today that I find very disturbing," she said, forcing herself to stay calm. If she didn't keep her emotions under tight control, she knew for certain they were going to betray her. And she'd rather die than allow Lane to see how badly he had hurt her.

His eyes narrowed slightly. "What did you learn?"

She could tell he anticipated what she was about to say. He had probably already formed a plan for damage control on the outside chance that she did figure things out. But as far as she was concerned, there was nothing he could say that she would find redeeming.

"You failed to tell me that you were put into the foster care system because you were a thief and a grifter." She shook her head at her own foolishness. "I should have trusted my instincts. You did swindle my grandfather out of half of this ranch, didn't you?"

"No." He rose from his chair to walk over and pour his beer down the sink. When he turned to face her, his expression gave nothing away. "I told you before, I've never cheated at cards."

"Sure. Whatever you say. You were good enough at swindling and stealing from people that it took a year for the authorities to catch you," she said, getting up from the table to face him. "You had to have been a very convincing liar to get all those people to believe your schemes. I know you had me fooled."

"I've never lied to you," he said, taking a step toward her.

Refusing to let him intimidate her, she stood her ground. "You must think I'm horribly gullible or more likely, you think I'm a complete fool. Did you have yourself a good laugh when I made it so easy for you to seduce me?"

"It wasn't like that, Taylor," he insisted. "Deep down you have to know that."

"To tell you the truth, at the moment I don't trust myself to know anything," she admitted. "I suppose I have you to thank for teaching me that my judgment is completely unreliable and more than a little flawed."

"Listen up, Taylor. You have a flaw, all right. It's jumping to conclusions before you have all of the facts." His voice held a steely edge and there was no doubt he was furious, but he didn't shout as she'd expected him to do. He didn't have to. His deadly calm tone was far more effective. "Yes, I withheld the information about my past for two very good reasons. Number one, I'm not at all proud of it. And number two, I knew how you would react."

"Were you ever going to tell me?" she asked.

"Yes." He took a deep breath. "I intended to tell you about the trouble I got into when I was a kid, as well as my reasons for doing what I did. But I was waiting for the right time."

"Are you going to tell me now?" she asked, wondering why she bothered to ask. He probably thought she was so gullible that he could tell her anything and she would believe him.

"No, I'm not," he stated, surprising her. "You have your mind made up about me and, at the moment, there's nothing I can say that will change it. I'll tell you everything tomorrow after you've calmed down."

"There won't be an opportunity tomorrow," she said determinedly. "I want you out of my house and off my property until after we play for the ranch."

"This place is just as much mine as it is yours," he pointed out, his voice still deadly quiet.

"This is an intolerable situation and one of us has to leave," she said, hoping he wouldn't call her bluff. Legally he had every right to stay and they both knew it. "You're the obvious choice because you can go stay with one of your brothers. I don't have anyone I can turn to."

He stared at her for what seemed an eternity before he finally nodded and started toward the hallway. "I'll go pack a bag and be out of here in fifteen minutes." Turning back, he added, "But don't think I'm giving up. This is my home now and I have every intention of living here for a *very* long time."

Taylor waited until he went upstairs to gather his clothes before she walked out onto the front porch and sat down in the swing. She didn't want to watch him walk out the door and run the risk of abandoning her resolve. It would be too tempting to tell him to stay and to ask him to give her a reasonable explanation for why he had turned to a life of crime after his father died, as well as why he'd lied to her—even if it was by omission.

Nothing would make her happier than for Lane to tell her that he had only been acting out as a normal teen would do after becoming the victim of a life-altering tragedy. He had lost so much in such a short time; she couldn't imagine how traumatizing it had to have been for him to find his father's dead body. He had only been thirteen at the time and she could tell that the incident still haunted him. But even if he told her that he'd been acting out, how could she be certain it was the truth?

The sudden slamming of a door and the sound of Lane's truck's powerful engine starting caused her eyes to burn with unshed tears. He was doing what she wanted, so why did she feel so miserable about it?

But when she watched the taillights of his truck fade into the darkness as he drove away from the ranch toward the main highway, she couldn't hold back her emotions any longer. Tears ran unchecked down her cheeks as the only man she could ever love drove away from her.

"I'm staying here with you for a few days," Lane announced two hours later when T.J. opened his front door.

"Uh-oh. Something tells me there's trouble in paradise," T.J. said, standing back for Lane to enter the house. "What did you do?"

"What makes you think I did something?" Lane demanded.

"We're guys," T.J. answered. "We screw up all the time and women just love to point that out. So what did you do?"

"I don't want to talk about it," Lane ground out. The last thing he wanted to do was rehash what had taken place with Taylor. The woman was as stubborn and frustrating as a green-broke mule and his gut still burned with anger from their encounter.

"Let's go into the man cave," his brother said, nodding. "You look like you could use a drink."

"That's a given," Lane muttered, following his brother to the back of the house.

When they entered T.J.'s game room—decorated to look like an old-time saloon—Lane took a seat on one of the stools while his brother went behind the bar to get their beers. Lane stared at the miserable-looking man in the huge mirror on the wall behind the bar. He looked like hell. For that matter, he felt like it, too.

"So are you going to tell me or am I going to have to drag it out of you by playing twenty questions?" T.J. asked, breaking the silence.

Lane drained the bottle in his hand and just as he'd anticipated, his brother set him up with another one. "There's nothing to tell. She's pissed off and I'm staying with you. End of story."

"Well, you know I'd be the last one to pry into your personal business," T.J. said, as if choosing his words carefully.

"Since when?" Lane asked. "You've been the nosiest one of the six of us for as long as I've known you."

T.J. grinned. "It's something I'm good at. And I've always been of the opinion that if a person is good at something, they should do it often."

"This is one time you need to back off, brother," Lane warned. "I'm not in the mood and I'd hate to have to kick your ass."

"That must have been some argument," T.J. said, shaking his head. "You're usually the cool, calm and collected one of the bunch."

"Not tonight." Lane finished his beer. "I'll take another one."

T.J. got him another beer and set it in front of him. "You must really have it bad for Taylor if she's got you this tied up in knots." He frowned. "I don't think I've ever seen you drink that many beers so fast."

"Well, you might see me drink four or five more before it's over with." Maybe if he drank himself into oblivion he would find some peace from the burning ache that went all the way to his soul.

"She found out about your past, didn't she?" T.J. guessed.

Glaring at his brother, Lane took a swig of beer. "Shut up, T.J."

"How did she find out?" T.J. pressed.

"I don't know." Lane shook his head. "She didn't tell me and I didn't ask. Hell, it doesn't matter. She found out before I could tell her myself and jumped to the conclusion that I cheated her grandfather out of half of the Lucky Ace."

T.J. whistled low. "Even I've got better sense than to joke about you cheating at poker, let alone openly accuse you of doing it."

Nodding, Lane finished his beer and stood up. "Which room do you want me to take?"

"I've got six spare bedrooms," T.J. said, following him toward the stairs. "Take your pick."

As he climbed the steps to the upper floor, he knew

as surely as the sun set in the west each night that T.J. was already dialing the phone to let their other four brothers know what was going on. But it was the first time the phone tree of sympathy had been activated because of him. And he didn't like it one damned bit. He knew they would all be supportive and any advice they felt compelled to pass along would be out of concern for him. But he didn't want to hear it. Not tonight. Not tomorrow. Not ever.

Unfortunately, he didn't think there was anything they could do or say that would make the situation better anyway. Taylor had her mind made up and until she calmed down, the devil would be passing out ice water in hell before she listened to reason.

She'd been the same way about playing poker for the Lucky Ace. When he had learned that she didn't know the first thing about poker, he'd tried to call off the game, but she wouldn't hear of it. She had made up her mind that she could beat him and that was what she was determined to do. Dammit! The woman was way too stubborn for her own good.

Letting himself into the first bedroom he came to, Lane dropped his duffel bag on the floor, stripped off his clothes and headed straight for the shower. As he stood beneath the steamy spray, he closed his eyes and forced himself to put things into perspective. If he didn't love her so damned much, he might be tempted to throw up his hands and call it quits. She overreacted to just about everything and when she believed she was right about something, she was as determined to see it through as a dog fighting over a juicy ham bone.

But it was that very passion that he loved the most about her. When she committed herself to something, she gave it 150 percent, whether it was cooking a gourmet meal or making love with him.

Turning off the water, he grabbed a towel and dried himself off. She might have won tonight's hand, but he knew something about himself that she obviously didn't. He could be every bit as stubborn as she was and he wasn't about to give up on them so easily.

When he walked into the bedroom to stretch out on the bed, he stared at the ceiling. Even though he was still stinging from her lack of faith in him, he couldn't stay angry with her. He could understand how the evidence against him had to have looked to her. Considering his history and the fact that he hadn't told her about his past up front, he had to admit that it probably did appear that he had swindled her grandfather. Added to Taylor's tendency to jump to conclusions, it would have taken a miracle for her not to find him guilty of everything she had first suspected him of doing.

As he lay there thinking about how much he loved her and trying desperately to come up with a way he could make things right between them, a plan started to take shape. He knew exactly what he could do to convince her of his sincerity and control the outcome of the insane situation they found themselves in. And there wasn't a doubt in his mind that he was going to get what he wanted.

Folding his arms behind his head, Lane smiled determinedly. He hadn't expected to fall in love with her, had even tried to deny it was happening, but he was all in. He was going to do whatever it took to make her see they belonged together and she was just going to have to get used to it.

Nine

On Friday, when Lane arrived at the End of the Rainbow Casino, he went straight to Cole Sullivan's private office. "Is everything ready for the game?" he asked.

"It's good to see you again, Lane," the casino manager said, rising to his feet to shake Lane's hand. "The VIP room is ready and I have a dealer waiting to start the game as soon as Ms. Scott shows up."

"Good." Lane couldn't wait to get started. The sooner they settled control of the ranch, the sooner he could sort out matters once and for all with Taylor.

"How have you been?" Cole asked as he pulled an envelope from his desk drawer.

"Pretty good," Lane answered, checking his watch.

He hadn't seen or talked to Taylor for the past several days and it felt more like they'd been apart for years. He missed her, missed holding her and making love to her.

After he had gone to T.J.'s the night Taylor had confronted him with his past, he'd spent the next three days coming up with a plan of action and how he intended to execute it. He wanted to talk to her, needed to hear her voice. He had even picked up the phone a couple of times and started to call her, but he'd decided against it for one very important reason: what he wanted to say to her wasn't something a man told the woman he loved over the phone.

"I have this letter Ben left with me just before he went to California last fall," Cole said slowly, interrupting Lane's thoughts. "I was instructed to give it to both of you together. Would you like to see it before or after the game?"

"After," Lane said decisively. "It might be upsetting for Ms. Scott and I'd rather not have either of us distracted by whatever it says."

His friend nodded. "Can't say that I blame you." Cole paused a moment, then went on as he tucked the envelope into the inside pocket of his suit jacket. "I was left with the impression that Ben knew he wasn't going to make it back from his trip to California and he wanted to be sure the two of you were clear about his last wishes."

Lane couldn't imagine why Ben had included him in something that should have been a personal letter to his granddaughter. But then, there were a lot of things that Lane hadn't understood about the man. He knew for certain that Ben had had more than enough money on hand to cover his wager last fall. But instead of betting the cash, Ben had chosen to put up half of the Lucky

Ace. It hadn't made sense then and it didn't make any more sense to Lane now.

"Ms. Scott has arrived," Cole's secretary said through the intercom.

"Mr. Donaldson and I will be right out," Cole answered. He looked at Lane. "Are you ready to get this show on the road?"

Rising to his feet, Lane nodded. "The sooner the better."

As they walked out of the office into the reception area, he immediately spotted Taylor, sitting poised on the edge of a chair as if she was ready to bolt for the door. She looked nervous and if the dark circles under her eyes were any indication, she hadn't been sleeping any better than he had. But God, she looked good to him. It was all he could do to keep from crossing the room to take her in his arms.

"Taylor," he said, touching the wide brim of his hat and giving her a nod.

"Hello, Lane," she said, her tone cool.

An awkward silence followed until Cole cleared his throat. "If the two of you are ready, I'll show you to the VIP room and you can get started with your game," he announced.

As they followed the casino owner through the main floor to the private room, Lane gave her a sideways glance. "Are you doing all right?"

Staring straight ahead, she nodded. "Couldn't be better."

Her false bravado made him want to give her a hug of encouragement. He managed to resist. She wouldn't welcome the gesture and he wasn't sure he would be able to keep it friendly. What he really wanted to do was pick her up and carry her off to some place private where she would have to listen to his explanation—before he kissed her until they both collapsed from lack of oxygen.

When they entered the room, he held her chair for her to seat herself before he found his own place across the table from her. "Good luck, Taylor," he said, smiling.

"As you told me when you taught me how to play, luck has nothing to do with it," she said, throwing his words back at him. "Whoever has the better playing skills will decide the outcome of the game."

"But even highly skilled players make mistakes," he advised. "That's when you need to give your opponent the benefit of the doubt." He wasn't talking about playing poker and he could tell from the slight widening of her eyes that she knew it.

As they continued to stare at each other, Cole spoke up. "Edward will be your dealer today. There will be a five-minute break every hour until the game is finished. I'll be the observer and verify the results of the game." Taking his seat at the table to watch them play, the man added, "Good luck to both of you."

Lane knew the game wouldn't take long enough for them to reach the first break. He had a plan and as soon as he knew he held the winning hand, he intended to execute it.

Fifteen minutes later, he glanced at the hold cards he'd just been dealt, then at the three flop cards lying faceup on the table. The moment he had been waiting for had arrived.

"Your bet, Taylor," he said, calmly.

Watching for the slightest show of one of her tells, he knew immediately when she hesitated with her bet that she was calculating the odds of her having the winning hand. It was all he could do to keep from smiling.

When she placed a small bet, she smiled. "Your turn."

"All in," he said, shoving his entire stack of chips into the pot. He had won more chips than she had, but that was part of his plan. If she matched his bet, it would set her up for the game to be over with the next hand.

As he watched her, Lane was proud that Taylor wasn't nibbling on her lower lip as she tried to decide if she should match his bet. But from the cards he held and the cards showing on the table, he knew she had nothing to worry about. "All in," she finally said, shoving all of her chips into the pot.

He could tell she was more than a little apprehensive by the slight quiver in her voice. Nothing would have pleased him more than to take her in his arms and kiss her nervousness away.

They both turned over their hold cards as they waited for the dealer to reveal the last two community cards. He had a pair of nines, while she had a possible straight.

His heart thumped hard against his ribs as Edward dealt the turn card and then the river card face up. Thankfully, they were of no help to him, but she did end up with the straight she was hoping for. "I thought my pair had you beat," he said, hoping that he looked and sounded convincing.

For the first time since sitting down at the table, she smiled at him. "Apparently not," she said as the dealer raked her chips and most of Lane's to her side of the table.

Left with just enough chips to make his play convincing, Lane waited until the dealer finished dealing the flop before he looked at his hold cards. When he did, he almost groaned aloud. He had a pair of kings and odds were she had a lesser hand. He could only hope that she beat him with the community cards.

Placing his bet, he shoved all but one chip into the pot. "As long as I have a chip and a chair, I have a chance," he said, smiling. When she hesitated, he held his breath. It would have been much easier to fold if he'd been dealt cards he knew would lose. But as he stared at her across the table, he knew his choice was the easiest one he'd ever made. Taylor thought they were playing for the ranch. But he knew there was much more at stake than a thousand acres of Texas dirt. And for the first time in his life, he was going to throw a game and hope that it was enough to get what he wanted.

"I'll match that bet," she said decisively and without hesitation.

The dealer dealt the flop—two tens and a king. Lane's heart felt as though it would jump out of his chest. He had a full house. Why the hell couldn't she have gotten his hand?

The competitor in him wanted to play the cards and

win. But as he stared at her across the table, his heart told him he had only one choice.

Taking a deep breath, he shook his head. "I fold," he said, leaving his hold cards face down as he conceded the game and picked up his remaining chip. "You win, Taylor."

Lane ignored the startled look on Cole Sullivan's face as he stood up and offered to shake her hand. "Congratulations. The Lucky Ace is yours and yours alone." When she placed her small hand in his, it felt as if a jolt of electric current passed between them. He'd done the right thing—the only thing he could do. He only hoped his plan worked and it wasn't the last time he would be allowed to touch her.

"It was a good game and you played quite well. I'm proud of you, Taylor."

"I had a good teacher," she said softly. The sadness in her emerald eyes was almost his undoing.

"Enjoy the ranch," he said as he slipped the poker chip into his jeans pocket and turned toward the door.

Forcing himself to move before he changed his mind, Lane walked away without so much as a backward glance and headed for the casino exit, leaving the only woman he would ever love behind.

Saddling Cinnamon, Taylor mounted the buckskin mare and headed south toward the creek. Her emotions were a tangled mess and she didn't see how she could feel any worse. Hopefully she could think more clearly and somehow draw strength from the place where she and her grandfather had gone fishing so many times.

The place where he had asked her grandmother to marry him. The same place she and Lane had picnicked the day they went riding.

Her confused feelings had begun the night she confronted him with what she had learned about his past and had only gotten worse this afternoon after Lane had walked out of the poker room. She knew it was a rule that once a player folded his cards, they were dead and other players weren't supposed to look at them, but she hadn't cared. Her instincts had told her that beating Lane shouldn't have been that easy. And she'd been right. He'd folded a full house, which would have easily beaten her three of a kind.

Why had he done that? Why had he thrown the game and given her his share of the Lucky Ace? And why did finally having all of the ranch make her feel as if she was the one who'd lost more than she had gained?

When she reached the creek, she dismounted and ground tied the mare. Walking over to the creek bank, she lowered herself to the grass and took the letter from the pocket of her jeans. Cole Sullivan had given it to her just before she left the casino, but she hadn't read it yet. On the front of it her grandfather had written both her name and Lane's. But she had no idea if or when she would ever see Lane again.

She closed her eyes and took several deep breaths. Just the thought of never seeing him again, never being held by him or having him love her so tenderly, caused tears to spill down her cheeks. She loved him more than she had ever dreamed she would love anyone and she'd driven him away.

The night she had ordered him off the ranch, Lane had been right—she did tend to overreact and refuse to listen when someone tried to explain things to her.

Taylor opened her eyes to stare at the crystal-clear water in the creek. The day after Lane left the Lucky Ace, she had realized that she should have given him a chance to explain. But she had thought there would be time after the ownership of the ranch was decided to apologize and tell him she was ready to hear his explanation. Unfortunately, he had walked out of the casino before she'd had the chance.

Now she didn't even know where he was. She supposed she could call one of his brothers to find out where he had gone and how to get in touch with him. But she'd decided against that. She wasn't comfortable with getting his family involved. For one thing, she wasn't certain they would tell her. And for another, she wasn't like her parents. She would prefer to keep her and Lane's differences private. A sudden thought caused her to suck in a sharp breath. Was she repeating the mistakes of her parents? Feeling more miserable by the second, she realized that was exactly what she had done. Her mother and father always overreacted to the slightest problem and were both too stubborn to listen to reason. That's why their differences always escalated into shouting matches.

But Lane had refused to lower himself to that level. He had remained calm and tried to discuss the issues she had with him in a reasonable manner, even though she could tell he had been furious about her accusations.

Needing a distraction from her disturbing self-discovery, she swiped at her eyes with the back of her hand, broke the seal and opened the flap of the envelope. When she removed the folded sheet of paper, she recognized her grandfather's handwriting immediately, causing a fresh wave of tears to flow down her cheeks.

Finally managing to bring herself back under control, she felt worse than ever as she read his message. Lane had been telling her the truth all along. He hadn't cheated to win the game he'd played with her grandfather. Ben Cunningham had thrown the game in order for Lane and Taylor to meet.

As she read on, Taylor was amazed at the lengths her grandfather had gone to in playing matchmaker. He had choreographed the entire ranch ownership fiasco. From his request that Lane move into the ranch house to telling her that he wanted her to leave California and live on the Lucky Ace, her grandfather had set them up because he felt they would be a good match—much like he and her grandmother had been.

Taylor wasn't sure how long she sat on the creek bank staring at the slow moving water, but a rustling sound caused her to turn and look behind her. Lane had ground tied his gelding beside her mare and was walking toward her. She'd been so lost in her misery she hadn't even heard him ride up.

Her heart skipped several beats just from the sight of him. In the black jeans, white dress shirt and black Western-cut sports jacket he had worn for their poker game, he had looked good to her. But now, dressed in his worn blue jeans, a chambray shirt and black leather vest, Lane couldn't have looked more handsome. He looked like the cowboy she had come to know over the past several weeks—the man she had come to love more than life itself.

"When I didn't find you at the house, I figured you might be here," he said, lowering himself onto the grass beside her.

"What are you doing here, Lane?" she asked. She hadn't meant to be so blunt, but after the way she had acted the night she had ordered him off the ranch, she was having a hard time believing he would even want to see her, let alone take the time to search for her.

"I stopped by to bring the papers Ben and I signed when I won half of the ranch," he said, taking some folded documents from the inside of his black leather vest.

He looked so good to her and nothing would please her more than having him take her into his arms and tell her that everything was going to work out. But she knew that was never going to happen—not after the accusations she'd made.

"I—I forgot there would be legal papers to sign," she said, barely resisting the urge to reach out and touch his lean cheek.

She watched him turn the documents over in his hands as he stared down at them. "Before I give these to you, I want you to listen to what I have to say," he said slowly. "And I'd really like for you to hear me out before you comment."

"All right." She nodded. "I have something I need to say to you, too." Admitting that she had been wrong wasn't easy for her, but she owed him an apology for accusing him of swindling her grandfather, as well as overreacting when she discovered the truth about his past.

He took a deep breath, then raising his gaze to meet hers, he shook his head. "I wasn't trying to hide what I did when I was a kid," he said. "It's not something I'm proud of and I prefer not to think about it, but I did intend to tell you about it at some point."

"After the things I had accused you of the night I arrived, I can understand your reluctance." She had unknowingly brought up his past that night and given her insistence that he was guilty, she couldn't blame him for being hesitant about sharing his youthful mistakes.

He shrugged. "I don't know how much you know about it, but my dad embezzled a fortune from the people who trusted him to build their savings. That's why he took his own life. He knew he was facing the rest of his years in prison and he wasn't man enough to face the consequences of his actions."

"I read about your father's crimes in the article from one of the Houston papers," she admitted.

"My mom wasn't aware of what he had been doing, but by the time he died, my father had squandered all of their savings, as well as run through millions of his clients' money." He stared off into the distance. "I'm not sure why he did it, but I suspect he was trying to project an image of being a huge success."

"He might have thought it was important for the type of job he had," she suggested gently.

"Probably." Lane shook his head. "Anyway, after he died my mom found a job as a receptionist in a big corporate office and we had to move out of the suburbs and into an apartment in Houston because we didn't have a car. Both of our vehicles were sold along with everything else at the court-ordered auction."

"That had to have been a huge adjustment for you and your mom." She could only imagine how hard that had been for both of them.

He nodded. "Everything was going along okay and we were squeaking by until my mom found a lump in her breast." His expression hardened. "Because of the treatments she needed, she couldn't work, and along with losing her job, she lost her health insurance."

"That has happened to a lot of people," she said, thinking how unfair it all was. "How old were you?"

"I was fourteen and suddenly thrust into the role of being our sole means of support," he said, taking a deep breath.

"Couldn't your mother apply for assistance from some of the state agencies?" she asked.

"She did," he admitted. "But they had a backlog of cases and we needed money right then." He gave her a meaningful look. "Some landlords don't give a damn what people are going through. They want their money when the rent is due or they'll toss you out in the street. Same thing goes for grocery stores. If you don't pay for the food, you don't eat."

"I'm so sorry for what you had to go through," she said, feeling worse than ever. When she found out about his past, she had assumed he stole things for the fun of it or had been rebelling as a lot of teenagers do. But that hadn't been the case. Lane had turned to crime as a way to survive.

"I wasn't old enough to get a real job and it didn't take long for me to figure out that mowing lawns and doing odd jobs wasn't cutting it," he continued. "I had to find a way to make some real money."

"That's when you started—"

"Yeah, that's when I became a thief," he interrupted. "I stole whatever I thought I could resell, went door-to-door selling magazine subscriptions that people were never going to get and solicited donations for charities that didn't exist. I did whatever I could think of to make ends meet."

"Did your mother know?" Taylor asked, her heart breaking for what he'd had to do.

"If she did, she was too sick to care," Lane answered. He glanced down at his hands. "She died six months after her diagnosis and it wasn't long after that I was caught trying to sell an expensive silver tray to a pawn dealer."

"Is that when you became a ward of the state?" she asked.

He nodded. "When my case came up in court, the judge looked at the evidence against me, and after asking me why I had done the things I had done, he took pity on me. He said that if I pleaded guilty to the charges, instead of a juvenile detention center, I would be put into the foster care system and sent to the Last Chance Ranch." Looking directly at her, he smiled. "That was the best thing that ever happened to me."

"That's when you met your brothers," she said,

knowing how important they had become to each other. The Last Chance Ranch had saved him and enriched his life in so many ways.… She was just beginning to understand why he wanted to own part of the Lucky Ace.

"Yes." Lane reached out and took her hand in his. "I gained siblings and a dad who took the time and cared enough to help me move past what had happened." His tone changed to one of fondness. "Hank Calvert had his hands full with the six of us. But he used ranch work and rodeo competitions to keep us busy and help us work off some of the anger we had to deal with." Chuckling, he added, "And the words of wisdom he passed along were priceless."

"What did he tell you?" she asked, loving the way her hand felt in his.

"Oh, things like being polite and dusting your hand off on the seat of your jeans before you shake hands with somebody," he said, grinning. "Then there was the lecture every time one of us had a date about how to treat a lady. If I heard 'don't forget to open her doors' once, I heard it a thousand times." Laughing, he added, "Another one he was particularly fond of telling us was, 'unless your arms are broke, you'd better carry whatever it is she needs carrying.'"

"Is that the reason you always hold my chair when I sit down?" she asked, smiling back at him.

"Yup." His grin widened. "Hank had a laundry list of things he said made a man into a real man. He called it the Cowboy Code, and I can honestly say he lived by everything on that list."

"He sounds like he was a wonderful man," Taylor

said, wishing she could have met the cowboy who had cared enough to help boys who might otherwise have continued down the wrong path in life.

"He sure was," Lane said fondly.

"Lane, I'm sorry for all those awful things I said to you the other night," she said, feeling horrible about her accusations. "I should have let you explain everything instead of demanding that you leave. I really need to work on controlling my tendency to jump to conclusions and overreact first without listening to reason."

He nodded. "You're a very passionate woman."

"That's no excuse for my behavior," she insisted. "Please accept my apology."

"Don't worry, Taylor," he said, his smile sending shivers up her spine. "All is forgiven."

They sat in silence for several long moments before she asked, "Lane, why did you fold your hand today? You had me beat and we both know it."

When his dark brown gaze met hers, her heart skipped a beat. "I knew that you wanted all of the Lucky Ace." With her hand still in his, he gave it a little squeeze. "And I realized that you and your happiness were more important to me than a thousand acres of Texas dust."

"Lane, I—"

Placing his index finger to her lips, he shook his head. "You said you'd listen to me." He replaced his finger with his lips to give her a kiss that robbed her of breath. "I have another business proposal I'd like to run past you."

"Okay." His kiss felt wonderful and having spent

four days without it, she wanted more. "What do you have in mind?"

"I was thinking that if you don't mind, I could stay here for a while and help you run the ranch," he offered. "Do you think that's something you would be interested in?"

Hope began to rise within her. "Yes, I would really like that."

He gave a short nod. "And what would you say to me living in the house with you?"

"That would be nice," she said as her pulse sped up.

"How would you feel about having the master bedroom remodeled and redecorated?" he asked, looking thoughtful. "Is that something you would be open to doing?"

"That would be a good idea," she said, nodding.

He seemed to consider her answer for a moment before he asked, "After it's redecorated, would you be open to making it your bedroom?"

"I suppose that I should," she said, wondering where he was going with his suggestions.

"And if I promise not to snore too loud, would you be open to me staying in there with you?" he asked, raising their entwined hands to his lips to kiss the back of her hand.

"I would love that," she said, meaning it. She started to move closer to him, but he raised his hand to stop her.

"Just wait," he said. "You haven't heard the rest of my proposal."

"All right, you have my attention," she said, grinning. He was going to stay at the Lucky Ace. That's all she cared about.

"Would you be willing to sign a document that states I have the right to live here with you on your ranch?" he asked.

She frowned. "I guess that would be all right."

"I would want witnesses," he warned.

"I think most legal agreements are witnessed," she said, nodding.

When he pulled her into his arms, the feeling of once again being held by the man she loved brought tears to her eyes. "How would you feel about changing your name?" he asked, his handsome face breaking into a grin that sent her heart soaring. "Or maybe hyphenating it."

"What are you asking?" she asked, unable to draw in enough air.

"I love you, Taylor, and I'm asking you to marry me," he said, the light in his eyes reflecting a love she had never dreamed possible. He handed her the poker chip he had picked up before he left the casino in Shreveport. "I want you to keep this and every time you look at it, I want you to know that you're the woman who inspired me to give up my professional playing status."

"You mean it?" she asked. "I'm the woman who tempted you to quit playing? And you're willing to put up with me and the way I jump to conclusions and overreact?"

"Your passion is one of the things I love about you, babe," he said, kissing her until they both gasped for breath.

"And you really love me?" she asked, afraid to believe it was true.

"More than life itself," he said without hesitation. "Now, are you going to keep me waiting with your answer, or are you going to tell me you love me, too, and that you would be happy to be my wife?"

"Yes, I love you," she said, kissing him. "Yes, I'll marry you. And yes, I want to sleep in the master suite with you every night for the rest of our lives."

"Thank God!" His arms tightened around her as if he never intended to let her go. "When do you want to get married, Taylor?"

"Whenever you do," she said, happier than she'd ever been in her entire life.

"As far as I'm concerned, I'd like to make you mine as soon as we can get a marriage license," he said, kissing her again. "But I'm sure you'd like a wedding, and that takes time to plan."

"I'd like for my parents to be here," she agreed. Even though they fought constantly, she loved them and they loved her. Surely they could put their differences aside for one day.

"Why don't we go back to the house?" he asked, standing up, then helping her to her feet. "The sooner we get started on those wedding plans, the sooner we can get married and start working on a full house."

She laughed. "How many children do you want?"

"I don't want any for a while," he said, putting his arm around her as they walked over to the horses. "I want to spend some time just being me and you. But when we do start having kids, I can guarantee you that I'll be more than happy to give you all you want."

"Oh, I almost forgot to show you the letter from my grandfather," she said as they mounted the horses and started across the pasture.

"I'll look at it later," he said, giving her a smile that lit the darkest corners of her soul. "Right now, I want to get home and make love to the hottest woman I've ever met."

"I love you, Lane Donaldson."

"And I love you, babe. More than you'll ever know."

"I think we've settled the matter of whether the Lucky Ace is your ranch or mine," she said thoughtfully as they mounted their horses.

"We did that when we played that poker game today," he said, grinning. "It's yours."

Shaking her head, she grinned back at the man she loved with all her heart and soul. "No, Lane. The Lucky Ace belongs to both of us. It's *our* ranch."

Epilogue

"**W**ho won the pool about me and Taylor getting married?" Lane asked his brothers as he watched his beautiful wife join in the line dancing with Bria, Summer and Mariah. She was the most gorgeous woman he had ever seen and he couldn't believe she had agreed to become his wife.

"I took this one," T.J. spoke up, grinning from ear to ear. "I said it would be the fourth of July."

"How much longer before the fireworks start?" Nate asked, checking his watch. "I have a phone call to make."

"You have about an hour," Lane said, eyeing his brother. "You got a new woman on the string?"

"Something like that," Nate said evasively as he took his cell phone from his pocket. "I think I'll go make that call now. I should be back in plenty of time for the fireworks."

"Who's the lucky lady?" Ryder asked when Nate strolled off with his phone to his ear.

"He and that little blonde down in Waco are talking again," Jaron answered, sounding distracted.

Lane noticed that Jaron hadn't taken his eyes off of Mariah since he'd arrived for the wedding. "Still haven't changed your mind about being too old for her?" Lane asked, taking a swig of his beer.

Jaron shrugged. "Nope."

"You're hopeless," Ryder said disgustedly as he shifted little Katie to his shoulder.

"You could at least ask her to dance," Sam pointed out.

Jaron shook his head. "No sense starting something I don't intend to finish."

"Damn, but you're a stubborn cuss," T.J. said, laughing.

"And you're full of bull," Jaron shot back. "What's your point?"

"So who's going to be the next brother to take the plunge?" Lane asked, smiling at his new bride when she lifted her wedding gown to do a series of dance steps, revealing a pair of white cowgirl boots. He couldn't wait for the reception to wind down so he could spirit her away for their first night as husband and wife.

"Not me," T.J. said, shaking his head. "I'm a confirmed bachelor and likely to remain so."

"You mean you haven't cozied up to your neighbor?" Sam asked, grinning. "Now that her stallion is staying on his side of the fence, I thought the two of you were getting along better."

"Not even on a bet," T.J. said vehemently. "I like her just fine as long as she stays on her side of the fence and I stay on mine and I don't have to deal with her. She's the kind of trouble I don't want or need."

"I think he's protesting just a little too much, don't you guys?" Lane teased.

"I think you're right," Sam agreed.

"I think you're both full of bull roar and buffalo chips," T.J. shot back. "My money is on Nate taking a trip down the aisle next."

"He does keep going back to the blonde in Waco," Ryder admitted.

While his brothers continued to speculate on which one would be the next to join the ranks of the blissfully hitched, Lane set his beer bottle on a table and walked over to the band. After making his request, he waited until they struck up the first chords of the song before he crooked his finger at Taylor. Looking like an angel in her full-length wedding gown, she smiled and floated across the dance floor toward him.

"I'd really like to dance with you, Mrs. Donaldson," he said, smiling as he took her in his arms.

"I love the way my new name sounds," she said, putting her arms around his neck.

"Donaldson?" he asked, raising an eyebrow.

She laughed. "No. The Mrs. part."

"How much longer before we can leave?" he asked, hoping she agreed to their departure sooner rather than later.

"I'm ready now," she said, kissing his chin. "The dinner is over with, we've cut the cake and we've danced. I'd call that good."

"As soon as this dance is over, we're out of here," he said, unable to stop grinning.

"Oh, my word, Mr. Donaldson," she teased. "You're giving away your tell. From the look on your face, I know exactly what you're thinking."

Laughing, he nodded. "I guess I'll have to work on hiding that."

"Don't you dare," she whispered, sending a wave of heat from the top of his head to the soles of his feet. "I like knowing that you want me as much as I want you."

His body tightened to an almost painful state and to get his mind off what they would be doing later, he nodded toward her parents, dancing just a few feet away. "Your folks seem to be getting along pretty well."

"I know." She smiled. "I've never seen them this relaxed. They actually seem pretty happy tonight."

When the song finally ended, Lane took her by the hand, led her across the dance floor and straight to the house, waving to his brothers as they walked past them. He held her hand as they climbed the stairs, then stopped at the door with the poker chip he'd given her attached to it—the door to the master suite.

"I've been wanting to make love to you in this bedroom ever since it was finished," he said, picking her up to carry her across the threshold of their newly decorated room. They had agreed to wait to make love in their new bedroom until after they were man and wife.

"Oh, I forgot about the fireworks," Taylor said when

he started to unbutton the tiny buttons at the back of her wedding gown.

"Don't worry about it, babe," he said, giving her a kiss filled with all of the love in his heart. "We'll make some fireworks of our own."

And as the night sky outside their bedroom window was lit by an array of colored starbursts, they did just that.

* * * * *

A sneaky peek at next month...

Desire

PASSIONATE AND DRAMATIC LOVE STORIES

My wish list for next month's titles...

In stores from 16th May 2014:

❑ The Texan's Forbidden Fiancée – Sara Orwig

& My Fair Billionaire – Elizabeth Bevarly

❑ Expecting the CEO's Child – Yvonne Lindsay

& Baby for Keeps – Janice Maynard

❑ A Bride for the Black Sheep Brother
   – Emily McKay

& A Sinful Seduction – Elizabeth Lane

2 stories in each book - only £5.49!

Available at WHSmith, Tesco, Asda, Eason, Amazon and Apple

Just can't wait?

Visit us Online

You can buy our books online a month before they hit the shops! **www.millsandboon.co.uk**

Hot reads!

These 3-in-1s will certainly get you feeling hot under the collar with their desert locations, billionaire tycoons and playboy princes.

**Now available at
www.millsandboon.co.uk/offers**

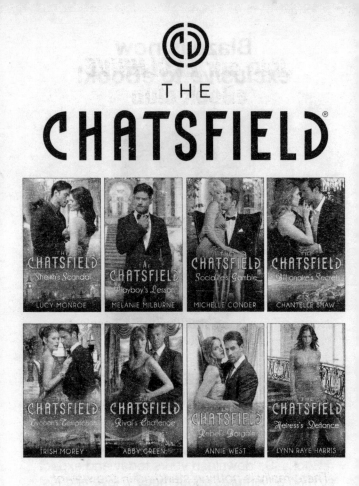

Join our *EXCLUSIVE* eBook club

FROM JUST £1.99 A MONTH!

Never miss a book again with our hassle-free eBook subscription.

★ Pick how many titles you want from each series with our flexible subscription

★ Your titles are delivered to your device on the first of every month

★ Zero risk, zero obligation!

There really is nothing standing in the way of you and your favourite books!

Start your eBook subscription today at www.millsandboon.co.uk/subscribe

The World of Mills & Boon

There's a Mills & Boon® series that's perfect for you. There are ten different series to choose from and new titles every month, so whether you're looking for glamorous seduction, Regency rakes, homespun heroes or sizzling erotica, we'll give you plenty of inspiration for your next read.

By Request
Back by popular demand!
12 stories every month

Cherish™
Experience the ultimate rush of falling in love.
12 new stories every month

INTRIGUE...
A seductive combination of danger and desire...
7 new stories every month

Desire™
Passionate and dramatic love stories
6 new stories every month

nocturne™
An exhilarating underworld of dark desires
3 new stories every month

For exclusive member offers go to
millsandboon.co.uk/subscribe

Which series will you try next?

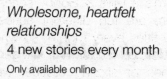